Praise for *The Uninvited*

"Part ghost story, part love story, part historical fiction, this tale set in a small Midwestern town during the Great War is compulsively readable, beautifully written, and populated with characters that will hover in the air around you long after you've set the book on your nightstand. I finished this story and wished very much I had written it. Bravo, Cat Winters."

—Wendy Webb, author of *The Vanishing* and *The Tale of Halcyon Crane*

"Evocative and lushly written, *The Uninvited* also features a twist I never saw coming."

—April Henry, *New York Times* bestselling author

"Dark and romantic [. . .] The author effectively captures the dangers of the period, and yet Ivy finds bastions of human kindness and acceptance. Her compelling voice carries this gothic coming-of-age story, at once horrifying and tender, toward a revelatory yet hopeful conclusion." —*Publishers Weekly*

"*The Uninvited* is an affecting novel, dark in fiction and in fact. Set in 1918 against the parallel epidemics of the Spanish influenza and an equally terrifying strain of 'superpatriotism,' Cat Winters's latest offers resonant characters, a stunning twist, and an emotional, satisfying conclusion."

—Michelle Gable, international bestselling author of *A Paris Apartment*

Yesternight

Also by Cat Winters

The Uninvited

Young Adult

In the Shadow of Blackbirds
The Cure for Dreaming
The Steep and Thorny Way

Yesternight

CAT WINTERS

wm

WILLIAM MORROW
An Imprint of HarperCollins*Publishers*

HarperCollins books may be purchased for educational, business, or sales promotional use. For information, please email the Special Markets Department at SPsales@harpercollins.com.

FIRST EDITION

Designed by Diahann Sturge

Photograph on title page and part titles © Stefan Holm/Shutterstock, Inc.

Library of Congress Cataloging-in-Publication Data

Names: Winters, Cat, author.
Title: Yesternight / Cat Winters.
Description: First edition. | New York: William Morrow Paperbacks, 2016.
Identifiers: LCCN 2016016049 (print) | LCCN 2016022728 (ebook) | ISBN 9780062440860 (softcover) | ISBN 9780062440853 (ebook reflowable)
Subjects: LCSH: Women psychologists—Fiction. | Child psychologists—Fiction. | Reincarnation–Fiction. | Paranormal fiction. | BISAC: FICTION / Historical. | FICTION / Horror. | FICTION / Occult & Supernatural. | GSAFD: Mystery fiction.
Classification: LCC PS3623.I6743 Y47 20016 (print) | LCC PS3623.I6743 (ebook) | DDC 813/.6—dc23
LC record available at https://lccn.loc.gov/2016016049

ISBN 978-0-06-244086-0

16 17 18 19 20   RRD   10 9 8 7 6 5 4 3 2 1

For Betsy Martin and Kathie Deily, two teachers from my past who encouraged me to make writing my future

Acknowledgments

I'm incredibly thankful for both my agent, Barbara Poelle, and my editor, Lucia Macro, who believed in this book from the moment it was first discussed as a basic idea. Thank you to the rest of the HarperCollins team: Leora Bernstein, Pamela Jaffee, Molly Waxman, Diahann Sturge, Ingrid Dolan, Nancy Fischer, K. Stuckey, and everyone else who played a role in this book's editing, production, promotion, and overall success.

Thank you to my always-supportive Wednesday morning coffee and writing crew, as well as to longtime writing friends Kim Murphy, Francesca Miller, Susan Adrian, Ara Burklund, The Lucky 13s, SCBWI Oregon, and so many others who have been there for me.

Thank you to the Oregon Historical Society for promptly providing what I needed, even if it was a tiny article in an obscure publication from the 1920s. I also appreciate the input of Dr. Jarret Lovell, a friend and professor of criminal justice who suggested I investigate the history of psychology for my female protagonist's profession. Thank you to my husband, Adam, a high school math teacher, for looking over the calculations that appear in the novel, and my sister, Carrie, for her enthusiasm and valuable input on the earliest draft. Any mistakes concerning history, psychology, mathematics, and any other academic field discussed in *Yesternight* are entirely my own.

Thanks also to the countless friends and family who have cheered me on through every single book. Meggie and Ethan: as always, I appreciate your patience, love, and support!

Dreamt I to-day the dream of yesternight,
Sleep ever feigning one evolving theme,—
Of my two lives which should I call the dream?

—George Santayana, "Sonnet V," 1896

Part I
JANIE

ॐ CHAPTER 1

November 11, 1925

I disembarked a train at the little log depot at Gordon Bay, Oregon, and a sudden force—a charging bull—immediately slammed me to the ground. Rain pelted my cheeks, my hair, and my clothing, and for a moment I just lay there on the concrete in front of the passenger car, stunned, panting, *drenched*.

Once I gathered my wits enough to realize that gale force winds, and not a bull, were to blame, I rolled onto my hands and knees and pushed myself to my feet. Another blast of cold air smacked me in the face, and the burgundy wool cloche I bought when I first signed on with the Department of Education shot off my head. The poor hat sailed into the distance without ever touching the ground—a stain of red swallowed up by a palette of gray. My short hair slapped at my cheeks and stung my eyes.

The train whistle shrieked through the commotion of the storm, and the porter shut the door behind me. He may have asked if I was all right—he might have been the reason that my bags now sat three feet away from me on the platform—but the wind and the rain howled across the air and drowned all voices and sense. My only link to civilization on the other side of the mountains clacked away down the tracks to the south.

I grabbed the handles of my traveling bags and used the hundred pounds of dresses and toiletries packed inside to anchor myself against the winds. I then lifted the luggage, as well as my black leather briefcase, and staggered to the shelter of the depot's overhang, but not without skidding to my left as the gales continued to bully me. The soles of my galoshes squeaked and slid against concrete. The town of Gordon Bay itself seemed to be fighting to spit me back out.

Somehow, I lumbered over to the safety of a wall and secured myself against the sturdy logs with my bags still in hand. Despite the woolen gloves shielding my hands, my fingers ached down to the marrow of my bones from the bitter cold and, even worse, from the dampness. Oh, my Lord, that infamous Oregon November dampness—three times worse on the coast than what I experienced in Portland. Rainwater streamed down my face, iced my cheeks, and smeared my lips with the briny taste of the nearby Pacific. I closed my eyes, buried my face against the wall, and endured the wind screaming past my ears.

I believe I may have cried a little. I know I swore, *profusely*, at all of the PhD students—mostly male, of course—who had gotten themselves accepted into toasty, cozy universities, while I was doomed to roam the far reaches of the earth with a briefcase full of intelligence tests. My renowned fearlessness in working with students categorized as "delinquent" or "frightening" failed to transfer into bravery against the elements.

"Miss Lind?" called a man's voice from a distance that sounded to be the opposite end of a tunnel.

Another gust of wind whacked me in the back and pressed my chest against the logs. Rain blew sideways and soaked my shins through the cream-colored stockings that my coat didn't quite cover.

"Miss Lind?" asked the voice again, this time a tad closer.

I raised my head and saw a man in his late twenties or so pushing his way toward me through the storm. He wore a midnight-black coat and a gray fedora, the latter of which sprang off his head and flew into the distance—the same fate as my cloche. His exposed hair, blond, trimmed short in the back with longer strands in the front, fluttered about like rippling blades of grass, but within a mere matter of seconds the rain slicked every lock flat against his scalp.

"Are you Miss Lind?" he called, pulling his coat farther around himself, bending forward to plow through the tempest.

I nodded. "Yes."

"Welcome to Gordon Bay," he said, and he smiled. His eyes—either blue or green—smiled, too, and a little dimple appeared above the right side of his mouth and made him look about ten years old, even though he stood close to six feet tall. Rain poured down his face and caused his lashes to stick together. "Here . . ." He offered his right hand. "Let me help you with your bags."

"Thank you," I shouted into the wind, "but I think I might need to carry them to keep from blowing away. The storm already knocked me to the ground once."

"That's our friendly coastal weather for you."

He put a hand to my back and helped to coax me away from the log wall. I didn't even realize I needed any coaxing until I took my first step and found my heart racing.

"Come along," he said. "I'll help you."

I felt like a toddler learning how to walk again, my steps heavy and ungainly, my torso tipped forward while my backside stuck out behind me. I wore eye makeup and suddenly realized that ghoulish dark lines probably streaked my face.

A black car—enclosed, and with lovely rain-proof windows— sat at the nearby curb, but the task of plodding toward it through the winds felt like a ten-mile journey, underwater, while cloaked in chains.

"I don't think we've formally introduced ourselves," I said with an attempt at a lighthearted tone, although the storm whipped my words over my shoulder and carried them away as briskly as it had stolen our hats.

"How's that?" asked the fellow, leaning his head toward mine.

"We didn't formally introduce ourselves."

He clasped me against his side as another arctic blast tried to shove us off our feet. "I'm Michael O'Daire."

"And I'm Alice Lind. It's nice to meet you."

"Nice to meet you, too."

"They told me I was to meet a Mr. O'Daire," I said, "and I actually worried I wouldn't be able to tell which fellow you were in the crowd of people at the depot."

He laughed with a sound that cracked across the air. "There's never a crowd at this depot from September to June. *Never.*"

We reached the car, and Mr. O'Daire leaned forward and used both of his gloved hands to pry open his passenger-side door for me. He succeeded in the endeavor, and rain showered against the front seat's leather, forming a small puddle. I plopped myself down with a splash and sighed in relief when he shut the door against the commotion outside. He then opened a back door and tossed my bags onto the seat behind me.

"Thank you," I called over my shoulder, but he closed that door and sprinted around to the driver's side without hearing me.

I wrapped my arms around myself and shivered inside my red winter coat. An agonizing chill throbbed deep within my bones and numbed my ears and hands.

My companion jumped into the seat beside me, slammed his door shut, and yanked off his sopping-wet gloves. The wind rocked the vehicle back and forth, and the rain beat against the windshield in an unyielding rhythm. If the town of Gordon Bay rose up before us, I could not see it through the deluge.

A cylindrical object of some sort soared into view.

"What's that?" I asked, and the object smacked the glass in front of me so hard, I jumped and screamed.

"A bucket," said Mr. O'Daire, and we whipped our heads over our shoulders and watched the projectile blow away behind us.

"Good Lord." I shifted back around in the seat. "Is the weather always this temperamental on the coast in the fall?"

"This is a particularly devilish storm."

"I hope it's not a bad omen for my arrival."

He chuckled. "I doubt it. But I think, if you don't mind"—he combed both of his hands through his hair, splattering water across his coat—"I'll wait a few minutes before driving through this mess. The worst might pass in a few minutes."

"That's fine with me." I hugged my arms around my middle and slouched down in the seat.

"Here . . ." He swiveled around and half-crawled into the back-seat with his rear end jutting into the air beside me. It was a fine rear end—trim and well-shaped—but, still, I turned my face away.

"I think I might have a blanket," he said, his voice a little muffled.

"You don't need to—"

"Already got it." He dropped back down in the seat with a *thump.* "Please, warm yourself up. What a rotten way for a town to greet a lady."

He handed me a plaid blanket with fuzzy green fabric hairs sticking up all over the place. The thing reminded me of a mangy old mutt that my sisters and I once tried to convince our parents to take in when I was seven or eight.

"Thank you." I tucked the blanket around my shoulders and arms. The fabric scratched at the bottom of my chin and smelled a little musty, but it, indeed, thawed the chill. "Much better."

"You're welcome." He relaxed against the seat, and we both stared out at the rain that hammered away at the windshield as though fighting to break through the glass.

"So"—Mr. O'Daire drew in a long breath—"you're a psychiatrist?"

"Psychologist," I corrected him. "School psychologist. It's a relatively new position in the fields of both education and psychology."

"And you travel around, administering . . . *tests*?"

I met his eyes, unsure what his emphasis on that last word implied. "Yes."

"Hmm." He nodded in a noncommittal way and rubbed his lips together.

I cocked my head at him. "Do you work for the schoolhouse here in Gordon Bay, Mr. O'Daire?"

"No, I'm the proprietor of a local hotel."

"How, then, did you get this glamorous task of fetching me from the depot in a typhoon?"

He smiled, but not with as much vigor as before. "I volunteered. My daughter attends the school, and the schoolteacher is her aunt from her mother's side."

"Well, thank you for not leaving me to flounder about on my own. Your kindness is much appreciated." I wriggled my shoulders to keep the blanket from slipping. "Did Miss Simpkin tell the parents I'd be coming?"

"It's not a secret that you're here, is it?"

"Not at all. I'm here to help the children. I'll be using a measurement called the Stanford–Binet Scale."

"An intelligence test?"

"Yes." I shivered again—from the cold, not the tests. "If I find students who are unable to thrive in their current environment, then I'll confer with Miss Simpkin and the Department of Education about the possibility of creating a special school—or at least a separate classroom—to meet the needs of the struggling children."

"The feebleminded children, you mean?"

"Oh, I'm not fond of that particular term, but, yes, I'm here to identify children who are inclined to repeat the same grade levels, some of them doing so year after year. It's a widespread problem that the state is striving to fix."

"What about other types of children?" Mr. O'Daire returned

his gaze to the windshield and the rain. "Others who are smart, but still . . ." He ran his tongue along the inside of his right cheek.

I waited for him to continue, for I had learned not to feed people words. It tainted the thoughts they were attempting to decipher and articulate. I peeled my wet gloves off my hands while he excavated the right phrase himself.

He wiped water off his brow with the back of his right index finger. "Children who are *different*."

"Ah, well, I'll also be evaluating students for hearing, vision, and speech deficiencies, and a physician will be coming to Gordon Bay—"

"That's not quite what I meant about different."

I shook out the discarded gloves and again waited for him to elaborate.

He grabbed hold of the steering wheel. "Have you ever dealt with children who defy explanation, Miss Lind? Children who unsettle adults?"

I tried to swallow, but my throat muscles tightened. I would not have been the "troubled child" expert sitting in that automobile in Gordon Bay—I would never have gone into the field of psychology to begin with—if I myself had not unsettled adults as a young girl. Naturally, I didn't mention such a thing.

"Actually," I said, "I've become rather famous in Oregon for my ability to work with challenging pupils. In fact, I hope to devote the rest of my life to unlocking the mysteries of the minds of haunted children."

"'Haunted'—that's certainly a way of putting it." Mr. O'Daire's fingers tightened around the steering wheel. "Have you ever examined a student whose problems seemed . . . illogical? Or, well, quite frankly . . . supernatural?"

"I have, indeed," I answered without hesitation. "I've tackled a case of a supposed demon possession."

"Really?"

"Yes. The poor child, as I discovered, had suffered from abuse, which led to that upsetting situation. I've also worked with several children who've claimed to have experienced ghosts and monsters, but most of them were coping with bereavement, or were influenced by superstitious families."

"You don't believe in ghosts or demons yourself, then?"

"No." I smiled. "I don't. In my experience, supernatural entities say more about the people believing in them than they do about the mysteries of the afterlife. Haunted *people* are far more predominant—more interesting—than genuine haunted houses, despite what the recent fashion for séances might suggest."

Mr. O'Daire drummed his thumbs against the steering wheel's leather and clenched his jaw. The rain softened, as though sitting back to allow him to speak—to turn those fidgety movements into words.

And yet his tongue remained silent.

"As a parent," I said, "do you have a concern about one of the children here in Gordon Bay?"

He peeked at me from the corner of his eye. "How old are you, Miss Lind?"

"Old enough to hold a master's degree from the University of Oregon, Mr. O'Daire."

He smiled and nodded, as though appreciating the straightforward zing of my retort. He couldn't have known how much that question grated; how many fellow graduate students had called me "girly" and "kiddo," making me feel like a child who only pretended to understand psychology.

Another violent gust shook the car, and for a moment I worried we had drifted out to sea. I squinted through the window to my right and saw the blurred outline of the log depot. Beyond it roiled gray ocean waves. Liquid steel.

"I don't want to say what I think is happening with my Janie," said Mr. O'Daire with a conviction that startled me.

I turned his way again. "It's your daughter who concerns you?"

He pursed his lips and pleaded for help with his eyes—eyes now seemingly more blue than green, a sharp contrast to the ebony of his coat. "I would like you to listen to her yourself. Tell me what you think of her without me affecting your opinion."

"How old is she?"

"She turned seven in July."

I nodded. "Do you think your concerns about her will show up in an intelligence test?"

"No. She's . . ." He cracked a grin that caused a second dimple to pucker the skin above his lip. "Janie's smart as a whip. No, that's not the way . . ." He ran a hand through his hair, smoothing it against his scalp, although it popped straight back up again in the front. "Please ask her about her earliest memories."

I nodded. "Yes, of course. Early memories are typically a crucial component in unlocking enigmatic behavior."

He kept taming down his hair, patting and combing and fussing. "I'm not going to say anything more about her right now."

"You don't have to." I folded the top half of the blanket down to my lap. "Thank you for your deep concern as a father. Involved parents such as yourself and your wife—"

"Oh, Janie's mother and I aren't married anymore," he said, and he pulled back on the parking brake, as though checking to make sure he'd set it all the way.

"Oh. I'm sorry."

"We disagreed about what's happening with Janie. It killed our marriage. It killed me."

Before I could say a word in response, he popped his door open and dashed around to the front of the car, where he turned the crank with the rain beating down on the back of his head. I watched him, my eyebrows knitted, wondering what early memory from Janie's past—what seemingly "supernatural" behavior that resulted because of it— could have broken up a marriage and caused a father to drive through hurricane winds to speak to a woman who might save the girl.

The engine sparked to life beneath the hood of the car, and the floor vibrated against the rubber soles of my galoshes. Mr. O'Daire ran back toward his side of the automobile, his wet hair hanging in his eyes. With a sigh, he dropped down in the seat beside me and slammed the door shut.

"Off we go!" He threw the clutch lever forward, and off we indeed went, puttering into gray and waterlogged Gordon Bay.

I peered out the rain-streaked windows at souvenir shops and restaurants, most of which sat dark and empty. "I don't know if anyone told you, but I'm to stay in the boardinghouse."

"The boardinghouse is a dump. You're not staying there."

"But—"

"Gordon Bay blooms in the summer and dies a lonely, miserable death every fall, so I have plenty of rooms available in my hotel. I'll let you stay for free."

"Oh, I couldn't . . ."

"Miss Lind . . ." He looked my way, water streaming down his cheeks from his hair. "You don't know how long I've been waiting for someone with a background like yours to show up out here."

"Are you certain? I am here to examine all of the children, not just Janie."

He ignored my words and drove us past the last buildings of that hiccup of a town. Open grasslands lay before us, between the sea and foothills coated in Douglas firs and mist.

I folded my hands beneath the blanket and endured the tips of my fingers tingling back to life. "Mr. O'Daire, did you hear what I said?"

"If you're being forced to travel out to this godforsaken region of the world in the middle of storm season just to help our kids, then the least I can do is give you a comfortable room with a fireplace."

He steered the car around a bend, and a three-story structure—a Swiss chalet-style beauty—rose into view on the edge of a cliff above the churning sea. Fog devoured the top halves of a dozen or so chimneys; gables and exposed beams lent the place a dashing European air. The moody sky hovered impossibly close to the ground, and the building seemed to have slipped straight out of the clouds.

"Is that your hotel?" I asked.

"Do you like it?"

"And how! Did you build it?"

"My father did, as soon as the railroad linked us to Portland thirteen years ago. Before that he constructed houses."

I leaned back against the seat and marveled at the architectural masterpiece. My skin longed for the heat of the fireplaces attached to all of those half-hidden chimneys. "Honestly, I'm used to simple boardinghouses, even ones considered 'dumps.'"

"It's no trouble at all. I swear." He drove us around another bend, and the hotel disappeared from sight behind a thicket of pines. "Not that a person who doesn't believe in ghosts would care," he added, "but the place isn't known to be haunted, nor does it have any tragic tales of murder attached to it."

"Why did you expect me to ask about that?"

"I didn't, but one of our competitors brags that his inn is inhabited by the ghost of a sea captain's widow, so everyone expects the same of us."

I sighed and shook my head. "I blame the séance frenzy I was just talking about. That and our culture's bizarre fascination with sideshows and amusement parks. Over the summer, my oldest sister dragged me to the Winchester house down in San Jose, California. Have you heard of it?"

"No, I haven't."

"Sarah Winchester, heiress to the Winchester Rifle fortune, lost her life no more than three years ago, and people have already turned her mansion into a tourist attraction, complete with a guide who tells stories about spirits driving the woman mad. My sister adored the theatrics. I, however, spent the entire time rolling my eyes."

I bit my lip, for I realized Mr. O'Daire displayed no discernible reactions to my views on Mrs. Winchester's house, despite his talk about ghosts. He stared ahead at the road, his expression now contemplative, his lips pressed shut. I also realized what a boring bluenose I sounded.

However . . . the fellow did need to know that I in no way intended to diagnose any of the Gordon Bay schoolchildren as suffering from paranormal phenomena, despite whatever he believed about his daughter.

The hotel reemerged, and Mr. O'Daire steered the car onto a driveway that wound around to the front entrance in the shape of an elongated *S*. Through the dance of the squeaking windshield wipers, I spotted the words GORDON BAY HOTEL spanning a wrought-iron archway. The car dipped through a pothole and knocked my elbow against the door. I braced my hands against the seat.

"The weather is hard on the property," said Mr. O'Daire with a tone of apology. "Half my job is maintenance."

I returned my hands to my lap. "Well, the hotel is awfully beautiful, I will say that. And it looks far dryer than that overhang under which you found me huddled."

"Good Lord, I hope your stay here doesn't compare to *that*."

We both chuckled, and he brought the car to a rattling stop beside a cement sidewalk, just a few short yards from the hotel's front door.

"I'll help you out"—he set the brake—"and get you settled inside before fetching your bags."

"Thank you."

More dashing about in the wind and the rain ensued, although this time the gusts refrained from knocking me to the ground, and the distance was so short, it took just a few swift sprints before I found myself standing inside a bright yellow lobby radiant with heat from a fire that crackled in the hearth. Stained-glass chandeliers flooded the room in electric light, and a rust-colored sofa and armchairs, devoid of any guests, occupied the center of a space large enough to hold a party of at least forty people.

A broad-hipped woman with a silver serving tray in hand traipsed down a staircase located behind the front desk. Her hair—waved in front, pinned in back with the help of a tortoise-shell comb—matched Mr. O'Daire's coloring, only with streaks of white threaded through the gold.

"Good afternoon," she said, her voice rich and earthy, as though deepened from smoke or drink. She sized me up with eyes like Mr. O'Daire's—large, luminescent eyes that also couldn't decide if they preferred to be blue or green. "I was a little worried when you didn't come straight back, Michael."

"The storm was hell. I took my time driving back." He groomed his hair with his hands again. "Miss Lind, this is my mother, Mrs. O'Daire. She helps run the place from time to time."

"So nice to meet you." I walked over to my hostess with the thick heels of my brown oxfords echoing across the walls. "I'm Alice Lind, a school psychologist who's come to evaluate the children of Gordon Bay."

"Yes, so I've heard." She accepted my hand with a firm shake, and I smelled a tea rose perfume that reminded me of my own mother's. "I've already got a fire started in your room, and I just delivered a pot of tea."

"Oh?" I looked back to Mr. O'Daire. "Then you both decided I was coming here before I even knew I was to be staying."

"Someone wanted to stick her in the boardinghouse," said Mr. O'Daire with a snort.

"Oh no, that won't do at all." His mother placed a hand upon my shoulder. "Would you like me to draw you a bath?"

"No . . . no, thank you. I was hoping to quickly change and go straight to the schoolhouse to introduce myself to Miss Simpkin."

"I'm driving over to fetch Janie and some of her friends in fifteen minutes," said Mr. O'Daire with a gesture of his thumb toward the door. "Let me go grab your bags. You can change and warm up for a moment, and then we'll head over. You can meet Janie."

Before I had time to agree—or to contemplate if the best time to meet his daughter was right then and there—he threw open the door and jogged back out into the rain.

"Come along, then." Mrs. O'Daire steered me around by my shoulders and lured my wet coat off my arms. "Let's get you dried and warmed before you catch your death of cold. I've put you on the second floor, where you'll have a fine view of our lovely, restless Pacific."

I opened my mouth, half-tempted to bring up Janie with the woman—she was the girl's grandmother, after all. I thought better of it, however, and sealed my lips shut.

Before I knew it, the O'Daires had tucked my belongings and me inside a charming room with a white double bed, white-paneled walls, and white ruffled curtains. A fireplace warmed the space, particularly the left side, and a blue and gold rug gave the room its one jolt of color. I blinked at the stark brightness of the quarters after drowning in the murk of the storm.

Once left to my own devices, I kicked off my shoes and poured myself a cup of much-needed tea. A stray drop scalded my wrist, warning that the beverage required cooling. While I waited, I grabbed a towel from a stack of linens on the bed and dried my hair in front of the dressing table's oblong mirror.

"Good heavens!" I said in response to my drowned-rat appearance, brought on by five and a half hours spent on a train, in addition to the damage from the storm. A bob, I discovered, was not attractive at all when it dripped rainwater onto one's sweater and hung to one's chin like limp brown shoestrings. My eye makeup stained my face, as I'd worried. My bangs stuck to my forehead. My neck, roughly the same width as my head, appeared even more mannish than usual with my hair too short to hide it and water glistening across it.

But this is all for the children, I reminded myself, rubbing my hair dry with the towel. *The Department of Education specifically requested that you be the one to administer the Gordon Bay examinations—you, Alice Lind. Not a man. Not someone with more experience. Just remember how much you wanted a person like yourself to appear out of the blue and help you when you were young. Just remember . . .*

My eyes shut. In my head, I heard a sound that often followed me around whenever my confidence faltered—a cruel skipping rope rhyme, chanted in the voices of neighborhood children.

Alice Lind,
Alice Lind,
Took a stick and beat her friend.
Should she die?
Should she live?
How many beatings did she give?

Something rustled near the hotel room's door. I spun around, and my eyes darted about, on the hunt for tiny movements—not from spiders or mice, but from eyelids, blinking as someone, perhaps, spied on me through a hole in the wood.

Of all the fears I carried with me—a terror of gunshots, a wariness of the dark—the paranoia that people were watching me in rooms where I undressed and slept perplexed me the most. My heartrate tripled, and my hands went clammy and cold, even though I had never once, in my conscious memory, experienced an actual Peeping Tom.

"Is . . . is someone there?" I asked.

No one responded.

I half-wondered if Mr. O'Daire stood outside the door, a new hat in hand, waiting to take me to see his Janie. I imagined him bending down on one knee and peering through the keyhole with one of his captivating eyes, his breath fluttering against the wood.

"Is someone—?" I shut my mouth, chiding myself for giving into that old stab of anxiety. It had manifested two years earlier, when I first embarked upon the job of traveling around to rural schoolhouses, and it had made for countless sleepless nights on the road.

"Always face your fears, Alice," I whispered to myself, as I often did when paranoia attacked. I gritted my teeth and pulled my tan sweater up past my shoulders and over my head, exposing my arms, my satin slip, and a birthmark the shape of a nickel at the top of my left breast, three inches below my collarbone. "No one wants a crackpot evaluating their children—and no one cares to gawk at your naked body."

CHAPTER 2

The rustling I heard, it so happened, derived from someone leaving a cotton laundry bag on the dark wood floor outside my door. Not a Peeping Tom.

"Did you find the bag I left?" asked Mrs. O'Daire from around a bend to my left, at the far end of a pristine white hallway dotted with golden knobs on four-paneled doors. She climbed into view from the top of the staircase, drying her hands on an apron she now wore over her simple brown dress.

"Um . . . yes." I lifted the bag.

"It's for your wet clothing."

"Ah." I nodded. "Thank you."

"Slide them inside"—she headed toward me, pantomiming the movement of sticking clothing into a sack—"and I'll wash them up for you."

I smiled. "You and your son are far too kind, Mrs. O'Daire."

"We just feel so awful about our weather. Michael said he found you clinging to the wall of the depot, soaked to the bone, shaking."

"Yes." I laughed. "I was just thinking how much I must have resembled a drowning rat. I'm sure my hair still looks a fright."

"You look fine." She patted my upper right arm—she was one of those people who liked to touch, it seemed. "I admire you young women who possess the courage to march into the dangers of the world on your own. I hope you had time to warm up with your tea."

"Yes. I'm now toasty on both the inside and the outside."

"Good." She imparted one final pat, this time to my left shoulder. "Now go fill up that bag so I can attend to your clothing. Then you can run straight back into the rain and meet Miss Simpkin and the children. My son is waiting for you downstairs."

"Mainly I'm meeting Miss Simpkin today," I said, just to clarify. "I'll start working with the children tomorrow."

She squished her lips together and nodded, and again neither of us mentioned little Janie.

THE DRIVE TO the schoolhouse proved to be far less traumatic than our previous trek through the streets of Gordon Bay. A light rain spat against the windshield, and the bruise-black clouds rolled westward, over the crests of the Coast Range, away from town. The sky overhead gleamed from the sun hiding behind the lingering gray, and the winds pushed against the car with more of a nudge than a shove.

Mr. O'Daire drove us along a street that ran perpendicularly to the main section of town. We passed two more souvenir shops and one eatery, every one of them closed.

"As I told you before," he said, following my gaze to the wilted-looking buildings, "Gordon Bay dies every autumn. It's a dramatic, crumbling death that strikes right after the beginning of September."

"So I see," I said. "It must be a struggle for everyone to make ends meet during the rest of the year."

"It is, unfortunately."

Up ahead, in front of a barber shop, a scarecro
a plaid cap teetered on the edge of the sidewalk. An auburn beard
that resembled tree moss rambled down to the open collar of his
olive coat, indicating that he most certainly had not just visited the
barber shop behind him.

"Is that man all right?" I asked.

"That's Sam, one of our local veterans." Mr. O'Daire slowed
the car to a stop and rolled down his window. "You all right, Sam?
You're standing a little close to the edge of the road there, buddy."

Sam gave a salute and swayed to his left. "I'm fine, Mikey. Just
trying to keep my feet dry."

"Get yourself out of the rain. Have a cup of coffee, why don't
you? Do you need a dime?"

"Just trying to keep my feet dry," said the fellow again, and his
right foot plunked into a stream of water flowing through the gutter.
His shoes weren't tied, so he soaked his laces.

"Sam?"

"I'm all right, Mikey."

Mr. O'Daire shook his head and rolled up the window. "I'll
check on him later—make sure he's not still standing there."

"Is the poor man drunk?"

"Probably, although he acts that way when he's sober, too." He
sighed and drove us onward.

Not more than a quarter mile farther, in an empty field of mud-
matted grass, stood our destination: a whitewashed schoolhouse
that looked like dozens of other schoolhouses I had already visited
in my brief career as a traveling test administrator. A bell tower
with a pointed peak stretched high above a set of doors, reached by

wooden steps in desperate need of sanding and painting. I could practically smell all of the odors waiting for me within: dusty blackboard chalk; damp shoes; a sooty fire in a potbelly stove; the sour stink of children who hadn't bathed in the past week.

"Did you say the schoolteacher, Miss Simpkin, is your former sister-in-law?" I asked.

"That's right."

"Might I inquire what your current relationship with her and your ex-wife is like? Are you all on speaking terms?"

Mr. O'Daire offered a strained smile that failed to involve those charming dimples of his. "As much as people can be in this sort of situation."

"Miss Simpkin doesn't mind you coming to the school?"

"Don't worry"—he shifted the car into a lower gear—"you won't witness any squabbling. We're civil to each other, even if we all have different opinions on what's best for Janie."

He pulled his vehicle alongside a long black motorbus inhabited by a heavyset driver who puffed on a cigar.

"Oh, how nice," I said in the direction of the bus. "I presume this is transportation for the children who live too far to walk?"

"It is." Mr. O'Daire stopped the car and climbed over the back of the seat once again, knocking objects about down on the floor behind me.

I met the eyes of the driver beside us. He smiled and nodded and didn't seem to question the upside-down person next to me. Primarily, he looked to be avoiding an early death of hypothermia. A pythonesque scarf encircled his neck, and a wooly gray hat consumed his hair, eyebrows, and ears.

"You might want to duck," said Mr. O'Daire.

I did as he asked, and something fluttered over my head. When I sat back up, I found him clasping a green umbrella.

"Hold tight." He opened his door and then the umbrella, everything whooshing and blowing and reminding me again of my dramatic arrival on the depot platform. "I'll come around and get you," he said, and he did just that.

I grabbed my black leather briefcase and joined him under the umbrella, which covered the both of us, but only if we tilted our heads two inches apart from each other. I smelled his rich shaving soap—a peppery, gingery aroma—and clutched my briefcase against my left side, doing my best not to look him in the eye at that close of a range. I once ended up in the bed of a fellow graduate student after sharing an umbrella in precisely that manner.

We hurried up the short staircase and, after Mr. O'Daire tussled with the collapsing mechanism and closed the umbrella, we dove into a cloakroom that housed satchels, lunch pails, and jackets of various sizes and thicknesses. Through the open doorway to the classroom, I spied children sliding out of their seats at the wooden desks and gathering up books. They ranged in age from about five to eighteen—a mustached young man may have even been nineteen—and I moved my head about to try to see past the taller ones in the back and find a girl who may have been seven-year-old Janie O'Daire.

One girl seemed a likely candidate: a wide-eyed thing with nut-brown hair cut just below her ears. She cradled her books against her chest with her shoulders stooped, and she lined up behind a redheaded girl with posture so impeccable that the brunette disappeared behind her, even though the brunette was taller. The children trooped our way, and I waited for Mr. O'Daire to introduce me to the hunched little urchin.

"Hello, Daddy," said the redhead in front of her instead.

"Hello, Janie." Mr. O'Daire scooped his arm around the confident-looking child and pulled her out of the line.

The brunette fetched her coat and lunch pail with the rest of the children.

"I want to introduce you to Miss Lind," said Mr. O'Daire, beaming down at his daughter. "She's a kind lady who will be helping out at your school for the next week or so."

From beneath a fringe of bangs cut straight as a paper's edge, Janie peered at me with eyes more intense in color than both her father's and her grandmother's, even though they all shared the same bluish-green hue. It was as if someone had squeezed more paint out of the end of a brush when creating the girl and allowed her to show up a little brighter in the world. A splattering of freckles formed a tidy constellation across her cheeks and turned-up nose.

"Hello, Janie." I offered my hand to her. "It's a pleasure to meet you."

Janie maneuvered her books beneath her left arm and accepted my handshake. "I'm pleased to meet you, too." Her bobbed red hair swayed at her chin line.

Her father kept a hand on her shoulder. "Miss Lind is here to give all of you children a fun test to see what you're best at."

Janie peeked up at him with a grin that showed off a fascinating jumble of teeth—big ones, baby ones, and three missing eyeteeth. "We already know what I'm best at, Daddy."

"Well, you can tell her all about that when she tests you."

Mr. O'Daire grabbed a little navy blue coat from a hook. "She's here specifically to listen to you. Talk to her about anything you want."

Janie closed her mouth and nodded.

A young woman with curls even redder than Janie's locks sauntered our way, her eyes switching between Mr. O'Daire and me.

"You must be Miss Lind," she said.

"Yes. Are you Miss Simpkin?"

"I am." She offered her right hand and spread a powdery layer of chalk against my palm. "I'm so sorry about our weather. I worried the wind might cause our windows to implode, so I'm sure it was quite a shock for you."

"I survived," I said, "thanks to Mr. O'Daire."

"Yes, Mr. O'Daire was keen on being the first to meet you." She dropped her hand to her side.

Beside me, Mr. O'Daire helped Janie into her coat. "I'm going to gather up some of Janie's friends," he said. "I'll drive them home in case the weather acts up again."

"Take Janie straight to her mother after you deliver the others," said Miss Simpkin.

"Of course." His gaze shifted to me. "Do you want to chat with Miss Simpkin for a while? I could come back and fetch you after I get them delivered."

"Would that be all right?" I asked the schoolteacher. "I brought the test materials to show you, if you'd care to take a look before I start administering the evaluations tomorrow."

"Yes, a chat would be lovely." She reached out and patted Janie on the head. "Tell your mother I hope she weathered the storm safely. Look after her, all right?"

"I will." Janie rose to her toes and kissed her aunt on the cheek.

Mr. O'Daire escorted the child out of the schoolhouse, but not without a quick glance back at me. I turned away, having nothing yet to offer him about Janie. He closed the door, and I heard their footsteps, as well as those of three other students, galumphing down the stairs outside. The sudden silence of the emptied-out schoolhouse made my ears hum.

"Please, come in." Miss Simpkin swiveled on her heel and led me down the aisle between rows of desks with seats attached to the fronts of the desks behind them. The words ARMISTICE DAY dominated the blackboard, and I remembered for the first time that day that I'd arrived on November 11. No rain-drenched Gordon Bay parade appeared to be celebrating the seventh anniversary of the Great War's end, however. I thought again of poor veteran Sam, teetering on the edge of the sidewalk.

Miss Simpkin scooted a spare chair in front of her desk, near a wood-burning stove. "Please, have a seat."

"Thank you." I sat down with the briefcase on my lap.

The schoolteacher circled around to the other side of the desk, her movements brisk yet stiff. From the look of her, I'd say her age was close to mine, mid to late twenties, but her face and figure possessed a roundness and softness that made her seem more womanly, more maternal, than me and all of my sharp angles. The halo of red curls framing her face resembled those of the film star Greta Nissen, whom I had recently seen with my sister Bea in the tolerable comedy *Lost: A Wife*.

She plopped down in her chair with a sigh, and all those curls rustled, as if taking a breath themselves. "Do you mind if I have a smoke?"

I shook my head. "Not at all."

"I truly thought we were all going to die today." She slid open a desk drawer and fetched a red and white box of cigarettes and a silver lighter. "Storms plow through this area all the time, but from the way the wind wailed through this old schoolhouse and rocked us about, I thought for certain the roof would blow off and suck us all out."

"I don't blame you. The wind literally knocked me to the ground as soon as I stepped off the train this afternoon. You should have seen—" I burst out laughing at the memory of my body splayed across the platform and my hat shooting off my head. "Oh, but it was dreadful. Thankfully, Mr. O'Daire showed up and assisted me to his automobile."

Miss Simpkin's eyes lost their pep at the mention of my driver. "Well, I appreciate you coming all this way. I don't know if the Department of Education told you, but I specifically asked them to send a test administrator familiar with children who are."—she shook a cigarette out of the red box—"*perplexing.*"

"Yes, they told me."

"You've had experience with difficult cases?"

"I have, indeed. Ample experience."

Miss Simpkin gave a flick of the lighter and set a flame to the end of the cigarette. Her eyebrows puckered. She inhaled a deep smoke and then removed the cigarette from her mouth and asked, "What did Mr. O'Daire say about Janie?"

"Is Janie the reason you requested me?"

"What did he say?"

"Well . . ." I thought back to our conversation. "He told me that you're Janie's aunt and his ex-wife's sister. And he made it quite clear that something about the child concerns him."

"Did he say what?"

"No, he said that he'd like for me to speak to her myself before he told me anything more. He wanted to avoid affecting my diagnosis of her."

"Hmm." Miss Simpkin took another puff and rocked back in her chair with a squeak of the wooden joints. "I'm surprised he felt that way."

"To be most honest, I'm not sure if simply talking to Janie, or even testing her using Stanford–Binet, will give me any insight into his worries. I saw her just now." I nodded toward the cloakroom. "Whatever it is that concerns him about the child isn't something that's overtly apparent."

Miss Simpkin's eyes moistened. She blinked several times in a row and held the cigarette with trembling fingers.

"Usually," I continued, "a parent—or a teacher—will speak to a psychologist about a troubled child's disconcerting behaviors before the child is approached. Most children won't simply start talking about their fears, or past tragedies, or whatever it is that's haunting them."

She nodded. "I suppose that makes sense." Another smoke.

I kept my gaze fixed upon her and her dependency on that cigarette for comfort, even though she had stopped looking at me.

"Why did you request the assistance of someone like me?" I asked. "What is it about Janie that has you all worried?"

She rubbed her right thumb against her bottom lip. "Her mother doesn't know I requested special help, but other children— other parents—they started coming to us over the summer, saying that Janie frightened them. It seemed wrong to ignore what's happening any longer."

I scooted forward in my chair and laid my right hand upon her desk. "Please, if there's a concern that needs to be addressed, I want to know as much as possible about Janie. If this concern is showing up in her relationships with her friends or in her schoolwork, then we should definitely make sure Janie is safe and happy."

"You're right," she said, her voice cracking. "You're completely right. If this were any other child . . ." She sniffed and parked the cigarette in an ashtray. "Well . . . how should I begin?"

"Take your time." I folded my hands on the top of my briefcase.

Her lips twitched, as if deciding whether they should smile. "There's something I could show you. It—it definitely demonstrates the mystery of our Janie." She slid open the desk's bottom drawer and seemed to hold her breath while doing so. "During the week of Halloween, I asked all of the children to write a composition on the theme of 'The scariest thing that's ever happened to me.'" She rustled out a sheet of wide-ruled paper and laid the page in front of me. Her hand shook against the top edge, giving the paper the appearance of the fluttering wings of an insect caught beneath her fingers. A dying moth. "This is what Janie had to say."

I picked up the composition and read.

The scariest thing that ever happened to me was when I used to be called Violet Sunday and lived in Kansas. I was deep in the water and couldn't swim back up to the surface. My heart hurt. It felt like it was about to blow up. Even though I loved numbers so much, I didn't even feel like counting to figure out how many seconds I was under the water. All of my number happiness left me, and I just

*sank and sank until everything went black and I died. I
was nineteen. I died, and it hurt.*

I swallowed and peeked up at Miss Simpkin, who leaned her
hands against her desk.

"Did Janie used to have a different name?" I asked.

"No. She's always been Janie O'Daire."

"Did she almost drown when she was younger?"

Miss Simpkin shook her head. "No."

"Are you quite certain?"

"Quite." She picked up her cigarette and took another puff.

I peered down at the fine display of penmanship—the neat
lines, the full, round curves of letters printed in pencil.

*All of my number happiness left me, and I just sank
and sank until everything went black and I died. I was
nineteen.*

I cleared a heavy feeling from my throat. "Do you know if
anyone who might not have been entirely . . . *competent* has ever
watched over Janie?"

"You mean other than her father?"

I glanced over my shoulder to the empty space where Mr. O'Daire
and I had greeted Janie. I turned back to Miss Simpkin. "You don't
believe Mr. O'Daire is a competent father?"

"I don't think he'd ever hurt her, but . . . his current business practices are"—she tapped ash into the tray—"*unsavory*, to say the least."

I smoothed out the edges of the paper against my briefcase and
reread the paragraph once more.

"Janie, she's . . ." Miss Simpkin rested her left elbow on the desk and held her head against her hand. "She's talked about her life as Violet Sunday ever since she was two years old. The story's always been the same. She was born in Kansas and drowned at nineteen. She loved mathematics."

"She's spoken about mathematics and Kansas since she was two?" I asked.

"In one way or another, yes."

"Has she ever been to Kansas?"

"She's never left Oregon."

I wrinkled my brow. "Do you believe she's remembering a previous life? Is that the great mystery everyone's dancing around?"

Miss Simpkin tapped more ash into the tray and rocked her knuckles across her lips. "I often wonder if her father is feeding her that tale and convincing her that she used to be a dead woman from the 1800s."

"Why do you think he'd do that?"

"I don't know." She shrugged. "Money, I suppose. Fame. He's not a war veteran, or a respected business owner, or even a married man. He's just the spoiled son of a successful hotel proprietor who inherited his daddy's business."

I shifted my weight in my seat and strove to remember Mr. O'Daire's mannerisms when he spoke to me about Janie. The drumming of his thumbs against the steering wheel in the rhythm of the rain came to mind. And yet the genuineness of his love and concern for his child had also made an impression on me.

"May I keep this paper?" I asked.

Miss Simpkin squirmed. "I haven't yet shown that particular writing sample to either of her parents. As I said, her mother doesn't even know about you yet, other than the fact that a person would be arriving to survey the children's ability to learn inside a classroom."

"I'll keep the composition to myself for now. I simply want to use it for comparison, in case Janie feels like talking to me about this story of hers."

"All right." She rubbed her forehead and closed her eyes, as though battling a wicked headache. "At a friend's house, Janie drew a detailed picture of a woman drowning—a macabre illustration that included blue skin and a horrific expression on the woman's face. Her friend's mother asked Janie to stop coming over because of it, and now my sister worries that people are hinting that the child requires institutionalization."

"I honestly don't believe anything close to an asylum would be necessary. To me"—I lifted the paper—"this is either a case of a child with a rich imagination or the suppressed memory of a trauma that's trying to be understood."

Miss Simpkin drew another long puff and blew smoke out of the right side of her mouth. "Do you believe in past lives, Miss Lind?"

"No, I don't. I've studied psychology long enough to know that the human mind is a delicate work of art that sometimes plays tricks upon us. It talks us into believing in the extraordinary when ordinary explanations are to blame."

"What can you do to help Janie?"

"Allow me a little extra time with her during her examination. I'll speak to her and get to the source of this strange story of Miss Sunday from Kansas." I unfastened the clasp of my briefcase. "The good news is that Janie is a child who is obviously loved and well cared for. That palpable concern for her health and happiness will make everything much easier for her. I will, however, explore the possibility that her father is talking her into this tale."

"Thank you. I'd appreciate that." Miss Simpkin snuffed out the cigarette. "Shall we move on to the subject of those tests, then? I'm going to need to soak my feet in steaming-hot water soon."

"You and I both," I said with a smile, and I slid Janie's composition into my briefcase, while the name of her tragic drowning character sang through my head like another skipping-rope chant.

Violet.

Violet Sunday.

A darling name. A name that most certainly sounded as though it had been plucked from the imagination of a child—and not from the mystical memories of a dead woman.

CHAPTER 3

Just as Miss Simpkin and I were concluding a discussion about arranging a quiet space for the examinations, Mr. O'Daire opened the door to the schoolhouse, the green umbrella at his side, his blond hair tamed and combed.

"Did I return too early?" he asked.

"Not at all," I said. "Your timing was rather perfect, actually." I packed my notebook full of colors, drawings, and dictation samples into my bag and turned back to Miss Simpkin. "Thank you again for allowing me to chat with you before starting with the students tomorrow."

"It was a pleasure." She shook my hand without once looking at Janie's father across the classroom.

I left the warmth of the schoolhouse's potbelly stove and followed Mr. O'Daire back out to his car. The rain had subsided, so we no longer needed to huddle beneath his umbrella. The frigid dampness of the air remained.

Mr. O'Daire opened the passenger-side door for me without a word, but the expectant look in his eyes, the slight lift of his golden-brown eyebrows, seemed a request for my thoughts about Janie.

"I'll speak to you more about your daughter after I examine her tomorrow," I said, and I climbed into the car.

He leaned his elbow against the top edge of my door. "Did Miss Simpkin say anything about her?"

"Tomorrow, Mr. O'Daire." I tucked my skirt beneath my legs on the seat. "Today was solely meant for introductions."

He nodded, with some reluctance, and shut my door.

To my relief, he didn't press the subject any further, although he did once again drum his thumbs against the steering wheel. We didn't see Sam and his threadbare coat either.

"Is that man all right now?" I asked after we passed the barbershop.

"You mean Sam?"

"Yes."

"I don't know." Mr. O'Daire's eyes softened; the drumming ceased. "Hopefully, he found shelter."

"Does he have a home?"

"He sleeps at his folks' house, but they don't know what to do with him. They've been stuck with him like that ever since he came home from France."

"It's such a shame there's not more psychological help out here on the coast."

"There's not *any* psychological help in this part of the coast. Aside from you, that is." He peeked at me with an expression loaded with optimism.

I sincerely hoped I'd be able to live up to that optimism.

"Were you in the war?" I asked.

"I trained at Camp Lewis, but they signed the Armistice right before my division was about to ship overseas. I can stab a sandbag with a bayonet better than anyone, though, so if you need a sandbag killed, Miss Lind, I'm your man."

"Sandbags are a common hazard to my profession"—I smiled and tucked a wayward lock of hair behind my ear—"so I'll most certainly keep that in mind."

He laughed, and his cheeks flushed with color.

I dug my teeth into my bottom lip and scolded myself for sounding so inexcusably flirtatious.

A moment later, my stomach growled, and my attention switched to eating and sleeping, the lack of both being the true hazard of my profession. Mr. O'Daire must have heard the caterwauling from my insides, for as soon as he pulled his automobile to a stop at the curb in front of the hotel, he said, "If you don't feel like trekking back into town for supper, you can eat here. We entertain local townsfolk and fishermen down in the hotel basement every night."

"Oh?"

"We'll be serving ham sandwiches, along with pretzels and pickles and drinks." He set the parking brake and extinguished the motor. "It's a large ham tonight, seeing as though it's Armistice Day. I'll have Mom deliver a sandwich to your room if you'd prefer to recover from your travels."

"Ham and pretzels, you said?"

He nodded.

I refrained from asking aloud, *The type of food served to whet customers' thirst for liquor in a speakeasy, you mean? Nice and salty?*

"Would you prefer something else?" he asked.

"No. It sounds lovely. And I think I would prefer to eat in my room."

He stepped out of the car and rounded the front of the vehicle while straightening the lapel of his black coat. His ability to earn a living with an empty hotel, the smart threads that he wore in a town crippled by rain and poverty, Miss Simpkin's characterization of his practices as "unsavory"—they all suddenly made sense. My host in Gordon Bay was more than just the concerned parent of a peculiar child. He was the owner of a "blind tiger," or so people called such establishments that spit in the face of Prohibition. A man who clearly knew how to succeed in the face of adversity.

Might he also prove to be an indispensable collaborator in getting to the root of his daughter's "Violet Sunday" tale, if he's so ambitious and resourceful? I wondered. *Or is he a handsome roadblock I'll need to steer around in order to solve this problem?*

Even worse, is he the problem?

UP IN MY hotel room, I situated myself in an armchair and ate my sandwich and pretzels with my feet defrosting in front of the fireplace. Poor Mrs. O'Daire had to leave my doorway with a rejected pickle wrapped in a napkin, for I couldn't stand the smell and taste of cucumbers in any form, pickled or otherwise. I also loathed carrots, green beans, peas, turnips, rutabagas, and radishes, and my persnickety behavior had vexed my mother my entire life, even at our most recent family gathering, just that past summer.

"An infantile aversion to vegetables," Mother had called it, while my middle sister, Margery, nodded in agreement, shoveling strained peas into the mouth of my six-month-old nephew, Warren. The baby's tongue pushed out an avalanche of rejected green vegetables, and I was forced to cover my mouth with a napkin to conceal my gagging.

Despite the momentary pickle encounter, my private supper in

Gordon Bay proved much more palatable and peaceful than any family dinner in Portland. Rain pinged against the windowpane; the hearth-fire glowed and shimmied with satisfying little pops of the logs. Down below my window, in the blackness of night, waves splattered against the shore, and over the rumpus of the sea, I heard automobiles rumbling to a stop in gravel. I had to wonder if Gordon Bay law enforcers cared at all that Mr. O'Daire and his mother entertained "local townsfolk and fishermen down in the hotel basement." In all honesty, I craved a glass of wine. Or gin.

Instead, I sipped my tea and licked pretzel salt from my lips.

It's all for the good of your future, Alice, I told myself yet again, and I sat up a little straighter in the chair. *Something to bolster the old university application. Field experience. Another chance to save children.*

My black briefcase caught my eye. It lay slumped against the wall to my left, by the room's door, and although I couldn't actually see the contents, Janie's composition beckoned to me from within. My front teeth crunched into the middle of a pretzel, dusting my sweater with crumbs. I stared the briefcase down, still able to re-member the first lines of the child's queer paragraph verbatim.

The scariest thing that ever happened to me was when I used to be called Violet Sunday and lived in Kansas. I was deep in the water and couldn't swim back up to the surface. My heart hurt. It felt like it was about to blow up.

The more I thought about Janie's selection of Kansas, of all the regions in the world, the slower my chewing grew, the deeper my brow creased.

So strange, I thought. *Kansas. But . . . I wonder . . .*

In my own childhood, I had gobbled up L. Frank Baum's delicious stories of Dorothy and Princess Ozma . . . and *Kansas*. In fact, I had drawn my own maps of Kansas to mount upon my wall, pored over the Kansas page in the family atlas, and struggled to construct a hot air balloon out of bed sheets so that I might fly away to Dorothy's home state, which I imagined to be a portal to adventures dark and wondrous. Whenever people asked where I was born, I even claimed to be from the prairie, and once again Mother would tut and sigh at my strangeness and say, "The child is obsessed with books."

I grabbed a notebook out of my briefcase and scribbled down a note to myself: *Ask Janie what books she enjoys reading. Another Oz fanatic, perhaps?*

On the following line, I added, *Inquire about fears of the bathtub, the ocean, or other water. Memory suppression highly likely. Does she mean she was nineteen months old, not nineteen years? Why nineteen?*

I leaned my elbow against the armrest and rubbed my right index finger across my lips.

Memory suppression, I wrote again in my notebook, my hands shaking, and I gulped another sip of tea, now lukewarm and bitter from a collection of leaves that must have slipped through the strainer. *If Janie doesn't know what happened, the mother* must *be contacted, despite her fear of the possibility of institutionalization.*

I sighed and scratched my forehead.

Sometimes, traumatic memories liked to keep the doors to their chambers wide open so that their victims would never stop hearing, seeing, and sensing the horrors of their past. The memories roared and clawed and sank sharp teeth into a person's brain, and as hard as the sufferer tried, she could never slam the door shut without someone—someone like a trained psychologist—to help.

In fact, shutting the door wasn't even the solution. The memories themselves needed to be weakened. Tamed. Shrunken down to minuscule granules of dust that could no longer clamp down and destroy a person's life.

Other memories, however, preferred to hide behind closed doors with thick metal locks. From behind the wood, they snarled. They growled. They pounded their fists against the barriers and threatened to kick the doors wide open to reveal their monstrous faces when their sufferers least wanted to see them. And yet they remained a frustrating mystery. Unconquerable until viewed and faced.

One of those closed doors existed inside of me.

Something happened to me when I was quite young. Whenever I asked my family about the incident as an adult, they'd lower their eyes and murmur useless phrases such as *It was simply a difficult period for you, Alice.* Or *That was such a long time ago.* Even my oldest sister, Bea, my confidante, refused to discuss it.

When I was four years old, I attacked several neighborhood children. An anger that emerged out of seemingly nowhere swelled inside me. It grew. It purpled. It howled and exploded. I struck my victims with a tree branch thicker than my arms and as heavy as a stepping stone. Not gentle taps, mind you—*merciless beatings of their heads.* Most of the children bled. I marveled at the sight of their shocking red blood that matted their hair and caused them to cry. "Devil Girl" is what their older siblings called me in the aftermath.

> *Alice Lind,*
> *Alice Lind,*
> *Took a stick and beat her friend.*

And yet no one ever explained what had happened to me to instigate such violence. No one would tell me if someone had beaten me and, therefore, inspired my need to beat others. I had come to believe I'd once been kidnapped. I sometimes dreamt of a mountain of a man with a beard like a thicket of tumbleweeds. He'd kick open our front door with the heel of his boot, aim a rifle at my chest, and pull the trigger with a ground-trembling eruption of gunpowder that I tasted on my lips.

Yet no one explained to me what that dream meant, or why such unspeakable violence burned through my blood.

Even sitting there in my Gordon Bay Hotel room with a half-finished sandwich and broken remainders of pretzels waiting by my side, I could feel my stomach tightening over whatever unfathomable tragedy lay buried inside my subconscious.

I will not leave until I'm certain Janie O'Daire is not suffering from a past trauma, I wrote in my notebook. *I will not.*

CHAPTER 4

The following morning, a wall of fog pressed against my hotel window. From the world beyond came the rush and the roar of the ocean, as well as the bellow of a fog horn, yet the only sight I could see was a motionless mass of white that did not seem inclined to depart anytime soon.

Behind me, a soft knock rattled the door. My shoulders flinched, and I dropped the curtain I'd been holding open.

"Who is it?" I asked.

No one responded. My hands tingled with that debilitating old fear again—the paranoia of being observed through a keyhole by an ogling eye. I took a breath, shook off such nonsense, and opened the door.

Down on the floor sat a silver tray of food—buttered toast, a hard-boiled egg, sausage patties, and a bowl of fruit, as well as a steaming mug of coffee that smelled divine. I poked my head into the hallway and looked both ways, expecting to hear the patter of retreating foot-steps. Not a sound met my ears, but I called out, "Thank you," and collected the food.

After shutting the door, I maneuvered the tray onto the dressing table. Again, Miss Simpkin's warnings about Mr. O'Daire's role in Janie's story pestered me:

I often wonder if her father is feeding her that tale and convincing her that she used to be a dead woman from the 1800s.

And . . .

He's not a war veteran, or a respected business owner, or even a married man. He's just the spoiled son of a successful hotel proprietor who inherited his daddy's business.

I lifted my chin and eyed the breakfast before me, along with the pristine white room. The food, the fireplace, the car rides, the O'Daires' fuss over my safety, the fog boxing me in—everything suddenly seemed suspect. A trap. Perhaps I had insisted upon sweeping Miss Simpkin's words aside too swiftly, tried too hard to tie my own muddled past to Janie's experiences, while ignoring the looming possibility of a swindle. Now more than ever, Mr. O'Daire—attractive Mr. O'Daire with his smiling eyes and boyish dimples—struck me as a fellow who had pushed his way through the storm to reach me, not as a compassionate father rescuing his daughter's savior, but as a con man stalking toward his prey.

I ate the breakfast with some reluctance, as though the bitter taste of bribery tainted the food.

Down in the hotel lobby, Mrs. O'Daire brushed ashes from the fireplace grate. Her back faced me, and every time she bent forward, the strings of her apron came a little more untied. Her hand went to her waist, and she stretched with a crack of her spine that made my own vertebrae tingle.

"Good morning," I said from behind her, and I descended the last step of the staircase. It would have seemed nonsensical and cowardly to attempt sneaking past her, especially when I carried a small cloth purse, in addition to my briefcase, and it jangled with coins that the children would need to count during the examinations.

She peeked over her shoulder. "Ah, good morning, Miss Lind. I trust you slept well."

"Yes, thank you." I scanned the lobby, in search of signs of her son. "Would it be all right if I borrowed an umbrella in case the rain starts in again? I'm planning to walk to the schoolhouse this morning."

"Oh no—that won't do at all." She laid the dustpan against the hearth's blackened bricks. "Have you seen the weather out there?"

"Well . . . yes . . ."

"If I allowed you to step foot out there alone"—she pushed herself to her feet—"I'd worry about you getting lost. Michael is currently in his room down the hall. I'll go fetch him and let him know you're ready to go."

"Thank you, but I'd prefer to walk. I'll just follow the road back into town."

"Miss Lind!" She put her hands on her hips. "No one will be able to see you out there."

"But—"

"Someone might come up behind you and smack you with his car—kill you right on the spot."

"Please, don't worry about me," I said with a laugh, even though I feared that very thing might occur. "If you have an umbrella . . ." I glanced toward the hallway, down which Mr. O'Daire apparently lived. "I'd prefer to leave as soon as possible."

"Does my son make you nervous?"

"I . . . I beg your pardon?"

"I know that Michael . . ." She peeked toward the hallway as well; her voice dropped to a whisper. "I know he told you he's no longer married. And I know how divorced men sometimes make women uncomfortable . . ."

"I'd actually prefer to go on my own for the simple reason that I'll be examining Janie this morning. I'd rather wait to see Mr. O'Daire again *after* I speak to the child."

"Ah." She closed her mouth. "Still, it's not worth the risk of getting hit by a car."

A door opened down the hall.

I tightened my grip on my bags. "I appreciate your concern, Mrs. O'Daire—truly I do. But I must be off."

IMMEDIATELY, I REGRETTED my decision to walk to the schoolhouse. My pride prohibited me from wheeling around to seek help, and yet I struggled to find my way through that freezing-cold mass of mist that impeded my view of any object farther than five feet ahead. Just in case an automobile roared around the bend, I adhered to the leftmost edge of the road, one foot on dirt, one on pavement, both legs poised to spring out of the way at a moment's notice. Waves crashed somewhere beyond the haze to my left. I feared I might veer onto a path that would dump me straight over a cliff.

At one point, a car engine, indeed, puttered up from behind. I sidled into the slick grasses at the side of the road and planned how I would explain to Mr. O'Daire that we needed to remain apart for the sake of the morning's test.

Instead of my host's vehicle, the autobus toting the schoolchildren crawled into view; I could just barely make out three tyke-sized heads in back. The cigar-smoking driver either didn't see me or avoided me, for he drove the vehicle onward, where the fog swallowed them whole, like an arm disappearing into a sleeve.

I pressed onward, as well.

The world smelled of rain and the ocean, everything damp and briny and bitter cold. Invisible droplets of moisture pricked at my cheeks like tiny stabs of sewing needles, and the chill in the air again bothered my bones, especially in my fingers, which made me worry about frostbite. My nose and eyes insisted upon running.

The real possibility of dying out there alone turned my thoughts to Janie O'Daire and her aunt's inquiry into my opinions on reincarnation. Every Sunday of my young life, my parents had steered me into the corner church, most especially during my unholiest of moments. The concepts of heaven and hell formed my early belief system, but not once did anyone speak of the transmigration of souls from one body to another. Nowadays, admittedly, I wavered between atheism and agnosticism, but the religion of psychology ruled my way of thinking more than any other dogma.

During my first year of administering intelligence tests, I met a six-year-old girl who claimed to speak to her deceased mother every night, as well as a nine-year-old boy who insisted that his late grandfather lived in his attic. My training in childhood grief allowed me to assist those children with their losses, and not once did I believe that they actually communicated with ghosts. The demon-possessed child I had referred to with Mr. O'Daire—ten-year-old Frankie of Pike, Oregon—proved to be a terribly tragic case of molestation by an uncle. Frankie horrified his teacher and classmates with his violent mutterings and his thirst for cutting other children with scissors, but I allowed his parents to see that church exorcisms were not the solution. The devil was a member of their own family.

Psychology, in short, explained *everything*.

By the time I lumbered into the town center of Gordon Bay, the fog had lifted. Without freezing or collapsing or losing my fingers, I managed to arrive at the little white schoolhouse, whose bell tower shone in a glimmer of sunlight that muscled its way through the clouds.

Inside the cloakroom, I found Miss Simpkin arranging a small round table and two chairs, assumingly for me and my examinees.

"Good morning," she said with a peek at me from beneath a cluster of red curls that hung over her forehead.

"Good morning." I lowered my bags with a rattle of the coins. "I see the cloakroom is transforming beautifully into our examination room."

"I hope you like it." She put her hands on her hips and exhaled a breath that jostled the curls. "It's awfully squished in here though, isn't it?"

"I've worked in much tighter spaces, I assure you. Ideally, we should be giving these examinations in a private office, but that's simply not possible in most of the towns that I visit."

"If you're sure it's all right . . ."

"It's just fine." I removed my coat.

She scooted the backmost chair farther away from the wall. "Is there a particular order you'd prefer for testing the children?"

"I usually start with the youngest and work my way up to the oldest."

"We have twenty-five students total, although some of them attend only sporadically."

"What I can't finish this week, I'll finish next week." I slipped off my gloves.

Miss Simpkin stood up straight and brushed her palms across the sides of her gray skirt. "Janie isn't one of the very youngest."

I blinked, almost having forgotten little Janie after my anxiousness of getting situated in yet another new schoolhouse. "I beg your pardon?"

"If you're especially eager to speak with her . . ." She nodded, as if hoping she need not say anything further.

"I would like to speak with her as soon as possible, yes." I hung my coat on one of the curved brass hooks. "But I can wait until I've finished with the five- and six-year-olds. I prefer examining the children from youngest to oldest."

"I hope Mr. O'Daire isn't being too charming." She smiled—or grimaced—as though she'd just swallowed a spoonful of castor oil.

"I actually haven't seen Mr. O'Daire since he drove me home yesterday afternoon. I holed myself up in my room for the rest of the day and then walked over here before he could offer to drive me."

"Smart girl."

Before I could respond, our first pupils pushed their way through the door—two tow-headed boys in overalls, possibly twins, most certainly brothers, both loud and springy and bubbling over with laughter. The type of children who would need a firm dose of coaxing and guidance to keep them seated for a forty- to fifty-minute examination.

I firmed up my shoulders and shoved aside my growing curiosity over the O'Daires. It was time to turn myself into Mighty Miss Lind, No-Nonsense Test Taker and Wrangler of Children.

MISS SIMPKIN INTRODUCED ME to the twenty-one children who swarmed inside the schoolhouse that morning, including Janie, who arrived without her father walking her inside.

"Miss Lind will take each of you, one at a time, to the table and chairs you saw sitting in the cloakroom," said Miss Simpkin in a voice far more animated and musical than the one she used with me. She even moved her hands about with the grace of an orchestra conductor. "She'll then give you a test that's meant to find out what you know and how well you know it. Do your best, but do not be worried. Much of the time it will feel like playing a game."

The first child I received back in my makeshift office was a five-year-old boy with chestnut-brown hair and a runny nose that required a bit of plugging with my handkerchief. As my training taught me, I spent the first several minutes establishing rapport with the child, asking him about his pets (a cat named William and a turtle named Slowpoke), his toys (his favorite was a hand car he drove with the push and pull of a handle), and his family (a mother, a father, two older brothers who were at that very school, and Myrtle Ann, a noisy, gassy baby sister). When I asked him, "What is the name of that color?" and pointed to papers mounted on white cardboard, he identified red, yellow, blue, and green without any struggle. When I asked, "Which of these two pictures is the prettiest?" and showed him drawings of two women, he called the more attractive one the "prettiest" and added, "but the ugly one sure looks like Grandma Prudence."

I bit my lip to avoid laughing and gave my usual, scripted answers of "fine" and "splendid"—everything coached and uniform and supportive. All responses went into the record booklet provided by the test makers. The boy's examination took thirty minutes, a standard amount of time for a child of five.

Next I saw two six-year-olds, a boy I diagnosed as being colorblind and a girl with a lisp who hesitated to speak to me. The boy's examination took forty-five minutes; the girl's an hour and a half.

We stopped for lunch, and then, unable to resist a moment longer, I said to Miss Simpkin, "Please let Janie O'Daire know that she'll be the first of the seven-year-olds whom I examine."

Miss Simpkin nodded, and the girl was fetched; the dice, rolled.

I sat up straight in my chair and readied myself to enter into the world of "Violet Sunday."

CHAPTER 5

Janie," I said in a voice that I strove to make as warm and welcoming as the classroom's little potbelly stove, "please tell me about your family."

The child tucked a lock of red hair behind her ear in a manner that struck me as rather grown-up. "Well, I live with Mommy and my aunt Tillie. Miss Simpkin is Aunt Tillie."

"So she said!" I folded my hands upon the closed record booklet. "What is it like having an aunt for a schoolteacher?"

"It's heaps of fun."

"Is it?"

"Mm hmm." Janie nodded, and her eyes glowed. Her short hair swung against her cheeks. I heard the backs of her feet knocking against the legs of her chair.

"Who else is in your family?" I asked.

"Daddy. And Nana."

"Nana? Is that your grandmother?"

"Mm hmm." Again, she nodded. "She works with Daddy."

"Do your father and grandmother live with you, too?"

"No." Her feet banged the chair harder, loud enough to poten-

tially interrupt the students in the classroom. "Daddy lives in the
hotel, and Nana lives in another house. Aunt Tillie lives with us."

"Ah, I see," I said. "You have several family members in the
area, but not all of them live in the same place. Is that correct?"

"Yes." She dropped her gaze to the table and rubbed her lips
together. Her feet stilled.

"Have you ever lived in the hotel with your daddy?" I asked.

"No."

"Have you always lived in the same house here in Gordon Bay?"

She shook her head and picked at the edge of the table. Her
shoulders tensed.

"Where else have you lived?"

She didn't respond.

I cleared my throat and steered the conversation elsewhere.
"What is your favorite subject in school, Janie?"

"Mathematics," she said without hesitation, and her eyes—
brightening again—returned to mine.

"You like working with numbers?"

"Mm hmm."

"In a few minutes . . ." I waited for a sudden peal of laughter in
the classroom to subside and for Miss Simpkin's steady voice to rule
the schoolhouse once again. "In a few minutes," I continued, "I am
going to ask you to count the value of five coins. Do you think that
will be something you'll enjoy?"

"Yes." She scooted up higher in her chair. "It'll be so easy, but yes."

"How long have you enjoyed mathematics?"

"Since . . . forever."

"Forever?" I asked.

Janie's strawberry-red lips spread into a coy smile. *"Forever."*

I shivered, in spite of myself. The child's voice had changed—deepened, matured, even taunted and teased. She stared at me without blinking, as though daring me to ask more.

Go ahead, she seemed to nudge. *Ask me what I mean.*

I gave a little cough into my right hand and chided myself for getting so ridiculously spooked. "And . . . who first taught you arithmetic?" I asked.

"A teacher."

"Miss Simpkin?"

Janie shook her head.

"Your parents?"

At that she laughed and became a regular child again. "No! Mommy and Daddy aren't so good with numbers."

"Another schoolteacher, then?"

She averted her eyes from mine and scratched at a chip in the table's surface. "My first-ever teacher helped me to see my talent for math. His name was Mr. Rook."

"Mr. Rook?"

"He had one of those"—she pushed a finger against her chin—"*lines* in his chin."

"A cleft chin?"

"Yes." Janie nodded and removed her finger from her face. "And he carried a pocket watch with an etching of a castle on the back."

"Ah, I see. You remember him well, then."

"Mm hmm."

I crossed my legs beneath the table. "Did he teach here before Miss Simpkin started teaching?"

"No. Somewhere else."

"Where?"

Janie squeezed her lips together and refused to answer.

I forced myself to refrain from mentioning "Violet Sunday" without Janie bringing us around to the subject herself. A glance at my watch revealed that the five minutes of establishing rapport was dwindling, and yet I couldn't abandon the conversation.

"Do you enjoy addition in particular?" I asked.

She shrugged. "It's *really* easy, but I like it."

"What's two plus two?"

Janie snorted. "Four, of course."

"And four plus four?"

"Eight."

"Eight plus eight?"

Janie rolled her eyes. "Sixteen."

"Six—"

"Thirty-two," she said before I could even utter "sixteen plus sixteen."

"Splendid." I nodded and smiled, but inwardly I shouted, *Holy hell! Why on earth is this astounding girl stuck in a one-room schoolhouse in the middle of Nowhere, Oregon?* Many of the seven-year-olds whom I typically interviewed couldn't even count to thirteen, let alone add beyond two plus two.

"And how about thirty-two plus seven?" I asked on a whim.

"Thirty-nine, of course," said Janie.

"Of course." I gulped. "This is, indeed, easy for you, isn't it? And you're just . . ." I peeked at the list of the pupils' names and ages in my record booklet. "You *are* just seven years old, correct?"

"That's right. You can ask me a harder one if you'd like."

"All right, then." I folded my arms over my chest. "Let's get really tricky, just for the fun of it, but there's absolutely no pressure to answer correctly, understand?"

"Yes."

"Tell me"—I wiggled my chin back and forth while bouncing various number combinations around in my brain—"what is two hundred fifty-seven plus forty-eight?"

Janie peeked up at a corner of the room behind me and closed one eye. "Three hundred five."

My jaw dropped at the confidence of her tone. I fumbled around in my briefcase to find a blank piece of paper. While she waited patiently, her hands flat against the table, I scribbled down the equation and added up the columns.

The answer: *Three hundred five.*

I gasped. "How on earth did you calculate the equation so quickly, Janie?"

"I saw the numbers in my head"—she closed her eyes—"and I used the tens and the ones places to figure things out. I do that with everything—addition, subtraction, multiplication, division, fractions . . ."

"You know how to calculate fractions?"

"Yes." She giggled and leaned back in her chair. "That's pretty easy, too, if you really think about it."

My mouth went dry from gaping. I stammered and fussed with my papers, slicing a thumb on a sharp edge of one of the pages, and I managed to sputter up one more equation: "What do you get when you multiply four fifths by seven eighths?"

Again, Janie peeked up at a corner of the room and squinted with one eye closed. I peeked over my left shoulder, just to make sure that her father wasn't standing there, an abacus and a slide ruler in hand, mouthing the answers to her.

"Seven tenths," said Janie with a nod, and she gave another little tuck of her hair behind her right ear.

I jotted down the equations and dithered for a moment, forcing myself to remember how to multiply fractions. My brow sweated; my nose itched from all the eraser flakes showering my paper as I rubbed away mistakes.

The answer that emerged at the end of all my pencil scratches: *seven tenths*.

I looked up at Janie, who smiled and resumed swinging her heels against her chair.

"See?" she asked. "I like numbers."

"S-s-splendid," I said, and with shaking fingers, I opened the record booklet and tried to remember what the devil I was supposed to do with rickety old Stanford–Binet, which didn't seem at all like a proper test for a child such as Janie O'Daire.

I maneuvered us through all of the regular sections of the examination—the color identifications, the coin counting, the scrutiny of an illustration, the comparison of two objects from memory. Janie spoke with eloquence, answered all questions with ease, and demonstrated the intelligence of a person at least four to five years older than herself. Her math level was equivalent to that of a person fifteen years old or above.

Fifteen years old or above!

"What is your earliest memory, Janie?" I asked before she could leave her chair and skedaddle off to her seat in the classroom.

She scratched the tip of her freckled nose, and I couldn't help but wonder if her father had coached her in the answering of this particular question, even if he hadn't been responsible for her impressive feats of calculation. He was the one who advised me to ask it, after all.

"How far back can you remember?" I asked again with a tilt of my head. "For most people, memories start around the age of two or three, although some people insist they can remember being babies. I myself—" I bit my tongue and refrained from projecting myself into the situation.

"I remember being a baby," said Janie, and she peeked up at me from beneath her golden-red lashes.

Out in the main section of the schoolhouse, the children applauded a student who must have given an oration or performed some other act of classroom bravery, and for the first time since Janie sat down, I became truly aware of the rest of the school.

"And . . ." My heart beat to the rhythm of the second hand on my wristwatch. Janie's patience would soon wear; Miss Simpkin might poke her head around the corner to check on the welfare of her niece. "Is that as far back as your memory goes?"

"I remember." Janie licked her lips and turned her eyes toward the window beside us, through which sunlight shone for the first time that day. "Mother tied a creaky wire contraption around her waist—a bustle—and it made her . . ." Janie snickered and covered her mouth with her right hand, her shoulders shaking. "Her backside looked like it was trapped in a birdcage. My sister and I laughed so hard we fell off Mother's bed."

"Oh?" I sat up straight. "You have a sister, then?"

Janie merely blinked, still gazing out the window. A pinkish-yellowish light glowed across her cheeks and hair.

"You didn't mention her when I asked about your family," I said. "Does she live with you and your mother and aunt?"

Janie drew both hands into her lap. "I haven't seen her in a long time."

"How long?"

"Very long."

"What is her name?"

Janie sunk her teeth into her lower lip. "Eleanor."

"And . . . is Eleanor older than you?"

She swiveled to her left in her chair and pointed her knees toward the entrance to the classroom.

"Janie?" I swallowed. "Is Eleanor still alive?"

I could only see a sliver of Janie's profile, but I witnessed the downward turn of her mouth, the pursing of her slender red eyebrows.

"Oh . . . I'm sorry," I said in a voice a hair above a whisper, assuming the sibling to be deceased.

"I don't know if she's still alive," said Janie, swallowing. "She'd be an older woman now."

I leaned forward in my chair. "I'm sorry; I think I might have heard you wrong. Did you just say that your sister would be an older woman?"

"Probably fifty-three or so."

I drew a short breath and strove not to laugh. "Fifty-three?"

"She would have—" Janie blinked and whipped her head my way with her mouth wide open, as though catching me in the act of eavesdropping on a private conversation. "May I return to my desk now?"

"Yes." I froze, startled by her shift in character. "We're done with the examination. But, Janie, if you—"

The child shot off her chair and tore around the corner, back to the classroom.

CHAPTER 6

I examined two more seven-year-olds that afternoon: a sullen boy with the mental age of four and the little brunette whom I'd mistaken for Janie the day before. Not surprisingly, no one matched the mathematical acrobatics of Janie O'Daire.

"Most of the children I tested today seem to be operating within average IQ ranges," I said to Miss Simpkin when we conferred at her desk after the children went home. "The pupil I'm most concerned about is Dale Gage. His IQ is fifty, which is more typical of a child of four, not seven."

Miss Simpkin tutted over poor Dale, and we discussed the need for him to be placed on the list of students who would benefit from a class or school designed for subnormal children in the region. Unlike the previous afternoon, Miss Simpkin did not pull a cigarette out of her desk drawer, but she chewed on the end of a pencil as though hungering for a smoke. I discussed the color-blind boy and the girl with a lisp, both of whom demonstrated average mental abilities for their ages and grades, despite their particular impediments. Flames sputtered in the stove next to the desk, and a fresh afternoon rainstorm jackhammered the roof and tossed about the pine branches outside the window.

"And what about Janie?" asked Miss Simpkin. She bit down on the pencil with a discernible *crunch*.

"Ah, yes, Janie." I ran my index finger across the line on my records containing Janie's responses, quite certain that Miss Simpkin saw straight through my attempt to pretend I didn't immediately remember her niece's results. "I have to ask"—I glanced up at her—"who is Mr. Rook?"

She drew the pencil out of her mouth. "Mr. Rook?"

"Yes. Janie, as you probably know, demonstrated an astounding knack for mathematics. When I asked where she learned such impressive skills, she said a Mr. Rook had been the teacher who helped her discover her talent for numbers."

Miss Simpkin shuddered. "That, Miss Lind, is a prime example of Janie's disquieting behavior. *I* am the only person who has ever been Janie's schoolteacher."

"How interesting . . ." I crossed my legs. "Janie described the man as having a cleft chin and a distinctive pocket watch. Is there anyone she knows who meets those descriptions?"

"No one I can think of. There is no Mr. Rook in Gordon Bay. Even the name alone gives me the willies. I'm imagining a dark cloak made of feathers and beady little bird eyes."

"Who *did* teach Janie advanced mathematics, then? How can a child of seven multiply fractions in her head without writing a single number down on paper?"

Miss Simpkin slid the pencil between her teeth again. "She's simply been good at numbers for as long as I can remember."

"She calculated *fractions*, Miss Simpkin. You must know how miraculous a feat that is for a child as young as she."

"I do, and none of us understands it. Her intelligence isn't the part that concerns me, however—unless Michael parades her around in front of men of science or newspaper journalists because of it."

I arched my brows. "*Has* he gone to the newspapers?"

"He once lured reporters to Gordon Bay, not long before he and my sister separated. He claimed he wanted to use the papers to find other parents with children like Janie, but my sister sent the newsmen packing. She doesn't want any fuss or exposure—that's why we must be so careful about the way we approach all of this." Miss Simpkin fumbled to open a lower drawer in her desk.

I tucked the record booklet into my briefcase. "I would like to speak to the girl's mother."

"Rebecca won't speak to you."

"Are you certain?"

"Quite certain. She's hoping Janie's eccentricities simply settle down and disappear." Miss Simpkin gritted her teeth and continued tugging on the drawer, which sounded to be jammed. "We just want this to all go away, but I'm so frightened that it won't."

"No, it won't, I'm afraid. If her father . . ." I peeked over my shoulder to ensure that Mr. O'Daire hadn't entered the schoolroom behind me. "If Mr. O'Daire is feeding the child these Violet Sunday stories, as you suggested yesterday, then there certainly can't be a resolution until someone speaks to him about his motives. On the other hand, if there's been a trauma—a near-drowning in Janie's past, for example—then her fears, I'm sorry to say, will continue to beleaguer her until someone helps her to cope with the tragedy."

The drawer burst open, and Miss Simpkin jerked backward with a small cry. She then lunged toward the desk and fished out the box of cigarettes.

"Besides," I said, clearing my throat, "I should like to speak to Mrs. O'Daire about long-term plans for Janie's supernormal intelligence. We'll need to ensure that the child is being challenged. We may even need to arrange for her to attend a special school for advanced children in the near future."

Miss Simpkin slid a pure white cigarette between her lips. "Rebecca would never send Janie away."

"Well, we might be able to establish a school for above-average children in the coastal region, just as we would for the children who struggle to keep up with their peers."

With a flick of her lighter, Miss Simpkin set the end of the cigarette aglow. "I think . . ." She paused to take a puff with the cigarette wedged between her teeth, forcing her to speak out of the left side of her mouth. "The first thing you need to do, Miss Lind, is to remove yourself from Michael O'Daire's hotel."

I blinked. "I . . . I beg your pardon?"

"I'm not suggesting that anything untoward would happen between the two of you . . ." She gave me the once-over, prompting me to cross my arms over my chest. "But Rebecca isn't going to like hearing from Janie that she's being evaluated by a woman who's sleeping under Michael's roof. If you want my sister to trust you, if you want to have *any* hope of speaking to her"—she took another smoke, her eyes fixed upon me—"then please, immediately, stop letting her ex-husband pamper you."

CHAPTER 7

That afternoon, I entered the hotel lobby with every intention of checking out and avoiding trouble. Unfortunately, no one else occupied the premises at the moment, or so it seemed. Halfhearted flames lapped at the fireplace logs, but the wood needed stirring, and the room lacked heat.

"Mr. O'Daire?" I called out.

No one responded. Rain tapped against the windowpanes, and a log slipped in the grate.

I ventured past the front desk and down the main hallway. To my immediate left, an open doorway led to a small closet outfitted with bookshelves and a few dozen cloth-bound novels, primarily sea-themed adventures—*Moby-Dick*, *Treasure Island*, *Two Years before the Mast*, etc. Ten Sherlock Holmes books, including my favorite, *The Hound of the Baskervilles*, added a dash of mystery to the collection. To the right of the shelves hid another door, within the closet, oddly enough, and it also stood ajar.

"Mr. O'Daire?" I asked again, in the direction of this mysterious second doorway. "Are you in?"

"Down here," he called from somewhere deep in the bowels of the hotel's underbelly. "I'm just putting tonight's ham in the oven."

"Ah, yes." I smiled. "The ham." I stepped into the closet and found a flight of stairs leading down to the shadows of the basement.

"Come down, if you'd like," he called, still out of sight, still muffled.

I grabbed hold of a splintered rail and clambered down the wooden steps, each board whining and wheezing from the pressure of my feet. The farther I descended, the mustier and boozier the air smelled, as though I were lowering myself through the neck of a whiskey bottle.

Down in the basement, six round tables, surrounded by a hodgepodge of chairs, filled a dim room lit by smoky copper lamps that hung from thick beams crisscrossing a low ceiling.

Mr. O'Daire stuck his head through a square opening that separated the main room from an area that must have been a kitchen, for I heard a pot bubbling and caught a glimpse of a wooden icebox behind him.

"I see you survived your adventure of wading blindly through the fog this morning," he said.

"Yes, I did."

"Why wouldn't you allow me to drive you? I'm surprised you didn't get hit by a car."

I turned my gaze to the glass-shaped rings marking up the wooden tabletops. "I didn't want to trouble you for a ride. And the walk did wonders for my legs after traveling for so many hours yesterday."

"You're a terrible liar."

I glanced back at him. "Why do you say that?"

"Because someone telling the truth would never describe a walk through freezing fog as a 'wonder.'" He smiled and pulled his head out of the opening.

I laid my briefcase on the nearest table and debated the best way to tell him I was checking out of the hotel, without causing offense.

"May I get you a drink?" he called, again out of sight.

"Mr. O'Daire . . ." I cleared my throat. "I can no longer be a guest in your hotel. I'll be spending the rest of my stay in Gordon Bay at the boardinghouse."

He meandered around the corner, a glass in hand, his brow furrowed. "Why?"

"May I be honest?"

"Please do."

"Miss Simpkin dislikes me staying here. I'll be collaborating quite closely with her over the course of the next week, and the last thing I want to do is to make her uncomfortable."

He set the cup down on the table beside him. "Did she offer you a bed at her place?"

"No."

He rolled his eyes. "That's typical of her."

"I'm sorry." I removed my gloves. "That's simply how it is."

He stepped closer, tucking his hands inside his pockets. "Did you talk to Janie today?"

"Yes, I examined her this morning."

"Did you ask her about her earliest memories?"

I laid the gloves on top of my briefcase and smoothed down the wool until the fingers lay flat. "I know about Violet Sunday."

"She told you about her?"

"Miss Simpkin prepared me for the situation, actually, and Janie . . ." I met his eyes. "Janie demonstrated her mathematical prowess to me. She also told me some stories that seem to correlate to the Violet Sunday tale."

"It's not a tale."

"*Who* is Violet Sunday, then?"

"She's Janie." He looked straight at me without blinking. "She's who Janie was before she was born into this life."

Keeping my own face stoic, I gauged the sincerity of his expression—the steadiness of his eyes, the stillness of his lips, the even pattern of his breathing, which neither accelerated nor slowed.

"Do you believe in past lives, Mr. O'Daire?" I asked.

"I didn't used to."

"But you do now?"

"Yes. Without a doubt."

I fussed with my gloves on the table again. "What is it about Janie's story that has you so firmly convinced that this isn't a case of childish fantasy?"

"Janie's mother and I have kept a record of all of the details she's given about her previous life. Would you care to see it?"

"Yes. Most definitely."

"May I serve you a drink before I run up to my room to fetch it?"

I inhaled the sharp sting of alcohol in the air. "I'm an employee of the Department of Education. I'd lose my job if I purchased a glass of liquor."

"I never said I sell liquor."

"But, I clearly smell—"

"I wouldn't dream of offering you booze, Miss Lind. How about a soft drink?" He smirked, and his eyes laughed, as though he knew full well what I smelled—as though he believed me to be too persnickety for bootlegged whiskey.

I shifted my weight and debated whether a glass of soda pop would meet Miss Simpkin's definition of being "pampered" by her former brother-in-law. I surveyed my surroundings—the unfinished planks of the dark walls, the weak haze of light exhaled as yellow steam from the bulbs of the copper lamps, the bare tabletops ringed in those octopus-tentacle-like suction marks from all the glasses and bottles of evenings past. Enjoying a carbonated beverage in a dank basement could hardly be described as "pampered," one would think.

"All right," I said. "A soft drink would be lovely. Thank you."

He backed toward the kitchen, his hands still wedged inside his pockets. "Root beer? Orange Quench? LimeTone?"

"Orange Quench, please."

"On the rocks?"

"Why not?"

"Coming right up." He disappeared into the kitchen, but I could see him moving about through the opening in the wall. He wore a cornflower-blue shirt with the sleeves rolled up to his elbows, and his back faced me, so I viewed the sturdy breadth of his shoulders and the bobbing movements of his elbows as he fetched a bottle from the icebox. His blond hair tapered to a sharp point above the nape of his neck. A slick black belt encircled his trim waist.

I heard the pop of a bottle cap and a contented sigh from the bottle as he poured a stream of liquid. He then strode back out to me with a glass bubbling with a neon-orange beverage that smelled of penny candy.

"Enjoy." He set the drink next to my bag and gloves. "I'll be right back with the journal."

"Thank you." I sat down and watched him jog up the rickety old staircase, his black shoes thumping out of sight.

Up above my head, the ceiling soon creaked with the sounds of him hustling about somewhere on the ground floor, and I tried to envision what he was doing up there, pondering if he was just then opening a blank notebook and scribbling down this so-called "record" of Janie's previous life. And yet, I strove to remain open-minded. My job at the moment was to stay neutral and to collect any and all facts pertaining to the child in need.

Roughly two minutes later, Mr. O'Daire returned down the steps with a confident gallop, a book tucked beneath his right arm.

"In June 1921"—he walked up to my table—"Rebecca, my former wife, first started using this notebook to keep track of Janie's stories of the past. Janie was about to turn three at that point, but she'd already been speaking of her life as Violet for at least six months."

On the table before me, he laid a brown leather notebook about the size of a paperback novel, but half as thick. The book reminded me of a travel journal that I carried with me whenever Bea and I took one of our excursions down to California, including the recent trip to that Winchester tourist attraction with the séance room and the tales of vengeful spirits.

"When Rebecca began jotting down her notes," said Mr. O'Daire, "I had been back from the army for over two years. I left for Camp Lewis a little over a month after Janie was born, but since my return in March 1919, I've witnessed everything Janie did with my own eyes. I can corroborate all of the incidents Rebecca chronicled, except for the ones that occurred when I was here at work."

I pulled the notebook closer. "Where is your mother right now?"

"At her house, in town. She only helps now and then during the non-summer season. Her back isn't as good as it used to be. Why?"

"I want to ensure that we're speaking in confidence right now. I want you to be able to talk as openly and honestly as possible about the contents of this journal. About Janie."

"Of course." He lowered himself down in a chair across from me. "I want to get to the crux of what's happening with my daughter, Miss Lind. I've been going out of my mind with worry about her. How do you help a girl who insists she's homesick for a place she's never even visited? How do you calm a small child who screams out in terror about the horrors of drowning, when she's barely ever dunked her head underwater?"

"She's suffering, then?"

"Oh, God, yes." He gestured toward the notebook with his head. "Read our notes. You'll see what I mean."

My eyes shifted back down to the scuffed brown leather of the journal's cover. The lower-right-hand corner had worn away to the palest shade of tan, almost white, as though the book spent a great deal of time sliding in and out of bookshelves and getting gripped by a firm thumb. I took a breath and opened to the first page.

An entry written in an elegant cursive hand awaited.

June 7, 1921

> *I fear what may come of describing on paper the curious goings-on with our daughter, Janie O'Daire, but it's the only thing I can think to do to sort out her peculiarities. I am planning to use this journal as a map; a means of navi-*

*gating my way around Janie's stories and nightmares—
around her very head—so that we might see if there are any
inconsistencies, or any possible truths, to her stories.*

*Here is what happened just this morning. Janie was
playing with her Victorian dollhouse that my parents gave
to her last Christmas. I brought a basket of clean laundry
into her bedroom to put away, and she turned around and
peered at me with the strangest mournful expression.*

"I want to go home," she said.

*"You are home," I told her, but she burst into tears and
said, "No, my other home. Not the one with the man in it,
but my real home. The pretty one with red flowers on the
wallpaper."*

*When I told her she has never lived in such a place, she
threw one of the chairs from her dollhouse across the room.*

*"The Kansas home!" she cried out. "My real home. Why
must I live here instead of there?"*

*Janie is not yet even three years old. Her birthday is in
a couple of weeks. She has never lived in Kansas. She has
never traveled any farther east than the foot of the Coast
Range right here in Gordon Bay, Oregon. The little toy chair
made a dent in the wall, she was so vexed when she threw it.
Why does she insist on saying she used to live somewhere else?
She has been fabricating these tales for as long as she could
first string words together to make sentences.*

Why?

I turned to the next page. Across from me, Mr. O'Daire folded
his hands on the tabletop and breathed without a sound.

June 8, 1921

> *Another bad nightmare. Janie woke up, screaming, "Drowning! Drowning! Drowning! Too cold! Too cold!"*
>
> *When I asked her about the dream in the morning, she said she could not remember what she had been dreaming about, but an hour or so after breakfast she wandered into the kitchen behind me and said, quite eloquently, "Do you think someday we ought to go to Friendly, Kansas?"*
>
> *"Where?" I asked her.*
>
> *"Friendly," she repeated. "I want to go back to Friendly. That's where my pretty house is. I don't mean the one with the man in it."*
>
> *"And where is the house with the man in it?" I asked with a smile. "In Mean, Kansas?"*
>
> *Her face darkened, and she balled her hands into fists. "It isn't a joke!" she cried out, and she stormed out of the room. I then heard her sobbing upstairs.*
>
> *Fifteen minutes later, she skipped back into the kitchen and asked about lunch, seemingly forgetting all about "Friendly, Kansas" and the house "with the man in it."*

I chewed on the fingernail of my left pinkie, debating whether the child might be suffering from a multiple personality, as her sudden switches from one persona to the other suggested. Or perhaps paramnesia, a condition in which a person remembered events that never actually occurred, more commonly seen in elderly, senile patients, not children.

I raised my eyes to Mr. O'Daire's. "'Friendly, Kansas'?"

He pressed his lips together and nodded. "I know—it sounds like a make-believe town. She's talked about Friendly ever since that day Rebecca first wrote about it, though. And she'll fly into a fit of crying whenever we tell her we can't take her there."

"Have you checked an atlas to see if such a place exists?"

"Of course."

"And?"

He shook his head. "I've never found it on any map or in any book stocked in our nearest library. Although, to be fair, Gordon Bay is also too puny to appear on most maps."

I flipped through more pages of the notebook, still chewing on that nail, still worrying that a multiple personality was at work in the mind of such a small child. The farther I traveled into the journal, the shorter and more succinct the notes grew.

November 22, 1921—Today Janie claimed that she clearly remembered the drowning dream. She described seeing the man from the other house watching her struggle in thick underwater grasses that yanked at her ankles and skirts.

January 17, 1922—Today Janie asked if I enjoyed calculating square roots. She turned three and a half last month! Nobody in this house—not my husband, not I, not her visiting grandparents or aunt—has ever discussed mathematics much at all, aside from perhaps mentioning the cost of a bill. Square roots!

May 4, 1922—Janie spoke of her drowning dream again this morning. "Why do you think you drowned?" I asked. She lifted eight of her fingers and said in a voice that made my blood run cold, "Eight. Eight. Eight. Watch out for the number eight!"

June 23, 1922—Janie's fourth birthday. When I asked what she wished for after she blew out her candles, she stated, "I wish someone would take me back to Friendly. My other family must be worried sick."

December 25, 1922—Michael asked Janie to make a Christmas card for me. She signed it "Violet Sunday." Oh, how tired I am getting of hearing about Violet Sunday! Janie's eccentricities are starting to remind me of Mother's, and I am frightened this queerness will continue forever.

When I questioned Janie about the mistake on the card, she told me that signing that name came naturally, although the Sunday part was a mistake, now that she thought about it. She told me she wonders what the man in the other house would think of her signing her name that way.

"What do you make of this somewhat sinister-sounding 'man in the other house'?" I asked Mr. O'Daire with another lift of my head. "Janie speaks of him so frequently, and yet he seems to remain an unnamed mystery in the journal. Unless . . ." I thumbed ahead to the second half of the notebook, where I discovered a completely different set of handwriting, one more linear and slanted, more rushed. The dates ranged from August 1923 to the present year. "Whose handwriting is this in the second half of the book?"

"Mine," said Mr. O'Daire.

"Why did your wife stop writing?"

He rubbed the back of his neck and winced, as though the forthcoming answer caused his muscles to ache.

"Mr. O'Daire?" I asked, and my stomach sank, for I thought once more of Miss Simpkin's insistence that this was all a swindle. "Why didn't she continue the journal herself?"

"The idea of writing down anything that would make Janie sound insane started to sicken her. When Janie was five years old, Rebecca's mother was . . ." He lowered his hand from his neck and picked at a rough spot on the table's wood. "They had to commit my former mother-in-law to an asylum."

"Oh." I swallowed. "Oh, I'm so sorry. May I ask why?"

"Severe melancholy. Rebecca and her sister couldn't even convince their mother to get out of bed sometimes. She'd want to—and she once even tried to"—he scratched at the wood with one of his nails—"take her own life."

"Did their mother demonstrate these symptoms from an early age, do you know? Or did they manifest as she got older?"

"Rebecca always told me she grew up fearing her mother's dramatic shifts in moods. Her father was the captain of a whaling ship and traveled out to sea for long periods of time. They lived in a remote house to the south, and every time Captain Simpkin left, according to Rebecca, her mother would simply . . . *unravel*."

"Hmm . . ." I smoothed out a curled-up corner on the bottom right-hand side of the page. "It sounds like prairie madness."

"How's that?"

"Many of the pioneers who settled in the Great Plains couldn't tolerate the loneliness of such an isolated way of living. They turned melancholy . . . and sometimes violent."

Mr. O'Daire shifted in his chair and crossed his right leg over his left.

"Is Captain Simpkin still alive?" I asked.

"Yes. And still sailing out to sea."

"Did he ever come close to drowning? Could the risks of his occupation perhaps have led to this fear of drowning in Janie?"

Mr. O'Daire shook his head. "I've never heard of him experiencing a brush with death. Janie has never expressed concern over his safety either. A 'tough old barnacle' is what she knows him as."

I smiled at that comment and flipped through more pages. "Was your mother-in-law ever left alone with Janie?"

"She never harmed anyone but herself, if that's what you're wondering."

"Yes," I said. "It's precisely what I'm wondering. As I said about prairie madness—"

"No one has ever hurt that child, Miss Lind. I swear. I wouldn't let them."

"I just want to make absolute certain."

"Everyone loves that girl. Everyone's always fussing over her and making sure she's safe and content, including my parents and Rebecca's parents."

"I'm glad to hear that." I softened my voice. "Janie hinted that her other grandfather, your father, is no longer alive. Is that correct?"

"My father died of cancer the same year we institutionalized my mother-in-law." Mr. O'Daire placed both hands, palms down, flat on the table. "It was . . ." He laughed—one of those coughing types of laughs that rattles out of a person when he's astounded by his own rotten luck. "It was an awful year. Rebecca grew to hate me for wanting to get a professional's opinion of Janie. I caught her with a fellow who had been her first sweetheart—someone who was purportedly consoling her over her hardships with me. I inherited this hotel and moved out of my own home. Tillie moved in with

Rebecca to help her with Janie. And . . . now . . ." He shrugged. "Now, here I am, spending my evenings entertaining other lonely saps. Still desperate to prove that Janie once lived another life as a lady mathematical genius."

I cocked my head at him. "Why do you want to prove this reincarnation theory so desperately?"

He leaned forward, digging his elbows against the table. "If you had a child who screamed in terror most nights because she claimed to have drowned thirty-five years ago, wouldn't you do the same? Wouldn't you do whatever you could to help that child return to the place where she claims she came from—to help her find peace?"

"You believe that if Janie returns to this 'Friendly, Kansas,' she'll find peace?"

"Why would a child plead to go to a place year after year after year if it didn't mean something vital to her?"

I redirected my attention back to the journal, knowing some rational explanation, miles away from the possibility of a past life, waited to be discovered within all those crinkling pages marked up in lines of black ink.

I circled back to the theory of paramnesia.

"Does Janie ever strike you as being paranoid?" I asked, scanning a page that detailed Janie's fears of bath time.

"No. Only when she's in the throes of one of her nightmares. Why?"

I shook my head, knowing it was far too soon to mention any possible diagnoses to her father. I reread two of the entries that most haunted me:

May 4, 1922—Janie spoke of her drowning dream again this morning. "Why do you think you drowned?" I asked. She lifted eight of her fingers and said in a voice that made my blood run cold, "Eight. Eight. Eight. Watch out for the number eight!"

And . . .

November 22, 1921—Today Janie claimed that she clearly remembered the drowning dream. She described seeing the man from the other house watching her struggle down in the cold, dark waters while her heart burst to pieces.

I pressed out a crease in the paper. "I don't know what to make of this number eight business, do you?"

"She's always been obsessed with that number."

"Does she seem frightened of it?"

"Not entirely. She writes it quite a bit, sometimes over and over, especially when she gets into one of her dreamier moods."

"How interesting." I turned to the later entries, spotting the words *the man in the other house* yet again. "As I was saying before," I continued, "Janie seems to fear a specific individual. A man." I met Mr. O'Daire's eyes. "Can you think of any men in her real life who might have frightened her?"

He clenched his jaw. "For the last time, Miss Lind, no one's ever hurt Janie in her current life. For crying out loud, I wouldn't even let anyone abusive in the same breathing space as my daughter."

"You're positive? When she was a baby, there weren't any friends or—"

He slammed the heel of his right palm against the table, making me jump. "Her mother and I have done nothing but taken the best care of her. We lost another baby—a stillborn—a year before we learned Janie was on the way, and we swore we would lay down our own lives before Janie would ever face any harm. No one has ever hurt that little girl."

"I'm sorry." I closed the book, my heart sinking—clenching, *shattering*—over the idea of a deceased baby. "I . . . I'm sorry for your loss. And for upsetting you. I can tell this entire puzzle surrounding Janie has frazzled everyone's nerves. But you must understand that I, as a psychologist, must seek out rational, behavioral explanations before I can even begin to consider the reincarnation theory."

He ran the same hand that had just whacked the table through the short strands of hair above his right ear. A gold band encrusted with a blue gem gleamed from his right ring finger—a high school class ring, if I had to wager. His left hand demonstrated no lingering indications of his former wedding band.

"Janie mentioned having a sister," I said.

"Eleanor?"

"Yes, that's the name she gave."

"That's Violet's sister." He bent forward and took the notebook, paging back to the beginning of the records. "Rebecca wrote down several cases of Janie mentioning Eleanor and their mother and father, as well as a little terrier named Poppy." He scooted the book back in front of me and poked at an entry with his right index finger. "See?"

I looked down and, indeed, read an account of Eleanor.

August 19, 1922—When I was brushing Janie's hair this morning, she said that her other mother had "a ghastly time" trying to brush all the curls in her sister Eleanor's hair. "My hair was straight and brown as an acorn shell," she said, "but Eleanor's was blond and springy and tangled. I used to envy her hair. She looked like a princess after it was brushed. Oh my, how I wish I could tell Eleanor that none of this was her fault. There was nothing she could have done."

I shook my head and breathed through my nose, continuing to remain perplexed.

"Did you learn about anything like this in your university studies?" asked Mr. O'Dairc.

"About reincarnation?"

He nodded.

"No. This is the first time I've ever encountered this particular type of claim."

He tapped his left fingertips against the tabletop. "Do you have any recommendations—anything at all—for what I could do to help her?"

"Before I can do anything further, I would like to read more of this journal, to obtain a more complete picture of what Janie is trying to say through her Violet Sunday stories."

Again, he nodded, with some hesitation. "All right."

"I would also like to investigate the existence of Friendly, Kansas—or a place with a name that strongly resembles Friendly.

I think the sooner we rule out the reincarnation theory, the better it will be for . . ." I stopped and bit my bottom lip, unsure which name to add to the end of that sentence.

"Better for who?" asked Mr. O'Daire, his forehead wrinkling. "For you?"

"I didn't say that."

"Are you worried about being viewed as a laughingstock if you help my daughter?"

I slid my right thumb across the layer of condensation frosting up the glass of soda pop in front of me. "I'm already considered a laughingstock by some, Mr. O'Daire."

"Why?"

"Because I'm a woman in a man's field."

He leaned back in his chair and dangled his right elbow off the armrest. "Is the chauvinism that bad?"

"Every single doctorate program I applied to turned me down, even though my grades were higher than those of most of the male students around me. Those cocky, lucky dunderheads got accepted and moved on, whereas I—" I met his eyes and closed my mouth, realizing I had veered into the territory of complaining. "I'm sorry. I know that's none of your business. The chauvinism I face, however, is one of the very reasons I go beyond the normal duties of a test administrator to help the most troubled of students."

"Miss Sunday encountered that same barrier."

I blinked. "I beg your pardon?"

He nodded toward the notebook. "She was a female mathematician trampled by a world lacking equality. And I'm sure she'll face the same prejudices in this life as Janie O'Daire."

I lowered my eyes back to the book, for I found it hard to look at a man who so wholeheartedly embraced the idea of reincarnation. The sincerity of his belief embarrassed me, to be most honest. It felt like meeting a high-school-aged boy who still believed in Santa Claus.

"My understanding, Miss Lind, is that you came to Gordon Bay to ensure that our children are in the right place."

"Yes." I nodded. "That's precisely why I'm here."

"Janie feels misplaced."

"Yes, but that's not—"

"I'll pay you to help her, if that's what you'd require."

"No, that's not necessary. In fact"—I got to my feet, nearly knocking my chair backward—"you've already done far too much for me. If you don't mind, I'll read this journal in my room for the next hour, and then I'll gather my belongings and head to the boardinghouse, as Miss Simpkin suggested."

"Sailors stay in that boardinghouse." He stood up as well. "It's a flophouse, and it doesn't typically host educated young women."

"Well . . ." I tucked the notebook beneath my left arm and cleared my throat. "I'm a big girl. I'll simply—"

"You'll be bathing and taking meals amid the stink of fish, in the company of foul-mouthed fishermen who spend most of their lives elbow-to-elbow with other fellows out at sea."

"I'm sure I'll be fine."

"If you'd prefer, I could ask my mother to house you."

"Thank you, but I'm afraid that's still too similar to you hosting me yourself. At least, I'm sure that's what Miss Simpkin and her sister might think." I picked up my briefcase and gloves. "I'll read for an hour and then be on my way. I'll contact you again after I've had time to collect my thoughts and search a bit for this region of Kansas myself."

"How do you plan to search for Friendly?"

"My oldest sister works at the Central Library in Portland. I'll send her a telegram first thing tomorrow morning and ask if she can find a detailed map of Kansas, or perhaps even Kansas census records that might provide some assistance."

"Really?" He shrank back, as if my kindness had caught him off guard. "You'd . . . you'd do that?"

"Bea adores solving mysteries—as much as your friend Sherlock Holmes in that collection of books I saw on the way in."

His posture relaxed. "Thank you," he said—a near-whisper; a sigh of relief.

Without warning, something bubbled over in the back room, startling us both. The kitchen belched a cloud of steam.

"Do you have a pot boiling on the stove, Mr. O'Daire?"

"Oh, damn! My hard-boiled eggs!"

I smiled. "Go, tend to your food."

"I'm not joking about that boardinghouse." He backed toward the kitchen, pointing in what must have been the direction of the establishment. "You'll be surrounded by sex-crazed sailors who don't get much of a chance to consort with women. Lock your door, or you'll find them crawling into your bed like cockroaches."

"It sounds like my years spent in graduate school with my fellow psychology students," I said, and I added, after fetching my briefcase, "but at least the fishermen won't all insist that I'm suffering from penis envy."

I left Mr. O'Daire standing there in the steam in front of his kitchen, still pointing, his face blushing redder than beets, while the pot boiled those poor eggs to bits.

CHAPTER 8

I read the O'Daires' journal for well over an hour and penned five pages' worth of notes about Janie and her various claims, which had flowed out of the child at irregular intervals throughout the years, with no apparent warning signs to precede them. The same key elements appeared over and over in her tales—a death by drowning, a love of numbers, a sister named Eleanor, the mysterious "man in the other house," the dire need to return to Friendly, Kansas. On more than one occasion she mentioned being born around 1870.

Little, specific details emerged as well: the color of the dress Violet wore on her tenth birthday, Violet's mother's lemon-verbena perfume, Violet's love of a candy called almond drops. When the handwriting changed from that of Mrs. O'Daire to Mr. O'Daire, the stories remained the same; they were simply written in a more straightforward style, and in sloppier penmanship.

I attempted to transfer as many of the details as I could into my own notebook, just in case Friendly, Kansas, could, indeed, be located on some sort of highly detailed map or atlas; in case I actually managed to track down a family with the surname Sunday.

Nothing aside from the claim of drowning in a lake led me to any more clues about a trauma in Janie's real past.

Once I felt satisfied with my notes, I packed up my belongings and left my hotel room with the leather journal and an envelope filled with three dollar bills to cover the rate for one night's stay, whether Mr. O'Daire wanted my money or not.

"For you," I told him down in the basement, handing him the book and the envelope. My luggage waited upstairs in the lobby.

He took both of the items without any particular hurry. "Are you certain I can't persuade you to stay?"

"It would be far easier if I obeyed Miss Simpkin's wishes."

"Easier for her, not you. She still gets to sleep in a comfortable house."

"If I learn anything about Friendly, Kansas, I'll contact you immediately."

He sighed and rubbed at his chin. "Let me at least drive you to the boardinghouse."

"No, you've been far too kind already. And, truly, I'm used to taking care of myself."

"You've never been married?"

"I'd prefer to stay single until I get myself more established in my field. It wouldn't be fair to drag a husband around to all of these little Oregon towns."

He cast me a sidelong glance, as though debating whether I teased about dragging a man around the state.

I wasn't.

I pulled my gloves over my fingers. "Good-bye for now, Mr. O'Daire. Enjoy selling your 'soda pop' to townsfolk this evening."

"Enjoy the smell of your fishermen housemates."

I chuckled, even though the idea of sleeping in close proximity to such men left a sour feeling in my stomach.

I ENJOYED A bowl of clam chowder and a thick slice of sourdough bread at a shadowy little table in a corner of Gordon Bay's only open restaurant. The place smelled of fish and sawdust, with a whiff of despair, and no other customers joined me in the dining room, which was roughly the size of a shack.

After dining, I asked the waitress for directions to the boardinghouse.

She pointed to her right with a sturdy arm squeezed into a sleeve the color of mustard caked on a bottle cap. "Head north for two blocks and turn right. It sits on the edge of town, butted up to the creek." She dropped her arm to her side. "I hope you're not lodging there."

I forced a smile. "Is the place truly as atrocious as everyone's making it out to be?"

"Are you married?"

"No."

"And you ain't got anyone to stay with around here?"

"Well, I'm here for work, actually."

"Work?" She placed a hand on a hip. "What type of work takes you to the flophouse?"

"Well, I'm a—"

"Honey, if you say 'whore'—"

"No!" I jumped, I was so startled at her accusation at first, but then the question made me snicker. "Do I look like a prostitute?"

We both glanced down at my plain brown sweater and the little teacup-shaped lumps for breasts beneath.

"Not really." She snorted. "You look like a schoolmarm."

"You're close—school psychologist. I'm here for a week to evaluate the local schoolchildren."

"Can't you stay in a hotel? There's a nice place around the bend called the Gordon Bay Hotel. It looks like a castle on the edge of a cliff."

"Hotels cost too much for my budget." I fussed with the collar of my sweater, pretending that my neck wasn't sweltering over the idea that the local "schoolmarm" had banned me from said hotel because of her ex-brother-in-law. In fact, Miss Simpkin's lack of trust in me was starting to grate on my nerves—to remind me a bit of my middle sister, Margery, begging me to keep my "panties on in the future" after I stupidly confided in her about a late and painful menstrual period I knew to have been a miscarriage.

The waitress took my empty bowl of chowder. "How about staying with the schoolteacher if you're a school psych . . . psychia . . ."

"*Psychologist*. Miss Simpkin didn't invite me to stay with her."

"She lives in a house on Fourth. Shares it with her sister and niece."

I raised my chin with interest. "Do you know Miss Simpkin and her family?"

"Oh, everyone knows everyone in this dinky place, hon. Tillie Simpkin used to be engaged to a boy here in town, the son of a good friend of mine. But"—the waitress fetched my bread plate with a hefty sigh—"the poor fellow came home from the war not right."

"Shell shock?"

"Mm hmm. Sometimes you'll see him roaming around out there." She nodded toward the darkened road beyond the window to my left. "He just sort of mutters and whistles to himself, lost and confused, nosing around for booze."

"Are you talking about Sam?"

"Yeah, 'Simple Sam.'" She shifted my bowl to her other hand. "You've met him?"

"I've seen him."

"He's not the only local doughboy who's had troubles from the war, but he's about the worst, poor devil." She knitted her thick eyebrows. "And poor Tillie Simpkin getting stuck a spinster because of him."

I studied the empty street bathed in the fluid shadows of night and remembered Mr. O'Daire slowing his car and calling out to Sam when the fellow tottered on the edge of the curb. I wondered if they'd all been chums when they were younger, he and Sam and Miss Simpkin and her sister. Another thought—a disturbing one—stabbed at my gut like the tip of a knife. Perhaps Sam was the source of Janie's fear of drowning. Perhaps the O'Daires had allowed him into their house after he returned from the war a broken man, and Sam had harmed the girl . . .

"Do you know Mrs. O'Daire and Janie?" I asked the waitress.

She shrugged. "Not well. But I do know Rebecca had a fling with the mayor's son, Harry Grady, a glassblower, of all things." The woman gave a dramatic roll of her eyes. "It made the local newspaper. And, oh, how the jokes soared about Harry's talented lips luring that redhead away from Mikey O'Daire."

I picked up my coin purse from the floor, not wanting to pursue that line of questioning with a person who clearly delighted in gossip.

"How much do I owe you?" I asked.

"A dollar fifty."

I pulled out two dollars and laid them on the table. "Thank you for the chowder. It was divine."

"You're welcome. It's not every day I get to serve a hoity-toity psychologist." The waitress sauntered away while clanking my dirty dishes together. "Sorry I called you a whore, sweetheart."

"You're not the first," I murmured under my breath, and I slipped out the door.

Gordon Bay proved to be a town so apparently safe that a person could leave a schoolhouse unlocked and unattended late at night. I discovered this information after running up to the silhouette of the school building with my bags jostling by my sides and my gaze periodically flitting behind me for signs of "Simple Sam" or drunken fishermen. Without as much as a strand of moonlight to guide me, I squeaked open the schoolhouse door and sidled inside the empty cloakroom like a cat burglar—like Irma Vep, scampering across Paris rooftops in a skintight black suit in an old serial film that my sisters and I adored when we were younger.

"Oh, dear God," I said to myself, peering around at the darkness. "What has happened to your life?"

Nothing other than a stark and chilling blackness responded.

After much fumbling and tripping and bruising, I stumbled upon Miss Simpkin's desk and managed to procure a candlestick and a box of matches. Neither Sam nor fishermen—nor any mice or raccoons—inhabited the schoolhouse, thank heavens, so I lit a fire in the stove and curled up on the floor beside it, pulling my coat over my shoulders as though it were my beloved Pendleton blanket that waited for me at my parents' house. Amid the scents of chalk and dust and the lingering stink of dirty feet and wet socks, I lay with my eyes wide upon, my head propped upon my leather brief-case with all those hard and bulky testing supplies bulging against my left cheekbone. I thought of untimely deaths and a Kansas lake and Janie and Michael O'Daire. I thought how ridiculous and dangerous to my career it would be to pursue the preposterous theory of reincarnation.

My mind also wandered to the two young men I had slept with in graduate school—dark-haired, green-eyed Tommy Morris, who shared both his umbrella and his bed with me, and blond and athletic Stuart Ayers, who had led to that short scare of a pregnancy after he failed to pull himself out, as promised. Tommy now pursued his PhD at Columbia. Stuart zipped off to Johns Hopkins straight after obtaining his master's—just like his father, whom he told me he loathed. Neither of my former lovers shivered on a schoolhouse floor, worrying what to do about a seven-year-old girl who claimed to be a dead woman, or the father desperate to save her.

CHAPTER 9

What on earth are you doing down there on the floor, Miss Lind?" asked a voice that sounded vaguely familiar.

I opened my eyes to find Miss Simpkin gaping down at me, her curls dangling across her milky forehead in a striking contrast of red against white. In fact, all of the colors in the schoolhouse looked wrong—too bright, too saturated and blinding. Sunlight poured through the windows and rendered the muted palettes of the room unrecognizable. Even the chalk letters and date on the blackboard glowed with a phosphorescent shine. Never before had I witnessed the classroom in full sunlight.

Miss Simpkin removed her gloves with jerky movements, her fingers snagging inside the wool. "You didn't sleep here last night, did you?"

"Yes, I did." I pushed myself up to a seated position and winced at a crick in my neck, as well as a chalky layer of grime coating my tongue. "Everyone kept warning me that foul-smelling fishermen would force themselves upon me in that boardinghouse, so where else was I to go?"

"Oh, Lord." She dropped her hands to her sides. "I didn't mean for you to leave the hotel to become a hobo."

"Not a hobo. Just a woman who's trying not to get herself embroiled in a family squabble."

"You sound angry."

"Quite frankly, I'm beginning to feel like a pawn in your family's game of chess." I pushed myself to my feet. "I seem to be both desperately needed and viciously unwanted."

"I can assure you, it's not a game, and you're not unwanted." She unbuttoned her coat and turned her face toward Janie's empty desk. "This is all simply a bit overwhelming for me. Before this past September, I never thought I would ever be placing Janie in front of a psychologist."

I brushed chalk from my skirt and understood why my mouth felt as though it had consumed dust all night long.

"Do you know about the journal that Mrs. and Mr. O'Daire kept?" I asked.

Miss Simpkin wiggled her shoulders out of her coat. "My sister kept that journal for a while, and then Michael took it from her, against her wishes, after she decided to stop recording Janie's stories."

"What did you think of the journal before your sister stopped writing in it?"

She hung the coat on a hook behind her desk and plumped up her curls, now darkened by the shadow of the American flag hanging beside her. "The Violet Sunday tales always struck me as odd, naturally," she said. "It didn't make sense that a child would claim so desperately to have lived so far away, so long ago."

"Did you ever witness firsthand Janie talking about her life as Violet?"

"Yes." She lowered her head and rubbed the back of her neck. "I still do, although not as frequently as before."

"How does Janie typically sound when she's telling such tales?"

"A little dreamy. Sometimes angry and desperate, if I'm not re-acting as though I believe her. I've asked her directly if her father told her to say such things, and she staunchly defends him."

"Hmm." I nodded, not at all surprised, considering most seven-year-olds' devotion to parents who treated them well. "And you're one hundred percent sure no one has ever hurt her in the past?"

"I am."

"No other relatives or friends of the family have ever struck you as suspicious?"

She shifted her face away, still cupping her hand over her neck.

I thought again of her former fiancé, Sam. Her shoulders stiff-ened, as though detecting my suspicion.

"I'm positive," she said. "Violet Sunday seemed to emerge com-pletely out of the ether. I don't want to think of Janie as a liar, and I don't truly want to imagine her father putting her up to this behavior. But above all, I'm terrified she might be—" Her voice caught in her throat. "You see . . . I've seen the inside of an asylum, Miss Lind. I would rather die than send Janie to a hell like that, and so would her mother."

"As I told you yesterday, I don't believe an asylum would be needed."

"I know about multiple personalities. I know that's what might be wrong with her."

"The field of psychology is rapidly changing." I stepped forward with my hands squeezed together. "First and foremost, we strive to get to the source of a patient's problem through psychotherapy.

We're learning more and more about the role of memory and the ways people become prisoners of their pasts if they don't seek help."

Miss Simpkin's eyes moistened. She pinched the bridge of her nose between her fingers and breathed as though crying, although no tears spilled.

"Janie is still so young," I told her in the voice I used to soothe the most anxious of children who took my tests. "If we help her now, while her earliest memories are easiest to reach, before they've damaged her relationships and her psyche, then she can still lead a normal and successful life."

"How do you propose helping her?"

"I want to start by investigating the existence of Friendly, Kansas."

"How?" She dropped her arm to her side. *"Why?"*

"To rule out the reincarnation theory—to keep that particular path from distracting everyone. Also, if Friendly, indeed, exists, I would like to explore exactly where in the state it is located. That information might allow your family to remember why Janie knows about the region."

Miss Simpkin pulled down a box of matches from a shelf mounted on the wall beside the stove. Next to the shelf hung a map of the United States, colored in tea-stain shades of brown.

"There's a Finney County, Kansas." She struck a match and squatted down in front of the stove. "But no map that I've ever seen, including this one here, shows a place called Friendly." She tossed the match into the stove and set fire to a crumpled sheet of paper on the logs. "It's a made-up town." She stood up. "The name doesn't even sound real."

"I agree—it's likely a fictional creation. However, after I tidy myself up, I'm going to send a telegram to my oldest sister, Bea, who works at the Central Library in Portland. If anyone can find a mysterious town that's hidden in the center of the United States, it's she."

"You won't find it, Miss Lind."

"Well, we'll simply wait to see what comes of my sister's Sherlockian skills." I opened my luggage to scrounge around for a fresh sweater, when I remembered Mr. O'Daire's collection of Sherlock Holmes novels in his hotel library.

A glance up at Miss Simpkin told me that, she, too, associated Holmes with Michael O'Daire. With a frown, she grabbed a poker and jabbed at the half-charred pile of wood that sputtered and popped in the stove.

AFTER I DRESSED and tidied myself, Miss Simpkin directed me to the local post office for my telegram purchase. Another rainstorm attacked, and I sprinted instead of walked to my destination—a little brick building on the edge of town, across from the railroad tracks. Once inside, I peeled off my coat to cease dripping all over the tiles and breathed in the perfume of crisp envelopes and fresh ink.

To obtain the cheapest rate, I chose to purchase a ten-word telegram. Never possessing much talent for the clipped and punctuation-free style of telegraphese, it took me a solid five minutes to decide upon my phrasing. After much consideration, much pencil tapping—remembering my own childhood obsession with Kansas and Bea's potential concern over my mental hygiene—I settled upon the following sentence:

URGENTLY LOOKING FOR FRIENDLY KANSAS
FOR STUDENT DOES IT EXIST

I paid extra to allow Bea to send me a ten-word reply, and then I ran off again, back into the cold and splattering rain, back to the schoolhouse for another round of intelligence tests.

THE CHILDREN ARRIVED. Janie traipsed past me in the parade of pupils that had finished depositing coats, galoshes, and lunch pails in the cloakroom, but aside from a brief, shy smile darted my way, she paid no attention to me.

In spite of myself, as I stood there, waiting for the students to pass through the room, I pictured the imaginary Violet Sunday as having an actual face and a figure. I envisioned a young woman wearing the style of dress seen on my mother in sepia photographs from the late 1880s, before she met my father—the tapered sleeves, the ruffled skirts, the bustles, the endless buttons, the frills, and the fuss. I imagined dark hair fanning out into the depths of green-brown water like streaks of spilled ink; black eyebrows set against pale skin; bubbles rising to the surface from a prim little turned-up nose that resembled Janie's herself. In my mind's eye, Violet Sunday formed into a conglomeration of *Hamlet*'s Ophelia, a beautiful dark-haired classmate named Emma from my high school years, and a grown-up version of Janie. A mythical creature. A frustrating distraction that kept my mind from focusing on rational diagnoses.

If I hadn't been a psychologist—if I didn't find the idea of reincarnation so absurd—I would have wanted Violet Sunday to exist.

A female mathematical genius.

A *Victorian* female mathematical genius.

What an absolutely delicious idea.

ON THAT PARTICULAR day I tested the eight- to eleven-year-olds. No one struck me as needing a remedial curriculum or as suffering from a serious mental abnormality. The children all appeared to be quite ordinary, as a matter of fact. Janie O'Daire had spoiled me. The routine of intelligence testing had never seemed so rote; so dull and uninspiring. I felt unnecessary.

By the time Miss Simpkin dismissed the students, rain fell by the bucketful, and lo and behold, there was Mr. O'Daire again, breezing through the front door with his green umbrella fountaining all over the floor, offering to drive home the children who normally walked instead of riding the autobus. Miss Simpkin was so busy helping children squeeze into coats and mittens to pay any heed to his offer, or to his presence in general, and I busied myself with assisting one of the five-year-olds to simultaneously blow his nose and stuff his feet into boots. In my peripheral vision, I saw Mr. O'Daire standing there in that black coat of his, his blond hair slightly mussed from the cap he had just removed, his posture erect and confident. He jumped in and attended to the students who needed help with scarves and gloves, and then he opened the door for the mad dash to the automobiles. Mud squelched beneath shoes, wind yanked at umbrellas, and children shrieked and whimpered, but we managed to cram twelve of them into the vehicles, while a handful of older students jogged off into the storm with their satchels shielding their heads.

As soon as the men closed the car doors, Miss Simpkin and I ran back into the schoolhouse and gasped for air inside the cloakroom.

"Again," she said, "I'm so sorry about our weather."

"Please, don't apologize. It isn't as though we never get any rain or wind in Portland." I closed the black umbrella I had borrowed and nearly got walloped in the elbow from the front door opening beside me.

Mr. O'Daire poked his head inside the cloakroom. "Do either of you ladies need a ride?"

Miss Simpkin shook her head. "I'm still working for at least another hour."

"I need to finish some business with the tests," I said. "But thank you."

"How did you like the boardinghouse?" he asked with a lift of his eyebrows.

Miss Simpkin and I exchanged a look.

"Well . . ." I slid my coat off of my shoulders. "I actually didn't stay there last night."

"Oh?" He stepped farther inside. "Where did you stay, then?"

Miss Simpkin turned and clip-clopped into the classroom.

"I . . . um . . ." I lobbed the coat onto a hook. "I slept here."

Mr. O'Daire slammed the door shut behind him. "You *what*?"

"I decided, after hearing horror stories about the boarding-house from both you and a waitress, that I would stay here instead."

His gaze darted about the cloakroom. "On what, for Pete's sake, did you sleep? The floor?"

I cleared my throat, my face burning with humiliation. "Well . . . yes."

He balled his hands into fists. Before I could ask him to refrain from getting upset, he marched into the classroom.

"Tillie!"

Miss Simpkin plopped into the chair behind her desk. "What?"

"What's wrong with you, making a woman—a respectable psychologist who's helping *your* pupils—sleep on a filthy schoolhouse floor?"

"Oh, Christ, leave me alone, Michael." She wrestled her cigarettes out of the desk. "If Rebecca ever learns you were housing Miss Lind, she would think *you* were the one who brought her to this town, and that's not going to help anyone."

"Don't punish Miss Lind for Rebecca's paranoia."

"It's not paranoia. Something's wrong with Janie, and we all know it."

A knock came from behind me. I gasped and spun around, terrified I'd find Janie reeling over her aunt's blunt words.

When I opened the door, I instead encountered a bundled-up young man no older than some of our teenage students. The oily-faced chap wore a dripping-wet cap with a Western Union messenger badge pinned to it. A red bicycle rested against the railing at the bottom of the steps. Mr. O'Daire's automobile full of children waited several yards behind the fellow, rain pecking at the black roof, heads bobbing about beyond the closed windows.

"May I help you?" I asked the boy.

He wrestled a tan envelope out of a leather bag that was slung across his chest. "I have a telegram for Miss Lind."

My mood perked up. "I'm Miss Lind."

"Here you are, ma'am."

I took the paper, the edges now damp. "Thank you."

"You're welcome. Good day." He maneuvered down the slick steps to his bicycle, and I ensured he didn't slip before I attended to the message.

"Is it from your sister?" asked Mr. O'Daire from the classroom behind me.

"I assume so, unless it's a message from the Department of Education." I turned away from the door and the rain. "Whatever the case, please don't get your hopes up."

"Open it, please," he said.

I trod toward the two of them in the classroom while opening the envelope with the nail of my right index finger. Mr. O'Daire's breathing quickened. Miss Simpkin released a gust of smoke out of one side of her mouth with the *whoosh* of a deflating tire.

I drew out the paper from within and, indeed, spotted the name BEATRICE LIND, typed on the sender's line. "Yes, it's from Bea!"

"What does it say?" asked Mr. O'Daire.

My sister had addressed the telegram to "Nell"—an old nickname she'd been calling me for as long as I could remember.

My jaw went slack at the rest of her words:

YES MY DEAR NELL FRIENDLY IS A NE KANSAS TOWN

"Well?" Mr. O'Daire staggered toward me with his hands braced against the sides of his head. "You're killing me with this suspense, Miss Lind. What does it say?"

I drew a breath and raised my eyes to his. "It says that Friendly, Kansas, is real."

Miss Simpkin choked on smoke.

Mr. O'Daire collapsed to his knees on the floor and beamed as though I'd just announced the birth of a new child.

My mouth opened, but no further sounds materialized—not even a feeble gasp or a gurgle.

"Oh, God." Mr. O'Daire struggled to stand back up. "Does this mean you'll consider it, then? You'll consider reincarnation?"

"What do we do?" asked Miss Simpkin, still coughing. "What on earth do we do now?"

"Give . . . please . . ." My brain and mouth failed to coordinate. I pressed the telegram to my chest and tried to remember how to properly breathe. "Give me a day or two . . . to collect my thoughts. I need to think. I need to think before I can say anything more. This could mean nothing." I peeked at Bea's message again. "It could mean everything. I don't know. Give me time. I must have time."

 CHAPTER 10

The telegram inspired further questions.

My notes, jotted down in the cloakroom after Mr. O'Daire drove away in a dazed state of wonder, read as follows:

If Friendly—a town in northeastern Kansas, unknown to anyone looking at the maps available in Gordon Bay—truly exists, how did Janie know about it? Did Mr. O'Daire meet someone from Friendly while in training for the war? Did he meet a family with the surname Sunday, by chance?

What is the meaning behind Janie's strong desire to travel to Friendly, Kansas? Is it make-believe? Is it a wish planted in her head by a parent? Has she been there, even though everyone insists that she hasn't?

Would Janie be able to name other towns in the area of Kansas surrounding Friendly? According to my memory, larger cities in the northeastern section of the state include Kansas City, Topeka, Lawrence, Leavenworth, and Manhattan.

Perhaps make a list of towns that exist throughout Kansas— Hutchinson, Marysville, Oakley, Independence, Liberal, Goodland—

and ask her to point to the ones that sound familiar. Throw in some made-up names to test if she's pointing to the words at random. Make notes of her mood as she surveys the list.

"It can't mean anything, can it?" asked Miss Simpkin, emerging in the opening between the cloakroom and the classroom. She held the frame of the entryway for support, and her face lacked its usual pinkness. "Someone *had* to have told her about Friendly. Hadn't they?"

"I was just wondering the same thing." I read through the notes I'd just written. "Did Janie's mother ever investigate whether the town actually existed?"

"Of course she did. When Janie first started speaking of her other life, we all tried to find the place. The name sounded so silly and childlike, though." She leaned her right shoulder against the doorjamb. "We felt foolish going to any great lengths. And we certainly couldn't seek the help of any libraries as well-equipped as the one in Portland."

"None of the men who were involved in the war ever came across a fellow from Friendly, did they?"

"I don't . . ." She squeezed her eyes shut and rubbed at the lids. "I suppose Michael could have."

"Or . . . what about Sam?"

A flash of pain seized her face. She opened her eyes. "How do you know about Sam?"

"I saw him in town when Mr. O'Daire first drove me out here." I rolled my pencil between the balls of my right thumb and middle finger. "Did Sam ever come in contact with Janie?"

"No. Sam isn't quite right in the head anymore. No one would have brought Janie in contact with him. Unless . . ." She stiffened.

"Unless Michael allowed him to be with the child. They were close friends, before the war. I don't think . . ." She shook her head. "No, I don't think poor Sam has anything to do with this." She hesitated in the doorway, blinking, wrinkling her brow. Then she slipped back into the classroom.

I massaged a dull ache in my forehead and read through my notes again, my eyebrows pinched, my elbows planted on the table. I debated writing to the postmaster of Friendly, Kansas, and asking him to deliver a message to the family of a woman named Violet Sunday. I pondered if Michael O'Daire might be in cahoots with a family named Sunday, the members of which would promptly send me a letter in reply.

But why would Mr. O'Daire go to all of that trouble? I asked myself. *Why?* The benefits reaped from such a con game—a game in the works for the past *five years*—would not outweigh all of the effort and the risks involved with plotting with a family that lived two thousand miles away. So far, Mr. O'Daire had gained seemingly nothing from this so-called ruse.

Miss Simpkin's footsteps again pattered my way. She came around the corner, her arms crossed, a lit cigarette tucked between the middle and index fingers of her right hand.

"You can stay with us tonight," she said, still pale, her voice fluttery. "But, as I told you, I've sworn to my sister that you're simply a test administrator, not a true psychologist."

"When I first met Mr. O'Daire, he knew that I'm a psychologist and said as much."

Miss Simpkin took a smoke and twisted the upper half of her body toward the window.

"How did he know if your sister didn't?" I asked.

She withdrew the cigarette from her lips and exhaled smoke from flared nostrils. "Michael overheard me discussing your arrival with the local truant officer earlier this week. I had been stressing to the officer how important it was that all of the children attend school while you're here, and, without me realizing it, Michael showed up to fetch Janie out here in the cloakroom."

"I see." I swallowed, my throat dry. "And he didn't breathe a word about my credentials to his ex-wife, I assume?"

Miss Simpkin shook her head. "If he had, Rebecca would have kept Janie home from school the entire time you're here. He must know that."

I put a hand to my lower back and stretched my spine with an audible crunch.

She cringed. "Oh no! That's from sleeping on this awful old floor, isn't it?"

"Well—"

"Please, let me compensate for last night by hosting you. I absolutely detest thinking of you curled up on the ground in here. Children tromp into this schoolhouse after working in fields and horse stables and . . ." She shuddered. "God, when I think about the filth that's dragged into here on the bottoms of shoes . . ."

"I don't know . . . Your sister would watch me like a fierce mama bear."

"Don't mention your university degrees. She'll feel at ease once she gets to know you."

"But—"

"Please, Alice," she said, her eyes imploring. "Stay with us. I feel terrible about booting you out of the hotel when you're working so hard to help us." She took another smoke. "May I . . . did you mind that I called you Alice? I'm not much for formalities."

I cast my eyes toward my notes and debated whether it would be wise to allow myself to be drawn any farther into this family.

Miss Simpkin brushed aside a red curl that had coiled across her right cheek and rubbed her lips together. She watched me with eyes wide and eager—eyes framed in heavy copper lashes—and I couldn't help but feel that everyone involved with Janie was seducing me into joining their own side of the mystery. My eyes even strayed to the way the bodice of Miss Simpkin's green dress opened just above her collarbones to expose her bare, white throat. She smelled of smoke and jasmine perfume and reminded me a little of a girl I once kissed, while drunk, one lonely winter as an undergraduate.

"Well . . ." I said, my mouth dryer still.

Miss Simpkin continued to rub those plump lips together.

"I suppose . . ." I nodded, unfolding my hands and spreading my fingers across my notes. "All right, yes. As long as your sister isn't put to any trouble, I would be pleased to stay at your house."

Miss Simpkin slid the cigarette into her mouth and smiled. Her fingers shook.

WE WALKED THROUGH the rain-soaked streets of Gordon Bay beneath a twin pair of black umbrellas, each of us lugging one of my suitcases. Lamps glowed in a weak yellow haze along the darkening roads. Storm clouds and twilight bleached out all other colors in the neighborhood. The plunking of raindrops against our umbrellas, as well as the heels of our shoes striking the sidewalks, proved to be the only sounds.

"It's just up ahead," said Miss Simpkin, nodding toward one of the shadowed homes in a row of five Victorians.

I readjusted my grip on my luggage and the umbrella. My heart sped up in anticipation of whatever unknown scene awaited behind the closed door of whichever house we would approach. I envisioned Mrs. O'Daire as a stouter version of Miss Simpkin—a woman who would scream at me to leave her and her child alone, the veins in her forehead bulging, a fireplace poker hoisted in the air like a weapon. My brain even hurt from all the imagined shrieking and fuss. I also braced myself for the distinct possibility of finding Janie engaged in a morbid style of play—perhaps pretending to drown her dolls in the kitchen sink or creating more pictures of blue ladies with anguished faces, floating underwater. She might lash out in violence if anyone expressed doubts about her stories, maybe even pelt people in the head with blunt objects, just like . . . like . . .

Like you, Alice, I heard my sister Margery say inside my mind. *Like you as a child, beating defenseless children with a stick as though you wanted to smash their little skulls. What was wrong with you, Alice? What dark demon possessed you? You terrified me.*

I stopped for a moment to catch my breath.

"Are you all right?" asked Miss Simpkin with a peek at me from beneath her umbrella.

"I'm simply tired." I readjusted my grip on my suitcase. "Exhausted, actually."

To the west a door opened. I looked up and spotted the figure of a little girl in the doorway of the next house over. A light from behind the child illuminated short red hair that looked to be Janie's, as well as a midnight-blue dress with a hem that grazed the tops of her knees.

"Aunt Tillie?" she asked.

"Yes, it's me, Janie." Miss Simpkin gestured with her head for me to follow her. "Come along. Let's get you warm and fed."

"Thank you." My feet clopped after her through a pathway of puddles that led up to the house, and we climbed three porch steps, up to where Janie stood.

Miss Simpkin brushed her fingers through the girl's short locks. "I've brought a special guest to stay with us, Janie. Where's your mother?"

"In the kitchen." Janie peered up at me with her wide turquoise eyes. "It's Miss Lind from the school!"

"It is, indeed." Miss Simpkin closed her umbrella. "I've offered her a room with us for the rest of her stay. What do you think of that?"

"I could show her my bedroom."

"No!" cried her aunt.

Both Janie and I startled.

Miss Simpkin cleared her throat and parked her dripping umbrella on the porch swing. "I mean, we'll have to speak to your mother before we give Miss Lind any tours of the house."

Oh, my, I thought. *How that bedroom now intrigues me.*

Miss Simpkin wiped the bottoms of her shoes on a doormat. "Come inside, Miss Lind. I can feel the heat of the fireplace already."

I placed my umbrella beside the other one on the swing, wiped clean my own soles, and followed the schoolteacher and her niece into a home that resembled most other middle-class houses I had entered, with no signs whatsoever of supernatural phenomena, ugly divorces, or grandmothers whisked away to asylums. Everything looked clean and dusted and cheerful, from the golden-orange wallpaper the color of Monarch butterflies to a menagerie of porcelain forest animals perched on a table in the entry hall. Nothing made the hairs on the back of my neck stand on end. The only unpleasant feature was a trace of dankness—an odor which I assumed to inhabit most of the houses on the coast.

I lowered my bags to the floor, and Miss Simpkin and I removed our coats and hung them on a rack next to the front door. Miss Simpkin then promptly grabbed my hand and steered me down the hall toward a kitchen that smelled of roasting chicken.

"Rebecca," she called, her fingers sweating against my palm. "We have a guest I would like for you to meet."

"A guest?" called a female voice that sounded far more hospitable than I would have expected. From around a bend strolled a slender woman with finger-waved, strawberry blond hair, cut just below her ears. She had a nose that turned down a little oddly at the tip on an otherwise pretty face, and the long and graceful neck of a ballerina. She dried her hands on a dishtowel and smiled, but her movements slowed as she took in the sight of me. "Hello," she said, her voice still welcoming, despite the stiffening of her face.

"This is Miss Lind," said her sister, "our test monitor."

Heavens! How I fought off the urge to object at that new title she'd given me—a greater demotion than even "test administrator."

"And you must be Mrs. O'Daire," I said with an offer of my hand.

"It's so lovely to meet you, Miss Lind." Janie's mother reached out and shook my hand with fingers as warm as the kitchen heating the air from around the corner. "Will you be joining us for supper?"

"Well," said her sister, her voice rising an octave. "*Actually*, I was wondering if she might stay with us during the rest of her work assignment here in Gordon Bay."

"Oh." Mrs. O'Daire jumped as though someone had pinched her in the bottom. "Well . . . I . . ."

"If it's too much trouble," I said, "I can try to find another family to house me."

Miss Simpkin cleared her throat. "There's been some confusion about her lodging situation, you see, and—"

"No, it's no trouble at all." Mrs. O'Daire's voice also climbed an octave. "We have an extra bedroom downstairs, as a matter of fact." She nodded vaguely to her right. "Why don't you show Miss Lind where she can put her bags, Janie, while Aunt Tillie and I get supper on the table? Show her to the extra room."

"Yes, ma'am." Janie beckoned with a little index finger for me to follow her. "This way, please."

I turned to join the girl and cast a glance back at the two women, expecting to catch Mrs. O'Daire baring her teeth at her sister. Instead, the ladies moseyed around the corner in the midst of talk about the chicken and a new seasoning that Mrs. O'Daire had decided to try.

I picked up my bags and allowed Janie to lead me through a square front room bedecked in glorious built-in bookshelves made of a fine red mahogany, stocked with hundreds of cloth and leather spines. My eyes strayed to a five-foot-long sturgeon mounted above a brick fireplace.

"That's Chuck the Fish," said Janie with a nod to the gaping monstrosity. "Grandpa Simpkin caught him."

"Well, isn't he lovely?" I tore my attention away from Chuck and instead surveyed the bookshelves we passed. "Are any of these books yours, Janie?"

"No. They belonged to my grandparents."

"Have you ever read any of L. Frank Baum's novels about little

Dorothy Gale, such as *The Wonderful Wizard of Oz*, or *The Emerald City of Oz*?"

"No." She opened a door to the left of the fireplace and stepped into the middle of a small bedroom.

I sidled through the doorway after her and took in the sight of a warm and comfortable-looking bed, covered in a patchwork quilt, along with walls papered in a pale lavender hue.

"What a darling room," I said. "Thank you for showing me the way."

"The bed in here is kind of old." Janie wrapped a hand around a brass bed knob and scratched her left ankle with the inside of her right foot. "It was Mommy's when she was little. She was saving it for a new brother or sister for me, until Daddy moved away."

I lowered my bags to the floor. "I know it's extremely difficult when parents divorce, Janie, and if you'd ever like to talk—"

"I'm not sure why no brother or sister ever came." She rested her chin on the knob and blinked.

I put a hand to my chest, remembering the stillborn that Mr. O'Daire had mentioned. That child would have been older than Janie, I realized, but, clearly, the girl pined for a sibling.

"It's really easy to be born if you find the right parents," she continued. "If you want it badly enough."

I shivered, in spite of myself. "What do you mean by that?"

"It's just easy." She shrugged. "Anyone can do it if they feel like giving it a try. I chose Mommy on purpose, you know."

"You did?"

"She looked so kind and pretty, and I could tell how much she wanted a baby." Janie lifted her head from the knob. "Did you choose your mother?"

I shook my head, my eyes watering. "No, I . . ." I emitted a nervous laugh. "I don't know if I did. I don't think so. That's not quite how it works, you see . . ."

"That's how it worked for me. I waited and waited, and there she was."

Before I could even consider a response, Janie swung around with a swish of blue skirts and skipped out of the bedroom.

I just stood there with gooseflesh prickling my arms, unsure if I had just witnessed a performance, a delusion, or a miracle.

MRS. O'DAIRE AND MISS SIMPKIN served us supper in a dining room adjacent to the kitchen. They insisted that I call them "Rebecca" and "Tillie," respectively, and seemed to want to call me "Alice," even though I feared such informality would demolish all semblances of respect for me. Not only had I been demoted from school psychologist to "test monitor" in the breadth of an evening, but I now seemed to be dwindling from test monitor to "just a visiting girl that Tillie happens to know."

"Yes, certainly, call me Alice," I said with my lips stretched into a tight smile, hoping the use of my given name would at the least put Rebecca at ease and allow me to speak further with Janie.

We discussed Gordon Bay's weather, Tillie's decision to become a schoolteacher, Rebecca's brief career working as a cook in one of the local restaurants before she married Michael O'Daire, and the pros and cons of growing up on the coast compared to my childhood in the city of Portland. I avoided the boiled carrots and peas on my plate by nudging them behind my potatoes, not daring to share my repulsion toward vegetables.

Occasionally, I would glance across the table at Janie, who, unlike me, ate all of her food without hiding any of it. She sat in relative silence and never once lifted her head to stare across the table at me with a chilling gaze reminiscent of my "possessed" student, Frankie—as I feared she might. Nor did she seem troubled by any dark, or puzzling, or ingenious thoughts. She was simply a child eating supper with her family and a guest.

"What is your favorite thing about living on the coast, Janie?" I asked while cutting through a slice of chicken. "What is your best memory of living here by the sea?"

"Flying kites," she said, poking her fork into a mushy potato, "on the beach."

Her mother nodded. "My ex-husband's parents used to design kites in the off-season. We have a whole collection of their creations out in a shed in the back."

"What a wonderful hobby," I said. "Are you a designer of things, too, Janie?"

"Well . . . I wouldn't say a 'designer.'" The girl lifted her eyes to mine. "More of a solver."

She popped the potato wedge into her mouth.

"And what types of things are you solving?" I asked.

She chewed and swallowed. "Equations."

"Ah." I nodded. "That's right. You like numbers."

Her aunt shifted in her chair, but her mother continued eating as though unfazed by my line of questioning.

I cleared my throat. "Is there a particular type of equation that you—?"

"Do you ever attend the theater when you're in Portland, Alice?" asked Miss Simpkin.

I smiled at the obvious turn in the conversation's course. "Why, yes. Sometimes. My oldest sister, Bea, and I are fascinated by dark family dramas and horror. We try to make an evening of Ibsen or Shakespeare whenever we get the chance."

Mrs. O'Daire laughed in a manner that resembled a sniff. "Family dramas and horror are the last things I would seek for entertainment."

"I'm afraid that my normal life is rather boring." I smiled again. "I need to partake in imaginary dramas to enliven things a bit."

"I've loved the Brontë sisters' novels ever since I was about fifteen," said Tillie, "although nowadays I would never marry a Heathcliff or a Mr. Rochester. Can you imagine?"

"Ah, yes, those dear, wonderful Brontës and their brooding heroes," I said with a laugh. "Bea started bringing ghost and crime stories home from the library when I was far too young to be listening to those sorts of things, and I devoured them as if they were milk and cookies."

"Drama in real life isn't all it's cracked up to be," said Mrs. O'Daire without looking at me, cutting close to the bone of a chicken thigh. "Everyone always says how desperately they long for excitement, but I think there's a certain beauty to normalcy and calm."

"Perhaps you're right." I took a sip of my water and studied the current sense of tranquility reigning over the table, the gentle clinks of the silverware tapping against plates, the silent chewing and breathing, the relaxed postures.

And yet I could almost hear the pressure—the undeniable *roar*—of the turbulence roiling beneath the O'Daire family's surface.

CHAPTER 11

After supper, I retreated to the guest bedroom and fetched a fountain pen from my briefcase, along with two sheets of Department of Education letterhead. Using a wobbly little bedside table as a desk, I set the first piece of paper before me and penned a letter to the postmaster of Friendly, Kansas.

November 13, 1925

Dear Postmaster:

I work as a psychologist in the state of Oregon, and I have been given a rather fascinating case of a young child who insists that she knows a family from Friendly. More specifically, she longs to reach out to the family of a deceased Friendly woman by the name of Violet Sunday.

If such a family indeed exists, I would be most grateful if you delivered the enclosed letter to the surviving members. I apologize for not possessing an exact address. The child has mentioned the possibility of Violet having a sister named Eleanor.

> *Thanking you in advance, I am,*
> *Yours truly,*
> *A.M. Lind*

On the second sheet, I wrote the following:

November 13, 1925

Dear Sir or Madam:

I apologize in advance for the rather peculiar nature of this letter. I work as a psychologist for the Oregon Department of Education, and I have come across a seven-year-old girl who claims to know your family. Normally, I would not think it unusual for a child to say she knows people in another state; however, this little girl speaks as though she once lived with your family.

I do not mean to pry into your personal history, and I certainly do not want to stir up painful memories from your past, but this child is rather insistent—and specific—about her life in Friendly, Kansas. She claims that her name was Violet Sunday and that she excelled at mathematics. She states that she had a sister named Eleanor and a dog named Poppy, and she says that she drowned at the age of nineteen.

If there is any truth behind these statements, if a woman

*named Violet Sunday genuinely existed in Friendly, please
write to me at my home address in Portland, Oregon, listed
above. If your family has been in contact with the child's
father, Michael O'Daire, please also include that information in your letter. Whether this reincarnation mystery is
a hoax, or a childhood fantasy, or the symptom of a suppressed memory from the child's own past, I would like to
solve the puzzle soon and help the girl find peace of mind.*

Respectfully yours,
A.M. Lind

AROUND EIGHT O'CLOCK, someone knocked on the bedroom door.
I packed away all letters and notes and called out, "Come in."

Miss Simpkin opened the door. "Would you like me to draw
you a bath?"

"Oh, that sounds divine," I said with a long sigh, and my entire
body melted over the idea of warm water and cleansing soap.

"Stay here," she said. "Relax. I'll get it started."

"Is everyone doing all right out there?" I asked before she could
shut the door.

She paused with her hand on the tarnished little doorknob.
"Yes. I don't think you need to worry about a thing."

"Well, thank you." I reached down and took off my right shoe.
"It does feel nice to be lodging inside an actual house for a change."

"Good." She smiled and closed the door behind her.

DURING MY SOAK in the O'Daires' claw-foot tub, I thought I heard
someone snicker on the other side of the bathroom door.

I bolted upright and cupped my hands over my breasts.

"Is someone there?" I asked.

Silence ensued. I bit my bottom lip and sank back down into the steaming water, disappointed in myself. Nothing stood outside of that bathroom door other than my own anxieties—my stupefying fear of people seeing the naked and hungry side of me. The sexual side.

Keep your panties on in the future, my sister Margery had said, and my Lord, how she glared, as though I'd harmed both her and her children through my behavior. *You're an unmarried woman. You can't behave that way. You simply can't!*

I draped a washcloth over my forehead and attempted to clear my mind of all worries—the intelligence tests, the pressures of an upcoming Thanksgiving dinner, the enigma of Janie, the ridiculous complexity of just finding myself a damned bed in which to sleep.

Minds do have a way of staying active, however. They don't always agree to blissful meditation. As I reclined there, nude, in the house of strangers, my brain decided to stray toward the subject of blond-haired Stuart from graduate school and his crowded little university apartment that smelled of coffee grinds and wine. I didn't even know why I had agreed to join him in his bedroom; we didn't know each other well. He was a handsome flirt, and I had already discovered my fondness for sex after my brief, romantic entanglement with Tommy, the boy with the umbrella. Stu and I simply gravitated together, drawn by primitive desires and master's theses stresses.

During our little petting party on his lumpy bed, as demurely as possible, I had asked Stu if we could try pleasures of the oral and manual variety to avoid a pregnancy. Tommy had taught me such delights, for he was a young man of the world—a lady-killer—and I had quite enjoyed the sensation of his velvety lips between my legs. Stu blushed and said he couldn't do such a thing with a lady, but he swore, with a childish cross of his heart, that he would remove his "John Thomas" in the nick of time—which, of course, he didn't.

I slid the washcloth off my eyes and stared up at mildew stains that dotted Mrs. O'Daire's bathroom ceiling. My anger during that short pregnancy reawakened. A door inside my head shot open.

A nasty altercation had followed that sexual blunder.

I had confronted Stu about the baby. I yelled at him in his apartment, and he just shrugged and said, "What do you want me to do about it, Alice? I'm certainly not going to go and marry a girl like you."

"I don't want you to marry me," I had shouted. "I just want to have a future, but you ruined that for me. You ruined everything!"

He threw up his hands and turned away. "Aw, you're so loose, some other chap was bound to knock you up anyway."

Without even realizing what I was doing, I kicked off my right shoe, lunged at Stu, and smashed the thick heel against the right side of his head—not once, but twice. He cried out in pain and dropped to his knees with a hand cradling his skull. Blood seeped through his fingers, and I felt *good*. I hit him a third time, just because I could.

I slapped the washcloth back over my eyes and forced myself to slam that memory shut. What an appalling moment to dredge up in the middle of a bath after such an exhausting week. Stu never pressed charges. He didn't want to have to admit to anyone that a *girl* had beaten him up. I lost the baby just a week or two later and spent the remainder of graduate school avoiding the sight of Stu and his fine blond hair.

I still wore the shoes with which I had struck him, for they were my favorite pair. Brown slip-on oxfords with a rounded toe. Warm. Sturdy. Comfortable.

Rust-colored stains flecked the squared-off right heel, but I simply walked around upon it and pretended the blood wasn't there.

IN THE MIDDLE of the night, a child's scream pierced the air.

I awoke, entangled in blankets that didn't smell familiar, engulfed in darkness. My knee smacked a wall I couldn't see.

Another cry shattered the silence, this time emerging as a word: "No!" And shortly afterward—"Help! No! Help me, I'm stuck! I'm stuck!"

Someone raced across the floor above me.

I fought my way out of the web of bedding and stumbled across the unfamiliar room, arms outstretched, hands grabbing for obstacles that might guide me. I remembered where I was, as well as the location of the bedroom door.

"I'm stuck, I'm stuck!" shouted a child—*Janie*, I quickly realized—from somewhere in the house. "Drowning! Drowning! It's so cold!"

I opened the door and navigated my way around the front room occupied by that horrible mounted sturgeon. The fish's gray mouth gaped in a slip of moonlight that sliced through the part in the curtains, but it was the only thing in the room I could see.

Someone turned on an electric lamp upstairs, which transformed the staircase into a beacon of light. I scrambled toward it.

Again, Janie screamed, "Help me! Too cold! Too cold!"

"Janie," said her mother. "Janie, wake up."

Miss Simpkin flew past the top of the staircase as a blur of red hair and a green robe. I followed after her, rounded a corner, and tripped into a bedroom that froze me in my tracks.

Someone had written numbers all over the bright-yellow walls. No, more than numbers—letters, fractions, parentheses, integers, vertical lines, dashes, square roots, subsets. I didn't know entirely what I was looking at, but it appeared as though an intelligent, frustrated soul had regurgitated the inner workings of her mind across the paint. A bedside lamp cast a dim golden light that made the penciled scribblings look like warnings scrawled across the depths of a cave.

"What is she doing in here?" asked Mrs. O'Daire from the edge of a bed.

I blinked, only then noticing the others in the room—Janie, curled beneath a pink bedspread, crying, her eyes squeezed shut; her mother, with her strawberry hair in curlers, sitting beside the child, gawking at me; Miss Simpkin, huddled over Mrs. O'Daire, her hand on her sister's back. And beyond them the equations. Endless equations. Obsessive calculations.

"Get out of this room." Mrs. O'Daire jumped up and spun me toward the doorway. "Stop looking at the walls. Stop looking at them!"

She pushed me out to the hallway and slammed the door shut behind me.

I swayed and lost my balance, but even when I steadied myself, I couldn't stop seeing Janie's writing. I closed my eyes and pressed a hand against my ribs, but the scattered numbers and algebraic letters hovered in front of me, begging me to solve the problems of their creator, pleading with me, *Do something!*

DOWN IN THE kitchen, I paced the floorboards and longed for a swig of coffee or a shot of mind-numbing liquor. I paced with enough of a commotion for people upstairs to hear me, and sure as rain, once Mrs. O'Daire calmed her daughter down, she thundered down the staircase and blew into the kitchen.

"I don't want you in my house anymore!" she hollered, barreling toward me. "I want you to leave. Tonight."

"We need to talk, Mrs. O'Daire."

"No, we don't." She came right up to me, fists clenched, her curlers wobbling and clicking together. "I know you're not just a simple test moderator. Janie told me the types of questions you asked her at school. And I know my ex-husband is well aware that you're here in Gordon Bay."

I raised my chin and refused to back away. "I want to talk to you about your daughter."

"You're not going to take her away."

"No, I'm not. You're absolutely right."

A board creaked. I looked up and spotted Miss Simpkin peeking around the corner.

"Rebecca," she said, her voice small and whispery. "I think you ought to listen to her."

"You're the worst one of all, Tillie!" Mrs. O'Daire wheeled toward her. "Inviting this *psychologist*"—she spat out the word—"into your classroom and then into our house. I was polite during dinner. I was kind and patient, and look what happened."

"I'm sorry."

"Please, go upstairs!" She pointed to the doorway. "You're risking me losing Janie."

Miss Simpkin darted an apologetic glance my way before backing out of view.

I put out my hands. "Mrs. O'Daire . . ."

The woman spun back around. "I don't want to hear one word about those numbers on Janie's walls. I don't care how curious or horrified those scribblings make you feel, but you're not coming near my daughter ever again."

"But I know you're curious about her intelligence, too. I saw the journal."

She recoiled; her mouth twisted into a horrified grimace. "He—he showed it to you?"

"I swear to you, I don't want to take Janie anywhere. I just want to free her of these nightmares and ensure she's receiving an education worthy of that brilliant young mind of hers."

"He showed you the journal?" she asked again, splotchy patches of color now rising in her cheeks and neck. "What else did he tell you about our family's private secrets? Did he tell you about my mother—poor, crazy Mrs. Simpkin, locked up in a loony bin?"

"Mrs. O'Daire . . ."

"Did he?"

I closed my mouth and swallowed.

"Did you sleep in his bed?" she asked.

"What?" I shrank back.

"I know you stayed in his hotel, all alone, just the two of you. Are you sleeping with him?"

"I'm a professional psychologist working with schoolchildren."

"Did he tell you *his* secrets, or is he only sharing our daughter's problems with the world?"

"Mrs. O'Daire"—I reached out to her left arm, not quite touching her—"please, take a breath. Calm down."

She smacked my hand away. "He sells booze to rummies in that hotel he inherited from his daddy. He barely does a lick of work. All he wants to do is read his goddamned mystery stories and sleep with anything with tits."

"I'm not here to discuss your marriage."

"Everyone hates me for betraying him, but he's the one who screwed a nurse at his training camp during the war—while I was raising our baby daughter here at home. Did he tell you *that*, Madame Psychologist? Did he tell you that our curiosity over Janie's stories was the only thing that kept this marriage together for as long as it did?"

I rubbed my arms, now as cold as the air outside. "No. I didn't hear those details."

She put her hands on her hips and turned her face away. Her throat rippled with a swallow.

"I want to help you," I said. "I imagine it's been a terrible strain for you, wondering about your daughter's well-being in the middle of your marital troubles."

A tear rolled down her left cheek. "I know it's not sane for a child to write across her walls that way. I know, it's not . . ." She closed her eyes. "Tillie and I paint over the numbers, but she keeps writing them, over and over. She says she's working on a geometric proof that she's been trying to create for years. She says the number eight keeps getting in the way."

My neck chilled. Nothing I had ever learned in any of my courses could explain why a child of seven would do such a thing.

"Have you ever brought in a mathematician to look at her equations?" I asked. "A professor, perhaps?"

"I don't want experts of any sort seeing what she's like," she said, her voice deepening, sharpening, like the blade of a knife. She opened her eyes. "Whether she's a genius, or insane, or a reincarnated woman from the last century—I don't care what she is—someone will want to take her away from me and study her. Or Michael will put her on display as a freak of nature."

"If he hasn't done so by now . . ."

"He hasn't done so because he's lazy. He's been waiting for someone like you to show up and do the work for him."

"I assure you, I don't want to put Janie on display. I want to help her."

She shook her head. "I simply don't believe you. I can smell the ambition rolling off of you, Miss Lind. You're drenched in it, from that chic Colleen Moore hairstyle to your fine city clothes."

"Please . . ." I took a breath. "How can I be of help? What can I do to put you at ease?"

"You can leave this house." Her eyes locked upon mine. "First thing tomorrow morning."

"But—"

"That's my final word."

I nodded. "Yes, of course. If that's what you truly wish."

"It is." She turned and left the room.

⤫⤬⤭ CHAPTER 12

*M*rs. *O'Daire is unwilling to help,* I penned in my notes the following morning before repacking my bags. *The child writes complex mathematical equations all over her bedroom walls. She claims she is working on a geometric proof. SHE IS SEVEN YEARS OLD!!! I am still no closer to decoding the enigma of Violet Sunday.*

It was Saturday, which meant no school and ample time to decide where to lodge before embarking upon my final week in Gordon Bay. I trekked to the post office with my luggage and my black briefcase, the latter of which now contained an envelope addressed to the postmaster of Friendly, Kansas. The cream-colored paper slid from my gloved fingers into the left hand of the Gordon Bay postmaster, and all I could think of were the numbers and symbols scattered across Janie's yellow walls.

The postmaster tossed my envelope into a bag of outgoing mail.

The next phase of my investigation commenced.

Back outside, an eastbound wind blew the taste of sea salt across my lips and tossed hair into my eyes. Oh, how I missed my poor wool cloche! I even turned toward the north and scanned the train tracks down the way, wondering where my hat and Mr. O'Daire's fedora had traveled off to, envisioning them shacked up together in one of the hedges by the sand.

Oddly enough, I heard Mr. O'Daire's voice behind me just then.

"That's not a sight I wanted to see again," he said.

I shifted his way, confused, a bit offended if he was referring to the sight of me. "I beg your pardon?"

"You, traveling around with your suitcases, I mean." He strode closer, a smile inching across his face, his hands stuffed inside the pockets of his black coat with its turned-up collar that made him look like a dapper young police detective. "Please don't tell me you slept on another floor last night."

"No, I didn't. I—" I shut my mouth and waited for him to venture closer to avoid shouting out the details of my sleeping arrangements.

He came to a stop in front of me, his feet spread apart. "Where did you sleep last night?"

"I stayed with your daughter and former wife."

A flicker of apprehension glinted in his eyes. "Did . . . did Tillie invite you to stay with them, after all?"

"Yes."

"And . . ." He scratched at his cheek. "Did that go well?"

I lifted my bags in response.

He winced. "Rebecca kicked you out?"

"She did, but"—I lowered the bags—"I stayed long enough to witness something that I would very much like to speak to you about."

"What?"

"Let's not discuss it out here in the open." I gestured down the road with an elbow. "I'd prefer to speak elsewhere."

"All right, then." He pulled an envelope from his left coat pocket. "Let me just slip into the post office for a moment and send off this bill."

"Certainly." My gaze dropped to the address on his envelope, verifying that he, indeed, intended to send the correspondence to a local bank, and not an individual in Kansas. "I'll wait here with my bags."

"You and your bags are returning to the hotel, Miss Alice Lind." He backed toward the post office door, pointing at me with the bill. "Let's end this nomadic lifestyle right here and now and treat you like a respected member of our community."

He pushed open the door and strolled inside.

I rested my bags on the sidewalk and kept a watch on the road and sidewalks, fearful of Rebecca catching me standing there, waiting for her former husband.

Did you sleep in his bed? she had had the gall to ask me with her curlers shaking in her hair. *Are you sleeping with him?*

Seagulls cried out overhead, soaring eastward, escaping another storm brewing over the Pacific. However, no human beings—Rebecca O'Daire or otherwise—appeared.

Mr. O'Daire soon rejoined me and picked up my bags. "I hope you don't mind walking to the hotel this time around. I decided to get some exercise this morning."

"You really don't need to host me."

"Let's make this the last-ever conversation about your lodging situation, shall we?" He sauntered toward his hotel to the south. "How much longer are you working in Gordon Bay?"

I grabbed my briefcase by its handle and caught up to him. "I should be finished by the end of next week."

"Then you're to stay in the Gordon Bay Hotel until that point. Not another word about it."

"Well . . . thank you."

He smiled. "You're welcome."

Across the street, a portly fellow in a white cook's coat moseyed out of a restaurant that had been closed the night before. "Good morning, Mr. O'Daire," he called, lifting a broom in the air in lieu of waving with a hand. "Fine weather we're having this morning."

"Morning, Gus," said Mr. O'Daire. "Another storm's on its way. I wouldn't spend too much time sweeping up leaves, if I were you."

I marveled at the fact that everyone in small towns genuinely did all know each other, as I'd always heard.

A middle-aged couple in a black Buick cruised our way, and, naturally, Mr. O'Daire waved at them, too, and called out, "Good morning, Mr. and Mrs. Pruitt."

"Good morning," they called back, and they ogled me with curiosity.

"I haven't seen your friend Sam around in the past day or so," I said, ignoring the couples' questioning eyebrows.

"Hopefully, that means he's seeking shelter in the house of his mother. Hopefully, he's not dead."

I frowned. "That's awfully blunt."

"It's the truth." Mr. O'Daire led me across the street. "Poor old Sam seems doomed."

"Psychotherapy would benefit him. Memories of war are far too traumatic for a person to endure on his own."

"I'm curious, why did you go into the field of psychology?"

"Just"—I took great care not to trip on the curb on the next stretch of sidewalk—"a personal interest in the field."

"Do you know someone like Sam or my mother-in-law?"

"Why do you ask?"

"Is that your 'personal interest'? You're close to a lunatic?"

"Oh, don't call them that. I don't like when ugly words get applied to people who are suffering."

"You do know one, then?"

I didn't respond. The only "lunatic" that I personally knew, of course, was myself.

He added, "I have a feeling you're about to grill me with questions of a far more personal nature than that, Miss Lind."

My silence continued.

"After staying with my ex-wife, I'm sure you know all about my flaws and sins."

"Let's continue to wait until we get farther past town before speaking of delicate subjects," I said. "I'm not fond of eavesdroppers."

A few feet ahead of us, the red awning of a bicycle rental shop rippled with a wind that whistled across the rooftops. I pulled my coat tighter around myself and, again, strands of my hair flapped against my cheeks. To our right, the sky squirmed with menacing black clouds that looked like they didn't give a damn about anyone stepping out for exercise.

Another minute or so later we reached the section of the road that ran through open grasslands, away from the buildings of town. I felt it time to bring up Janie and her bedroom walls.

"Have you seen Janie's room lately?" I asked.

"No. Rebecca doesn't allow me into the house anymore."

"She doesn't?"

He readjusted his grip on my bags. "Driving Janie home from school now and then is about the best I can do."

"That's the only time you see her?"

"Oh, I'm willing to bet that Rebecca told you all about her fears of me kidnapping Janie and rushing her off to the circus. She's gotten it into her head that I'm planning to somehow make millions off of our child."

"What *would* you do if the reincarnation story proved to be genuine?"

He shrugged. "I honestly don't know. I'd be flabbergasted, I suppose. I'd hope, for Janie's sake, that somehow a chance to visit Kansas would become a real possibility."

"Have you ever tried, on a whim, writing to the postmaster of Friendly, even when you didn't know whether the town existed?"

"I have."

I raised my brows. "Really?"

He nodded.

"And what happened?"

"No one ever responded."

"And yet you still believe that such a family exists out there?"

"Of course. No one living with Janie can't not believe in the Sundays. Not even her mother . . . no matter how much she balks at the idea nowadays."

I thought again of Janie's bedroom. "When you still lived with Janie and Mrs. O'Daire, how did Janie decorate her bedroom walls?"

His pace slowed. "Why do you ask?"

"Please tell me, what did you see in her room?"

He stopped walking altogether, and his face sobered. His shoulders tensed. "She wrote . . . *numbers* all over her walls."

"What types of numbers?"

"I don't know what they were. They didn't make sense. *That* part worried her mother to no end, even when she was still openly speaking of Janie's past life."

The clouds prowled closer, blocking the sun from view, casting us both in shadow. I realized I'd been squinting and relaxed the muscles around my eyes. "Why did that part in particular worry her?"

"It seemed too much like insanity to her. On the one hand, I agreed—it, indeed, resembled a crazy person's room. On the other, I felt it looked to be the realm of a genius. Did you see it?"

"I did."

"And how do you explain *that* away with regular psychology? How on earth can anything other than reincarnation be at work when a seven-year-old girl is working to create proofs?"

I switched my briefcase to my left hand. "She could very well be a child prodigy."

"I've thought about that," he said, "but it wouldn't explain how Janie became aware of all of those complex mathematical symbols to begin with. Even prodigies need to be shown that sort of thing before trying out proofs, I would think."

"Has anyone given her advanced books on mathematics?"

"Her aunt has, but not until *after* Janie started writing the proofs."

"Are you absolutely certain it was after?" I asked.

"Quite. Primarily, Tillie wanted to show Rebecca and me the books so we could try to comprehend what the devil Janie was writing."

"I'm afraid I don't know how to explain it, then." I shook out my right arm, which tingled from carrying the case. "It simply doesn't make sense. Many children Janie's age in these schoolhouses can't even count to thirteen."

"Say that again," he said, leaning his right ear toward me.

"Say what again?"

His eyes brightened. "Did you just say, 'I'm afraid I don't know how to explain it' . . . as in, 'I don't know how to explain it in terms of psychology?'"

"Well . . . I . . ."

He raised his chin and smiled. "You believe."

"No. No, I'm not saying—"

"Yes, you are." He stood up tall. "You're coming around to the possibility that Janie experienced a past life."

"I'm sorry, Mr. O'Daire, but her behavior also shares traits in common with patients who suffer from a multiple personality."

"How did Janie acquire knowledge of advanced math, then? Do multiple personalities come equipped with a math tutor?"

"No, but—" I flinched as a sudden downpour of rain hit my face, shocking my eyes with cold flecks of water. I blinked and covered my head with my briefcase, upon which the rain plunked. "Well, then, here's the rain again, I see."

"Sorry. It crept up faster than expected."

I hustled onward, toward the hotel, still shielding my head.

Mr. O'Daire followed without a word, but I could hear him beaming, even without looking at him. I never thought it possible to actually *hear* someone beam, but I could tell by the briskness and cheerfulness of his step precisely how he looked. When I checked on him, there he was beside me, grinning the same way as when I had told him Friendly existed.

"I could lose all credibility for even pursuing this past-life theory," I said.

"I know. You've said as much before."

"This isn't one of your Sherlock Holmes mystery books." I increased my speed, for the rain strengthened, soaking my gloves. "There isn't going to be a tidy solution at the end of this investigation. Even if we prove the theory of reincarnation to be true, there's nothing we could do with that information."

"We could allow Janie to understand what's happening to her."

"I need to move on to another town at the end of this week."

"Then we'll have to work quickly."

Rain seeped into my shoes and froze my toes. I broke into a trot, spotting the hotel on the edge of the cliff up ahead.

"Your ex-wife doesn't want me near Janie again."

"That's going to be awfully difficult when you work in Janie's school."

"I'll bet you anything she keeps Janie home from that school until I'm gone."

"Then I'll contact the truant officer. Tillie specifically asked him to make sure the children attend during the testing."

My stomach knotted over the idea of the law's potential involvement. "I don't want to interfere with your family's dispute."

"For better or worse, you're already smack-dab in the middle of our dispute, Miss Lind. You may as well kick up your feet and make yourself comfortable."

We broke into a run. My right foot hit a puddle and splashed mud against my shin.

"Damn!" I said, even though I usually didn't swear in front of men.

"'Damn' for the rain?" he asked, peeking back at me as he sprinted ahead with my bags. "Or 'damn' because you're now completely embroiled in the bizarre world of Violet Sunday."

"Both. This is quite a predicament you've put me into, Mr. O'Daire."

"If you hated it so much"—he smiled over his shoulder at me, swinging the luggage by his sides—"if you weren't as curious as all hell about Janie, you'd be running in the other direction right now, not after me."

"It's simply my job."

"And what a job it is!"

A shot of wind whipped a blast of arctic air up my skirt, and I, indeed, ran after him, not away.

FROM BEHIND HIS front desk, Mr. O'Daire fetched a white towel and a silver key to the same room that I had occupied during my last visit. Room 22.

"Is your mother here?" I asked from the other side of the desk, more soaked mop than person by that point.

"No, she's at home." He handed me the towel. "Why do you ask?"

"I'd like to speak with her about Janie."

"Oh?"

"I'd like to hear about her interactions with the girl—her observations of the 'Violet Sunday' moments."

He nodded and kept his voice even. "I'll be fetching her later this afternoon so she can help with the Saturday-night supper and drinks."

"I'll speak to her then, if you don't mind."

"No, I don't."

I wrung out my hair with the towel and scanned the empty lobby—the vacant chairs, the coat stand lacking coats, aside from mine and Mr. O'Daire's. One of his sleeves protected one of mine—raven black against claret red. The jackets dripped in unison against a braided tan rug.

"Are we alone right now?" I asked.

"Yes," he said in a tone that sounded like a question.

"May I talk to you about your thoughts on reincarnation?"

He laid the key upon the front desk's polished wood. "What do you want to know?"

"Well, if past lives are a legitimate phenomenon—and I'm still not saying they are—what, in your opinion, was Violet Sunday's reason for coming back? And do you believe *all* souls are reincarnated into newborn bodies?"

He lifted his eyes to mine. "Are you sure you want my humble opinion on the great question of life after death?"

"If I'm going to even consider venturing into the realm of parapsychology, then I want to believe there's still some genuine psychology involved. What, in your opinion, as humble as it may be, do you believe would drive a human soul to be born a second time?"

"Unfinished business," he said without hesitation. "Or a tragic death, which would also create the sense of an unfinished life."

The hairs on the backs of my arms bristled. Again I thought of all the urgent mathematical writings marking Janie's walls.

He rested his palms against the countertop. "Reincarnation is very much in alignment with the popular belief that spirits remain tethered to this world to accomplish something they didn't achieve during their lives. Only, in the case of past lives, the spirit starts from scratch in a brand-new body."

I leaned my left elbow against the desk. "If this were true, might criminals and other nefarious people from the past also return?"

"Well . . ."

"For every Violet Sunday, mightn't there be a Jack the Ripper or Vlad the Impaler, returned to continue their murderous rampages?

And wouldn't we see them repeating their violent patterns in their new lives? Wouldn't we have already realized that reincarnation exists, if it actually exists?"

"I don't believe every vicious individual will become a criminal in his new life, nor will every good soul remain a good one." He toyed with the little key and its plain metal ring, jangling the two against each other. "From what I've seen, past life personalities are as fragile as candlelight. Often, the residual traces of Violet burn out, and Janie lives as just Janie, a girl shaped by her mother and me and her current surroundings."

"Well, then . . ." I straightened my posture. "Now you're venturing into the psychological territory of nature versus nurture."

"Am I?"

"I think your 'humble opinion' isn't as humble as you believe."

He folded his hands on the countertop and leaned against it. "I read quite a bit, that's all. And sometimes . . ." His face pinked up; he turned his eyes away from mine. "Sometimes, I even fancy myself a writer."

"Really?" I smiled. "What do you write?"

"Well . . ." He shifted his weight between his legs. "Nowadays, I gravitate toward dark, philosophical works. All these winters spent on the coast, all this business with Janie and the child that we lost, did that to me. I didn't used to be so introspective."

"If you died this very moment and had a chance to come back," I asked, a little startled at my own dark line of thinking, "do you think you would?"

"Yes." He nodded. "Most definitely. I would try to get things right the second time around."

"You don't think you've gotten things right this time?"

"Haven't you heard anything I've said about myself?" He smirked again, but the light in his eyes dimmed. "I sit here and write about grim and hefty topics. I'm a divorced man, banned from seeing his daughter, stuck in a hotel without guests nine months of the year. Does that sound like 'getting things right'?"

"I'm sorry." I drew back. "I didn't mean to upset you."

He stroked a hand through his damp hair. "No, that's just me taking out my frustrations on the wrong person. I'm sorry. It's just a vexing way to live, stuck in this place, pressured to keep it running the way my father did, restricted from helping my own daughter."

"You are helping your daughter by speaking to me. Not every-one finds the courage to seek the aid of a psychologist." I picked up my leather briefcase from the floor beside me.

"And how about you?" he asked.

"I beg your pardon?"

"Would you come back for another life, given the chance?"

I sighed and rolled back my shoulders. "Only if someone could guarantee I would return as a man." I reached back down and hoisted up my suitcases as well.

"Here"—Mr. O'Daire hustled around the desk—"let me help you with those; they're monstrous."

"There's no need. As I just said, I wish I had been born a man. No one would feel obligated to make a fuss over anything I do."

"All right, then." He lifted his hands and stepped away. "Carry on, Mr. Lind."

"Now you're making fun."

"Not at all. You're the saint who verified the existence of Friendly for me. You can do anything you please, as far as I'm concerned."

"Well . . . thank you." My face warmed. "Would you mind if I borrowed a book from your little library? I think I might weather the storm in my room until your mother arrives."

"What is it you're hoping my mother will say?"

"I want to obtain a complete picture of the family—and to see what all of Janie's relatives have to say about their experiences with her."

He paled and asked, "A 'complete picture of the family'?"

"Yes."

"What do you mean by that?"

"When working with a child, it's important to know the full background of her parents' relationship"—I averted my eyes from his—"warts and all."

"Ah." He nodded. "So . . . Rebecca, indeed, dragged out all of our dirty laundry."

"She had some things to say about you."

"Ask *me* about my infidelity, Miss Lind. Not my mother."

I swallowed. "All right, then. *Were* you unfaithful to your wife when you were married?"

"I told you, I haven't gotten things right." He picked at the front edge of his desk. "Rebecca and I fought before I left for Camp Lewis, even though I had no choice but to leave her and Janie to serve the country. She was terrified of Janie dying; I was terrified of all of us dying. I entered the army an unhappy, frightened young man, and I made a stupid mistake."

"I'm sorry to hear you left home in that state of mind."

He lowered his face and ran his tongue along the inside of his left cheek. "Our marriage was already in shambles. Everything was so much better before we lost that first little one."

My throat tightened. For the briefest of moments, my mind

slipped back to the moment when I myself discovered a stabbing pain in my abdomen; blood in my underclothes.

I clenched my hands around the handles of my bags. "Well, thank you for your honesty. The loss of a child is the most painful experience a parent can ever face. It's not surprising that you and your wife struggled in the aftermath."

"I should have been a better husband. Rebecca didn't deserve that."

I didn't pass judgment on either of those statements.

He raised his head. "I have a feeling you don't have many warts in your own past. Do you?"

"My own past," I said, altering the way I held my suitcases to keep them from slipping out of my damp fingers, "has nothing to do with my business here in Gordon Bay."

"I suppose not." He nodded. "I'm just not used to baring my soul to a person without knowing a thing about her."

"This is simply how the world of psychology works, Mr. O'Daire."

"I suppose it does." He tucked the key between my right thumb and index finger. "I'm sorry for prying."

When I could think of nothing more to say—when it became all too clear that both of our pasts elbowed their way between us in that hotel lobby—I turned and lugged my bags up the stairs.

 CHAPTER 13

In my notebook, I recorded Mr. O'Daire's accounts of Janie's wall writings, as well as his theories about reincarnation.

She wrote . . . numbers all over her walls . . . That part worried her mother to no end . . . On the one hand, I agreed—it, indeed, resembled a crazy person's room. On the other, I felt it looked to be the realm of a genius.

Reincarnation is very much in alignment with the popular belief that spirits remain tethered to this world to accomplish something they didn't achieve during their lives . . . the spirit starts from scratch in a brand-new body.

I don't believe every vicious individual will become a criminal in his new life, nor will every good soul remain a good one.

Past life personalities are as fragile as candlelight . . . the residual traces of Violet burn out . . . Janie lives as just Janie.

No new psychology-based diagnoses sprang forth from his statements. The past-life possibility, however, hovered in front of me, a filmy screen blocking the truth, distracting me with its outlandish yet undeniable presence. I increasingly wanted to believe in its existence. As ludicrous as the rational side of my brain still knew reincarnation to be, I longed to hunt down the real Violet Sunday and discover a murder in a lake that had, for three decades, silenced a brilliant mind. The back of my neck prickled just from thinking about it. What a discovery that would make—proof of the immortality of personalities. Proof of the undying potency of the human memory.

Memory is the strongest component of the human psyche, I wrote below my records of Mr. O'Daire's statements. *Not even death can weaken it. It propels us forward. It holds us back. It refuses to let us go.*

Rain suddenly battered my window with a sound that jarred. I lifted my head and gave a shiver. My room, I realized, lacked a fire in the grate, and the temperature couldn't have been any warmer than fifty degrees.

I rose, fetched a cardigan sweater, and then wandered over to the window while threading my arms through the thick sleeves. Down below the rocky cliff, white-capped waves slammed against slick black boulders. The water smacked the rocks with a satisfying *thwack* and promptly retreated to the gray and swollen sea, only to lunge straight back at the shore.

A bout of loneliness gripped me as I stood there, contemplating, dreaming, theorizing in the cold. I debated heading out to catch the train back to Portland and spending the night at my sister Bea's apartment. Sometimes, Bea hopped on trains and surprised me for weekend visits in whichever town I happened to be stationed. Neither of us had married. I strongly suspected that she preferred women over men, romantically speaking, but neither of us ever spoke of such a thing, and I certainly wasn't going to broach the subject with my parents or Margery. Bea currently lived with a blonde named Pearl who also worked at her library. She would have enjoyed hearing about my foray into the supernatural. I imagined her leaning close, her deep brown eyes narrowed and intent, as she formulated her own astute conclusions about the O'Daires.

THE STORM PASSED over the hotel's gabled rooftop and moved on to cannonade the mountains to the east. I grabbed an umbrella from the brass holder in the lobby, and without alerting the currently unseen Mr. O'Daire to my departure, I walked back into town with the rubber heels of my galoshes squeaking against the wet road. I ate lunch. I rummaged around the bushes near the depot in a futile search for my burgundy cloche. I browsed a bookstore and bought a copy of Mary Roberts Rinehart's *The Breaking Point*, simply because I believed I would have spoiled the expectant-looking owner's day if I had left his sleepy little business without a purchase.

Upon my return to the Gordon Bay Hotel, I found Mr. O'Daire adding logs to the lobby's fireplace.

"Oh." He sat back on his feet with the last log cradled in his arms. "I thought you were still in your room."

"I ventured out for a bit of exercise and lunch." I stuffed the umbrella back into the holder with three others. "Sitting around in hotel rooms disquiets me."

"Too much traveling from town to town?"

"I beg your pardon?" I asked.

"Is that why you don't like hotel rooms? Your gypsy lifestyle?"

"Precisely." I unbuttoned my coat and let that explanation do.

He grabbed a poker from a stand of black tools. "I'm planning to drive over and fetch my mother in a few minutes." He prodded the logs, pulling back when a flame snapped at his wrist. "Would you like to speak to her at her house or here at the hotel?"

"If you don't mind, I'd prefer to speak to her here, where there's plenty of room for a private conversation. I want her to be able to speak openly about her experiences with Janie without feeling self-conscious."

"Fair enough." He got to his feet. "I'll fetch her right now."

"Thank you. I'll wait down here in front of the fire if you don't mind."

"Would you care for another Orange Quench?"

"That won't be necessary. Just your mother will do."

I INTERVIEWED JANIE'S paternal grandmother in one of the guest-rooms on the topmost floor—her idea for an ideal location for chatting, not mine. She didn't want to be a bother in my own room, and, as she said herself, "these pretty little quarters are just sitting up here, bathing in dust." We drank tea and spoke of Janie and all of the various Violet Sunday anecdotes from the past five and a half years.

"The stories have never changed since she was just a wee thing," said Mrs. O'Daire, warming her fingers around a china cup painted in daffodils. "They've simply grown in detail and emotional depth. That's what makes them so believable, in fact. They're consistent."

"Oh, that's interesting," I said, and I jotted down *Stories believable because consistent* in my notebook, which lay on a small table to my left.

Mrs. O'Daire sipped her tea, while I stirred my own cup and waited for her to say more.

"Janie never alters anything," she continued after a spell, cra-

dling the teacup in her lap. "She simply expands upon the memories, recalling items like the fragrance of the pencils with which
she wrote or the particular lace on a dress that she wore. The older
memories—the childhood events—seem the strongest, and everything grows a little hazier in the later years of Violet's life. She seems
confused about what precisely happened to make her drown."

"And, as far as you're aware," I asked, "Janie never experienced
any moments of falling underwater since her birth in 1918?"

"No, there've been no brushes with drowning. Whenever
I helped bathe her in the early years, she always hated when we
rinsed her hair after a shampooing—she'd fly into a tizzy about
water going up her nose. But I do seem to remember her father
fussing over the same exact thing as a child."

"Do you have any reason to believe that Janie experienced any
severe accidents or abuse?"

"Heavens, no! That child is as protected and loved as a prized
peach."

Once again, I wrote in my notebook, *a relative insists that Janie's
past is devoid of any trauma.*

And later, after Mrs. O'Daire left the room, I added, *Nothing
else can be done, I'm afraid, unless I speak more to Janie or someone
comes forward with a concealed moment of tragedy in the child's life.
Unless I receive a return letter from Friendly, Kansas.*

IN MY OWN room that evening, with a blanket tucked around my
legs, I sat on the bed with my legs crossed in front of me and perused every single line of the notes I had compiled during the past
three days. I reread the specifics of a possible test I had considered
devising.

Perhaps make a list of towns that exist throughout Kansas—Hutchinson, Marysville, Oakley, Independence, Liberal, Goodland—and ask her to point to the ones that sound familiar.

Following my own advice, I, indeed, created such a list. Mining my own knowledge of Kansas, which I had formed during the years I spent in rapturous awe of the worlds of Dorothy and Princess Ozma, I wrote down the names of northeastern towns in the state. Interspersed between them, I included names fetched from my immediate family . . . and from my own imagination.

Kansas City
Topeka
Lawrence
Margery
Leavenworth
Rustic
Manhattan
Yesternight
Junction City
Marysville
Ottawa
Beatriceville
Abilene
Salina

I tittered over "Margery" and "Beatriceville," knowing Bea would appreciate my incorporation of her name into my investigation.

Oh, Nell, she would probably say with a flip of one of the neckties she always liked to wear with her blouses, *you always did like a*

*good puzzle. Maybe you should go find that handsome daddy of Janie's
and discuss Sherlock Holmes with him while playing footsie in front
of the fire. Just don't let him knock you up like that last one. Don't hit
him in the head.*

I closed my eyes and rubbed at my eyelids, forgetting how little
sleep I had managed to snatch over the past forty-eight hours. My
brain somersaulted, and all that pondering and speculating and
decoding throbbed within my temples. Rain tapped against my
window yet again—the sound of fingernails incessantly rapping
against glass—and I swear, I smelled the dampness of the outside world through the pane. The scent of water made me think
of drowning, which put me into that far-off lake somewhere in
the northeastern corner of Kansas. Skirts billowing and undulat-
ing. Ice-cold water rushing inside Violet Sunday's ears. A blurred
man, standing on the shore, peering into the water, while branches
dragged her down, down, down into a dark and gaping mouth. Into
eel-like grasses that lapped at her legs like long, wavering tongues.
And then blackness.

Followed again by light.

I REMOVED MY shoes and resigned myself to a much-needed nap,
but no more than two minutes after stretching across the downy
white bedspread, someone knocked on my bedroom door. I crawled
off the mattress—ill at ease over the idea of a person standing right
outside the place where I was just about to sleep.

The keyhole spied with its narrow dark slit for an eye.

"Who is it?" I asked in a voice that came out quieter than I
intended.

No one answered. I stepped back and stiffened over the ridiculous notion that the man with the tumbleweed beard from my recurring dream waited on the other side, preparing to kick open the door and blast a bullet through my chest. The taste of iron coated my tongue. A mental image of my legs covered in blood flashed through my mind.

Beneath the bottom edge of the door, I spotted the shadows of two feet.

I swallowed. "Who is—?"

"It's just me, Miss Lind," said Mr. O'Daire from the other side. "I'm sorry to disturb you. I brought you some dinner and a drink. Mom told me she thought you looked exhausted and malnourished, and . . . well . . . mothers are usually right about that sort of thing."

I squeaked open the door and found my host standing out there in the hallway, dressed in a pressed white shirt and an evening coat, along with a necktie and trousers the same charcoal-gray shade as the coat. He held a silver tray, topped with another one of his famous ham sandwiches and a side of pretzels, but no pickle this time. Also on the tray sat a glass of clear liquid that smelled as piney sweet as gin.

The dimples I remembered from his heroism at the depot re-emerged. "Yes, it's gin," he said. "You're not buying it from me, so you wouldn't be doing anything illegal if you drank it. I figured you might need a little hooch after all that we're putting you through in our tempestuous seaside hamlet."

"Hmm . . ." I eyed the glass brimming with liquid temptation. "Is your little blind tiger alive and kicking down in the basement right now?"

"What blind tiger?" The dimples deepened. "This is a fine old family establishment you're talking about, Miss Lind." He lifted the tray. "Shall I bring it in or hand it to you?"

"I'll take it, thank you." I procured the tray with care to avoid sloshing the gin and steered the food and drink toward the dressing table.

"Did your chat with Mom lead to any more answers?" asked Mr. O'Daire from the doorway.

"No, it didn't, I'm sorry to say. Although I greatly appreciate her speaking to me."

"She didn't seem to mind."

"I was just thinking about Janie's claims about drowning, as a matter of fact." I adjusted the tray's position on the table, scooting it just so. "I wondered if she's ever provided any clarification about a certain aspect of her nightmares."

"Which aspect?"

"That 'man in the other house'—she claimed to have witnessed him standing above the surface of the water, watching her drown." I licked a drop of gin from my right thumb and tasted the sweetness of juniper berries. "But has she ever said *how* she got into the water in the dream? Did he push her in—and if so, wouldn't she have bobbed straight back up to the surface?"

"Well . . ." Mr. O'Daire jangled coins about in his pockets. "I've always wondered if he had tried to kill her and was attempting to dispose of the body."

"*How* did he try to kill her, though? Has she ever mentioned memories of any other violent moments?"

"No, but I suppose he could have—" He blinked, his eyes dampening. He turned his face away and smiled in an embarrassed sort of way. "This is harder to talk about than I expected. All I can imagine now is Janie's little face underwater."

"Oh. . . . I'm sorry. I most certainly wasn't trying to put that image into your head."

"He—he could have done something without her realizing it, I suppose." Mr. O'Daire scratched at his lower lip. "Poisoned her, for example. Hit her over the head with something blunt, like a thick branch . . ."

Involuntarily, I gagged.

"Maybe he gave her eight blows," he added, oblivious to my disgust. "Maybe that's why she says, 'Watch out for the number eight!'"

Bile charged up my gullet. I doubled over and clamped a hand over my mouth, envisioning children's heads marred by blood in my front lawn.

"Miss Lind?"

I shut my eyes and saw a branch bashing a human skull, cracking bone. My own arm swung the branch through the air, striking my imagined version of Violet Sunday in the head—eight times in a row. *Eight. Eight. Eight. Watch out for the number eight!*

"Miss Lind?"

I gasped for air, still doubled over.

"What's wrong?" he asked.

"Why did you say that?"

"Say what?"

"The thing about the branch. Oh, Christ." I staggered over to the bed. "I'm going to be sick."

"Do you want me to get you a wastebasket?"

"No!" I waved him away. "I don't want you to see me."

"Should I leave?"

"Don't ever mention someone getting hit in the head again." I collapsed onto my side on the mattress and squeezed my arms around my middle. "I've seen it myself. It's horrifying."

"I didn't realize—do you want me to drive you to another town for the rest of the weekend? Is it too much to be stuck here?"

I dug my palms into my eye sockets and groaned.

"Miss Lind?"

"I'm sorry. This is so embarrassing." I laughed and burbled up tears at the same time.

Mr. O'Daire held the doorknob, his mouth tipped open, knees bent, as though he debated between propelling himself forward to assist me and escaping down the hallway.

"Don't worry about me, please. I'm fine." I sniffed and wiped at my eyes. "Thank you for the food and drink. Once my stomach settles, I plan to enjoy them and then lose myself in a long night's sleep."

"Is there anything else you need?"

I shook my head. "No. Thank you. Please go, so you don't have to keep subjecting yourself to this." I pushed myself up to a seated position with the swaying, erratic movements of a lush. Strands of my hair fell down over my eyes, reminding me of blood enmeshed in the locks of little children. "I'm fine."

Mr. O'Daire hesitated.

"Go. Please!"

He closed the door behind him, sealing me inside the room with my thoughts alone, which was never a good thing.

THE BOOZE AND the food and the rest helped immensely. I awoke the next morning feeling quite foolish for my behavior, and I even lost a great deal of my enthusiasm for the entire reincarnation line of thinking. Until proof from Kansas traveled west—if proof, in fact, was coming—I resigned not to believe in anything.

After dressing and fussing over my hair, I ventured out of doors and roamed the green grounds of the Gordon Bay Hotel, adhering to stone paths and sidewalks to avoid the swampy sections of mud and standing brown water. To the south, on the westernmost point of the cliff, I happened upon an overlook with a wrought-iron railing, below which the waves continued to perform their impressive display of swelling to great heights and smashing against boulders. The roar and swoosh of the movements reverberated deep within my chest. The water's spray salted the air with an invigorating zest, and it felt splendid to inhale it through my nose.

The scenery relaxed me so entirely, in fact, that I lost all track of time until Mr. O'Daire traipsed my way from some back exit of the hotel, asking how I was feeling. Much blushing and apologizing ensued on my part, and a great deal of "No, no, no, don't worry about it" tumbled from him. The whole exchange ended with him offering to drive me to one of the more populated towns to the north to have lunch with him.

The nail of my right index finger toyed with a patch of rust on the railing. "I can't," I said. "I'm not supposed to involve myself with any of the parents of the students whom I'm testing."

He leaned back against the railing, no more than three feet to my right. A breeze tousled his blond hair, mussing the careful comb lines that he looked to have just created before joining me out there. He appeared to have recently shaved, as well, his cheeks smooth, unblemished, with no traces of stubble. I smelled the ginger of his shaving soap.

"Who from the Department of Education is going to see you eating lunch out on the coast with me?" he asked.

"A parent from Gordon Bay might also drive up for a meal. Or one of the teachers with whom I'll be working at one of my next assignments will spot us and raise eyebrows when they meet me."

"It's merely a meal . . ."

"I would be risking my job. I would be compromising my work with Janie."

He wrapped his fingers around the rails behind him and sighed—a sound of frustration. Sexual frustration, to be precise, but I wasn't about to say as much. I wasn't entirely sure how we had wandered into such territory after a night in which he had nearly witnessed me vomit. Professors had warned against patients falling in love with their psychologists, due to the intimacy and comfort involved in psychotherapy, but they never suggested that a *school* psychologist might elicit feelings of amour in a parent. Perhaps my vulnerability had made me attractive.

"I wish I could get away for an informal chat," I said, "but it's simply not possible. Or wise."

He raised his gaze to mine, and we regarded each other with one of those too-long looks I knew so well.

I pushed away from the railing and retreated up the stone steps that led to the hotel's back lawn.

"What happens with Janie after you leave at the end of this week?" he asked from behind me, still at the overlook. "What do I do about the discovery of the existence of Friendly?"

I pivoted back toward him on my left heel. "I'm working on some ideas that I'm not yet prepared to discuss. If anything comes from them, I'll let you know."

"You'll be working in other towns, though."

"I know where to find you, Mr. O'Daire," I said with a smile. "I can guarantee that you'll be receiving a rushed telegram or an immediate personal appearance from me if another breakthrough occurs."

I turned and continued navigating the slick steps, holding out my arms for balance. "Don't worry," I added. "You'll likely hear from me again."

"Doesn't it get awfully lonely, this traveling psychologist life of yours?"

"Of course it does." I peeked over my shoulder. "That is precisely why I'm rushing away from you and your offer of lunch."

He let go of the railing, and his black coat fluttered like the feathers of a bird catching the wind.

I pressed onward, promising myself that I would grab the Mary Roberts Rinehart book I'd just purchased and hide away in a restaurant, or even the schoolhouse, if that's what it would take to while away the rest of the weekend without succumbing to my stupidity.

CHAPTER 14

Janie, to my surprise, appeared at school on Monday morning. Or, rather, to my surprise, Rebecca O'Daire *allowed* Janie to attend school, despite my continued presence in the building. The child did not smile at me, or wave, or even look my way when she entered the classroom with her fellow students, and I got the distinct impression that she ignored me on purpose. In fact, when she bustled by me to take her seat at her desk, she forced her irises to the far right corners of her eyes and kept her gait stiff.

The students settled into their seats, and Miss Simpkin led them in the Pledge of Allegiance. Thereafter, I devoted the rest of the morning to testing the twelve-and thirteen-year-olds with Stanford picture interpretations, bow-knot tying, the repetition of five to seven digits, counting backward from twenty, vocabulary testing, dictation, and "What's the thing for you to do?" scenarios. The examinations ran without much fuss; I offered my staple "fine" and "splendid" responses. And, all the while, the smooth right edge of my list of Kansas town names stuck out from the side of the record booklet. Waiting.

An hour before lunchtime, I entered the main classroom,

minding the loudness of my footsteps to keep from interrupting Miss Simpkin's animated reading of Longfellow's "The Song of Hiawatha."

Janie listened to the poem with her hands folded on top of her walnut-colored desk, her posture impeccable, shoulders lifted, spine straighter than Miss Simpkin's yardstick that hung from a nail on the wall. The child wore a purple ribbon that held her hair back from her pink little ears.

I stopped beside her desk and leaned down.

"Janie."

Her shoulders flinched. She peeked up at me with eyes round and bright green.

"Would you please join me at the back of the schoolhouse for one more question?" I asked.

Miss Simpkin ceased reading. "Didn't you already test Janie, Miss Lind?"

"I just have one more question to ask her. It'll take two minutes."

The schoolteacher gave me a small shake of her head, her eyes apologetic. "I'm sorry. Janie is just about to come up front to read."

"It's rather urgent. I think Janie will find it entertaining. It involves geography." I mouthed the word *please* to Miss Simpkin.

The teacher sighed. "I would like to review the question with you in the cloakroom first."

"Of course."

"Excuse me for a moment, class." She set the book on her desk and marched down the aisle behind me.

Once inside the cloakroom, I lowered my voice to avoid prying ears. "I'm still investigating Janie's link to Kansas. I've devised one more test to give her."

"You heard my sister—she doesn't want you speaking to Janie anymore. The only reason my niece is even in this classroom this morning is because she begged to come to school. I swore to Rebecca I would keep you two apart."

"I witnessed the severity of Janie's nightmares, Tillie. They won't disappear on their own."

"Rebecca doesn't want you interfering."

"It's not interfering. I'm a psychologist"—I slapped a hand to my chest—"hired to help children who don't have regular access to mental assistance. I see that Janie is suffering from sleep disturbances *and* in dire need of a more advanced curriculum. It's my professional duty to help her. You yourself called me here to help her. Let me give her one last test."

Miss Simpkin hugged her arms around herself and breathed through her nose. "What is the test regarding?"

"Kansas geography. I'm curious if any other towns in the state mean anything to Janie."

"And what will that prove?"

"It will show us how real Kansas is to her. Also, I'm conducting research to see if the Sundays actually exist."

"*How* are you conducting such research?"

"By writing letters to Kansas." I closed the record booklet sitting open on the table, not wanting any of my work on display. "You don't know what a risk this is for me, investigating the case of a potential past life. When you first told me of Janie's stories, I honestly wanted to laugh at its preposterousness. I knew I could never seriously go down that path if I wanted to keep my credibility."

Miss Simpkin's stance relaxed. "Are . . . are you now saying that you believe this to be a case of reincarnation?"

"Not just yet. However, I will say, at this point, I believe in the *plausibility* of reincarnation. I want to either rule out the theory so we can stop getting distracted by its glamour—or prove beyond a shadow of a doubt that Janie genuinely remembers a life lived decades ago in Kansas."

Miss Simpkin fussed with the collar of her blouse. "As you well know, Rebecca wouldn't ever allow you to put Janie on display at any lectures."

"I can't give lectures about reincarnation," I said with a curt laugh. "I'm struggling to be taken seriously as a woman in this field. If I'm suddenly a woman who's also spouting out psychical theories, I'll be laughed straight out of psychology."

"Then why are you doing this?"

"To help a troubled child—which is what the Department of Education pays me to do. I have no ulterior motives, and I'm most certainly not conspiring with Michael O'Daire to turn Janie into a profitable celebrity. I don't think that's what he wants either."

"Are you certain?"

"Quite." I rubbed my arms, which grew cold from a draft. "I know what it's like to be haunted by one's past, Tillie. I would love to free Janie of whatever it is that's perturbing her and let her live her life as just Janie."

"May I do the geography test now?" asked a small voice that came from behind Miss Simpkin.

The schoolteacher put a hand to her neck and spun around.

In the entryway to the classroom stood little Janie, hanging on to the doorframe. The stoic expression of her little rosebud lips conveyed no indication as to whether she'd just heard our conversation.

"May I?" she asked, her eyes focused on her aunt.

"Do you feel like taking another test with Miss Lind?"

Janie nodded.

"Well . . ." Miss Simpkin lowered her hand to her side. "All right, then. As long as it doesn't take too much time away from the other children's evaluations . . ."

"The test will be brief," I assured her. "Thank you for allowing Janie to take it."

Miss Simpkin laid her right hand over the breadth of Janie's head in a nurturing gesture. A protective gesture. After a brief peek back at me—her eyes pleading with me to avoid stirring up controversy—she returned to her pupils.

I pulled out the chair reserved for the subjects of my examinations. "Please, have a seat, Janie."

The child did as I asked, and I took my own seat on the other side of the table, in front of the record booklet, below five winter coats that smelled like leaky basements.

I clasped my hands together in my lap and sat up tall. "Janie, I don't know how much you heard of our conversation just now. I was telling your aunt how badly I want to help you to understand—to help you get rid of—these nightmares you keep experiencing. The drowning dreams."

Janie reached out and grabbed a nearby pencil. Using the tips of her fingers, she rolled it back and forth on the tabletop.

"Have you been having such dreams for a long time?" I asked.

Without looking at me, she nodded. The pencil's ridges whirred against the table's surface.

"I've heard that your dreams take place in Kansas, which is so interesting to me because I used to be drawn to that state myself. Have you ever been to Kansas?"

She inhaled a long breath and then nodded *yes*.

"Oh?" I asked. "Recently?"

She shook her head. *No*.

"And you're certain you've never read L. Frank Baum's books about Kansas and Oz?" I asked. "Or did your mother or father ever read them to you?"

Another headshake.

"They definitely haven't?"

The pencil slipped from her fingers and dropped to the ground. Janie leaned over and picked it up with a weighty sigh—the first sound to emerge from her mouth since she had asked her aunt about the test. She then sat upright and fiddled with the pencil again.

I tugged my list of Kansas cities out of the record book. "Janie"—I laid out the sheet in front of her—"I've listed various names on this piece of paper. Can you tell me if any of these words mean anything to you and the time you spent in Kansas?"

She made a sputtering sound with her lips, as though my question taxed her patience. Little bubbles of spit showered the paper.

Yet again, she shook her head *no*.

"I'm getting the distinct impression that you're not speaking to me at all." I offered her a smile that I hoped conveyed warmth. "Is your voice playing hide-and-seek with me today?"

She wiggled up to a straighter position in her chair and darted her gaze around the table, seemingly in search of something. She lifted the pencil in a position that indicated that she wanted to write with it.

"Here." I flipped over the paper in front of her. "You may write on the back of this page if you'd like."

With her left hand cupped in front of the paper to block my view of it, she leaned over and jotted something down. I folded my hands on the table and waited without a word. Out in the main classroom, Miss Simpkin questioned the children about "Hiawatha." Someone snored in the back row, on the other side of the cloakroom wall.

Janie lowered her hand and angled the paper so that I might read her words.

Mommy says no matter what I mustn't talk to you.

"Ah," I said, and my stomach squirmed over the idea of disobeying a mother's wishes.

And yet, I persevered.

I turned the paper back over to the list of towns. "Would you please, then, *circle* the names that mean something to you."

Janie put the eraser end of the pencil to her mouth and chewed on the metal band with her back left molars. The fillings in my own molars sang with pain from the remembered sensation of biting down on metal that very same way.

"If any of the names make you *feel* something," I added, "whether it is a good or a bad sensation, please specify which ones they are with just a little circle or a check mark."

Her attention strayed to the window, streaked and speckled from the rains. She tapped the heels of her shoes against the floor. The bottoms of my own feet vibrated from her movements.

"Janie?" I asked. "Do any of the names strike you as having a personal meaning? Are there any names that you like more than the others?"

She shifted her attention back to the paper and scribbled down another note.

I thought this was a geography test.

"It—it is," I told her, again smiling. "These are all the names of geographical places. I want to see what you know about them. Can you tell me about any of them?"

She simply stared at the names and blew air through her lips in a way that rustled her bangs. I began to wonder if she had ever before seen the names of any other Kansas town besides Friendly. I also fretted that this exercise was a pointless use of time. The test seemed to be going nowhere, and I felt an imbecile for creating it.

"Why don't you simply circle the names you like best?" I asked, struggling with all of my might not to influence her responses with my wording—to avoid creating significance where none actually existed.

With her other hand back in place to shield her response, Janie bent over and circled a name. The tip of her pencil squeaked against the paper as she did so. Next, she raised the pencil and let it hover over each ensuing word, her eyes moving back and forth. Little shots of anticipation tingled at the top of my spine.

She circled a second name, studied her work, and then let me see the results.

The towns she marked: *Kansas City* and *Yesternight*.

I furrowed my brow. Yesternight was one of the towns I had made up.

The child inserted the end of the pencil back between her teeth.

"Janie"—I cleared my throat—"would you please now write a short note next to those two names, explaining why you like them?"

She bent over the paper once again, her hair swinging forward, brushing the sides of her chin. The purple ribbon drooped down to a spot just above her right ear.

Once she finished with her notes, I craned my neck to read her explanations.

For Kansas City, she wrote, *It has the word Kansas in it. I like that.*

For Yesternight, she said, *Pretty name.*

"Splendid," I said, though unimpressed with the inconclusive findings. Clearly, the girl continued to be drawn to Kansas. She also liked my choice of an imaginary town name. That was all.

"Are you extremely bored by this test?" I asked.

Her lips crept into a cockeyed grin, and she nodded.

"Would you like to go back to your seat?"

She shrugged.

"May I ask you another question that has to do with a number, not geography?"

To that inquiry, she replied with a vigorous nod.

"What is your favorite number?"

Without hesitating, she wrote, *23.*

"Why twenty-three?" I asked.

She wrote, *My birthday is June 23.*

"Aha! I see. A good choice for a favorite number. And"—I crossed my legs—"what is a number you absolutely don't like?"

Her eyes shot up with a look of betrayal. A scowl crossed her face.

"Now you're glaring at me," I said. "Can you tell me how you felt when I asked you that question?"

"Did Aunt Tillie already tell you?" she asked aloud.

Her voice startled me so terribly, I banged a knee against the table.

"Your father was the one who first made me aware that a certain number bothers you," I said, rubbing the knee. "I learned that you associate the number with drowning. Do you know what 'associate' means?"

Janie lowered her face toward the paper without writing anything down. An invisible weight pressed down on her thin shoulders, and the shadow of her head seeped across the page. I wondered whether she saw the number eight written across all of the blank spaces on the paper. I envisioned a repressed memory heaving itself against the closed door within her head, the wood shaking, the locks clanking, rattling, loosening . . .

"Are you able to write the number down, Janie?" I asked, softening my voice.

She positioned the sharp tip of the pencil over the paper another time. After a long and languid blink of her eyes, using thick, dark loops of lead, she wrote the number.

8

I sat as still as stone to keep from twitching. "Why does that number bother you so?"

Below the digit, she wrote, *I don't know.*

I then launched upon an entire series of verbal questions, which she followed immediately with handwritten answers.

"Do you see the number eight in your dreams about drowning?"

Yes.

"Do you see it written somewhere?"

On glass.

"Is it on a window? Or a mirror?"

I don't know.

"And is there anyone else in these dreams? Someone besides you?"

Yes.

"Who?"

A man.

"What is his name? Do you know?"

Her eyes went bloodshot. She balled her left hand into a fist, which she used to hold down one side of the paper. Her right hand held the pencil above the remaining empty corner of the page. She released a breath, sending a shiver of a breeze across the edges of the sheet.

I leaned forward, watching, my own lips parting.

Janie lowered the lead to the paper and penned a single letter.

N

Immediately afterward, she lifted the pencil's tip back into the air and gawked at what she had just written, as if she, herself, were waiting for another letter to manifest. The purple hair bow slid another half inch closer to her ear.

She returned the pencil to the page and scratched out a second letter.

E

My heart galloped. Without drawing too much attention, I grabbed the table and waited for the name of "the man in the other house" to reveal itself. *Ned,* perhaps? *Neville? Neal? Nevan?* The key to the trauma in Janie's past glided into the lock of her closed mental door; I could almost hear the clicking of cylinders and gears. I would pry open the massive, smothering barrier of memory repression for this poor child.

Without a sound, the nib of the pencil returned to the paper. Janie wrote a third letter.

L

She set the pencil aside, flopped against the back of the chair, and exhaled a grunt of exhaustion.

NEL, she had written.

I turned the paper toward me to make sure I read it correctly.

Yes, *N-E-L*.

"N-N-Nel?" I asked, and blood drained from my cheeks. My lips lost all sensation. "Are . . . are you sure?"

She nodded, and her eyes fluttered closed.

Next to my left foot sat my black leather briefcase, and tucked within that briefcase sat the telegram from my sister, to which she had written, MY DEAR NELL.

My nickname since childhood.

Nell.

I shook my head, unsure how to even speak another word when such a distressing—and yet such an asinine—hypothesis blazed through my mind.

What if I was the man in the other house? I found myself wondering, of all the foolish things. *What if I hit Violet Sunday over the head with a blunt object—such as a hammer, or a branch—and pushed her into a lake to hide her body?*

What if that's what's been wrong with me all along?

I covered my mouth and forced myself to remain composed.

"Nel?" I asked again, and my own nickname caused me to shudder with a spasm that hurt my neck.

Janie did not nod that time. Her eyes remained shut, and she breathed as though sleeping.

"And what does Nel look like?" I asked.

"Brown hair," she said, again giving me a jolt with the unexpected reawakening of her voice. "Golden eyes." She lifted her lashes and focused on my own brown hair and golden-brown eyes. "Handsome. He sounds English. Or Danish."

I almost laughed in relief at that last comment. At the moment, the confusion over an English and a Danish accent sounded so comical—so utterly unrelated to me.

"I've never actually heard a Danish accent," I admitted.

"I heard him yelling my name."

"Which name?"

"He said, 'Violet, Violet, Violet!'"

"How did you end up in the lake?"

She leaned her elbows against the table and sunk her cheeks into her hands.

"Janie?" I asked. "Do you know how you ended up in the water?"

She picked up the pencil, and with her left cheek cradled in her palm, she wrote a figure over and over and over at the bottom edge of the paper:

8 8 8 8 8 8 8 8 8 8 8 8 8 8 8 8 8 8 8 8 8 8 8 8 8

"Did someone hurt you?" I asked, leaning closer, the bottoms of my toes pressed hard against the floor of my shoes. "Do you remember someone hurting you?"

She growled from deep in the bottom of her throat, and with a single stroke of her pencil, she dashed a line through all of those eights. The force of the lead ripped the paper.

"Janie?" I asked.

She shot to her feet, and the chair crashed to the floor behind her. "No one will take me to Kansas," she said through her teeth, her hands braced against the table. "Not Michael O'Daire, not Rebecca, not frustrating Miss Simpkin—so I am *never* going to remember what happened. Unless you can take me there yourself, Miss Lind, don't ever ask me again."

She knocked the paper to the ground and stormed out of the cloakroom.

✺ CHAPTER 15

At lunchtime, Janie grabbed her tin lunch pail and skipped outside with the rest of her classmates as though nothing were amiss. Through the chilled and frosted window, I observed her chatting and laughing with two other girls, the three of them perched on a log that looked to have been a spruce, their legs and boots swinging, hair bows flapping, their breaths crystallizing in the air.

Janie's aunt ate her own lunch in a sphere of blissful silence at her desk in the empty classroom. She flipped through a magazine, *McClure's*, and looked as relaxed as can be, until my footsteps disturbed the calm.

A shadow crossed her face. She closed *McClure's* and asked, "How did your chat with Janie go?"

I smoothed out my coat, which I'd slung over my left arm. "She wasn't keen on discussing Kansas with me."

Miss Simpkin nodded, as though she expected that answer.

"Has she ever mentioned Kansas City?" I asked.

"Not that I remember."

"Do you know of anyone named Nel?"

The schoolteacher dabbed her face with a napkin and contemplated my question. "No, I don't think so. Why?"

"Janie claims to have known a man by that name. She said he had brown hair and amber eyes, and he spoke with an accent that might have been English or Danish."

Miss Simpkin tried to smile, but the expression made her eyes moisten. "I can't think of her ever meeting anyone English or Danish."

"There wasn't even a Nels or a Nelson?"

"I'm getting so nervous that you are, indeed, seeing Janie as an insane child." She held the napkin against her bottom lip. "Despite what you just said about the possibility of reincarnation, after what you witnessed the other night, after hearing all of her strange ramblings, I'm so worried what you might think of her."

"I see her as a highly intriguing child who's reaching out for some sort of assistance," I said.

"I'm so torn between doing what's right for Janie and keeping my sister calm."

"I understand. I'm still here for the rest of the week and will do my best to keep an eye on the situation without pressing Janie for further information." I pulled my coat over my arms. "If you don't mind, I need to take a short walk into town and send another telegram."

"Is it a telegram related to Janie?"

I squished my lips together and debated whether I should lie and tell her it wasn't. "It's related to me," I said. "There's a little something that's worrying me, and I need to take care of it before I return to the other children this afternoon."

"You're not ill, are you? You didn't catch pneumonia when you slept on this atrocious old floor, did you?"

"No, I'm fine." I procured my gloves from the right coat pocket. "I just need to contact a family member about a little personal matter."

"Ah." She sat back. "I won't pry then." She reopened *McClure's*.

I walked away, tugging my gloves over my hands, my heart pounding.

I PAID FOR another ten-words-or-less telegram.

URGENT QUESTION HOW DID I GET THE NICK-NAME NELL

That time around I listed the Gordon Bay Hotel as my return address instead of the schoolhouse. Again, I paid for Bea to send me a telegraphed reply.

Upon leaving the post office, however, doubts attacked. My feet came to an abrupt halt on the sidewalk, and I almost swung back around to yell to the postmaster, *Stop! Never mind!* The phrase URGENT QUESTION now struck me as overly dire and worrisome—so terribly melodramatic. Bea might fret about my well-being. She knew the job often frustrated and exhausted me. I couldn't imagine what she might think if she learned the reasoning behind my question . . . if "reasoning" could be used to describe it.

I massaged my forehead with my wool-covered fingers and thought again of Mr. O'Daire surmising that someone had tried to kill Violet Sunday by hitting her over the head. I remembered

Janie circling my own made-up town name, "Yesternight." And, of course, I remembered "Nel."

I let the telegram travel on its way, unencumbered by me.

After I packed up my tests for the afternoon, I returned to the Gordon Bay Hotel and spotted Mr. O'Daire raking the inn's front path clear of yellow leaves. He wore a coffee-colored vest over white shirtsleeves and pinstriped trousers one shade lighter than the vest. The temperance of the day's weather must have prompted him to forgo his heavy black coat, and so he appeared to have shed a burdensome outer skin. He looked younger—more like a college fellow ready to hit the stands for a football game.

He lifted his head, as though catching my arrival out of the tops of his eyes. His raking stopped, and he stood up straight.

"You look like the Fuller Brush Man," he said with a smile, "walking up from the street with your bag and your determined expression."

"I'd make a terrible Fuller Brush Man." I readjusted my hold on my briefcase. "Too much chatting and flattering."

"You're not one to flatter people?"

"I make people feel better by first drawing out their flaws and fears"—I smirked—"not their strengths."

"No, I don't think you'll sell housewives many brushes that way. Maybe nerve pills."

I shifted my weight between my feet and cleared my throat. "Do you have a moment to chat about Janie?"

"Of course. I was just finishing up with this yardwork before I head over to my mother's. She's insisted upon cooking you a nice supper and asked me to fetch it for you."

"Oh, that's far too generous of her. You shouldn't have let her go to all that trouble."

"We're both just so grateful for all you're doing to help." He leaned both hands against the rounded tip of the cast-iron rake. "What did you need to tell me about Janie?"

"I spoke with her again this morning."

"Oh?" His fingers tightened around the rake. "And what did she say?"

"She told me that the mysterious Man in the Other House was named Nel, spelled N-E-L. Has she ever known a Nel?"

He cocked his head and rocked his jaw back and forth. "No, I can't think of anyone with that name."

"Has she ever met anyone Danish?"

"Danish? No. Why?"

"She claims this Nel to be Danish, or possibly English; she wasn't entirely sure which. She said he had brown hair and amber eyes."

"You see what I mean?" He tipped the rake's handle to his right. "This is precisely the type of thing that's been happening ever since Janie could talk. Little, specific details appear at random, as though a memory suddenly gets illuminated inside her mind."

"That's an interesting way to put it."

"It's what's happening."

I pulled my notebook and a pencil out of the briefcase. "Can you say that again?"

He smiled. "I don't entirely remember—"

"'Little, specific details,'" I said, jotting down the words, "'appear' . . . 'appear at . . .'"

"'. . . appear at random,'" he added, "'as though a memory suddenly gets illuminated inside her head.'"

I nodded and finished writing. "And does she bring those same new details up at a later date?"

"Usually, yes."

"And they're consistent with what she said earlier?"

"Always," he said without a trace of doubt.

"Your mother said as much, too. It's fascinating how tightly Janie adheres to her stories." I tucked the notebook back into my briefcase and stepped up to the brick stoop in front of the door. "If you do eventually remember someone by the name of Nel, or any name remotely close to it, please let me know. It would be extremely helpful."

"Certainly. Is that all there was from today's interview with her?"

"Well . . ." I fastened the clasp on my bag. "This might mean nothing at all, but Janie also showed an interest in Kansas City. Has that town ever arisen in conversation?"

"I don't believe so. Just Friendly."

"And does the word 'Yesternight' mean anything?"

"Yesternight?"

"Yes." My cheeks warmed, for I felt foolish discussing an item that had, I'd believed, originated in my own imagination.

"No." He raked aside three golden leaves that lay plastered against the bricks. "I can't think of her ever mentioning it. It's a word like *moonburn*."

"Moonburn?"

"I don't know if there's a name for it—a compound word that's a twist on a regular compound. Yesterday/yesternight. Sunburn/moonburn. I once wrote a short story called 'Moonburn' about a man who found it impossible to be awake in the daytime."

"Ah, that's right." I clasped the doorknob. "You're a writer."

"Rebecca claimed that particular story represented my pain over the change in Sam after the war." He swept aside another leaf with a screech of metal teeth. "I guess she was fancying herself a psychologist at the time."

"If you'd like, when I return inland, I can see if anyone I know is able to recommend a psychologist on the coast who might be able to help Sam. I would love to speak to him myself, but my specialty is children."

Mr. O'Daire peeked up at me with only his eyes. "As you've already seen, most people shun psychological help out here. They all assume emotional troubles equate to 'nuthouse.'"

"Sam is a prime example of what happens when a person doesn't receive much-needed assistance. People like your ex-wife should realize this and not fear me."

"I know that as well as you do, Miss Lind. Remember"—he raked away nothing at all—"I'm the one who rushed out into a storm to make sure you arrived here, safe and sound."

"Yes, I most definitely remember. And I'm still grateful for that feat of heroism." I twisted the doorknob.

"Where would you like your supper served?" he asked before I could disappear into the hotel. "There's a fire roaring in the lobby's hearth right now. I could arrange it for you there."

"In the lobby would be lovely. Thank you."

"I'm serving drinks again downstairs tonight. You're welcome to partake in that particular style of Gordon Bay Hotel hospitality, too."

I sighed and shook my head.

"I know, I know." He raked again. "You're a respectable employee of the Department of Education."

"One day, Mr. O'Daire, when I am long done working in

Gordon Bay, after I've solved the mysteries of Janie, I'll journey down into that basement of yours and enjoy a glass of booze with the rest of your regulars."

"A glass will always be waiting for you."

"Thank you." I smiled again and disappeared into the lobby with my briefcase bulging with notes about his daughter.

UP IN MY hotel room, I sat on the edge of the bed and stared at Bea's telegram from the week before.

YES MY DEAR NELL FRIENDLY IS A NE KANSAS TOWN

My mind dwelled upon the curious coincidence of a woman called Nell with a violent past investigating a girl potentially harmed by a Nel in another life. I couldn't shake the sensation that Janie had looked at me that morning as though she might have recognized her Nel in me.

A knock came at the door.

I crammed the telegram into my bag. "Who is it?"

"You have a telephone call," said Mr. O'Daire through the wood.

I froze, puzzled as to who would be calling me at the hotel. "I do?"

"It's a Miss Beatrice Lind."

All worries dissolved at the spoken name of my oldest sister. I jumped up from the bed and swung open the door. "My sister is calling?"

"I don't have an extension up here." Mr. O'Daire gestured with his thumb toward the staircase to his right. "You'll have to take the call down at the front desk."

"That's perfectly fine." I straightened my cockeyed sweater. "I wonder if she might have traveled to the coast as a surprise."

"I don't think she's calling locally."

"Well, in any case, it'll be splendid to hear her voice."

"Come along." He led me through the white hall, and I traipsed down the staircase behind him.

At his front desk, he handed me a black candlestick telephone and its bell-shaped earpiece.

"I'll go fetch your supper and give you some privacy," he said in a whisper. "I don't expect anyone to come seeking a room while I'm gone."

"Thank you," I whispered back. Both of our mouths lingered just a few mere inches away from the mouthpiece; Bea must have heard us, despite the hushed words.

He grabbed his coat from the rack.

I put the phone to my ear and asked, "Bea? Is that truly you?"

"Hello, sweetie," she said from the other end. "How are you doing?"

"I'm fine. I'm so happy to hear from you."

"You're in a hotel this time?"

"Yes, I am."

Mr. O'Daire peeked over his shoulder on his way out the door.

I waved and waited for him to shut the door behind himself before saying anything more.

"Alice?" asked Bea.

"Sorry. The hotel owner was just leaving for his mother's house." I sidled a foot to my right to better see him out the window. He bent down in front of his car and cranked the engine until it rumbled awake.

"Is it a very big hotel?" asked my sister. "Did he say he was fetching you supper?"

"Yes, his mother is cooking it for me at her house. There's been an entire to-do about my lodging situation here in Gordon Bay. The boardinghouse is tawdry, apparently, so I'm staying at a hotel owned by one of the students' fathers."

"That sounds more pleasant than the usual crowded lodgings the state squeezes you into, although I know hotels can make you anxious."

"I'm doing fine here."

"Are you certain about that?"

My mouth filled with a sour taste. "Why do you ask?"

"That last telegram of yours got me worried. It got me thinking a little harder about your original telegram."

I leaned my left hip against the front desk and deepened my voice, striving to infuse it with confidence. "A student with whom I'm working spoke of someone named Nel, and it merely made me curious about my own name."

"You said 'urgent question' in your telegram, Alice. Why did you say that?"

"I needed a swift reply, that's all. I would like to report the answer back to the student before I move on to the next town. Why . . ." My chin quivered; my voice acquired an unnatural chirp. "Why have you always called me Nell, Bea?"

She sighed. "You told us to call you that, Alice. You were quite insistent upon it when you were younger. I don't know why. Perhaps it came from the Christmas carol with the stocking for 'Little Nell.'"

My eyes watered. I tried to sputter up a laugh, but the sound burst from my lips as a sob.

"Nell?" she asked, slipping straight back into that old nickname out of habit. "Are you crying?"

I wiped my eyes with my fingers. "Did . . . did I ask to be called Nell when I was . . ." I grimaced. "When I was beating those poor children in the head?"

"Oh . . . no . . . don't bring up that bit of history, sweetie." She sounded so quiet now—so far away. "Don't dwell on an early-childhood incident that everyone else has forgotten."

"What was wrong with me, Bea? Please, tell me. You're four years older—you were eight at the time. Why did I hit them? What happened to make me lust for the sight of blood?"

It took a while for my sister to respond, and when she did, her voice sounded odd and uneven, as though she were being jostled about in a truck on a dirt road.

"I don't know. Perhaps . . . perhaps we read too many frightening stories at too young of an age. You always had a bit of a temper when you were little. Such stories might have put some naughty ideas into your head when you got mad." She attempted a laugh, but it came out a nervous bark.

I sniffed. "I have to ask you a question, one that involves a subject I don't think I've ever discussed with you before. I know our parents certainly never discussed this sort of thing."

"What subject?"

"Did I ever speak as though I lived a past life? A past life as someone else?"

Bea laughed in earnest that time, and even though I couldn't see her, I knew she had rolled her eyes.

"Don't laugh, Bea. I'm serious. When I insisted upon being called Nell, did I sound as though I had once lived as a person with that name?"

"I was so young, too, Alice. I honestly don't remember."

"Margery wouldn't remember, would she?"

"Don't ask Margery about any of this. She doesn't care to discuss difficult moments."

"Because she was one of the children I hurt, wasn't she?" I asked, and I gritted my teeth and closed my eyes. Down the center of our other sister's braided brown hair, a little white part line had lay exposed, and across that line I had brought down my weapon—my battering stick. Margery was two years older than I. She had been sitting in the shade of the old maple in our front yard, playing marbles with two other girls from the neighborhood, Ethel Pennington and Daisy West. The white line on her head had pooled with blood that turned to black in her hair, and she had screamed and clutched her head. All of the children screamed.

> *Alice Lind,*
> *Alice Lind,*
> *Took a stick and beat her friend.*
> *Should she die?*
> *Should she live?*
> *How many beatings did she give?*

"Don't fret so much about all of that," said Bea. "You never hit anyone that way ever again. It was only one troubling episode."

"I hit that boy Stuart—Stu—the one from graduate school. I bashed him in the head with a shoe after I told him . . ." I brought my lips closer to the mouthpiece. "After I told him about the baby. I hit him so terribly hard."

"Oh, Alice. Don't fret over that either. You said he responded to the news like an ass."

"The child—the girl I'm helping—she claims to have lived a past life as a young woman who drowned mysteriously, sometime in the past century. She claims a man named Nel was involved in her death. *Nel*, Bea!"

"Alice, no. You're exerting yourself with your work—I can tell. Come home. Take a rest."

"I can't."

"You're better than this job. You're too smart for it. It'll drive you crazy."

"I wonder if it already has." I wiped my left cheek using the back of my sleeve.

A pause ensued, during which I panted into the mouthpiece, my fingers strangling the telephone's black base. My fingernails pierced the fleshy heel of my left hand.

"You're not a murderer from the past century, for heaven's sake," said Bea. "Think about what you're saying—you, the woman who snickered all the way through the Winchester house!"

"I know." I nodded. "I know."

"I'm aware how much the situation with the baby hurt you."

I didn't respond. My eyes again watered. The air grew impossibly thick.

"Alice?"

"That was two and a half years ago, Bea."

"But it was traumatic for you. I know you want to pretend it didn't affect you in any way, but I was there in the hospital with you. I remember your pain and your grief, and I'm sure it's affected your desire to become intimate with men, as well as other aspects of your life."

I fussed with the wood on one of the corners of Mr. O'Daire's desk. "I'm a spinster, Bea. I'm not supposed to desire men in that capacity, remember?"

"Pfft. I'm not Margery. Single girls need that sort of thing now and then, no matter what the prudes say. You're a perfectly normal woman, Alice. A normal woman who shouldn't ever feel ashamed."

I bit down hard on my back molars to stave off more tears. "Thank you, Bea. You've made me feel much better."

"You're not being sarcastic, are you?"

"No, you truly are. Just hearing you say, 'You're not a murderer from the past century,' is a much needed slap across the face, to wake me up; to make me realize how foolish I'm being." I chewed the nail of my right pinkie. "Thank you."

"Are you going to be all right?"

"Yes."

"You're sure?"

I nodded. "Yes."

"And you're coming home for Thanksgiving dinner?"

"Of course."

"You had better be there to help protect me against Mother and Margery."

I laughed. "Oh, I'm sure they'll be bringing respectable, middle-aged bachelors for the both of us."

"Those 'bachelors' of theirs are almost always queers. Or ex-husbands whom other women tossed out like last week's garbage."

I drew my hand away from Mr. O'Daire's desk.

Bea made a kissing sound through the receiver. "Take care of yourself, Nell. I . . . I mean *Alice*."

"You, too, Bea. I'll see you Thanksgiving."

"I love you, funny face."

I smiled. "I love you, too."

She hung up with a *click* that sounded like a door closing deep within the recesses of my head.

Part II
VIOLET

CHAPTER 16

November 25, 1925

On the evening before Thanksgiving, I boarded a train in Salem, Oregon, elbow-to-elbow with political men and lawyers who, like me, journeyed from the state capitol to northbound relatives. The gentleman next to me repeatedly told me he was traveling to his "ancestral home" in Portland's West Hills for "feasting," as though he were a British lord returning to his manor. I simply smiled and closed my eyes, exhausted from the final days of testing in Gordon Bay and an ensuing trip to complete paperwork at the Department of Education. The intermingling aromas of colognes and newspapers and cigars made me feel I was traveling in a boardroom on wheels.

At my own "ancestral home" on the east side of the city—a gray and maroon Victorian, sandwiched between newer bungalows from the present century—I lugged my suitcases through the front doorway and inhaled the divine fragrance of pumpkin pie. Murmurs of parental excitement twittered from the back sitting room, and before long, both my mother and father bustled my way with broad smiles and shimmering eyes, their hair dusted with more gray than I remembered from my last stop at the house. Pop always seemed to be getting thinner; Mother, plumper, and broader in the hips.

"The first one's here!" said my mother in her little singsong voice she always used around us girls when excited. She clasped me to her chest, and her glasses bumped the top of my right ear. My father embraced me, too, although he stood taller, so his spectacles inflicted no harm.

Pop picked up my bags and hoisted them up the staircase while my mother brushed her fingers through my bangs as if I were two years old. She asked how I was eating and keeping my health with "that nomadic job of mine."

"I'm well into my twenties, Mother," I said. "I know how to take care of myself."

"When we encouraged all three of you girls to attend college, I didn't realize it would mean so many years of worrying about two of you running about on your own. And so few grandchildren."

I ducked away from her hand. "Margery gave you four grandchildren, don't forget. Much more than that, and you'll start forgetting everyone's birthdays."

"At least consider settling down in another year or so, like I did. A few years spent working is good for a woman, but husbands and babies are wonderful, too."

I moved down to the narrow side table where my parents collected my mail in a tidy pile. "Did a letter from Kansas arrive, by chance?"

"Are you expecting Dorothy to write you, like when you were little?" asked my father with a winded chuckle. He plodded down the staircase, his cheeks red from lugging my bags, his nose whistling. "Or the Tin Man?"

"No . . ." I smiled and sifted through letters from old friends and my newest issue of the *American Journal of Psychology*. "I wrote a letter on behalf of a student I was testing. If correspondence arrives from a town called Friendly, will you please immediately send me a telegram? I'll leave a list of all the schools where I'll be working over the next few weeks, and you can send the telegram there. Or, if the letter arrives at the beginning of my assignment, simply mail it to me. I'll pay for any postage or telegram fees required."

"Yes, of course," said my mother, "if it's that important . . ."

"It's highly important, Mother."

"All right, then. No need to snap."

"I'm not . . ." I drew a deep breath and put a hand on my hip. "I'm not snapping. I've been working quite hard these past few weeks and would like to finish up with a case that's been perplexing me."

"Would you like a glass of wine?" asked my father, tucking his hands into his pockets, a twinkle in his eyes.

"The father of one of his students is a minister," said my mother, her voice lowered to a conspiratorial whisper, all traces of offense now vanished. "He snuck your father a bottle of sacramental wine. He told him he deserved it for dealing with all of those high school hooligans."

"A glass would be nice." I unwound my woolen scarf from my neck. "But first I think I'll take a bath. That train this evening smelled like a pool hall, and now *I* smell like a pool hall."

"Yes, I was wondering if you'd taken up cigars." Mother fussed with a string on the left shoulder of my sweater. "I wouldn't be surprised if your oldest sister smokes them. She's wearing trousers this fall. That's her latest thing."

I shrugged. "If it makes her happy . . ."

"But . . . *trousers*, Alice. And her hair's cropped as short as a man's."

"Life's far too short to try to conform to everyone else's idea of fashion, Mother. Or, at least"—I sifted through the letters one more time—"I believe it may be short. And final."

Mother proceeded to complain about Bea, and in the mirror above the side table, I caught sight of the reflection of a framed photograph of my sisters and me from about 1903, when I was four, Margery six, and Bea eight. The image hung from a picture rail on the chestnut-colored wall behind me, just next to where Pop was standing, brushing lint from his sweater vest. All three pairs of eyes on our round childish faces peered across the hallway at me. Mother had put me in a dark dress with a sailor collar, and I wore a bow on one side of my long brown hair, which Mother parted on my right. Margery and Bea wore white dresses and ringlets, and they smiled for the camera, their teeth showing, little dimples like Mr. O'Daire's on prominent display.

I didn't smile. In fact, my expression carried an unnatural severity to it. A brutality. A coldness. Such a piercing stare—such hardened lips—did not belong on the face of a four-year-old child.

"I said, 'What's wrong, Alice?'" asked Mother, her voice suddenly loud. "Can't you hear me?"

I blinked. "Yes, of course. You're barking in my ear."

"Then why weren't you answering me?"

"I told you, it was a tiring journey. A tiring few weeks." I grabbed the handle of my briefcase, which hadn't yet made it upstairs. "I'll take a rain check for that glass of wine, if you don't mind, Pop."

"Did you even eat any supper?" asked Mother.

"I ate a sandwich before I boarded the train. I'm fine. I just need to bathe and get some sleep. Tomorrow I'll be fit and fresh for Thanksgiving, I promise you."

I lowered my eyes and hurried past the photograph.

LATER THAT NIGHT, tucked under all my familiar bedding, including my beloved red and turquoise Pendleton wool blanket, I thought back to my parting conversation with Michael O'Daire.

"I'll let you know as soon as I receive any new information related to my investigation," I had said on the platform of the little log depot. The train bound for the inland cities breathed plumes of steam against the backs of my legs, and the air smelled of grease and machinery, of travel and promises.

"Now you sound like a police detective," Mr. O'Daire had replied with a half-smile.

"No . . . as I mentioned before, I'm trying an experiment, and if anything comes of it, I'll telephone immediately."

He wiggled his tweed cap farther down over his head. "And . . . if nothing comes of it?"

"I'll still help Janie."

"How?"

"I'll speak with one of my former professors, a clinical child psychologist . . ."

"Do you think this is a form of insanity?" He tilted his head to his right. "Is that what you honestly believe?"

"I've been trained to investigate disturbances of the mind, Mr. O'Daire. That's why you were so keen on having me speak to Janie in the first place."

"I was keen on having you speak to her because I was curious if you would rule out all possible psychological explanations—which I believe you have. I believe you know in your heart what's happening with my daughter."

Down the way, the conductor called out, "All aboard!"

I shifted my head in the man's direction and observed, out of the corner of my eye, Mr. O'Daire lowering his face and clasping his hands around the back of his neck.

"I'm not a parapsychologist, Michael," I said, my gaze still averted from his. "I can only help her if there's something within her mind that's reachable by therapy."

He lifted his head. "Why did you just call me 'Michael'?"

"Because I'm worried there won't be anything else I can do for Janie." I swallowed and met his eyes. "If you're not willing to receive help from a person who possesses more experience in child psychology than I . . . if reincarnation is your only hope . . . then I'm afraid there's nothing more I can accomplish with this case." I offered my hand. "This may need to be good-bye."

His jaw tightened. He kept his hands on his neck.

"I'm sorry," I said. "I want to help her, desperately, but I'm not sure how."

"Well . . . at least you're being honest."

"I don't want to offer any promises I can't keep."

He gritted his teeth and gave a short nod, while my hand remained outstretched.

"Will you at least shake my hand?" I asked. "I'd hate to part in anger."

He reached out and wrapped his warm fingers around mine, giving them a firm squeeze. "You're breaking my heart, Alice."

"Don't say that."

"I had so much hope when you first arrived."

"Please, don't give up hope." I squeezed his hand in return, noting the smoothness of his fingers, the thickness of his high school ring. "You have a brilliant daughter with a remarkable future ahead of her." I withdrew my hand from his. "Allow her to receive as much education as possible, and she'll likely end up all right in the end. As a child, I myself experienced"—I cleared my throat—"*quirks*. And terrible nightmares, as a matter of fact. Both of my parents fully supported my education, however, and here I am today, a successful modern woman."

He nodded with his lips pressed together, his eyes damp.

I glanced over my shoulder at the awaiting locomotive. Wind shook through my skirt and my hair. "I had better get going."

"I wish you a safe journey."

"Thank you. Good-bye, Mr. O'Daire."

"Good-bye, Miss Lind."

I turned and left him behind on the platform.

MARGERY AND BEA planned to arrive late in the morning on Thanksgiving Day, which meant Mother and I were to be the sole cooks in the kitchen bright and early that Thursday. I strapped a ruffled apron around my waist and threw myself into stuffing, basting, stirring, seasoning, and baking. Mother gave her usual reports on all of the neighbors' latest health problems, and I did my best to use her gossip as a distraction to that unfinished business in Gordon Bay. Every once in a while I caught myself wondering what all of the O'Daires were doing at the moment—whether Janie spent any time with Michael on Thanksgiving or if she stayed with her mother and aunt. My own mother's voice would promptly startle me out of my ponderings, however, and send me straight back into tales of goiter and croup.

Margery and her brood arrived first.

"We brought vegetables," said my sister as she hugged me in front of the doorway. Beneath her right arm dangled both a sack of groceries and Baby Warren. "Prepare to be frightened, Alice."

"Why is Auntie Alice frightened by vegetables?" asked her round-eyed five-year-old, Bernie.

"Because she's a silly goose. She doesn't know what's good for her." Margery smiled with a show of her teeth, which were always a tad too large for her mouth, but not enough to detract from her pretty dark eyes and hair. She then leaned close to my ear and whispered, "Are you behaving yourself, Alice?"

"Please don't always ask me that," I said under my breath.

"I worry about you."

"You're ashamed of me."

"That's not true. I just wish you would track down a husband and settle down."

"Husband hunting season hasn't yet gone into effect this year, Margie. I've checked with the Oregon State Game Commission."

She rolled her eyes and handed to me Baby Warren, who smelled of strained carrots and soiled diapers. A bright-orange stain on the child's upper lip set off my gag reflex, so I swiftly swooped the child over to his father, Dr. Donald Osterman, a gangly fellow with squinty gray eyes and a thin mustache. Donald could never quite look me in the face after Margery asked if he would fit me for a diaphragm two years earlier—a request he vehemently denied due to my status as an unmarried woman.

"Happy Thanksgiving, Alice," he told me, speaking in the direction of Warren's bald head. "Work going well?"

"Quite."

"How nice."

"Yes."

I ducked back into the kitchen until Margery's oldest, Geraldine, shouted from the parlor, "Auntie Bea is here! And she's dressed like a man again!"

I sprinted back out to the front hall in time to see my oldest sister traipsing up the front path in a tan blazer, a bowtie, and loud checkered trousers. She wore her dark curls cropped so short and so slicked against her head, I would have, indeed, mistaken her for a man if I'd first seen her from behind. She carried a round cookie tin, as well as the large wicker handbag she used for toting around her wallet and books.

I scooted myself past Geraldine to be the first to greet Bea, who threw out her arms when she saw me and said, "There's the kid!"

"Hello, Bea." I wrapped her up in a hug, smelling perfume that wasn't hers, and pulled her toward the house by her elbow. "No potential suitors today," I whispered, "but I've received no less than two jabs at my lack of a husband since I first walked through the door."

"Are you feeling better than when I last talked to you?"

"Yes, but let's not bring that up right now." I took her cookie tin and yanked her into the house so I would no longer be the sole member of the family scrutinized for her questionable choices in life.

FEASTING COMMENCED AT a quarter past three, and everyone immersed themselves in conversations about childhood escapades and remembered grandparents and the time the roof leaked and rain flooded the attic. Margery handed me a bowl full of snap peas, which I promptly passed along to Bea, holding my breath as I did so. Peapods always reminded me of plump green fingers that had wiggled their way out of cold garden dirt. They smelled of rot. Of decay.

"Just eat them, Alice," said Margery through a strained smile, her voice lowered. "My children are watching. They'll wonder why *they* need to eat their vegetables and not you."

"I'm a grown-up, Margery," I replied with my own taut grin. "I don't need you to tell me what I should and shouldn't eat."

Aside from that one squabble, the meal sailed along on an even course, and I even managed to forget about Janie O'Daire and Violet Sunday and the nefarious Man from the Other House. Pop asked me once if I had come across any interesting students in my recent examinations, but I merely answered, "No. No one worth noting."

Only once did my thoughts glide back to Gordon Bay, to Michael O'Daire. I remembered the two of us watching the rain pelt his windshield as the wind knocked us about in the car. I recalled holding his fuzzy plaid blanket up to my chin and wondering if we'd get washed out to sea.

In some ways, I believed we had.

LONG AFTER MY sisters, mother, and I scrubbed the dishes clean, after the men returned the spare chairs to the sitting room and

Margery and Donald swept out the front door with the children, Bea joined me up in my room. We both lounged on my bed, she with her shoulders slouched against the damask wallpaper, her checkered legs crossed in front of her, and I against my headboard, an elbow sinking deep into my goose-down pillow.

"Here . . ." Bea unearthed a gleaming silver flask from the depths of her wicker handbag. "Don't ask how I obtained it, but I figured you could use a swig of juice."

"Oh!" I reached for the flask, which smelled of gin. "Bless you, bless you, Beatrice Lind!"

She snickered and handed over the metal container, which I unscrewed as fast as my fingers would allow. The gin burned down my throat like an antiseptic, but, oh, how sublime it tasted, like pine trees. Like Christmas. I licked excess drops from my lips, luxuriating in both the sweetness and the sting.

"I'd never call myself a lush," I said, "but I started craving hooch the moment I first stepped off the train out on that damn soggy coast."

"I thought you might have." Bea uncrossed her legs and sat up straight against the wall. Her short hair had lost some of its shiny slickness by then, and curls blossomed behind her ears. "I don't mean to sound like Mother and Margery," she said, tugging on one of the curls, "but have there been any men in your life recently? Any fun distractions from work?"

"I don't have time for men." I took another sip and leaned the back of my skull against the headboard with a *thump*. "Or fun. Or distractions." I smiled and closed my eyes, thinking of the letters I had written to Kansas, which I supposed could have been called "distractions," considering they had nothing whatsoever to do with intelligence tests. I pictured the envelope containing the correspondence as it passed through the rough hands of various postal workers until it landed in front of the postmaster of Friendly, two thousand miles away.

"Bea?" I asked.

"Hmm?"

"When you go back to the library"—I opened my eyes—"would you mind looking up the name of another potential town in Kansas to see if it's real?"

She blinked at me, all the mirth draining from her face. Her mouth stiffened, and the little smile lines that marked her age— almost thirty-one years—diminished.

"Bea, did you hear what I—?"

"What's the name of the town?" she asked.

"Yesternight."

Her face blanched. A groove formed between her eyebrows.

I screwed the cap onto the flask. "Have you heard of it?"

She exhaled a steady breath through her nose. "Yes."

"Where is it located?"

"Nebraska."

My fingers froze on the cap. "Nebraska?"

"Near a small train stop called Du Bois. There's a famous tale about a series of murders that occurred there."

I couldn't help but laugh—a nervous, abrasive titter that buzzed inside my head. "Infamous murders occurred in a town called Yesternight?"

"Not a town. An inn."

"An inn?"

She shuddered and rubbed at her forehead. "You don't remember discussing Yesternight when we were children?"

The edges of my furniture blurred, and the gin suddenly tasted vile—too sweet, too close to the smell of formaldehyde. "Was this when I . . . when I hit those poor . . ."

She swallowed, and her bowtie went a little crooked against the folds of her white collar. Her eyes pooled with tears.

I scraped my top teeth against my bottom lip and peered down at the flask in my lap. *Good God!* I thought. *Holy hell! Why on earth did Janie O'Daire . . . why did she identify the name of a place—a violent, bloody place—that I had spoken about as a child? Why did I speak of it?*

"The name . . ." I cleared my throat, while my fingertips sweated and slid across the flask. "It seemed to mean something to the child whom I examined. I don't understand why it would have if . . ." I shook my head. "I asked the girl which names she liked best. She circled 'Yesternight.'"

"Did she come up with the name on her own?" Bea lifted her head away from the wall. "Or did you introduce her to it?"

"She came up with—" I stopped myself and set the flask on my bedside table. A drop of gin plunked against the lace cloth that protected the wood, and I watched as the liquid bled into a stain the shape of a crooked heart. "No—it was a random name that I snuck into the middle of a list of Kansas towns, to see if she was fibbing when it came to name recognition."

"She must have fibbed, then."

"Unless she's been there, too. Unless she believes something heinous occurred to her there . . ." I squished my face between the palms of my hands and groaned from the barrel of my chest. "Oh, Christ, I don't know how to help that girl, Bea. Or her father. They both need me, desperately."

"Her *father* needs you?"

"When I first arrived in Gordon Bay, he picked me up at the train depot in the middle of a diabolical storm. He had such high hopes for me. He wanted me to rule out psychological explanations for the girl's behavior—he believes she lived a past life as a woman killed in the Great Plains. And she's so smart, Bea. She's written mathematical proofs all over the walls of her bedroom, and I can't think of any psychological diagnosis for that sort of behavior other than calling her a child prodigy. An astounding, odd, perplexing, terrifying prodigy." I grabbed the flask again and downed another drink, choking on gin.

"Whoa!" Bea held out a hand. "Slow down there, kiddo."

"I should go to Kansas. And maybe even . . . Nebraska, was it?"

"You have nothing to do with the murders at the Hotel Yesternight, Nell. Hell, you don't even have anything to do with the name 'Nell.' You were just pretending. Don't insert yourself into other people's stories."

"I'm not—"

"I know you, Alice. You're looking for answers to your own past through this child, but she doesn't have anything to do with you." She grabbed the flask from my hands and screwed the cap back in place. "Apply to PhD programs again. Stop trekking all over Oregon, giving tests far beneath your education. You deserve to be doing the type of clinical research you desire."

"The children need me. And it's not that easy . . ."

"Try!"

I scooted down on the mattress and curled onto my left side.

"You're miserable, I can tell." Bea nudged the back of one of my legs with her toes. "Do something about it."

I stared at my oak dresser across the room. A needlepoint version of the prayer "Now I Lay Me Down to Sleep," complete with an illustration of a blond-haired girl on bended knee, still hung above it in a cherrywood frame. I didn't know why I'd never replaced the thing with a grown-up decoration. I'd been too busy in recent years to care.

"I was tempted to sleep with the girl's father," I said in the direction of the prayer. "His name is Michael O'Daire, and he's been divorced for two years."

Bea lowered the booze to the floor. "But you didn't?"

I shook my head. "No. It would have been dreadfully unprofessional of me, and so harmful to the girl's case. I remained a chaste Mrs. Grundy."

"He was handsome, I presume?"

"Quite. He even asked me to lunch once, but I turned him down."

"Well . . ." Bea trailed off, not seeming to know if she should praise my restraint or pity my lack of human intimacy.

"I just left them both there . . . dangling." I sighed into my pillow, feeling the heat of my breath. "He told me that I broke his heart. Not because I refused to step out with him, but because I didn't know what to do about his daughter."

My sister reached out and warmed my right elbow with one of her hands. "Alice, your job is to test students to see if they're receiving the education they need. That's all. Unless a university finally smartens up and accepts you into its doctoral program—unless more men turn bold enough to hire women into their research clinics or the Department of Education pays you what you deserve—you don't need to be doing anything beyond test administration. And you certainly don't need to be diagnosing strange claims of past lives. Do you hear me? Despite your talent for investigating odd children, that's not what they're actually paying you to do."

I closed my eyes and squeezed my knees against my stomach.

"You're done with being little Alice Lind—you haven't been her in decades. And you're done with graduate students who acted like jackasses and all of the folks living in Gordon Bay. Let all of that go. Look ahead to the future. As George Eliot so wisely said, 'It is never too late to be what you might have been.'"

"That's easy for you to say. People don't mind lady librarians."

"I'm not allowed to be everything I want to be, kiddo." She gave my right shin a pat and slid off the side of the bed. "Which reminds me, I should be getting back home. Pearl doesn't like to be alone after dark. Her family's dinner was supposed to have ended by three."

"Tell her 'hello' for me."

"I will." She bent close and kissed my cheek. "Ugh! You reek of liquor. Best stay up here for the rest of the night."

"I will. Good night, Bea."

"Night-night. Don't let the bed bugs bite."

I smiled and allowed my eyelids to droop shut.

Before my sister's footsteps had even reached the bottom of the staircase, I drifted into a hazy stage of sleep and dreamed a horrible dream about my body soaked in blood.

✣ CHAPTER 17

*T*he case of Janie O'Daire is closed at the moment, I wrote in
my notebook on the Friday following Thanksgiving Day.
*No breakthroughs to report. No more chances to question
the girl.*

*I spoke to the Department of Education about forming a school
for accelerated students on the northern coast, but they do not feel that
the number of students who would benefit from such a school would
outweigh the costs.*

*I am frustrated and saddened that I failed to help young Janie. I
have failed myself as well.*

ON SATURDAY, I heard the distinctive flap of the brass mail slot
in my parents' front door and the whoosh of envelopes hitting the
floor mat. Immediately, I pounced upon the mail and searched for
a Kansas return address.

"What are you doing down there?" asked Mother from behind
me. I turned and witnessed her standing there with her hands
planted on her hips. She gasped and laughed a little at the sight of

me down on the floor on hands and knees, rifling through mail like a dog digging through trash.

"I told you"—I resumed my hunt—"I'm waiting for correspondence that's highly important. Darn!" I pushed myself to my feet. "It's not here."

"When it arrives, shall I open it and read it to you over the telephone?" asked Mother.

"No!"

"It's not a letter from a young man, is it?"

"Not everything revolves around young men." I bent down and picked up the scattered envelopes. "It's related to a child who requires my assistance, and if you don't contact me about it—"

"I already told you, I'll make certain you get the letter. Please settle down about it. What's gotten into you, Alice? You're not yourself this weekend."

"Please don't say that." I tossed my parents' mail onto the hall table. "Don't make me feel as though I'm going out of my mind."

"That's not what I said at all. What's bothering you so terribly? You've been prickly and short-tempered ever since you walked through the front door."

I closed my eyes. "Mother," I said with a sigh, "will you please answer a question that's been troubling me for a long while?"

She didn't respond.

I opened my eyes and peered straight at her. "Will you tell me honestly, without running away or dodging the subject, what was wrong with me when I was a little girl? What happened that made me so violent?"

Mother shifted her face away and didn't say a word. Her chest rose and fell, but the only audible sound in the house was the chair at my father's desk upstairs, squeaking against the floorboards.

"Did something traumatic happen to me when I was young?" I asked. "Did someone hurt me, or . . . or kidnap me?"

She shook her head. "No. We all kept you perfectly safe."

My skin chilled over how much her words echoed the O'Daires' insistence that no one had ever harmed Janie.

"Then why did I behave the way I did?" I asked.

Mother's brown eyes dampened; the edges of her nostrils turned pink. "I honestly don't know."

"Did you ever take me to receive mental help?"

"No," she said with a terse laugh. "People didn't do that sort of thing back then. The neighbor children's parents questioned what was wrong with you and suggested we send you away somewhere, but . . ."

I shrank back. "*Were* you tempted to send me away?"

She rubbed the right sleeve of her plum-colored dress across her eyes.

"Were you, Mother?"

She sniffed. "Most of the time you were a perfectly wonderful, bright young child. You often lost your temper when someone vexed you, but I have no idea why, at one point, you suddenly lashed out with such terrible violence."

"What did you think was happening to me?"

"Oh, Alice, don't ask that."

"What did you think, Mother?"

She fingered her lips, her hand trembling, so much so that it blurred like the wings of a hummingbird. "I thought . . ." She sniffed again. "Quite honestly, I worried . . . that you might have been possessed by the devil."

I tightened my arms around myself. "Bea said that I asked to be called Nell around then."

"Yes, you did."

"Did that ever frighten you?"

"Yes, I suppose so. Sometimes you insisted quite vehemently that your name wasn't Alice."

I pursed my lips together and reheard those last words a hundred more times. *You insisted quite vehemently that your name wasn't Alice.*

"Tell me, honestly . . ." I said, my voice breaking. "I won't laugh, and I won't tell Father, but you must tell me truthfully, did you ever believe I'd once lived a past life as another person?"

She clutched her chest with a whimper, and her skin suddenly looked so weathered and pale and paper thin, I feared I'd aged her in an instant with that single question.

"I know it sounds preposterous," I continued, "but did you ever believe in that possibility? Did you wonder if—?"

"Yes!" she said, her hand still braced against her chest. "I thought that all of the time."

My eyes expanded. "Did . . . did I ever say I had killed anyone in that past life?"

"Oh, Alice, stop." She turned on her heel and clopped down the hallway, away from me. "Let's stop speaking about this immediately."

"Did I?" I hounded her into the back of the house, smacking the kitchen door open with the flat of my hand when it swung toward my face. "Did I ever say that I murdered a woman?"

"Stop it, Alice."

"Did I?" I slammed my hands against the worktable in the middle of the room, launching a cloud of flour into the air. "Tell me, did I speak of murdering a person named Violet?"

"I don't remember," she said, kneading the skirt of her dress between her fingers. "I don't remember any names."

"What do you mean?"

"You bragged about killing dozens of people, Alice." She stepped back, still shaking, still pale, her eyes streaked with atrocious red veins. "You said there were dozens."

UP IN MY bedroom, I composed another letter.

November 28, 1925

Dear Sir or Madam:

> *I apologize in advance for the rather peculiar nature of this letter. I work as a psychologist for the Oregon Department of Education, and I have come across a small child who claims to have visited the Hotel Yesternight. Normally, I would not think it unusual for a child to say that she has visited a hotel in another state; however, this little girl's parents insist that the child has never traveled to Nebraska, and the child's sanity is in question.*
>
> *Would you be so kind as to confirm whether the Hotel Yesternight still exists somewhere in the vicinity of Du Bois? If so, does it still operate as an inn? Obtaining this*

information will dramatically assist me in solving this case.

> *Thanking you in advance, I am,*
> *Yours truly,*
> *A.M. Lind*

I addressed the letter to the postmaster of Du Bois, Nebraska, and I promptly marched it out to the nearest neighborhood mailbox. I shoved the envelope halfway into the slot, but my fingers froze, refusing to let the letter go. The paper quavered in my hand, the edges fluttering against the metal slot with the *flit-flit-flit* of a fly caught between a window and a screen. I remembered all the advice Bea had just given me Thanksgiving evening.

Don't insert yourself into other people's stories, she had said. *You're done with being little Alice Lind—you haven't been her in decades. And you're done with graduate students who acted like jackasses and all the folks living in Gordon Bay. Let all of that go. Look ahead to the future.*

My breath rattled through my teeth.

I yanked the envelope back out of the slot and tore it down the middle.

No matter what had prompted me to speak of a place called Yesternight and brag about killing dozens of people—whatever inspired me to beat children over the head with a stick that I could scarcely lift with my four-year-old hands—it was over now. The modern me wasn't a killer. Whether someone had molested me, or beaten me, or inflicted some other harm upon my body, whether I'd lived another life as a monster who took countless lives, possibly even Violet Sunday's, it was done. Best to brush the ashes from the past off my shoulders and press forward into the future.

The problem was, I realized as I pocketed the torn letter, the future looked to be either dull or frustrating. An endless sea of intelligence examinations. Weeks spent in boardinghouses and other unfamiliar beds that smelled of other people. Applications to doctoral programs declined. Dreams postponed. Relationships nonexistent. Advanced studies of memory suppression long delayed.

That's why I needed Janie O'Daire.

She made life instantly fascinating. She was precisely what I was looking for when I first entered the field of psychology with wide-open eyes and an urgent need to find someone who had suffered what I'd suffered.

CHAPTER 18

December 17, 1925

A letter arrived from Kansas.

The letter.

Mother had telephoned during the weekend of December 12 and said that the envelope appeared in the mail that afternoon; she told me she would forward it straightaway. I almost didn't believe in its existence. Mother may as well have said, *You've just received a postcard from a fairyland, Alice. Can you believe it?*

And now, there the crisp letter lay in my lap in another musty cloakroom inside another one-room schoolhouse. The postman had delivered the mail halfway through the school day, and it wasn't until after the children had filed out of the classroom with their lunch pails clanging against books, after I closed the examination booklet, that I allowed myself to drink in the sight of the envelope.

The letter writer had addressed the envelope to DR. A.M. LIND. She could not have known that just because I was a psychologist, I did not necessarily possess a PhD, but I found the respectful title of "Dr." to be kind.

However, it was the return address that ensnared my full attention.

> *Eleanor Rook*
> *289 Alamo Road*
> *Friendly, Kansas*

My eyes darted back and forth across all of the various names. The letters seemed to merge together and rearrange themselves and render the words familiar and strange all at once. I shivered from a brutal bout of chills.

Eleanor: The name of Violet Sunday's supposed sister.

Rook: Wasn't that . . . *Yes*, wasn't Rook the surname of the teacher who first purportedly taught Violet mathematics?

Friendly, Kansas: Good old Friendly.

Using the tip of a fingernail, I ripped the envelope open, taking great pains not to damage the contents within, yet still rushing to see what waited inside. My eyes watered in anticipation; my legs fidgeted. Pale-blue stationery came into view, and suddenly there I was, reading a letter penned a half-continent away in Janie O'Daire's wondrous world of Friendly.

December 1, 1925

Dear Dr. Lind,

> *As you can probably understand, I was quite taken aback when your letter arrived, and I have spent the past several days gathering the courage to respond. I have,*

indeed, received correspondence from a man named Michael O'Daire, but his letter unsettled me so deeply, I considered it a cruel prank and refused to pay it any heed. He contacted me back in 1921, and I tucked his envelope deep into a drawer and have not thought of it much since.

The receipt of your letter, however, has brought back that same flurry of emotions I experienced four years ago. I admit, this time around, curiosity has become my principal reaction.

I did, in fact, once have a sister named Violet. She was born and raised right here in Friendly, Kansas, and she died tragically one cold January in 1890 at the age of 19. Her married name was Jessen, but our maiden name was Sunday. We had a dog named Puppy, not Poppy, as mentioned in your letter. Poppy would have been a far more creative name, but I believe that I, the younger child, had insisted upon Puppy, and I tended to get my way. Violet married shortly before she died. She bore no children, and both of our parents are deceased. Aside from my grown children, I am the sole remaining member of my side of the family, and I am intrigued beyond words about this little girl who claims to have been my sister. I cannot think of any rational reason why a child living miles away on the shores of Oregon—a girl born decades after my sister's death—would say she had been our lovely Violet.

Yes, my sister was a mathematician, as the child in question has stated. Unfortunately, Violet lived in an era that prized female education even less than we do now, and my parents refused to pay for her to attend college.

She rushed into marriage instead and never got a chance to finish writing a geometric proof that had been perplexing her. Every single day I have wondered what she would have accomplished had she been allowed to live and continue her studies. When I think of Violet, I think of a book half-written, the ending an elusive mystery, out of my grasp, forever lost.

The more I write, the more I long to meet this child of whom you and Mr. O'Daire speak. I am a lifelong Presbyterian who has never been taught to believe in reincarnation, so what I am offering goes entirely against my upbringing. I invite you to bring the child to visit my house at your convenience. All I ask is for some notification in advance. We have a nice hotel in nearby Brighton, and I could arrange to have my husband pick you up and bring you out to see me. Take the Atchison, Topeka, and Santa Fe Railway to the Brighton Depot in eastern Kansas.

If you believe a visit would help this child, then please accept my offer. You have piqued my interest, Dr. Lind.

Yours sincerely,
Eleanor Sunday Rook

CHAPTER 19

Early that following morning, the first Saturday of Christmas vacation, I packed up my suitcases in a boardinghouse in the coastal town of Tillamook and climbed aboard a train heading northward, one that would pass through Gordon Bay.

During that second arrival at the little log depot, the wind merely whimpered. No forces of nature knocked me to the ground, but the temperature couldn't have been any higher than twenty-five degrees. The moist air chilled my earlobes, which poked out from beneath a gray hat I brought from Portland to replace my maroon cloche.

Despite the cold, my blood flowed with vigor. I gathered up my suitcases and walked the mile or two trek to the Gordon Bay Hotel.

The wrought-iron archway that bore the name of Michael O'Daire's establishment rose overhead on the driveway. In the graveled lot to the south of the main entrance, someone had parked a bottle-green automobile, indicating that an actual guest besides myself had decided to check in. A Christmas wreath made of fresh boughs of pine hung on the bare planks of the front door, and through one of the lobby's eight-foot-tall windows I spied a Christmas tree, festooned with glass ornaments and strings of popcorn. I smelled chimney smoke and another famous O'Daire ham, roasting down in the basement.

Inside, I found a young couple in fur coats of near-matching shades of caramel. They stood at the front desk with their elbows pressed against the counter, their backs facing me, and they spoke to Michael, whom I heard but couldn't see. Michael's mother waited at the base of the staircase with a pot of tea balanced on a silver tray, and her bottom jaw just about plummeted to her knees when she spotted me stepping into the lobby. Michael handed the guests a key and inquired if they needed assistance with their bags. From between the guests' heads, he caught sight of me as well. He startled and blinked, and then he combed his left fingers through his hair and asked, "Are—are you sure?" when the male member of the couple told him he didn't mind carrying the bags on his own.

"I'll show them upstairs, Michael," said his mother. "This way, please, and mind the third step. We've just discovered it needs mending."

The female member of the couple glanced over her shoulder at me with youthful blue eyes, her rouged lips slightly parted, as if I frightened her. I felt an ominous specter, lurking there in the lobby with my unannounced appearance, my frosted skin, and the letter from a past life tucked inside my coat pocket. The couple followed after Mrs. O'Daire. Michael braced his hands against the surface of the desk and tapped his right pinkie against the dark wood.

Without a word, I lowered my bags to the floor and walked toward him, tugging Eleanor Rook's envelope out of my pocket. Mrs. O'Daire and the guests journeyed out of sight up the staircase, beyond Michael, and soon it was simply he and I and the letter.

"You're back," he said. "I didn't think—"

"I have something you must see." I laid the envelope on the desk in front of him, next to a small potted Christmas tree. "It's from Friendly, Kansas."

"What?"

"Read it, please."

He regarded the envelope without touching it, his posture stiff, his hands still forced against the countertop. "Does it say—?"

"Just read it, Michael, please. I want you to verify that I'm not imagining its contents. I want you to swear you're not somehow behind it."

He sucked in his breath and then wiggled the sky-blue stationery out of the envelope. I watched as his eyes moved back and forth over Mrs. Rook's handwritten message. His rate of breathing increased. He must have read the letter at least twice, if not thrice—he perused it for ages without ever switching his gaze back to me.

"What do you make of it?" I asked.

He covered his mouth, still staring the letter down, still clutching the paper in his free hand. "Oh, God!" he said from behind his palm. "Oh, Jesus Christ!" He lost his balance and knocked over the little tree with his left elbow. The ceramic pot cracked, soil exploded across wood, and the air filled with the scent of damp gardens.

I propped the tree back in place on the desk. "Are you all right?"

Michael stepped backward. "I . . . I don't know what to make of it. Is . . . is it real? Is this truly happening?"

"Yes, it is. Can you believe it?" I leaned my weight against the counter. "How can we convince your ex-wife to allow me to take Janie to meet this woman?"

He shook his head. "I don't know if you can. But we've got to show her this. She'll faint dead away. Oh, Jesus!"

"Michael, tell me honestly—look me in the eye—"

He did as I asked, his lips and chin shaking.

"Did you instruct anyone in Kansas to write this letter to me?"

"No."

"Swear to me that you're not behind this. Swear to God."

"I didn't even know you contacted anyone in Kansas. When did you do this? *How* did you do this?"

"I wrote to the postmaster of Friendly the night that I stayed in the house with Janie. This is the idea I was telling you about." I laid a hand upon the blue paper. "I genuinely didn't believe anything would ever come of it. I was convinced I would need to put aside my investigation into Janie's stories forever."

"What is it?" asked Michael's mother from the staircase. She scuttled down the steps with her hands swishing across the banisters. "What's happening with Janie?"

"Read this." Michael grabbed the letter and shoved it at his mother.

She tucked her chin against her chest and eyed the paper as though it might be laced with arsenic. "What is it?"

"A woman claiming to be Violet Sunday's sister wrote to Miss Lind." He uncurled his mother's right fingers and crammed the letter into her hand. "Read it, please. This verifies that I'm not a lunatic for believing in Janie all these years."

Mrs. O'Daire tugged a pair of reading glasses out of her apron pocket and slipped them over her nose and ears. Michael backed away and covered his mouth again. His left hip whacked the front desk with a jolting *thump*, but he didn't flinch from the pain.

I gripped the edge of the countertop and longed to propel time forward—to convince Janie's mother to agree to put the child on a train to Kansas that very evening.

Mrs. O'Daire raised her face from the letter with enormous eyes. "Holy Mother of God."

"How do we get Rebecca to allow Janie to travel to Kansas?" asked Michael. "How do we stop her from being so terrified and convince her that this isn't some trick to make money?"

His mother removed her spectacles. "I'll speak to her right now. And you'll come with me, Miss Lind. We'll both show her the letter and talk to her as a concerned grandmother and psychologist."

Michael straightened his necktie. "I'm coming, too."

"No!" snapped Mrs. O'Daire. "You absolutely cannot offer to take Janie out of Oregon. You need to stay home, both now and during the trip to Kansas."

"But—"

"You must, Michael. For heaven's sake . . ." Mrs. O'Daire glanced toward the staircase and lowered her voice, assumedly to avoid disturbing the guests, who sounded to be running bathwater upstairs. "If Rebecca's greatest fear is that you'll take Janie away, then you cannot be any part of this."

"Join me for dinner later this evening, Mr. O'Daire." I slid a hand across his desk. "I'd like to speak to you about—"

"No!" said his mother with a bark that made me jump. "You two mustn't see each other anymore. The gossip around town is that you struck up an intimate relationship the last time you were here."

"What?" Michael gaped. "Who said such a thing?"

"*Everyone.* You know how this town is, Michael. You cannot appear in public together. You cannot speak to each other, and you most certainly cannot stay here anymore, Miss Lind. We'll tell Rebecca you came straight to my house with this letter, not his, and once we've made arrangements, we'll find you lodging elsewhere."

Michael rolled his eyes. "This is absurd. Miss Lind is going to great lengths to help Janie, and yet we're all expected to treat her as though she's a meddling, sex-crazed bitch."

"Michael!" His mother whipped her face toward the staircase. "Mind your language. The guests!"

"No, I won't mind my language. Goddamned busybodies are insulting both Miss Lind and her hard work, and I'm sick of it."

"Let's stop arguing and get back to making plans." I picked up the envelope with that all-important Kansas postmark. "I'm only on vacation until January 4. If this journey to Friendly is to occur, then it must happen soon. To be honest, I was hoping to board a train for Kansas either tonight or tomorrow morning."

Mrs. O'Daire sighed and thrust the letter back at me. "Neither of you are thinking clearly. Christmas is this upcoming Friday. If, by chance, Rebecca actually agrees to allow Janie to travel, then she most certainly won't want the trip to interrupt the holidays."

"Rebecca knows that Janie's greatest wish is to go to Friendly," said Michael. "If an immediate opportunity has arisen, thanks to Miss Lind and this Eleanor"—he tipped the envelope in my hand toward him—"Rook, is it?"

"Yes," I said. "And Rook was the surname of the teacher Janie told me about when I asked who had taught her mathematics. Isn't that interesting?"

"This isn't one of your Sherlock Holmes novels, Michael," said his mother, echoing my own words from my previous stay in Gordon Bay. "This isn't fun and games."

"You're not comprehending the importance of this letter, Mom. Christ, don't you understand what's happening here?" He jabbed a finger against the envelope on the desk. "We now have evidence that this mystery woman actually existed, right down to the name of Violet's sister and her astounding mathematical talents. Do you honestly believe that I'm just going to sit here quietly at home when we just broke through a barrier as monumental as this?"

"You're not thinking rationally, though."

"*This* isn't rational." He lifted the letter from my hand and held it in her face. "This one small piece of paper proves there's life beyond death. My own child has proved it. Don't you dare tell me I can't be a part of this." He rounded the front desk.

"Michael—"

"The one thing my daughter has ever wanted from this life was to visit the Sundays in Kansas. I'm going to make that dream of hers come true, even if it means I have to give up everything else on this earth." He snatched his coat from the rack. "We'll leave by tomorrow morning."

"Don't you dare kidnap that girl . . ."

"For God's sake, Mom, I'm not going to kidnap my own daughter. How dare you accuse me of such a thing?" He hoisted my bags off the ground with arms stiff and tense. "Mind the hotel. Make sure those guests up there have towels and soap and whatever else they need. I'm going to Rebecca's, and then Miss Lind and I will inquire about the purchase of train tickets."

Mrs. O'Daire put a hand on her hip and shook her head. "You're going to lose her."

"You're wrong." He shoved the front door open with an elbow. "I already lost her, long ago. Now's my chance to get her back."

CHAPTER 20

Michael drove faster than was probably wise. He shoved his foot against the gas pedal, and the engine howled with his desperation to reach his daughter. I braced a hand against the car door to steel myself against each turn and prayed I'd done the right thing by writing to strangers in Kansas.

At the O'Daire residence, Michael jogged up the porch steps ahead of me and rattled the brass knocker. He couldn't hold his body still; he shook out his hands and bobbed his legs.

"Be careful how you speak to her," I warned when I approached his side. "This is going to require the delicacy of a surgeon."

"I know." He pulled a handkerchief from a pocket and wiped sweat from his forehead, even though the air out there remained below freezing.

Footsteps approached us from inside the house. Michael drew a short breath, and Tillie opened the door.

"Oh!" Her shoulders jerked. "What are you both doing here?"

"We have proof, Tillie." Michael wrestled the letter from his breast pocket. "Violet Sunday was as real as you and I."

Tillie glanced at me, her forehead crinkling. "I don't . . . I don't understand."

"A woman named Eleanor Sunday Rook answered an inquiry I made to Friendly," I said. "I can't believe I'm saying this, but, yes"—I tapped the letter—"she, indeed, verified that a young, unknown mathematician named Violet Sunday existed. She claims to have been Violet's sister."

Michael edged his way inside the house. "Janie! Come here. I've got an early Christmas present for you."

"Please, do this carefully," I warned again.

"Janie!" he called, and two pairs of footsteps hurried down the staircase.

Rebecca stepped into view first, her eyes darting about between all three of us. She wore a small pearl comb in her strawberry blond waves, and for some reason the pretty little accessory made me worry all the more about knocking askew the normalcy of her life. From the look of her, she took great pains to keep everything neat and proper and sensible.

"What is *she* doing here?" she asked when she spotted me, and she pulled her button-down sweater more firmly around her chest. "What is all of this about, Michael?"

"Hello, Daddy," said Janie from behind her mother. She slid her left hand over the slick newel post and sprang off the last step.

"Janie!" Michael squatted down and put his arms out to his daughter, wiggling his fingers to urge her to approach him. "Come here. I have a Christmas present for you, baby."

Rebecca hooked a hand around the girl's right shoulder and kept her from moving. "I said, what is all of this about? Why are you both standing here in my house, unannounced?"

Michael, still squatting, lowered his elbows to his thighs and plunked one knee against the rug beneath him. "What is it that

Janie has always asked for since she could first speak? Where is it
that she's wanted to visit for as long as you can remember?"

Rebecca nudged the girl behind her. "I don't like this. What are
you getting at?"

"Mrs. O'Daire . . ." I inched forward, hating the sensation that
she considered us both threats. "We're here because I've received
a letter from a woman in Kansas—a woman named Eleanor who
once had a sister named Violet Sunday."

Rebecca's eyes veered straightaway to Tillie, who blanched.

"I wrote to the postmaster of Friendly, Kansas," I explained, "iden-
tifying myself as a school psychologist who's working with a girl who
insists that she knows a family named Sunday. I enclosed a second
letter and asked him to forward it to the Sundays if they, in fact, exist.
And"—I nodded toward Michael and the letter—"apparently they
do. Show her Mrs. Rook's correspondence, Mr. O'Daire. Please."

Michael passed the envelope to the pale and freckled hands of
his former wife.

Rebecca held the paper an arm's length away and gawked at
it without saying a word. The Friendly, Kansas, postmark sat on
prominent display, and she stared at the ink with bulging emerald
eyes, as though gazing at the seal of the devil. A clock chimed the
half hour from the nearby living room, bonging with a bellow that
rumbled across my stomach.

"Open it," said her sister in a whisper. "Please open it. What
does it say?"

Janie peeked around her mother and studied the envelope, her
lips parted, her breathing unsteady. The house itself seemed to
tremble around us.

Rebecca slid her fingertips inside the envelope and tugged the letter out. She then cleared her throat. "It says, 'Dear Dr. Lind, As you can probably understand, I was quite taken aback when your letter arrived, and I've spent the past several days gathering the courage to . . .'" She trailed off, reading the following two paragraphs in silence. Both the paper and her lips quivered. "Then she . . ." Rebecca swallowed. "She then says, 'I did, in fact, once have a sister named Violet. She was born and raised right here in Friendly, Kansas, and she died tragically one cold winter in 1890 at the age of 19. Her married name was Jessen, but our maiden name . . .'" Rebecca blinked in an obvious attempt to stave off tears. "'Our maiden name was Sunday.' Oh . . . my Lord." She dropped down to a bottom step on the staircase, pressed a hand over her eyes, and broke into tears.

"Mommy?" Janie perched beside her on the step. "Are you all right?"

Both Michael and Tillie looked to me, as though I might help the woman to cope with her emotions.

I tiptoed toward Rebecca. "Mrs. O'Daire . . . ?"

She leaned forward and bawled, and everything leaked—her eyes, her nose, her mouth. Her fingers squeezed a top corner of the letter, and I worried she might tear it.

"What are you feeling right now?" I asked her. "How can I help?"

Rebecca pushed the letter against her stomach and buried her whole face into the palm of her right hand. I heard gasping and slurping and sniffing and watched tears rain down on the pale-blue stationery.

Janie clasped her arms around her mother and pulled the woman against her small chest. "Why are you crying, Mommy? Why does the letter make you sad?"

"Because . . ." Rebecca reached out and cupped the back of the girl's head. "I've been waiting for this letter for years. I didn't think it would ever come."

Michael released a breath he might have been holding ever since Janie first spoke as Violet at the age of two. Tillie placed the back of her right sleeve against her lips and broke into tears, too. I nearly almost cried myself.

"As you read," I said, "Violet's sister, Mrs. Rook, wants to speak with Janie. I believe a visit to Friendly would be beneficial for both her and the child. We could compare notes. We could see if this is truly more than just a fantastical coincidence."

"Would you like to go to Friendly, Janie?" asked Michael.

Janie lifted her head and nodded. "Yes. Yes—please."

"This is all so sudden," said Tillie with a hiccup. "It's almost Christmas."

"What better gift to give Janie," asked Michael, "than a chance to see the place she's been pining for since the age of two? No toy can ever compare to this." He turned back to his ex-wife on the stairs. "What do you think, Bec? Should we give her Friendly for Christmas? I'll pay for everyone's tickets. I'll make the arrangements this afternoon and telegraph kind Mrs. Rook, who's been so generous about reaching out to us."

"I need to think about this." Rebecca dabbed at her nose with the left cuff of her sweater.

"We don't have much time," said Michael. "Miss Lind would need to accompany us, and she can only travel during Christmas vacation."

Rebecca sighed and peered back down at the letter. More tears leaked down her cheeks and chin.

Michael stepped forward and held his cap against his chest. "Come on, Bec," he said with an intimacy to his voice that prompted me to look away from the two of them. "Janie has needed this opportunity for a long, long time. You know that as well as I. We can bring Tillie with us. You don't even have to travel in the same railway car as me or sleep in the same hotel."

"She makes me nervous." Rebecca peeked at me and fussed with the letter, folding it along the crease lines. "I'm still worried . . ." More tears flowed. "There's that whole situation with Mother . . ."

"This letter proves that there's nothing wrong with Janie." Michael kneeled down in front of her. "It proves that something spiritual, not psychological, is happening here. The girl is as sane as can be. Isn't that marvelous?"

Rebecca wiped at her eyes. "Then why do we need a psychologist accompanying us?"

"Because," he said, "Mrs. Rook only felt brave enough to write when she learned a psychologist was involved. We can't show up without Miss Lind. We need a professional to be there, to make Violet's sister feel safe."

Rebecca sniffed and clasped the letter with both hands between her knees. "If I agree to this, then you've got to swear to me, Michael O'Daire . . ." She clenched her jaw and steadied her voice. "Swear to me you won't take Janie away from me afterward. Swear you won't parade her around in front of scientists, or journalists, or anyone else who might want to lay their hands upon her. If I lose her, if anyone harms her, so help me God . . . I'll kill you."

He drew back. "Rebecca . . . Janie's sitting right there . . ."

"I swear, Michael, I'll kill you." She glared at him out of the sides of her eyes with a stare that could have slain him then and there, and I knew there was no way on earth that this poor broken family would ever be mended, no matter what we discovered in Friendly.

CHAPTER 21

Michael drove me to a larger depot to the north—a proper railway station that consisted of more than just a sign and an overhang. An agent in spectacles and a blue cap showed us timetables and the route from the coast to Portland, then to Utah, where we would switch trains and join the Atchison, Topeka, and Santa Fe to travel southeastward to Kansas. Michael paid for five tickets, including mine. I sent a telegram to Mrs. Rook, and then one to Bea to explain that my work would prevent me from visiting at Christmas. The O'Daires, Tillie Simpkin, and I would be departing early the following morning. Our arrival at our destination would occur on the morning of December 23. Everything seemed to be rushing forward, like a motion picture propelled into fast motion, everyone walking and tipping their hats at twice their normal speed.

"Well, it's done, then," I said outside the station while watching Michael tuck four of the tickets into his billfold. I folded my own ticket into my coin purse. "Thank you for buying my fare."

"You're the reason this trip is happening." He crammed the

billfold into a back trouser pocket. "I'm in awe of your ability to accomplish the impossible."

"Oh, I don't think I've quite accomplished the impossible."

"You don't . . . ?" He leaned forward. "Are you joking? You convinced a skeptical stranger in Kansas to consider that my daughter may have been her deceased sister. You convinced stubborn Rebecca O'Daire to reexamine her former belief in reincarnation and allow Janie to travel halfway across the country." He pulled his cap farther down over his ears, which were brightening in color from the cold. "If those two feats aren't examples of accomplishing the impossible, then I don't know what are."

"I'm just so relieved that Janie's mother agreed. I feel we're so close to stumbling upon something absolutely extraordinary right now. My heart's been beating like mad ever since I first laid eyes upon that letter."

"Mine, too." He rubbed his gloved hands together. "Is there anything else I should be doing right now?"

"I'm planning to check myself into a hotel here." I glanced down the street, where I believed I had spotted some sort of inn. "Tomorrow morning I'll join the rest of you on the train, but for now, I'll leave you to go tend to your obligations and to pack for the journey. Do make sure to bring the journal along with you, as well as any other documented proof of Janie's Violet Sunday stories. Miss Simpkin showed me a recent essay that Janie wrote at Halloween time. Let's be sure that comes along, too."

"Sure, I'll take care of all of that."

I stuffed my hands into my coat pockets. "Shortly after we arrive at the Rooks' house, I would like to take Mrs. Rook into a separate room and ask her questions about Violet—questions that Janie has already seemingly answered. I'll investigate more about the number eight and this Nel, the 'Man in the Other House,' as well as all of the other little details Janie has given throughout the years. Comparing notes before Mrs. Rook and Janie start blending their stories together will be crucial in determining whether this is a genuine case of reincarnation."

"As long as Janie gets to experience whatever she needs to be happy"—he shrugged—"I honestly don't care what happens in Friendly."

"I'll do my utmost to ensure that she's happy."

"I'm sure you will. I'm going to be forever in your debt, you know."

"I'm simply doing what I was hired to do—assisting a child in need."

He shook his head. "You're going much farther than that, and we both know it."

"Anyone else in my position would do the same were he or she to receive a letter such as Mrs. Rook's."

A sudden flake of snow drifted past my eyes. A reverential hush—the type of ear-ringing silence that precedes a full-fledged snowfall—had stolen all birdsong and breezes from the trees around us, I realized, and the stores and restaurants across the street slept as soundly as those of Gordon Bay.

I lifted my face and witnessed a flurry of flakes careening toward us from the sky. "I never imagined it as snowing out here on the coast. I hope it doesn't slow down our travels tomorrow morning."

"What was it that you wanted to speak to me about?" he asked.

"How's that?"

"Back at the hotel, you asked me to join you for dinner so you could speak to me about something."

"Oh." My heart stopped. *"That."*

"What was it?"

"Hmm . . ." I drew my hands back out of my pockets and massaged the exposed skin of my neck between the woolen collar of my coat and the hat. I imagined the disappointment—the absolute *horror*—on Michael's face if I confessed my preoccupation with the coincidence between my childhood nickname and the name of the Man in the Other House. And, honestly, as I stood there in the stark white light of the day, I found it difficult to imagine that Violet Sunday's potential killer, in his new life, would just so happen to obtain a position as a traveling school psychologist in Oregon . . . and would just so happen to get assigned to the schoolhouse in which the reincarnated version of Violet—also now in Oregon—studied as a seven-year-old child.

Michael took a step closer. "Is something troubling you? Is it what my mother said about people assuming that the two of us—"

"No." My cheeks warmed. "The psychologist side of me is simply still wrestling with this puzzling, burgeoning parapsychologist side. I'm starting to reexamine another case of a child who experienced queer nightmares and behaviors when she was young."

"Do you mean yourself?"

I flinched at his astute guess, and then I laughed off his accuracy and fussed with my hat. "I beg your pardon?"

"When we parted ways before Thanksgiving, you described yourself as having 'quirks' and 'terrible nightmares.'"

"Now that I think about it, I do worry about those rumors circulating about us," I said—an obvious turn in the conversation, but a necessary one if the fellow was to maintain any semblance of respect for me. "We should sit separately on the train to avoid the risk of Rebecca rethinking her decision. I'm going to see if I can find some books to help pass the time. Or"—I raised my eyebrows—"if you want to perhaps bring along some of the novels that you've written . . ."

He reddened. "No. I won't subject you to *that*."

"Oh, come now. They can't be that bad."

He pushed his fingertips against his forehead, as though appeasing a sudden headache.

"Are you all right?"

"Just a little overwhelmed."

"That's quite understandable." I swiveled in the direction of that potential inn down the way. "Well, in any case, I'm going to check myself into a hotel and sort myself out—ensure that I have enough warm clothing for Kansas and all that. I'll see you bright and early tomorrow morning."

His lips formed a small smile. "Apparently you won't, if we're supposed to pretend we don't know each other."

"I'll at least make sure everyone made it onto the train."

"And then you'll sequester yourself in a corner and bury your nose in books for three days and nights?"

"That sounds about right." I brushed snow from my sleeves. "I'm rather boring, Mr. O'Daire. I'm surprised you haven't already realized that."

"You're boring like I'm a teetotaler."

I couldn't help but snicker.

Michael offered to help me with my bags, which were still sitting in the backseat of his car, and then he escorted me to the steps of the nearest hotel, a two-story structure, a porridge sort of beige, with empty flower boxes attached below each window. The building tilted slightly to the left and emitted the tantalizing aroma of Dungeness crab.

"Here . . ." Michael tugged Mrs. Rook's envelope out of a coat pocket and handed it to me. "I'll give you this so I don't have to worry about forgetting it tomorrow. Take good care of it—please."

"I will, I promise." I pocketed the letter inside my own coat. "Well . . . until tomorrow, then," I said, crisp and businesslike, and I gave his right hand a shake. "Here's to our upcoming adventure."

I moved to leave him, but he kept hold of my hand and tipped his face close enough that I could observe every fleck of green in his blue eyes, as well as a twin pair of minute moles that dotted his left cheek.

"I'm so impressed with you, Alice," he said, his voice far more natural, more relaxed and affectionate, than I'd ever heard it before. "Whatever happens in Friendly, know that to me you're a psychology miracle worker."

Before I could formulate any sound, he let go of my palm and turned back for his car. The clapping of his soles against the pavement echoed across the dormant shops and the porridge walls of the hotel behind me, and I just stood there, my hand stretched wide open, snow melting against my glove, while the words *psychology miracle worker* played through my head as a rich string sonata.

I NOW FIND myself on a journey to Friendly, Kansas, I wrote from the plush seat of an eastbound passenger train the following evening. *I do not know how I transformed from a woman who scoffed at the very idea of past lives to one who boarded a railcar to pursue the wild, uncharted frontier of reincarnation. And yet here I am, an eager investigator, thanks to a beguiling seven-year-old child. My entire way of viewing life and death, memory and behavior, violence and sanity, is tipping rapidly on its head.*

I plan to approach the coming days with caution, however. Above all else, I am a woman of psychology; an intelligent woman, hired to ensure the well-being of schoolchildren. I must not let my emotions, as well as unanswered questions about my own past, interfere.

✂⦿ CHAPTER 22

December 23, 1925

We rolled into the Brighton, Kansas, train station at 9:35 in the morning, two days before Christmas; three days after the O'Daires, Tillie Simpkin, and I boarded the first train of our excursion. During the connection in Utah, I had dispatched a telegram to Mrs. Rook, in which I passed along our approximate arrival time. I also asked if her husband might still pick us up.

The locomotive slowed to a stop, and I peeked out my window, finding a dozen or so people waiting beneath the overhang of a depot a bright canary yellow. They were all bundled in layer upon layer of winter clothing, and only their eyes and their noses peeked through heaps of wool. Even if I knew what Mr. Rook looked like—which I most definitely didn't—I might not have recognized him in the small crowd.

He had one of those lines *in his chin*, Janie had said of *her* Mr. Rook. *And he carried a pocket watch with an etching of a castle on the back.*

I stepped off the train and landed in a prairie world imbued with far more color than what L. Frank Baum had described in his writings of Dorothy's "gray" Kansas. Snow powdered the slanted rooftops of a row of red brick storefronts, and the scents of clean air, of winter wheat and horses, blended with the grease and steam of the locomotive. No mountains blocked the view of the white earth in any direction, and yet the land stretched to the horizon in gentle, rolling hills, not with the ironed-bed-sheet flatness I'd expected.

Down the tracks, Janie and her mother and aunt climbed down the stairs of another passenger car, their bulky luggage in hand. Woolen hats concealed their red hair, and scarves engulfed their necks and chins. Beyond them, Michael walked our way with a single leather suitcase, his tweed cap pulled down over his forehead, his long black coat fastened around the rest of him. I bustled toward everyone, relieved to find familiar faces.

Rebecca squinted at me through sunlight that glared down from the pale sky. "Where are we to go now?"

"Well," I said with a lift of my shoulders, "we're to hope that Mrs. Rook's husband, indeed, received our message saying we'd be arriving this morning."

"Do we know what he looks like?" asked Michael.

I strove not to wince; not to betray my lack of confidence. "Unfortunately, no. All I know is that his name is Mr. Rook."

Rebecca sighed. Tillie cringed.

What on earth have I done? I thought. *What are we all doing out here, smack-dab in the middle of the country—two days before Christmas?*

"That man over there looks like Mr. Rook," said Janie, pointing toward a somewhat older-looking fellow in a gray cap who stood at the edge of the awaiting greeters. "He's got that same line in the middle of his chin, although his cheeks sink into his face more than I remember. He used to shave much better and didn't look so whiskery."

Rebecca pulled her daughter to her side and squeezed her close. Michael, Tillie, and I shifted our gazes between the man in question and each other, all of us seeming to ask, *Should we believe her?*

"Well . . ." I readjusted my grip on my bags. "Let's go ask if it's him."

"Yes, let's." Michael picked up Janie's pint-sized suitcase for her and led us toward the fellow, who warmed his hands in his coat pockets and rocked back and forth.

I caught up to Michael. "Do let me speak to him first. I've got Mrs. Rook's letter right here. Is the journal nearby?"

"It's in my suitcase."

"I recommend taking it out in case we need it. Keep it handy." I fumbled with the clasp of my briefcase and rummaged around for the letter. With a semblance of authority, I then marched straight up to our potential host, who withdrew his gloved hands from his pockets.

"Good morning, sir," I said. "Might you be Mr. Rook?"

He nodded. "Yes, ma'am. That's me."

"So nice to meet you. I'm Miss Alice Lind"—I lifted the letter for him to see—"the school psychologist who wrote to your wife."

"Oh." He shook my right hand, his face pinking up. "We thought you'd be a man."

"No, I'm not." I swiveled on my heel toward the rest of my group. "I'm delighted to introduce to you little Janie O'Daire and her family. This is her mother and father . . ."

"Pleased to meet you." Michael reached out to the chap and imparted a brusque handshake. "Michael O'Daire."

"And this is her aunt, as well as her schoolteacher," I continued with a gesture toward Tillie, "Miss Tillie Simpkin."

"How do you do?" she said with a polite nod. She then picked at her lips and looked as though she craved a smoke. I think we all needed a cigarette.

Mr. Rook fussed with his cap, rocking again. "The missus is back at the house. We didn't think we could fit all of you into the car if she came along."

"It's so kind of you to fetch us," I said. "And so wonderful of you to agree to meet with us so close to the holidays. I know this is all a bit last-minute . . . and somewhat shocking—"

"Oh, it's shocking, all right." Mr. Rook eyed Janie. "Eleanor's not quite sure what to think of all this."

"*I'm* still not sure what to think of all of this," I admitted. "But I've never come across anything like this in all of my experiences of working with schoolchildren."

"Well . . ." He pulled out a gold pocket watch and checked the time. "It's mighty cold out here, and the missus will be expecting us. I reckon we should get you folks into the car and try to warm up."

"Is that an illustration on your watch case?" I asked.

"Well, yes." He tilted the watch so I could view the front of the case and its etching of a Medieval-style building that may have been a castle or a church.

My heart beat faster.

I closed my mouth. "How lovely. Thank you."

"How far is the house from here?" asked Rebecca.

"About twenty minutes. Will any of you require a drink or a trip to the powder room before we set off?"

None of us indicated that we did.

"All right." Mr. Rook nodded for us to follow him to a half-dozen cars parked near the depot, most of them black Model Ts with windows half iced over. "Let's head to old Friendly, then."

WE BOUNCED ALONG on an unpaved country road, our luggage knocking against the roof above our heads, the windshield wipers straining to scrape away particles of ice. I had squeezed in next to Mr. Rook in the middle of the front seat, and Michael sat on the other side of me, the journal tucked inside his left coat pocket, which bulged against my right side. Janie, Tillie, and Rebecca occupied the backseat, with Janie sandwiched between the two ladies.

Mr. Rook, a soft-spoken man, pointed out some of the local points of interest, such as the farm that had raised the dairy cows that won first prize every county fair, and a house that had been the home of two young bushwhackers who participated in the bloody 1863 massacre in Lawrence. I found myself nodding at everything he said, and Michael kept responding, "Now, isn't that interesting?"

The occupants of the backseat rode in silence during the first five minutes, until suddenly, out of nowhere, Janie piped up and said, "*Ohhh*, you're *Vernon* Rook, not William Rook. That's why you look different. You grew up and got old."

Mr. Rook snapped his face backward. The car swerved. A roll of hay the size of a shed shot up in our path in a field.

"Look out!" I shouted, and grabbed the man's arm.

The car skidded and jumped through the snow and tall grasses, but, somehow, Mr. Rook regained control and maneuvered us back onto the road, where we again jostled across frozen dirt.

Michael and I had clutched each other's hands, I realized, but I let him go and instead clasped my knees.

Sweat bubbled on Mr. Rook's brow. "What did you just say, little girl? H-h-how do you know me?"

Janie laughed the way one would with old friends. "I recognize your voice. You still sound like you, Vernon. Is your father still teaching?"

Our driver slammed his foot against the brake and threw us all forward in our seats.

"Jesus! Are you all right, sir?" asked Michael, rubbing his neck. "Do you need someone else to drive?"

Mr. Rook gripped the steering wheel and refused to look back at Janie, his face as white as the snow surrounding us. "Is this some sort of joke? Did you people come here to laugh at us?"

"No." I nudged at Michael with an elbow. "Show him the journal. Show him precisely why we're here and how we're just as stunned as he is."

"Did I say something wrong?" asked Janie, on the cusp of crying.

"No, darling." I turned toward her. "You're doing just fine. It's just that we adults aren't always as brave as you when it comes to you recognizing people like Mr. Rook."

"We shouldn't have come here," said Rebecca, her arm around Janie. "I knew in my gut this might lead to trouble."

Janie's eyes shone with tears. "Aren't we still going to Friendly?"

"Of course we're still going," said Michael. He stretched his arm across me to pass the journal to Mr. Rook. "Sir, these are the notes we've been compiling since Janie was two. She's been telling us about her life as Violet Sunday ever since she could first speak, but, I swear to God, this is the first time she's ever been east of the Coast Range in Oregon."

Mr. Rook's neck muscles tautened, and he refused to touch the book.

"Please, sir," I pleaded. "Read it. We've come so far. We've given up everything to travel here this Christmas and share this child's story with you."

Another fifteen seconds passed. Mr. Rook panted through his open mouth, as though he'd just sprinted across the field, but I nodded to urge him along.

He swallowed and accepted the journal from Michael, his lips now fixed in an expression of both doubt and terror. The thick thumbs of his tan gloves cupped the front cover, and I wondered if he felt that same sensation I experienced when I first encountered the journal—the sense of preparing myself to dive headfirst into ice water.

"Take your time," I told him, even though I shivered from the car's lack of heat. "I know this isn't easy."

Without a word, right there in the middle of that empty Kansas road, Mr. Vernon Rook opened the journal compiled by the O'Daires and embarked upon the fantastical tale that had bewitched the rest of us in that car. He cried silent tears, and he pored over at least twenty pages of Janie's life as Violet Sunday, while the rest of us huddled together to stay warm.

 CHAPTER 23

Janie passed the remaining ten minutes of the car ride by singing kiddie songs, accompanied by her reluctant-sounding aunt who half-sung at *mezza voce*. During the final stretch of the journey, they entertained us with "Animal Fair," an oddly catchy ditty that involved an elephant collapsing upon and killing a drunken monkey.

Mr. Rook steered us onto a gravel driveway that led to a white farmhouse parked in the middle of a field blanketed in three inches of snow. Tillie's voice fell off, but Janie continued singing about "the end of the monkey monk." The car swayed us back and forth, and gravel crunched beneath the tires with a sound not unlike the breaking of bones.

Windows framed by worn black shutters watched over us, and I spotted a woman's face peering through one of the panes on the second floor. A moment later, she dashed away. My stomach tightened.

"Is this where she lived all her life?" asked Rebecca from behind Mr. Rook. "Violet Sunday, I mean. Was this the house in which she grew up?"

Mr. Rook shifted the parking brake into a locked position. "Ask the girl."

Michael twisted around in the seat to face his daughter, who now sang "Lavender Blue."

"Janie," he said, interrupting her, "we're here. Do you recognize where we are?"

I swiveled around as well and watched Janie suck her bottom lip inside her mouth and peek out the window next to her mother.

"No." She sat back in the seat.

My heart sank.

"No?" asked Michael. "Are you sure? Did you get a good enough look?"

"I'm getting hungry."

"Janie, you ate on the train, not long ago," said her mother. "We're not here to eat. We're here to visit Mrs. Rook, whom you've repeatedly told us that you want to see."

Mr. Rook stepped out of the car and opened Rebecca's door for her. Michael spilled out of his side and held the door open for me.

"Why doesn't she recognize the place?" he asked me through gritted teeth. "She's been talking about this damn house all of her life."

"Maybe it's not the one Violet grew up in. Mr. Rook never did answer the question of whether it was."

Tillie swung her door shut, and, through her own clenched jaw, she said, "I'm sorry—I shouldn't have sang all those songs with her. It pulled her too far into the world of Janie."

"Hello," called a woman from up by the house.

I turned to find the same face I had witnessed in the upstairs window. It belonged to a petite woman with gray-streaked hair who looked to have been in her late forties or early fifties. She evaluated us with cautious eyes, and her thin lips formed a tentative smile. She had the type of deeply angled eyebrows that made a person appear perpetually concerned, so I wasn't entirely sure how to gauge her level of comfort with our arrival.

I approached her. "Mrs. Rook?"

"Yes." She nodded, those eyebrows still worrying. "I'm Eleanor Sunday Rook, Violet's sister."

"Oh, what a pleasure it is to meet you." I climbed the porch steps to where she stood and thrust my hand her way. "I'm Alice Lind, the psychologist from the letter. I heard that you and your husband were expecting a man."

"We were, but that's all right. Welcome to our home."

"Thank you. I'm so pleased to be here. Now, let me introduce you to the whole reason why we are here. Janie"—I beckoned to the girl with my right hand—"please come up here so that you may meet Mrs. Eleanor Sunday Rook. Bring your family along with you."

Janie stood closest to Michael now. She hooked one of her hands around his, and with cautious footsteps, walked toward us at his side. Her mother and aunt followed, gazing up at the house as though they expected to recognize it as well.

"Mrs. Rook, this is Miss Janie O'Daire," I said when the girl climbed up to the topmost step, the soles of her little boots scraping against the wood. "This is the child whom I told you about in my letter."

"Hello, Janie," said our hostess. "I'm Eleanor Rook."

"Pleased to meet you," said Janie with a tone of trained politeness.

Disappointment clouded Mrs. Rook's eyes. I could tell she had quite hoped for another sort of response. As did I.

I introduced the rest of the O'Daires and Tillie, and the Rooks invited us inside. We landed in an entryway wallpapered in a feminine pattern consisting of red flowers printed against an ivory background—just as Janie had described Violet's walls to her parents, according to the journal. We unwound scarves from our necks and shed gloves and hats, and I focused all of my attention on Janie's reactions to the surroundings.

"Would you like anything to eat or drink?" asked Mrs. Rook.

Janie's eyes lit up, and her mouth stretched into a smile that revealed a new gap between her teeth.

"I wondered," I said, "if I might perhaps speak with you in private, Mrs. Rook, before you and Janie even have time to interact. I would like to ask you a list of questions and see how your answers compare to the information Janie has told her parents about Violet."

Janie's smile faded. Her hand wilted out of Michael's.

Mrs. Rook exchanged a glance with her husband, who was removing his coat and gloves.

"If you think that would be the best way to proceed," she said, "then I'm certain Vernon could serve everyone else coffee and milk, or whatever they'd prefer."

"Sure." Her husband nodded. "I'll help."

I pulled my arms out of my coat sleeves. "Thank you. That's splendid of you. Are the rest of you comfortable with that plan? We can reconvene after my short interview with Mrs. Rook and share the journal with her."

The O'Daires nodded and voiced their agreement, and before long, I found myself following Mrs. Rook into a little back sitting room inhabited by a dozen pieces of taxidermy—stuffed ducks and geese mainly. The disembodied head of a buck hung above a fireplace, and his bulbous glass eyes glowed from the flames with unsettling flickers of life.

"Vernon likes to hunt," said Mrs. Rook.

"Ah, I see. That's an impressive pair of antlers on the fellow."

Mrs. Rook smiled, and I worried that my words had sounded dirty.

I brushed my bangs out of my eyes and sat down across from her in one of two checkered armchairs, angled in front of the fireplace. Quilted scenes of migrating ducks adorned the walls, and a plump mallard stood on a small end table, near my right elbow. Thankfully, the only smell to permeate the room derived from the logs burning in the hearth, and not the animals.

"Now . . ." I drew my notebook and fountain pen out of my briefcase on the floor. "Let me start by saying that I can't tell you how grateful we all are that you've allowed us to visit you today. As we already told your husband, Janie has been asking to visit Friendly ever since she was a child of two."

"Is that so?" asked Mrs. Rook, crossing her legs beneath a periwinkle skirt. "Two years old?"

"I'm so eager to speak to you right now, Mrs. Rook. Do you mind if I simply jump into my list of questions?"

"Please do. I'm eager to get on with things, too."

"I'm sure you are." I opened my notebook and pressed out a crease in the page of questions. "Are you ready, then?"

"I am." She wrapped her hands around her right knee and leaned forward. Her eyebrows persisted in conveying concern.

"All right." I took a breath and poised the nib of my pen above the paper. "So that I may record the basic information in my notes, please start by telling me the names of you and your sister."

"I am Eleanor Rook, born Eleanor Jane Sunday in 1872. My sister was born Violet Julia Sunday in 1870, but she married at the age of eighteen and became Violet Jessen."

I wrote down her answers, then asked, "Where were you both born?"

"Right here in this house." Mrs. Rook beamed at the room around her—the wallpaper peppered in those distinctive red flowers, the quilts, the knickknacks, the taxidermy. "When Vernon and I first married, we lived in a house in downtown Brighton, but I couldn't bear to part with this place after I lost both of my parents. I moved back here about fifteen years ago, when my children were almost old enough to head out on their own."

I nodded and made notes about the passing on of the Sunday house to Eleanor. "Did Violet ever live in any other house?"

"Yes, she lived in a small cabin on the edge of the property. 'The other house' we always called it."

I continued to write as though I hadn't ever heard of the "other house." My deteriorating penmanship betrayed the unsteadiness of my hand.

"And did she live with someone in that other house?" I asked.

"Yes, her husband, Nelson."

I lost my grip on the pen, which clattered to the floor and spit a drop of ink across the wood. "Oh no. I'm so sorry . . ." I bent over and erased the black dot with a thumb. "Did . . . did you say her husband's name was Nelson?"

"Yes, Nelson Jessen. His family was Danish."

"Really? Danish?" My eyes watered. I picked up the pen and righted myself in the chair, but my posture felt crooked and awkward. "Mrs. Rook . . ." I put a hand to my chest and struggled to catch my breath. "I must ask you, have you ever in your life met Mr. or Mrs. O'Daire?"

"You mean the girl's parents sitting out there?"

"Yes. The couple—or former couple. You don't already know them, do you?"

She swung her knees toward the room's closed door. "No. Why?"

"I want to ensure that none of you have ever spoken with each other—exchanged information."

"Did the little girl know about Nelson, too?"

"As a matter of fact, she spoke of a man named Nel who lived in a place she called the 'other house.'"

Mrs. Rook froze. I observed the dilation of her pupils and a purpling of her lips, as though oxygen failed to flow properly through her blood.

"When we're finished here," I said, "I'll show you those details in my notes, as well as in the O'Daires' journal. Did Nelson ever go by Nel?"

"We called him Nels with an *s*, but Violet sometimes called him Nel, or, jokingly, Nelly. He was the same age as Violet, but we all knew each other since we were little children. Vernon grew up with us, too. His father was the teacher at our schoolhouse."

"Vernon's father, the older Mr. Rook, taught Violet, then?"

"Yes, he taught all of us."

I shifted about in my chair, edging forward, switching which leg I crossed. "Did you and Violet have any other siblings?"

"No, it was just the two of us. We lived here with our mother and father and occasionally a dog or two, like the aforementioned Puppy."

"Tell me more about Violet's fondness and talent for mathematics," I said. "When did that start?"

"Early on in school. Violet was always calculating the prices of crops for our father, always helping him out. That's why it infuriated me when he wouldn't allow her to attend college. The girl was a genius; there was no doubt about it. She just happened to be a genius with a woman's body."

"You said she jumped into her marriage instead of going to college?"

"Yes, there was nothing else for her to do. She and Nels loved each other dearly, and he promised her he would help her earn money for tuition, even though they started with absolutely nothing." She sat back in the chair and stroked the armrests with slender fingers. "Violet and Nels married after they both graduated from school. He found himself a nice job as a clerk at a law office in Brighton."

"And you said he was the same age as Violet?" I asked, jotting down notes as I spoke. "He wasn't an older gentleman dangling money in front of a girl in need?"

Mrs. Rook laughed. "Oh no, it wasn't anything like that. Violet and Nels *adored* each other. She worked in the daytime, cleaning houses for a family in Brighton, just down the street from where Nels worked. And at night she'd scribble away in notebooks, formulating equations, sometimes even writing on the walls to map everything out on a larger scale. Oh my goodness"—she clapped her hands together and smiled—"you should see how much calculating that girl used to do on those poor walls. Nels would just shake his head and grin and say how proud he was of her. He excelled in math, too, but not quite like that."

"She—she wrote equations on the walls?" I asked.

"Yes. Shapes and numbers and all sorts of mathematical symbols that I never could quite understand. We left her writing up there in the other house, as a matter of fact. My parents never rented the place out to anyone else, and it seemed almost sacrilegious to erase all of her work." Mrs. Rook settled back against her chair again. "It's funny, I always imagined her coming back here one day, evaluating what she wrote, finding the answer staring straight at her."

I glanced at the door, listening for the sound of Janie among the low murmurs that filled one of the other rooms. "Janie O'Daire writes on her bedroom walls, too," I said in a voice more whispery than I'd intended.

Mrs. Rook gulped. "Does she, now?"

"Yes." I cleared my throat. "I think perhaps we ought to take her to the other house in a short while."

Mrs. Rook rubbed her thumbs along the edges of her armrests and nodded, her face doughy white. "Yes, I think I quite agree."

I recorded her statements about Violet's work as a housemaid, her equations on the walls, and her marriage to Nelson. My insides squirmed and burbled. The time to address Violet's death had at long last arrived. Time to unearth Nelson "Nel" Jessen's involvement.

"Mrs. Rook . . ." I swallowed and laid the notebook across the length of my lap. "Janie has given us several details about the day Violet died, but some key facts are missing."

"Oh?"

"I am going to now ask you some questions based on the information she has managed to tell us, to see if the specifics of her story match what actually happened. Do you mind speaking of your sister's death?"

"No, I don't mind." Mrs. Rook offered a tight smile. "I know from your letter that the child is aware that Violet drowned. Unless someone from Friendly told Janie about Violet, I honestly can't imagine how she would have learned that information. We didn't even list the cause of death in the obituary."

"What was the precise date of her death?"

"January 1, 1890. New Year's Day."

"How old was she?"

"Nineteen. Her birthday was December 2, so she was a young nineteen."

Nineteen years old. The *first* day of the *first* month. The *second* day of the *twelfth* month. Nowhere in any of those numbers did I hear her mention "eight."

"Do you know if a particular number troubled Violet?" I asked.

Mrs. Rook's dusky eyebrows shot up. "A number?"

"Yes. Was there a number that got in the way of her equations?"

"I don't believe so."

I wrote down Mrs. Rook's lack of knowledge in these matters. "Do you know where she drowned?" I asked.

She bit her lip, and I braced myself for the possibility that she might, indeed, say, *At the Hotel Yesternight, near Du Bois, Nebraska.*

"In a lake," she said instead, "just behind the other house."

"I see. And you're positive of that location?"

"Yes." She swallowed. "I know for a fact that's where she died."

"Thank you. Thank you for that information." I released a

silent breath of relief and wrote down her response. "Now . . . let's see . . ." My eyes struggled to focus for a moment; the words on the paper blurred in my lap. "Janie often suffers from nightmares about drowning, but what she doesn't seem to understand is how she got into the lake. She talks about a person being there, and a number written on glass, which is why I brought up the subject of the number to begin with. It seems to be a key to understanding her murder."

"Murder?" Mrs. Rook rose up tall in her chair. "Whoever said anything about a murder? Is that what the little girl is calling it?"

"Well . . ." I lowered my eyes to my notes and thought back to all that I knew about Janie's accounts of Violet's death. "She's never used the words *murder* or *killing*, but she's clearly troubled by the fact that a specific person is there, watching her drown. Was someone else with her, watching her?"

Mrs. Rook's forehead creased at those words, and, oh, how her eyes welled with plump tears. Her fingers clutched the ends of the armrests; her lips trembled, and I waited, simply waited, for all of those emotions to bubble over and transform into words.

She fetched a handkerchief from a pocket in the pale-green sweater she wore. "I was wondering if I might need this at some point." She blotted her cheeks, tittering a little. "It's been so long since we lost Violet, but still . . ." She sniffed and dabbed at her nose. "The grief has never completely gone away. The emotions always seem to be hiding behind other, brighter ones."

I nodded. "Difficult emotions do have a way of lingering, I'm afraid. Even when you believe they no longer hold any power over you."

She wiped at her cheeks and smiled in embarrassment. "I'm sorry."

"Please, there's no need to apologize, Mrs. Rook. I understand. I have sisters myself, and I—" I stopped mid-sentence, forbidding myself from shoving my own life into the situation. "Are you able to speak about the person who was with Violet when she died? Might it have been her husband?"

Mrs. Rook shoved her right elbow deep into the armchair's fabric and touched the handkerchief to her lips. "I haven't spoken about that day aloud in such a long, long time." She closed her eyes. "He was . . . Nelson . . . he was . . ." A shiver snaked through her. "He was, indeed, there. He watched her drown, I'm sorry to say."

I wrote those two sentences down in my notebook, my breaths ragged, my penmanship again faltering, ink smearing.

[Nelson] was, indeed, there. He watched her drown, I'm sorry to say.

My pulse drummed inside my ears. "And yet," I said, "you state that it was not a murder, correct? Nelson was there, but the family never suspected him of foul play?"

"No." Her voice broke with emotion. "We were all there. It was January. The lake was frozen. We were ice skating—Violet, Nels, and I, along with Vernon and a few of the other local young people. We were all so young then. Even though Violet and Nels had married, we were all just children, really, having heaps of fun on a cold New Year's Day."

My mind envisioned a serene scene of young men and women skating in the luminous whiteness of a Kansas winter. I thought of

Janie shouting through her house in the middle of the night, *It's too cold! It's too cold!*

"Oh no!" I said with a sudden stab of pain in my right side. "Did—did the ice break, Mrs. Rook? Is that what happened?"

She pursed her lips, and the tears brewing in her eyes spilled over to her cheeks. "It started off as a low and troubling *crack*. I called for Violet to watch out. I saw the gash forming. She must not have heard it—she was so busy gliding across the ice so beautifully, so peacefully. But then a sound like a gunshot exploded across the lake, and she plunged down into that freezing cold water. Another boy, Elmer, had a doctor for a father. He warned the rest of us not to jump straight in because of the sudden shock of the cold—he said it could stop a heart from beating in an instant. Nels tried to dive in to help her, but Elmer grabbed him by the waist and begged him to submerge himself with care or we'd lose them both. Violet had already stopped struggling down there. Poor Nels lowered himself down into the icy depths as quickly yet cautiously as he could, and he pulled my darling sister out."

I sat there with the tip of my pen hovering over the paper, unsure what to say; what to feel. Clearly, no version of me could have been responsible for a death like that, but the pang of Mrs. Rook's loss rendered me speechless. I suddenly missed both Bea and Margery to no end and experienced foggy memories of the two of them holding my hands in a hospital.

"We all loved her so much," said Mrs. Rook in a whisper. She balled the handkerchief in her right hand and tightened her fingers around it. "We all wanted to save her, but Elmer was right. The shock of the cold was too much. Even if we all had jumped in . . . she was gone so quickly. And I was so angry, afterward. So angry that a brilliant girl, a loving girl, lost her life because of something so silly as skating figures across an icy lake."

I blinked at her, and my mind took several seconds to process what she just said. "Did—did you just say, 'figures'?"

"Yes, she was skating figure—" Her lips formed the shape of the ensuing word, but she stopped herself and met my eyes.

Janie giggled from the other room.

"Was it a number?" I asked.

Mrs. Rook nodded. "Yes."

"Which number?"

Another discernible swallow rippled down her throat. "It was the number most people love to skate: eight, of course."

I jumped and involuntarily jerked my hands into the air, which sent the pages of my notebook fluttering like an eruption of flapping birds.

Mrs. Rook jumped as well. "Is that the same number the little girl mentioned?"

"Oh, God. Oh, my God." I scrambled to pick up my pen and pushed myself to my feet.

Mrs. Rook stood up, too, her legs unsteady. "Is this a significant coincidence?"

"Yes, yes, yes—oh, yes! We've gone well past coincidences by this point. It's time for you to come speak with Janie and her family." I beckoned to the woman with both hands. "You must read the journals her parents have kept over the years. It's all there. Aside from confusing 'Puppy' with 'Poppy,' she's right about everything—the red flowers on your wallpaper, your name, her name, her age, Friendly, your husband's watch, Nel from 'the other house,' the eights. Oh, my heavens, we've gone miles and miles beyond coincidences." I gathered up my notebook and briefcase, the papers rippling and crinkling and perfuming the air with fresh ink.

"Do you believe in it, then?" she asked. "Do you, a trained psychologist, stand by the theory of reincarnation?"

I stood up tall and held my belongings against my hips.

"Yes," I said without a shred of doubt in my mind.

CHAPTER 24

Mrs. Rook and I joined the others in the house's front parlor, a festive room decorated in Christmas garland and photographs of the Rooks and their children from throughout the years. A candle-lit Christmas tree stood in front of a bay window framed by curtains as green as the pine needles themselves.

The O'Daires, Tillie, and Mr. Rook sipped coffee and tea and dined on cinnamon rolls, and the sight of them all together—this growing family of sorts, connected by time and memories—sent a surge of emotion rushing up the middle of my chest. Of all the people in that house, I least expected me to be the one to cry that day, but there I was, suddenly covering my mouth, fighting to keep my emotions at bay.

"What's wrong, Miss Lind?" asked Janie, which made the lump in my throat thicken all the more.

"What is it?" Michael rose to his feet. "Has—has there been a mistake?"

"No, not at all." I blinked like mad to chase off tears. "Janie was so right about so much. Please, show the Rooks the journal. Show them everything."

MICHAEL TOOK THE journal out of his coat pocket and also helped
Tillie fetch Janie's school papers from one of the suitcases strapped
to the car. I collected my notes, and the Rooks unearthed photographs from a dust-laden cardboard box upstairs. Over cheese and
crackers and fresh slices of roast beef, we gathered around a low
table in the parlor and threaded together the tales of Mrs. Violet
Sunday Jessen and Miss Janie O'Daire.

"This is a picture of my sister at the age of eighteen," said
Mrs. Rook, and she passed around a portrait of a pretty brunette
in a dress with a high collar and a ruffled skirt that brushed the
floor. Violet's dark eyebrows didn't knit together as much as her sister's, but I noted a strong family resemblance in the eyes themselves
and in the fullness of the two women's mouths. Violet's right hand
rested upon the back of an upholstered chair, and behind her hung
a backdrop painted to resemble a backyard garden.

Rebecca handed the photograph to Janie, who ate her food
down on a maroon and gold rug, her legs crossed beneath the low
table. She glanced at the portrait of Violet for about two seconds
before setting it aside and returning to her munching. Boredom
dimmed her blue-green eyes. More photographs and mementoes
traveled her way, and we all held our breaths, waiting for her to
speak as Violet, but the food proved more important every time.

At one point I gained the courage to articulate a question I
hadn't yet asked of Mrs. Rook: "Does the name 'Yesternight' mean
anything to your family?"

Mrs. Rook shook her head, but her husband straightened
his neck and said without hesitation, "Do you mean the murder
house?"

His wife tutted. "Vernon! There's a child in the room."

The crackers and meat in my stomach hardened into stones. "You know about it, then?"

"Vernon has a fondness for sensational prairie tales," said his wife with a frown. "He could tell you all about the horrible crimes committed by the Benders of Labette County and Belle Gunness of Indiana."

"What precisely happened at the Hotel Yesternight?" I asked, and out of the corner of my eye I caught Michael lifting his head from a collection of photographs.

"Oh, the usual . . ." Mr. Rook gave a wave of his hand. "An isolated home. A touch of madness. Folks gone missing. This was all back in the mid-1890s. Nothing recent. I have a friend who travels around photographing infamous old houses."

I pressed a hand against my middle.

I was born in the late 1890s.

"Do you know if the house still operates as a hotel?" I asked. "And precisely where it's located?"

"It's in Nebraska," said Vernon. "Outside a tiny train stop called Du Bois." He pronounced Du Bois as *Do-Boys*.

"And . . . you're certain no one in this family, not even Nelson Jessen, found themselves visiting Yesternight?"

"Nels didn't travel much of anywhere after he lost Violet," said Mrs. Rook. "He suffered from frequent bouts of pneumonia."

"Do you have a picture of Nelson to show Janie?" asked Michael.

Mrs. Rook sifted through the black and white images in the box in her lap until she found a photo that, from my angle, appeared to be a wedding portrait. "Here he is"—she stretched her arm forward—"with Violet, on the day they wed."

Rebecca sat between Janie and Mrs. Rook and intercepted the photograph, as she had all of the others. She studied the picture for a moment, her forehead puckering, and then handed the image to her daughter. "Here you are, Janie," she said. "This is Violet and her husband, Nelson."

Janie took the photo and regarded it as though she were viewing the picture of a great-aunt she'd never met or even heard of. "Pretty," she said, and she laid the photo on top of the others. She again devoted her attention to her crackers.

"Janie . . ." Michael leaned forward in the rocking chair. "Does the man in the photograph look familiar to you?"

Janie peeked at Nelson and shook her head. "Nope."

"Are you sure?" asked her father. "You don't remember him from your dreams, or from anything else?"

Janie brushed at the cracker crumbs dusting the skirt of her dress. "How much longer are we going to stay here?"

"Janie!" snapped her mother. "We've come all these miles to be here because you've been asking to visit for years. For heaven's sake, why aren't you taking any interest in Violet Sunday's house?"

"It might simply be too much for her," I offered. "Best not to pressure her and—"

"You don't know that!" Rebecca spun my way in her chair. "You don't know anything about what she's going through right now because this is all new to you, too, isn't it? Don't pretend to be an expert on reincarnation just because you're an expert on everything else."

Her sister choked on her coffee. "Rebecca! Why are you attacking Miss Lind? She's merely trying to help."

"Because I know she's sitting there, formulating all of the things she's going to say about Janie in some hoity-toity psychological journal. She's scrutinizing my daughter as though the child were a monkey in a laboratory. Look at all of those notes she's taking." Rebecca pointed at the notebook in my lap, in which I was, indeed, scribbling at the moment. "She isn't going to let this go. Simply visiting isn't going to be enough for her."

"*Are* you planning to publish these findings, Miss Lind?" asked Mrs. Rook. "I personally wouldn't blame you if you did."

"That friend of mine I was telling you about," added Mr. Rook, "the one who photographs all of the old murder houses, he knows a doctor who moved to New York City to compile strange stories for the American Society for Psychical Research. I'm sure they'd take quite an interest in this case."

"No!" Rebecca put down her plate and rose to her feet. "I've agreed to come to this house solely to allow Janie to find peace of mind—nothing more." She balled her hands into fists. "I think we ought to go."

"Wait!" said Michael, rising as well. "Alice has already sworn she's not going to write up any articles about Janie."

"Why are you calling her Alice now, Michael?"

"Good Lord!" Michael stepped forward on one foot. "Don't start accusing me of things just because you're scared."

"What happened to Nel?" asked Janie from her seat down on the floor.

"My daughter will not become some laboratory toy for psychics, or teams of psychologists, or whoever else might be itching to get their hands on her. And, above all, you had better not contact any more newspaper men about this, Michael." Rebecca grabbed the child's hand and yanked her to her feet. "Thank you for your hospitality, Mr. and Mrs. Rook, but—"

"What happened to Nel?" asked Janie again, a little louder, and this time the room fell silent. Rebecca stilled, and the anger ceased blazing in her eyes.

Janie turned her freckled face toward Mrs. Rook. "Did he die, too?"

Mrs. Rook closed her mouth and swallowed. "Y-y-yes, dear. I'm afraid so."

"Why?"

Mrs. Rook gulped again. "He became deathly ill in January 1892, just two years after he became a young widower. As I told Miss Lind, my sister fell through a sheet of ice while skating figure eights on a lake in the back of our property."

Tillie and Mr. and Mrs. O'Daire all lifted their heads and exhaled the word *"Ohh."*

Janie blinked as though working to digest that information.

"No one killed her?" asked Michael with a glance at me.

"No, it was simply an accident." Mrs. Rook returned her gaze to Janie. "I'm sorry to say it, dear, but Nels's body and soul simply were never the same after he dove into that cold lake to fetch . . ." Her lips formed the word *you*, but she drew a short breath and instead said, "Violet."

Janie traced her left index finger along the bottom left corner of the photograph.

"Do you remember him, sweetie?" asked Mrs. Rook, cupping her hands around her cheeks. "I know it's been a long—"

"He was such a nice boy," said Janie.

Someone in the room sniffled as though he or she cried, but I could not pry my gaze away from Janie, who continued to study the photograph of Violet and Nelson Jessen.

"Yes, he was," said Mrs. Rook with a nod. "A very nice boy who loved you dearly."

Janie removed her fingers from the picture. I expected her to return to her lunch; to return to being Janie.

Instead, she slipped her hand inside Mrs. Rook's.

THE ENTIRE GROUP of us roamed through a field of green winter wheat that poked through the snow like patches of whiskers. The ground crunched beneath the heels of my boots, and the silent white sky stretched over the earth for endless miles.

Janie walked along in front with her mother, none of us thinking twice about the fact that this seven-year-old girl, this little stranger to the farm, led the way. Michael chatted with Mr. and Mrs. Rook about Violet's predilection for math, which left Tillie and me bringing up the rear.

Tillie slowed her pace so that we dragged at least twenty feet behind the others. She pulled a cigarette and lighter out of a coat pocket. "May I ask you a question?"

"I'm truly not going to publish an article about Janie," I said before she could even get the words out.

"That's not what I was going to ask."

"Oh?"

She stopped and lit her cigarette, and I waited for her to continue, my hands buried inside the folds of my pockets, a vicious chill chomping at my cheeks.

Tillie tucked her lighter away and exhaled a cloud of smoke that ghosted past my eyes. Her entire body relaxed, and her eyes rolled into the back of her head. "Boy, did I need that."

I snickered.

"You want one?"

"Oh, I don't smoke."

"Here." She handed the lipstick-stained end of the cigarette my way. "Try mine."

"I've tried them before and just ended up coughing and embarrassing myself. I'd hate to do that here." I trekked onward to keep from falling too far behind the rest of the group, even though they didn't seem to detect our absence.

Tillie caught up to me. "Here's what I was actually going to say." She sucked two more puffs into her lungs before asking, "Do you think you would be where you are today if you had been educated in a little one-room schoolhouse in a nothing town?"

"Where I am today?" I asked with a laugh. "Do you mean traipsing through a snow-dusted field in a remote corner of Kansas, trailing after two families I hardly even know—right before Christmas?"

"I mean, do you think you would have had the means to obtain a master's degree with an education like Janie's? And don't be too polite to give a blunt answer simply because I'm Janie's teacher."

I plodded forward three more steps and watched the snow break into chunks of ice beneath my feet. "It would have been much harder, I admit. My sisters and I attended city schools, and both of my parents were teachers. They've always been strong proponents of higher education for both men and women."

Tillie hugged her arms around herself. "Do you think Janie would benefit from an education in a city?"

"Is Rebecca considering moving?"

"You can't say a word to Michael, but yes. Despite fearing you, my sister has been inspired by you. She wants Janie to experience the same opportunities you've had."

I stopped in my tracks. "She absolutely must speak to Michael before making a decision such as that."

"What good will talking to him do? He'll only say no."

"You don't know that."

"Aren't you two coming?" asked Michael from up ahead.

My shoulders flinched at the sound of his voice. The little party now approached a cabin the shape of a shoe box with log walls and a shingled roof. The "other house," if I had to guess.

"We'll catch up in a minute," I called back.

Tillie, still hugging herself, dangled the cigarette from between two of her right fingers. I stole the thing out of her hands, shoved it between my lips, and breathed in the anesthetizing smoke until my chest expanded and my eyelids fluttered closed.

"You're not coughing, Alice," said Tillie in a throaty voice that told me she cracked a wry grin.

I opened one eye. "I might have smoked a little more than I let on."

"I have a feeling you've done a lot more things than what you've let on."

I smiled and passed the cigarette back to her. She promptly slid it between her lips and nudged me with an elbow.

"Please tell your sister to be careful," I warned, our heads bent close. "I admire her desire to advance Janie's educational opportunities, but she must also be cautious of the girl's mental health, especially after all of the emotions from this trip come crashing down back at home."

Tillie nodded. "I'll tell her."

We continued onward, switching the cigarette back and forth, our lipsticks smearing together into a rosy flowering of scarlet and magenta. It was the closest I'd come to kissing another person on the lips since my long-ago night with Stu, and the intimacy of it, the girlish silliness of it all, gave me the giggles. The O'Daires and the Rooks disappeared into the log cabin, and we stopped and hurriedly took more puffs before gaining the strength to join them.

"How are you going to go back to intelligence tests after all of this?" asked Tillie, nestling close to keep warm.

"I honestly don't know." I handed the cigarette back. "Despite how exhausted I am from all of the traveling, how routine the job often seems, I do enjoy helping the children. I know they need people like me, especially the tougher cases." I sighed and drew a line through the snow with the heel of my right boot. "However . . ."

"Ah, yes, the big 'however.'"

"I've wanted to study human memory on a more advanced level ever since graduate school. And now this . . ." I turned to face the cabin, inside which Janie now chirped about numbers written across the walls. "*This* opens an entirely new door to the uncharted limits of human memory. This changes everything."

We both stared at the cabin, hearing the cadence of the others' voices within.

Tillie dropped the cigarette to the snow and snuffed it out with the toe of her right boot. "Shall we go in?"

I nodded. "I suppose."

"Aren't you curious about Violet's writing on the walls?"

"Of course."

I followed Tillie to the cabin, realizing I didn't necessarily want to observe Janie's reaction to Violet's equations. I imagined her tracing her little fingers over the curves and the lines of the numbers and biting her bottom lip as she studied Violet's incomplete work, perhaps discovering missing components of her own theories. I even pictured her trooping onward with the families to the frozen lake on the property. I could see the graveness of her eyes as she peered out at the layer of ice shielding the waters that had claimed Violet's life, and I envisioned her marking the figure eight on the ice with the toe of her little brown boot.

And yet I couldn't do a single thing with that information. Frustration smacked me hard across the face out there in the brutal cold. The impotency of my situation was comparable to someone telling Thomas Edison, *Well, it's swell that you figured out how to create an electric lightbulb, Tommy old boy, but you can't breathe a word about it to anyone. You must sit in the dark and pretend as though you hadn't discovered it at all.*

Tillie stepped into the cabin first, and I poked my head through the doorway behind her, finding that the structure consisted of only one single room that smelled of damp wood. Two oil lamps burned on a table that looked to have been built from a barn door, and they cast a meager light across the backs of the families, who surrounded Janie in front of the farthest wall. I edged three feet farther inside and shivered at the sight of pencil markings scrawled across the lighter slabs of wood. Sure enough, the equations—a jumble of numbers, algebraic letters, and signs—resembled the markings on Janie's yellow walls. The more I blinked and allowed my eyes to adjust to the cabin's dimness, the more the calculations emerged on the boards, from floor to ceiling.

"Do you understand any of this, Janie?" asked Mr. Rook.

"Of course." The child giggled. "Why wouldn't I?"

Rebecca glanced over her shoulder and caught me watching them like a spy in the shadows. An intruder.

"I'm going back to the main house," I said, backing up.

"Are you sure?" asked Michael with a peek at me, his eyebrows knitted.

"It's time for the families to be together without me observing everything and getting in the way. I'll meet you all back there after Janie has seen and heard all that she needs to experience."

"Thank you, Miss Lind," said Rebecca, and she put a hand on Janie's left shoulder, the only part of the girl I could see from my vantage point.

I burrowed my hands back into my pockets and retreated across the field of snow, leaving the O'Daires, the Simpkins, and the Rooks to finish weaving their memories together without me.

DEAR GOD, I believe! I wrote in my notebook back at the house. *The evidence is astounding and conclusive: Janie O'Daire proves that reincarnation deserves serious research within the academic circles of the United States of America. I wish more than anything to be the person to conduct it.*

Countless obstacles stand in my path, namely a lack of authorized proof that I can present to a research clinic. However, I will not give up the fight for children such as Janie.

For former children such as me.

CHAPTER 25

Mrs. Rook invited all five of us to stay through Christmas. "It's been such an unexpected pleasure having all of you here," she said as we disappeared into our hats and coats in the entry hall. "Won't you consider staying with us? I'm sure Janie would prefer to spend Christmas inside a comfy house rather than in a hotel or on a train . . ."

"Three of us already own tickets for a train that's departing this evening," said Rebecca, which caused my fingers to fall still on the buttons of my coat.

Michael looked similarly flummoxed, his right hand frozen halfway inside his glove. "You're leaving this evening?" he asked.

Rebecca affixed Janie's hat on the child's head. "I appreciate the offer, Mrs. Rook, but Tillie, Janie, and I made plans for a Christmas escape in a lovely hotel elsewhere."

Michael still didn't move. His voice deepened. "You're not staying in Friendly any longer than today?"

Rebecca didn't answer him, and neither did her sister. They wound their scarves around their throats and refrained from looking at him, although Tillie glanced at me with anxious eyes.

Michael fitted his cap over his head with his gaze fixed upon his ex-wife. "Are you certain Janie has experienced enough of Friendly?"

"She's ready to go home," said Rebecca.

"Are you, Janie?"

Janie fastened her coat buttons and nodded.

"How did she react to the lake?" I asked Tillie beside me, my voice lowered to a near-whisper.

"She didn't want to stay at it for long. She started talking about wanting to go home."

I nodded and turned toward Janie, asking, "Do you have any last questions for the Rooks?"

"Nope." Janie brushed her hair off her cheeks. "I'm getting really tired. I want to go home."

Mrs. Rook bundled her nose beneath her handkerchief. Her husband wrapped an arm around her shoulders and swallowed, which, for some reason, brought my attention to that cleft chin of his that Janie had described as a Rook family trait way back in Gordon Bay. Again, the progress I had made disintegrated with the swiftness of sand sifting through my fingers.

We bid our hostess good-bye out in front of their house, next to the Model T that still bore our frosty suitcases upon its roof.

I shook Mrs. Rook's hand. "Thank you so much for allowing us to visit. You've been a tremendous help."

"I wish it had all lasted a bit longer." She lowered her face and wept into the handkerchief.

I stroked her right arm, below her shoulder. "If your sister truly did move on to the body of this little girl, then know that she has a bright and wondrous future ahead of her. She'll continue on with her mathematics and finish whatever it was she'd been starting. Her parents will see to that."

"Yes . . ." Mrs. Rook nodded. "I'm sure they will."

More handshakes ensued, although Janie climbed into the backseat of the car without saying good-bye to anyone. She looked exhausted. I reminded myself she was just a child. The sky purpled from the onset of twilight, which meant her bedtime likely neared.

Mr. Rook cranked the Ford to a start, and we all situated ourselves in the same seating arrangement as before. Mrs. Rook waved good-bye, and her husband steered the car around in the driveway.

To my surprise, Janie craned her head and watched the woman fall into the distance behind us. I observed the girl, wondering what thoughts coursed through her young mind, yet not daring to ask in front of her mother, who surveyed me with unblinking eyes.

We reached the end of the driveway.

Janie stiffened. "Stop the car!" she shouted. "Stop it quickly!"

Mr. Rook slammed on the brakes, and we skidded to a jarring, squealing halt.

"What is it?" asked Michael. "What's wrong?"

"I didn't say good-bye to Eleanor." She crawled over her mother's lap and grabbed the door's handle.

"Careful, Janie," said Rebecca, raising her arms for her to pass. "You're hurting me."

The child leapt out of the car and ran back up the driveway at a speed that caused her to skid twice on the snow. Mrs. Rook remained on the front porch, her posture erect, arms hanging by her sides, but in a matter of seconds, the child threw herself around the woman, and the two of them embraced with the fierceness of loved ones bidding each other good-bye. I turned away and gritted my teeth to refrain from crying. We all did. No one said a word.

A few minutes later, footsteps galloped our way, and Janie, out of breath, blew back inside the car with a gust of cold air.

"All right." She plopped back down in her seat between her mother and aunt. "I'm ready."

BACK AT THE Brighton Depot, Michael and Mr. Rook unloaded our suitcases from the car's roof.

"In case any of you are staying around here tonight," said Mr. Rook, "the hotel's right there across the street."

I took my bags from Michael and said nothing of the hotel. Originally, I had assumed that all five of us would be lodging in the establishment and returning to the Rooks' farm the following morning, or at least exploring the rest of Friendly. We hadn't even gotten a chance to view the main town.

Rebecca picked up her suitcase and Janie's. "Thank you for your help, Mr. Rook. We appreciate all that you've done."

"Is there anything else I can do for you folks?" he asked.

We shook our heads and told him we couldn't think of anything.

"Good-bye, little lady." He offered his hand to Janie. "It was quite an experience meeting you."

"Good-bye," she said, giving him a shake. "Thank you for the food."

He chuckled, his eyes crinkling. "You're welcome."

The rest of us thanked him and shook his hand, too.

A westbound train rolled into the station with plumes of white steam converting into languid gusts of frozen air above the smokestack. As its iron wheels glided to a stop along the rails, Mr. Vernon Rook—the schoolteacher's son, husband to Eleanor Sunday, witness to the death of Violet Sunday—stepped back into his car and chugged back home to Friendly.

I half-believed he'd been a figment of our imaginations.

Rebecca, Tillie, and Janie gathered up their suitcases and joined the other passengers who were lining up to board. They stood ten or so feet away from Michael and me, their backs toward us, not a single good-bye spoken.

"Isn't Daddy coming with us?" asked Janie with a glimpse over her shoulder.

"Watch my bags for me," said Michael to me, and he walked over to his family with his hands balled by his sides.

My heart flinched. I clutched my briefcase to my chest.

"Rebecca!" he called. "Why aren't you letting Janie say good-bye to me? Why are you lining up like I'm not even here?"

She turned toward him. "Please don't make a scene, Michael."

"Why would I make a scene?"

In response, she swept Janie behind her back with her right arm.

Michael's shoulders tightened. "Why are you hiding her from me?"

"I have something to tell you."

Tillie cast me a look of consternation. I inched toward them, my breathing shallow.

Michael shifted his weight between his legs. "What's going on?"

"As soon as we're back in Oregon"—Rebecca gripped Janie's right shoulder behind her—"I'm putting the house up for sale."

"Why?"

"We're moving to Salem, to be closer to Mother and to put Janie into a city school that will meet her needs as an advanced student."

Michael rubbed the back of his neck and rocked from side to side.

"I've come to realize how much potential she has." Rebecca's gaze flitted toward me for the breadth of a second. "I think the Violet Sunday stories might leave us one day. As I've told you, and as we all witnessed here, they're not showing up as frequently as they used to. But Janie's intelligence will remain."

"But—"

"It's not fair to keep her inside that little schoolhouse. I know that now, and I'm sure you know that, too. Tillie will join us at the end of the school year to find a nearby teaching job."

"Well . . ." Michael swayed for a moment, as though he might collapse, but he righted himself and grabbed his right ear as if it ached. "I'll . . . I'll come visit on Mondays and Tuesdays, then, when the hotel's not so busy."

"No," said Rebecca. "You won't."

"I beg your pardon?"

"I know you, Michael. You're going to keep hounding Janie about the Violet stories, even if she wants to let all of this go. You never give things up easily."

"That's not true, Rebecca. Jesus"—he reached for Janie—"stop hiding her from me."

Rebecca pushed the child farther away. "You make me nervous."

"What are you talking about?"

"I know you're going to continue associating with Miss Lind. I'm willing to bet money that as soon as we climb aboard this train, you're going to check into a hotel room across the street with her."

I stepped forward. "No, that's not true, Mrs. O'Daire . . ."

"Who cares if I do?" snapped Michael. "We're not married anymore, Bec. Miss Lind has sworn she's not publishing any papers about Janie, even though she's pouring all of her goddamn savings into this trip and giving up Christmas with her own family. Did you ever stop to think about that? Have you seen how much time and money this woman has invested into our child, while all you do is berate her and accuse her of having sex with me?"

The people ahead of Rebecca in line spun Michael's way with ugly glowers. A young mother clamped her hands over her little boy's ears.

"Step away from the line, Michael," said Rebecca through her teeth. "You're making a scene."

"Let me at least hug Janie good-bye."

"No!" She backed away with the girl. "I don't want you grabbing her."

"Let me hug my daughter good-bye!" Michael pushed Rebecca aside, which drew shrieks and gasps from the crowd.

"Could we get a police officer over here?" called a man toward the front of the line. "There's a man disturbing the peace. He's hurting a woman and her child."

"No! Christ, no!" Michael pulled away from his daughter. "Don't do this to me, Rebecca. Don't turn me into a criminal right here in front of Janie."

"You *are* a criminal, Michael. You run a speakeasy, for heaven's sake. You're lucky I've let you see Janie as much as I have. You're lucky I haven't contacted the Feds about you."

Tillie jumped out of line and squeezed my hand. "What should I do? Oh, God, how can I make this stop?"

A conductor with thick jowls tromped our way in a no-nonsense march, his fists swinging by his sides. "What's going on down here?"

"I just want to hug my little girl good-bye," said Michael, now in tears. "My ex-wife's taking her away from me, and she's telling me I can't even hug her before they leave."

"I'm scared he's going to grab her and run," said Rebecca, also in tears. "Please make him leave."

"I want to hug Daddy," said Janie, her eyes bloodshot, lips shaking. "I don't like that he's crying. I don't want you yelling at each other."

Michael shifted toward the conductor. "I'll hug her in her front of you, sir. You can all hang onto her shoulders—I really don't care. I just want to tell her good-bye." He reached for Janie again. "Please, Rebecca. Don't rip her away from me like this. I want the best for her, too. I only want the best for her."

Janie took hold of his outstretched hand and sidled around her mother. The conductor muscled his way around Michael and positioned himself next to the child with a meaty paw clamped around her right shoulder. Rebecca clutched Janie's other arm, and the girl resembled a wishbone, about to be broken into two. Tillie and I clung to each other's hands, holding our breath. I feared I'd instigated every appalling second of this family's present battle.

Michael managed to slip an arm around Janie and hug her. She leaned her red hair against his tweed cap amid the tangle of other arms, and Michael's shoulders quaked. I heard him crying without a shred of shame. The other passengers boarded the train with glances over their shoulders.

"All right," said Rebecca, tugging Janie back. "That's enough. We need to board."

Michael staggered to his feet. "You're a selfish human being for banning me from seeing her again, Rebecca. I hope you know that. A selfish bitch who's crazier than your fucking mother."

The conductor yanked him away by both his arms. "All right, sir. You're coming with me to the police station."

"No! Leave me alone." Michael shook the man off him.

"Tillie, what are you doing over there?" cried Rebecca, dragging Janie up the train's steps. "Hurry! We need to board."

"Go." I set Tillie's hand free. "Keep Janie safe. I'll stay and watch over Michael."

She nodded and ran after her sister and niece, while the conductor pulled Michael away from the train with his arms hooked beneath Michael's armpits.

"Let me go!" shouted Michael when Janie's head of red hair disappeared into the train and a porter closed the door behind her. "Let me go! I'm not going to kidnap anybody. I just wanted to tell her good-bye. Oh, God. Janie! I'm so sorry, Janie! I didn't mean to talk to your mother that way."

Michael broke away from the conductor and stumbled toward the train. The conductor latched onto his arm before he could reach the closed door.

"Come along, sir. Time to pay a visit to our friendly neighborhood police station."

The train chugged to a start.

"Jesus Christ," said Michael, "I'm not going to disturb the peace anymore. Look—she's gone. You let her take my little girl away." He squirmed and struggled to free himself again. "Just leave me alone. It's almost Christmas Eve, and I've just lost my daughter. Leave me alone."

The conductor loosened his grip, and Michael tripped sideways, holding out his arms to catch his balance.

"Watch my bags," he called to me. "Take them to the hotel for me. I need to think. Oh, Christ."

He turned and lumbered across the street. A car skidded to a stop to avoid plowing him down, but Michael kept going, disappearing into the night.

CHAPTER 26

I obtained two rooms at the Brighton Hotel but remembered nothing at all of the face of the man who'd jangled the keys my way, nor of the décor of the lobby, which may have included a Christmas tree. I paid the clerk to deliver Michael's bag to his room and whisked myself behind the closed door of another room, one story higher, where I dropped down on the edge of a bed that smelled of the colognes of strangers. My head throbbed from the echoes of Rebecca and Michael's war over Janie—the pushing and pulling, the tears, the pleas, the panic, the rage. I feared Michael had wandered off to die. I worried Janie now sobbed in that westbound train, traumatized even more than during her dreams of Violet's drowning.

I covered my face with my hands.

Oh, God, I thought. *What am I doing here? What have I done?*

All of the successes of the day spent with the Rooks shattered to pieces.

I debated calling Bea for advice, but thought better. She would only chastise me for giving up time with our own family. She would remind me of my status as an interloper.

Interloper.

That's what I'd become.

School psychologists did not climb aboard trains with students' families during the Christmas holiday. They did not bother strangers in other states to explore bizarre phenomena that would make ministers and regular psychologists quiver with discomfort. They did not cause women to shout lewd accusations about their sex lives in front of a crowd of people in railway stations. They did not consider throwing away their entire careers to jump headfirst into the world of psychical research.

And yet . . . part of me didn't care if that's what my life was to become—if that's how people viewed me.

Crazy reincarnationist.

Bossy go-getter.

Slut.

I had tried to be a good girl. Oh, my Lord, after hopping into boys' beds, how I worked until my brain ached; how diligently I had played by the rules. I had stopped seeing men altogether, dressed in skirts that fell well past my knees, and wed myself to a "female-appropriate" stratum of a male career.

And where had such sweetness landed me?

Tell me, I asked myself as I held my head between my hands in that stagnant hotel room that lashed me with its silence, *why should I care about my reputation, when my reputation is stifling me? Killing me? When everyone assumes the worst anyway?*

THE ONE FEATURE I remembered from the narrow hotel lobby was a wooden telephone with an attached coin box. Once I composed myself and powdered my nose, I ventured downstairs with my coin purse in hand, my chin raised, my footsteps steady. The scents of broiled steaks and seasoned soups drifted through an open doorway that led to an adjoining restaurant, just a few yards beyond the telephone, which hung on a dark wooden wall that separated the lobby from the staircase.

"Is there something I can help you with, miss?" asked the clerk from behind the front desk.

"I would like to use the telephone."

He nodded toward the phone. "Help yourself."

"Thank you." I walked over to the contraption and lifted the earpiece from the latch.

"Number, please?" asked a female voice at the other end of the line.

I moved my lips closer to the mouthpiece. "I need to place a station-to-station call."

"Please tell me the long-distance number you would like to reach, as well as your name and number."

"I'm trying to reach the Hotel Yesternight outside of Du Bois, Nebraska. My name is Miss Alice Lind, and I'm calling from"—I squinted at the numbers written on the phone's information card—"Sycamore 4322."

A short pause ensued, during which the operator must have been jotting down my information. "Thank you, Miss Lind," she then said. "Please hang up while I put the connection through. I'll call you back at Sycamore 4322. The charge will be twenty-five cents for the first three minutes of conversation."

"Thank you. I appreciate your help." I hung up.

Down the hall, the clerk lifted his head of thinning brown hair.

The youthful fullness of his face and smoothness of his skin indicated that he wasn't much older than I—perhaps thirty at most—but his hair, swept over a bare patch on top, fought to age him. That balding business was one of the only cruel jokes men's bodies played upon them, or so it seemed to me. I wondered if it was a fair trade for pregnancies and monthly bleeding, for drooping breasts and ballooning bottoms and the distinct notion that one was being punished with illegitimate children, while the chap involved simply got cozy with a brand-new girl . . .

I strolled over to the clerk on the thick heels of my oxfords. "Do you happen to have anything I could read for fun while I wait for the operator to call me back? I'm afraid I've already read all of the books I brought with me on the train."

"Um, well . . ." He pivoted around and bobbed about, as if he wasn't sure whether he should bend down and scrounge around for reading material on some lower shelf, or if he should just admit that he didn't have anything. "I have a railway timetable." He stood up straight and slid a folded piece of paper across the counter.

"That would be quite helpful, actually. Thank you." I picked up the schedule and gave it a cursory glance. "After I receive my call, I'm planning to eat in the adjoining café. If the man whose room I reserved—my brother—if he enters the hotel, will you please direct him to the restaurant? He's blond, in his late twenties, and stands close to six feet tall."

"Certainly, miss."

"You haven't seen him yet, have you?" I rose to my toes and looked out the window beside me. "I'm a little worried about him."

"It's not that large of a town. I'm sure he won't get lost."

"I'm sure you're right. Thank you." I meandered back down toward the telephone and opened the timetable to study my options for traveling to Nebraska. The telephone hovered in the corner of my right eye, but its little gold bells stayed silent.

With a sudden squeal of arctic air, a man opened the front door. I jerked my chin upward, but, instead of Michael, I found a young brunet couple, huddled together. The gentleman of the pair wrapped half of his coat around the young woman, like a bird nestling its young under a wing. I stepped over to one of the lobby windows and scanned the darkening streets.

Seven minutes later, the telephone rang. I lunged for the machine and grabbed the earpiece, and the operator instructed me to deposit my coins, which I did with sweating fingers.

After the money clattered into place, a male voice traveled down the line: "Hello, this is Mr. Al Harkey of the Hotel Yesternight."

I tottered; my knees buckled. Precious seconds of my three minutes flitted away.

"Hello?" asked the man again.

"Hello," I said, breathing into the mouthpiece. "I would like to inquire about the availability of rooms at your hotel."

"When would you like to stay?" he asked.

"As soon as possible. Are you closed for Christmas?"

"No, we only close for a week during March when my wife and I celebrate our wedding anniversary. We're open through Christmas, specifically for those of you Spiritualists who only have time to visit during the holidays."

"Oh, I'm not a—" I shut my mouth, not wanting to waste more time by explaining that I wasn't a Spiritualist exactly. "I plan to travel by train from Brighton, Kansas, to Du Bois, Nebraska, tomorrow. Would you happen to have a room available for me tomorrow night?"

"Yes, there's plenty of room. We had two other guests scheduled, but they canceled due to the weather. May I get your name?"

"Miss Alice Lind."

There was a pause at the other end. "Did you say 'Lind'? L-I-N-D?"

"Yes, I did."

"Now, that's odd . . . Just yesterday a telegram arrived for someone with . . . I believe it was addressed to someone with your last name."

"Really?" My heart gave a queer jump that made my fingertips tingle. "No one's expecting me to arrive there. Are you sure it was 'Lind'? It's easy to mistake the name for another one."

"I could be wrong. I'll have to ask my wife where she put it. How many are in your party, Miss Lind?"

I hesitated, glancing out the window once again. "One . . . perhaps two. My husband isn't sure if he'll manage to take time off work."

"Oh, I'm so sorry to hear that."

I cringed at my own lie—at my hubris for assuming that Michael might abandon his troubles and tag along with me. "Thank you," I said. "How would I best reach the hotel when I arrive at the depot?"

"A train arrives at a quarter past three. Try to get yourself on that one. I'll drive into Du Bois and pick you up."

"That's awfully kind of you. Are you sure you wouldn't mind?"

"Blizzard conditions are expected tomorrow night. I recommend you don't arrive any later than that particular train."

"I'll be there at a quarter past three. Thank you so much for your help."

"I'm looking forward to meeting you and your husband, Mrs.—or did you—did you say 'Miss'?"

"It's *Mrs.* Lind. Thank you. I'm looking forward to meeting you, too. Good-bye."

I hung up and attempted to walk to supper on legs that wobbled and bowed.

AFTER DINING, I inquired again at the front desk about the arrival of my "brother" but received a headshake and an apology from the clerk. Just to be certain Michael hadn't shown up without anyone noticing, I opened the door to his hotel room. Only his tan leather suitcase resided within those snug quarters.

"May I sit down here in the lobby and read while I wait for the gentleman?" I asked the clerk, a Willa Cather novel that I'd purchased on the coast tucked under my left arm. "I wouldn't be taking the chairs from any other guests, would I?"

Only two chairs occupied the lobby, scarlet ones, planted next to a small table bearing a three-foot-tall Christmas tree.

"Certainly you may read down here," said the clerk with a little brush of his fingers through that thin patch on top. "Most of our guests are out visiting family right now. They'll return once they tire of the relatives whose houses they didn't want to sleep in in the first place."

I chuckled and thanked him and noted that a clock mounted on the wall behind his desk showed the time as half past seven. I promised myself that if Michael didn't arrive by eight thirty, I would seek out the local police station.

Did he perhaps hop aboard the next train? I wondered. *Would*

*he have dared risking the ire of that bulldog of a conductor a second
time around?*

I seated myself in the rightmost chair of the two and leaned forward to better speak to the clerk from around the Christmas tree.
"Are there any speakeasies in Brighton?"

The fellow cleared his throat. "I wouldn't know that information, miss."

"All right. Fair enough." I sank back in the chair and read.

Eight o'clock arrived.

Eight fifteen.

Eight twenty.

The worst possible scenarios flooded my mind: Michael throwing himself off of a bridge. Michael strangling a woman who resembled Rebecca. Thieves strangling Michael. Bloodshed. Arrests.
Sanity trials.

At eight thirty, I shifted about and peeked out the window. The
lobby sweltered from the oppressive heat of a fireplace that blazed
as though fighting to warm a castle. I fanned myself with my book
and struggled to breathe air that seared my lungs.

"Are you all right, miss?" asked the clerk.

"Yes, I'm just worried about . . . my brother. It's getting awfully
late."

At that, the door opened.

Michael stumbled across the threshold with such a clumsy to-do
that his cap slid off his head and plopped onto the floorboards. He
laughed at the sight of the little mound of tweed splattered in front
of his feet.

"Michael!" I rose from my chair. "I was just telling this man
how worried I've been about you."

Michael flashed a grin and sauntered my way, reeking of liquor. His eyes had become two faint-blue life preservers, drowning in a bloodshot sea.

"Do you remember, Alice"—he pointed straight at me—"you asked me what Vlad the Impaler would be like if he returned for a second life?" He stopped in front of me and tottered. "Well, I figured it out. Good old Vlad came back from the dead as Rebecca Simpkin O'Daire, queen of the fucking whores."

"Hey!" called the clerk from down the way. "Mind your language, sir."

"Yes, please stop cussing." I brushed snow off of Michael's right shoulder. "I understand why you needed to drink so much—really, I do. But don't get yourself arrested. That won't solve a thing."

"You care about me so deeply, Alice. Don't you?" He placed his hands on both of my cheeks and leaned in so close, his breath stung my nostrils. "You really and truly care about me. And you care about my Janie."

"Yes, I do." I grabbed hold of his wrists. "So please don't say or do anything else that would spoil my compassion."

"You're an angel sent from heaven."

"No, not quite." I leaned my face away from his booze-soaked lips, which lingered rather close to my own mouth. "Do go to bed, Michael, and sleep off today. If you behave nicely, I'll be here to help you in the morning."

"I went to the depot . . . to buy a ticket back home." His eyes pooled with tears. "But that son of a bitch . . ." He glanced over his shoulder at the hotel clerk before lowering his voice. "That *conductor* was prowling around out there again. I don't understand why Bec took her away from me."

"I know . . ."

"I don't understand. I helped solve the mystery of Violet Sunday. I gave Janie everything—*everything*—she's ever needed, and I helped prove it, damn it. We proved she's not crazy."

Still holding his wrists, I lured his hands away from my face. "Mrs. O'Daire is no doubt in a state of shock after everything she experienced at the Rooks' house today. She needs time to sort out what she's feeling right now. And so do you."

"*You* wouldn't do that to a fellow, would you?" he asked. "Take away his child?"

"I'm in no position to answer that question."

"Do you know how badly I want to kiss you right now?" He cupped a hand around my neck, but I managed to duck my head and grab hold of one of his forearms before he could bring his mouth any closer.

"Is everything all right, miss?" asked the clerk.

"Yes." I gripped Michael by his biceps and wheeled him around. "I just need to steer my *brother* up to his room so he can sleep the day off."

"Alice . . ."

"Quiet!" I snapped at Michael, and I strapped his left arm over my shoulders. With some prodding and teeth-gritting and swearing on my part, I guided him up an endless staircase upholstered in fabric as green and slick as moss.

"Where are we going?" he asked in the landing, and directly thereafter he attempted to straighten a portrait of a bowl of fruit that didn't need straightening to begin with.

I shoved the key into the lock of the first room at the top of the stairs. "Here"—I swung open the door—"this is for you. Go inside. Collapse onto the bed. Sleep until you feel better. When you're conscious and sober again, I'd like to speak to you about my plans for tomorrow."

"Plans?"

"I'll tell you tomorrow."

"Oh, Alice . . . lovely Alice . . ." He stroked his fingertips through the ends of my short hair. "Come in here with me. Stay the night. I want you. You must know I want you."

"Go inside. Get some sleep."

"Where are *you* sleeping?"

"Never you mind." I nudged him into the room and shut the door before he could even think of slurring his way through any more professions of love.

 CHAPTER 27

In the morning, I kneeled down on the floor outside of Michael's room and slid a note beneath his door:

I intend to breakfast in the adjoining restaurant before boarding a late-morning train. Please join me. I am certain you could use a cup of coffee to boost you over the painful hump of that inevitable hangover, and I would like to speak to you about the next phase of my investigation. I am not yet ready to abandon the line of research that brought me here.

Sincerely yours,
Alice Lind

Downstairs, a waiter wished me a happy Christmas Eve and brought me a breakfast of grapefruit, French toast, and bacon. I nursed a bitter cup of coffee while gazing out the window at a nickel-colored sky that promised snow. No other customer dined in any of the wicker chairs surrounding me, but the solitude brought me solace. The soft clinks of pans the cook washed in the nearby kitchen reminded me of home, of Mother baking sweet mincemeat pies for the Christmas Day feast, and of Margery and Bea wrapping presents for Margie's children. The savory scent of the bacon somewhat mimicked the mulled spices the others would be enjoying in warm drinks after dinner. I craved roasted chestnuts and gingerbread—and the Christmas port my father somehow acquired every December.

"Do you mind if I join you?" asked a voice I almost didn't recognize.

I lifted my head to find Michael bracing his left hand against the curved back of the chair across from me. He squinted from the lamplight shining down on the table, and discomfort creased his forehead. A chalky paleness robbed his lips and cheeks of their usual color.

"Please"—I nodded toward the chair—"have a seat. I'll call over the waiter so we can order you some coffee."

"Thank you." He sank into the chair with the slowest of movements, as though lowering arthritic bones into a warm bath.

I ordered his coffee, as well as slices of hot, unbuttered toast to soothe his stomach. The waiter bustled away with his chin held high, clearly pleased to have someone to fuss over in that otherwise empty restaurant.

I cut through a slice of French toast and observed the manner in which my breakfast companion leaned his elbows against the table and cradled his head in his hands. I didn't dare point out that my mother always chided us for elbows placed on tables.

"How are you?" I asked.

He closed his eyes and groaned. "I'm not sure how to answer that question."

No more than two minutes later, the coffee and toast arrived, which perked Michael up a tad. He drew hesitant sips, his fingers wrapped around the white mug, and the wincing grew less frequent as the skin between his brows ceased puckering.

I allowed him to relish the silence for a while before asking, "Did you see in my note that I'm proceeding with my research today?"

"I did."

"I mentioned the subject last night, but I doubt you remember . . ."

"I remember some of the things you said . . . and what I said." His gaze flitted my way long enough to tell me what he remembered.

My neck warmed. I took a bite of French toast.

He cleared his throat. "Have you decided after all to write a paper about Janie?"

"No, I couldn't do that. I intend instead to explore another potential case of a child who may have experienced a past life." Another bite; another gulp. "I've booked a room at the Hotel Yesternight in Nebraska."

He raised his eyes. "Why on earth are you going there?"

"Do you remember how I said that Janie circled the word *Yesternight* when I gave her a list of Kansas names?"

"Yes . . ."

I fussed with my napkin on my lap. "I didn't tell you before, but I pulled that particular name from my own imagination, to see if Janie would choose random words with the same frequency as she would select real Kansas place names. Her identification of Yesternight intrigued me back when I tested her, but my interest flourished when I learned from my sister Bea that I spoke of a place called Yesternight when I was quite young."

"Aha!"

"'Aha,' what?"

Michael lowered his mug to the table, and his eyes brightened with the first glimmer of a smile since he and Rebecca had quarreled. "I was right after all."

"Right about what?"

"About you." He replanted his elbows against the table. "You're the child you spoke of the day before we boarded the train—the other girl haunted by a past life."

I dabbed the napkin against my lips. "Before meeting you and Janie, not once would I have believed that a past life lay behind all of my troubles—the nightmares, the strange behaviors . . ." I crossed my legs and debated which of my oddities to share with him.

Michael picked at the brittle crust of his toast and waited for me to continue, as though he had now assumed the role of school psychologist, and I the concerned parent.

"I would tell people I was born in the Great Plains," I decided to say, not daring to mention the beatings, of course. "And I insisted that my name was Nell, which for a short while caused me to worry that I might somehow be Nel from the Other House."

"You thought . . ." His brow furrowed. He leaned forward with a crackle of the wicker of his chair. "You believed you were Violet's husband?"

"Oh, that sounds so odd." I covered my eyes with a hand. "But, yes, for a brief moment, I did. This all occurred when Janie showed an interest in Yesternight."

"Why didn't you ever tell me?"

"I told Bea, and her reactions made me feel like a paranoid idiot. I most certainly didn't want you viewing me that way." I took a sip of my drink and took solace in the coffee's warmth bathing my insides. "In any case"—I cleared my throat—"now that I know more about Nelson Jessen, that theory is long gone. The fact that Mr. Rook described the Hotel Yesternight as an infamous murder house, however, has me all the more worried about my possible connection to it."

Michael chewed on his bread and studied me with a contemplative focus to his eyes—the same "should I believe this person?" sort of look that I used to direct toward him.

"Tell me the truth," I said, now bracing my own elbows on the table, "do you think my newfound preoccupation with my own potential past life is simply a desire to find the same peace of mind that Janie found? A trace of envy, perhaps?" I swallowed. "Or do my early childhood experiences sound at all similar to what you observed in her?"

He shook his head. "I'm not a psychologist. I don't think I can adequately answer those questions."

"I suppose I would like to find what Janie found in Friendly. That satisfaction she experienced when she climbed back into the car yesterday; those words she said—'I'm ready.' That's what I long to discover for myself . . . if, in fact, I'm somehow linked to Yesternight."

Using my fork, I stirred a piece of French toast through a pool of syrup and watched Michael sip his coffee. Our eyes met. My heartrate tripled over a question I found myself on the verge of asking.

I took a deep breath and simply asked it: "Would you care to accompany me to Nebraska?"

Color returned to his face. He lowered his mug to the table and breathed as though attempting to recover from a trace of shock. "Is that what you want?"

"I would prefer to have you there with me . . . as the person who first led me down this road. As the person who changed my entire system of belief."

"That was Janie's doing, not mine."

"You played a principal role in my transformation."

He nodded and gave a small smile. "I suppose I did."

I averted my gaze to the piece of toast that I continued to drown in syrup with my fork. "Furthermore," I said, "I don't believe that sending you back home on your own on Christmas Eve would be wise. I would like to ensure you're safe and well cared for."

"Aren't they expecting you to arrive alone?"

"I told them my 'husband' might be joining me if he can take time off of work."

He held his mug just below his chin, and I stirred and stirred and stirred.

"Where would I sleep?" he asked, but directly thereafter the waiter sidled over to our table and inquired how we were doing.

"We're fine," I told him, my face burning.

"Thank you," said Michael.

"Splendid. I'll bring the coffeepot around in a few minutes."

"Lovely."

The fellow strode away across the black and white tiles.

I gripped the handle of my fork. "You may stay with me."

"Are you sure?"

Again, I lowered my eyes. "I'd have some stipulations about the time we spend together."

"Oh? And what are they?"

"I can't discuss them here, Michael. Just know that I refuse to . . ." I checked to make sure the waiter remained in the back kitchen. "I absolutely cannot have a child. I have nothing in the way of precautions, so unless you do—"

"There are other things we can do," he said, and he brought his mug to his lips and took another drink, his eyes upon me.

I laid the damp fork on the side of my plate, where the prongs wept golden-brown droplets. A smile tugged at the right corner of my mouth.

The same smile inched across his face.

Oh, God, I thought. *What am I doing? What have I done?*

MICHAEL AND I huddled together beneath the yellow overhang of Brighton Depot, on the far right edge of a sparse collection of passengers who discussed the nip in the air and a storm stalking the rolling hills in the distance. Michael had hauled my hundred-pound suitcases for me and joked that I'd lugged my entire wardrobe with me, which, in fact, I had, due to my vagabond lifestyle. I'd toted his bag, which weighed nothing at all, as though he'd packed merely feathers.

Down at the far end of the platform, the conductor who had threatened to cart Michael off to the cops pulled a pocket watch out of his coat and checked the time. Michael turned us away from the man with his arm around me.

"He might not even recognize you," I said.

"I don't care if he does." He pulled me closer against his black coat. "He's not letting another beloved girl slip away from me."

We stared at each other for one of those searching types of moments—the "should I kiss you?" question in our eyes—and then he bent his face toward mine and kissed me for the first time. My entire body thrummed. We kissed again, until the conductor called out, "All aboard!"

We found our seats in the back section of the first passenger car, and again we nestled together and drank up each other's warmth, even though the train itself exuded heat. Michael smelled musky and bathed, his breath peppermint sweet, and I forgot all about the whiskey-soaked lips that had tried to kiss me the night before. Onlookers may have mistaken us for newlyweds. I felt like a newlywed, tucked up beside him, our mouths unable to stay away from each other for more than three seconds.

"You'll need a ring on your finger if we're to pretend that we're married," he said, and he twisted the high school ring with the sapphire off his right hand.

"I'm not sure it will fit properly . . ."

He glided the cold band over the knuckle of my left ring finger. It wobbled and slipped, and we joked about keeping it in place with chewing gum.

He then kissed the length of that newly adorned finger of mine and pulled me close again.

I pushed aside memories of him insulting and hollering at his ex-wife. I forgot all about my graduate school lovers. I even momentarily stopped thinking of Michael as a father. Life would begin anew. I would open a door to the next phase of my studies, perhaps even align myself with the American Society for Psychical Research. I would return to a time in which I allowed myself to love a man.

For the moment, we were Mr. and Mrs. Lind, a married couple journeying to a rural inn for the Christmas holiday, unfettered by our pasts.

Part III
NELL

CHAPTER 28

Christmas Eve 1925

A pale-faced young fellow in a black Homburg hat waved us down at the snow-capped depot in Du Bois, Nebraska. Michael and I were the only two people to disembark the train at a quarter past three that Christmas Eve, and yet I looked behind us to see if the young man might have been waving at someone else.

The fellow strode our way with his cheeks glowing bright pink from the cold—the pink being the only semblance of color on that sun-deprived complexion of his. He had twiggy eyebrows and coal-black eyes and appeared to have been no older than twenty.

"Mr. and Mrs. Lind, I presume?" he asked.

Michael coughed into his hand, as though trying not to either laugh or object at being called "Mr. Lind," but I stepped forward and said, "Yes, we're the Linds. Are you the man to whom I spoke on the phone? Mr. Harkey, was it?"

"Yes, Albert Harkey." He shook our hands. "Welcome to Nebraska."

I smiled. "Thank you. How kind of you to drive out here to pick us up on Christmas Eve."

"It's no trouble at all. Mabel, my wife, is cooking supper right now, and we've got a fire waiting for you in the hearth. It's an English tradition to tell ghost stories on Christmas Eve, you know, so you're arriving on a spectacular night."

"Are you English?" asked Michael with a sidelong glance at the rather rural-sounding Mr. Harkey, who most certainly didn't enunciate words like an Englishman.

"No," said the fellow, "but what with the blizzard coming in, and the Christmas Eve timing . . . I hope you're prepared to voyage deep into the diabolical past of our beautiful, wretched establishment tonight."

Michael and I exchanged a look, which Mr. Harkey must have noticed, for he swiftly added, "You *are* coming for the hotel's haunted past, aren't you? Oh, jeez—" His face sank; he pinched the rim of his Homburg. "I hope you're aware that this isn't just a regular old inn."

"We've heard about the hotel's reputation," I said, "but it's the history I'd like to explore; not ghosts."

"Well, you'll certainly get the history, ma'am. May I help you with your bags?"

"Yes." Michael passed one of my suitcases his way. "Thank you."

Mr. Harkey picked up my second bag from the ground at Michael's side and then wheeled around to guide us past the departing train. Up ahead, next to a patch of sidewalk caked in fresh, unshoveled snow, awaited a chocolate-and cream-colored vehicle that looked to have been a former delivery truck of some sort. On the enclosed back compartment, in flamboyant red lettering, someone had painted the name THE HOTEL YESTERNIGHT.

I lagged behind with Michael and asked him under my breath, "Does the hotel's name on that vehicle strike you as the type of lettering found on theater posters?"

Michael breathed a curt laugh. "We don't have any theaters in Gordon Bay, Alice."

"Oh. That's right."

"Why do you ask?" He slowed his pace. "Are you having second thoughts about this place?"

I sighed, still preoccupied with the melodramatic flourishes on the truck. "I'm worried it's going to be another tourist attraction that capitalizes on the allure of death and spirits, like Mrs. Winchester's house in California."

Michael squeezed my hand. "Aren't we here because of the allure of death and spirits? Isn't that what all of this is about?"

"It's not the same at all. What we experienced with Janie was so pure—so sacred and utterly untainted by commercialism."

"But—"

"We're investigators, Michael; not children buying tickets to an amusement park ride. I want my own experience with the past to be as sublime as hers." I tightened my grip on my briefcase and called out to our host, "Mr. Harkey, is the hotel still located on the same plot of land on which it was originally built?"

The fellow poked his head out of the back of the truck, into which he'd been cramming my belongings. "Yes, it is."

"Hmm . . ." I turned back to Michael. "I'd still like to go, then.

Surely the memories of the house itself would remain, despite any theatrics the Harkeys might have added."

Michael pressed his lips together and nodded. "All right."

Mr. Harkey bustled around from the back of the truck and opened the passenger-side door for us. "Please, make yourselves comfortable."

"Thank you." I climbed in first, adjusted myself in the middle of a hard wooden seat, and situated my briefcase on my lap.

Michael slid in beside me. We joined hands and watched Mr. Harkey pick up Michael's suitcase with a brisk waddle that caused the Homburg to slip down over his eyes. His breath fogged up the air in front of his face like plumes of Tillie's cigarette smoke.

Michael shook his head over the fellow. "How old do you think he is? Twenty-two at most?"

I was about to reply that young Mr. Harkey likely worked for his daddy, but I remembered Michael had embarked upon the hotel business because of his own father.

Mr. Harkey slammed the door to the back compartment shut, and the truck hiccupped forward with a wave of motion that made me momentarily seasick. Thereafter, he opened the driver's side door, adjusted one of the levers on the dashboard, and jogged around to the front of the truck, where he cranked the vehicle to a jolting start.

"Everyone ready?" he asked, jumping into the car beside me.

"Yes," I said, and I tightened my fingers around Michael's.

Mr. Harkey shut the door against the cold. "Off we go, then." He thrust the gear shift lever forward and sent us rumbling down the flat streets of Du Bois.

Before long, the town fell to the wayside, and we cruised into a pure-white expanse of endless countryside that stretched to a gray horizon. A handful of houses and stables marked the locations of farms in the distance, but a palpable sense of desolation—of trekking across a harsh and deserted planet—made me fear we were the only souls alive for miles. The temperature inside the truck dropped by at least ten degrees, and the skin beneath my gloves grew so frigid compared to Michael's fingers surrounding my hand.

"How long have you worked at the Hotel Yesternight?" I asked Mr. Harkey.

"Mabel and I bought the place, oh . . . let me see . . ." He scratched his smooth chin. "About two and a half years ago now. My grandmother grew up with Mrs. Gunderson in Kansas City, so I'd heard stories about the hotel ever since I was a youngster in knee pants."

"Who is Mrs. Gunderson?" I asked.

"She's the star of the show." Mr. Harkey smirked with mischief in his eyes. "You'll hear all about her tonight. For now, just sit back and enjoy the ride. We'll be there in about thirty minutes."

"Is it that much farther?" asked Michael.

"Oh, yes. Yesternight's desolation is the very reason behind its infamy."

I sidled closer to Michael, who leaned his lips next to my ear and whispered, "We should have gone to Kansas City and checked ourselves into a swanky hotel."

I whispered back, "Do you want me to ask him to return us to the station?"

"A blizzard is coming. I don't think there's anywhere else we can go."

"I'm sorry if this is too much . . ."

"I'm already feeling dark inside," he said. "I'm just worried."

"I'll take good care of you."

Michael shifted his focus to the barren countryside outside his window, and although he didn't utter a single word about Janie, his back stooped with the weight of the little girl's shadow.

THE HOTEL YESTERNIGHT arose on the edge of a snow-bound field. The slope of the shingled rooftop emerged first, along with a narrow chimney and the boxy silhouette of a structure that looked to have been a shed or an outhouse.

Mr. Harkey drove the truck down the slick road with great fortitude and care, but every twenty or so feet the tires lost traction, and we skidded and swerved, which made my heart jump about.

Another half mile or so farther, more details of the hotel manifested: a curved porch supported by Grecian columns; a half-dozen windows peering out from the front wall; an attic room tucked beneath an ornate gable; paneled siding painted one shade darker than the snow itself. The bare branches of sycamore trees stooped over the shingles, and in them sat a single crow, bringing to mind the old rhyme about the meaning behind magpies.

One for sorrow,
Two for mirth,
Three for a wedding,
And four for a birth . . .

I did not recognize the house as being a place I had visited in some long-ago past, but a cold sense of dread, of homesickness for Portland, froze my blood into liquid ice. Snow pelted the windshield and the vanishing road, both ahead and behind us, burying us deep into the prairie.

"Are you all right, Alice?" asked Michael, his voice lowered again so our driver wouldn't hear. "Do you recognize the place?"

"No," I said in a whisper. "I simply miss my family back home all of a sudden. I'm feeling a twinge of darkness similar to what you just mentioned."

He swallowed near my ear.

"Everything all right?" asked Mr. Harkey.

"Has the place always been in such tip-top shape?" asked Michael, presumably to lighten the mood. "Or did you and your wife restore it?"

"Oh, you should have seen the old girl when we bought it. She was *ghastly*. Windows missing, paint stripped off by sun and wind, the top floor collapsing into the bottom one . . . We paid a pretty penny to gussy her up." He slowed the truck and turned onto a driveway piling up with snow. Flakes as large as the palm of my hand slapped against the windshield, and the vehicle jerked forward with an erratic dance. "Well . . . here we are, Mr. and Mrs. Lind. The old Gunderson residence."

Anxiety gripped my chest at the sight of all those plain, tall windows staring us down. Michael fidgeted beside me, and I could tell by the way he peeked up at the attic level from the tops of his eyes that the house disquieted him, too.

"To the north lies a small lake that you'll hear about soon," said Mr. Harkey, fighting to maneuver the bucking vehicle the rest of the way across the drive. "And to the south you'll find the dormant fruit and vegetable gardens."

My neck ached from all of the jerking and grinding.

"My wife is quite the gardener," he continued, a little louder, over the whines of the engine. "She's become adept at pickling and canning ever since we moved here. She's a pip, as you'll soon see. Aw, hell!" He threw up his hands when the truck wouldn't budge another inch. "We're going to have to get out here. Sorry, folks." He turned off the motor. "I know the snow's a little deep here."

"That's fine." Michael unlocked his hands from mine. "I'll carry Alice if it's too much for her to wade through it."

"Now there's a chivalrous husband." Mr. Harkey smiled and shoved open his door, which had nearly frozen shut.

"*Do* you want me to carry you?" asked Michael after our driver left us. "I don't mind . . . if you'd prefer not to risk brushing your stockings against snow . . ."

I blinked to appease a stinging in my eyes, which refused to look away from the awaiting house.

Michael covered one of my hands with his. "What is it?"

"I feel so selfish." I gulped, my throat burning. "I've brought us both to the farthest reaches of civilization, just to figure out my own problems."

"You'll find answers here; I'm sure of it."

"My sister Bea would kill me if she knew what I was doing right now. Or she'd send me straight to an asylum, which is what this place reminds me of."

"I've seen an asylum, and it doesn't look like this." Michael forced his own door open and clambered out into the snow. His boots, along with the bottom six inches of his trousers, sank out of sight. "Come along. I'll help you out."

I took a breath and joined him out there in the cold, my galoshes sinking and crunching into the snow just like his. The flakes continued to accumulate, even as we stood there and gathered our bearings, and a sub-freezing wind pummeled my ears.

Mr. Harkey threw open the back door of the truck and fetched my two bags. Michael squished his way toward him and grabbed his own suitcase.

Up at the house, a woman appeared on the porch, a red scarf wrapped around her neck, short copper hair blowing in the wind beneath a knitted hat. "Do you need any help, Al?" she called.

"No, we've got everything, Mabel. Just make sure to add another log to the fire so these two can warm up."

The woman disappeared back into the house, and the rest of us waded through the snow toward the porch she'd just left. My legs ached from the cold with such unbearable pain that I forgot for a moment the nature of the place I sought to reach; I forgot why I was there. My brain focused solely on the promise of a fireplace—of heat and thaw and comfort. A stovepipe at the back of the house pumped out the aroma of a sweet-scented meat.

At the top of the porch stood the closed front door, painted a luscious shade of black, with an oval windowpane mounted in the center. Beside the door hung a wrought-iron sign bearing the hotel's name in golden letters, and below the sign I saw a verse from the Book of Hebrews, carved into a weathered slab of wood:

FORGET NOT TO SHOW LOVE UNTO STRANGERS: FOR THEREBY SOME HAVE ENTERTAINED ANGELS UNAWARES . . .

The quote assuaged my nerves a smidgen, but, still, I felt out of sorts.

Mr. Harkey jogged up the porch steps ahead of us with my bags banging against his outer thighs, his thick boots thumping with a ruckus that gave me a headache. He lowered the suitcases to the porch and swung the door open. "Please, step inside. Shed your damp coats. Warm yourselves."

Michael and I stamped our feet on a coarse brown mat, shaking small avalanches of snow from the sides of our boots, and we entered a long front hall, flanked on the right by a staircase that rose to a darkened landing. I determined the sweet roasting meat to be venison and also smelled mutton chops.

Mr. Harkey closed the door behind us, and with chattering teeth and violent shivers, we peeled off our coats, gloves, and hats. My body adjusted to that painful transition from numbness and constricted veins to defrosting skin and blood prickling back to life.

To our left, a room accessible by opened pocket doors radiated heat from a stone fireplace, to which the woman with the copper hair tended. Kerosene lamps flickered from walls the yellowish tan of tobacco-stained teeth—an ugly color I did not care for in the slightest. No pictures lined either the hallway or the parlor. Nothing about the place, aside from the fireplace, imparted comfort or hospitality.

The woman hung the fireplace poker on a rack of tools and got to her feet, revealing a young face with brown doe's eyes and plump cheeks. "Welcome, Mr. and Mrs. Lind." She came toward us, her right hand extended. "I'm Mabel Harkey. So nice to have you join us this Christmas Eve. Merry Christmas."

"Merry Christmas," we said in return, and we shook her hand, her skin toasty from the fire. She couldn't have stood any taller than four foot ten, and I felt an Amazon compared to her, even at five foot four.

"Mrs. Lind said they've come for the history," said Mr. Harkey, my bags still in hand.

"I've been interested in this hotel since I was a child in Oregon," I felt compelled to explain. Michael's gold band on my left ring finger slid over the hump of my knuckle, which sent a nervous quaver through my voice. "I finally acquired some time off of work to visit. This is the only week we could manage to travel here."

"You came from Kansas?" asked Mrs. Harkey.

"We did," said Michael, his voice as timorous as mine, even though his words weren't a lie precisely.

"You must want to freshen up after your travels, then." Mrs. Harkey put a hand to her husband's right shoulder. "Let's allow the Linds to get situated upstairs, shall we?"

"How much time until appetizers and drinks?" asked her husband.

"About fifteen minutes, but we can delay if these two need me to press any clothing before dinner. I can heat up the iron on the stove."

"That reminds me," added her husband, "I should warn that we have no electricity . . . and no indoor plumbing. I'm afraid you'll need to brave the elements to reach the outhouse or else use a chamber pot."

I forced myself not to grimace at those unappealing options, and out of the corner of my eye I caught Michael clenching his jaw.

"Bring down any garments that you might need pressed." Mrs. Harkey bustled down the hallway, calling over her shoulder, "I'll go heat up the iron right now."

Mr. Harkey lumbered toward the stairs with my bags. "Come along with me. I'll show you to your room."

Michael grabbed up his suitcase, and we followed our host up the staircase. Because it was an older house, the steps naturally creaked and bellowed below our feet and added to the drama of the establishment. Mr. Harkey plodded up with slow and deliberate steps, as though drawing gasping moans from the wood on purpose. I disapproved of him a little more because of it.

In the landing up above, the dim afternoon light bled into the shadows of evening. Our host led us to a room to our immediate right.

"Here you are." He opened an anemic wooden door and carried my suitcases to a space on the floor at the base of a four-post bed. A quilt the pale green of lime rickeys covered the mattress.

I entered the room ahead of Michael and again found bare walls and very little in the way of decoration. A bouquet of scarlet geraniums filled a thick vase made of crystal on a table next to the left side of the bed. Against the wall to my right stood an unassuming pine wardrobe, as well as a single chair. I smelled the venison from downstairs, but another odor—a dankness, a sourness—pervaded the air up there. It seemed to be a combination of mothballs and mildew, spoiled meat and stale perfume.

Mr. Harkey's lips edged into a grin, and his cheeks warmed with color. "You two get settled now. We'll see you back downstairs for drinks in about fifteen minutes."

"All right," said Michael. "Thank you."

Our host closed the door behind himself.

Michael turned the key in the lock, removing it thereafter, leaving a tiny lock-shaped hole in its place.

I sank down on the bed and released a breath I hadn't realized I'd been holding. "This is all a bit exhausting."

"Agreed."

I unbuckled my galoshes and yanked them off of the regular shoes hiding within the rubber casings, and then I slipped the second pair off of my feet as well. Michael sat on the bed behind me and removed his boots.

My eyes locked upon the closed bedroom door—upon that keyhole.

Something moved beyond the darkness of the slot; a flash of white. I sat up straight with a jerk of the bed.

"What is it?" asked Michael.

"I just saw something move on the other side of the keyhole. Do . . . do you think Mr. Harkey is still standing out there?"

"I heard his footsteps return downstairs."

"Are you certain?"

"I think this place might simply have you spooked, and I don't blame you one bit. It's giving me the heebie-jeebies, too." He lay down on his back across the mattress, which whined like a dying accordion. "Do you recognize the hotel from the inside? Does it seem familiar?"

I rubbed my hands across the tops of my thighs and kept my attention focused upon that door.

"Alice? Did you hear what I—"

"No, I don't quite know what to think of the house just yet. I wish I felt more certain."

He patted the mattress beside him. "Come here. Let's take a little reprieve from the topic of reincarnation. Settle our nerves."

I swung my knees onto the bed and crawled over to him with a swiftness spurred on by a sudden fear of someone grabbing my ankles.

Michael pulled me against his side and kissed the top of my head. "If you want . . ." Another kiss, one that spilled chills across my skull. "I could do something to help put you more at ease."

I chewed my lower lip and stared again at the keyhole. "Mrs. Harkey is waiting for us to bring her the garments that need ironing."

"I don't think there will be enough candlelight to expose any wrinkles in the fabrics." He rolled onto his side and kissed me, and I knew—I knew for absolute certain—I heard a rustling outside the door.

Michael didn't flinch, however, so I closed my eyes and willed my fear of Peeping Toms to die a harrowing and brutal death.

Michael coaxed my mouth open with his lips and ran his smooth tongue along mine.

"We must be careful," I said when we came up for a breath. "Please be careful."

"I will." He cupped a warm hand around my left breast, over my three layers of clothing—the sweater, a slip, and a bosom-binding brassiere that squeezed my figure into the boyish shape of a flapper. His mouth moved down to my neck.

"They'll be back at the door in a few minutes," I said, my voice nothing more than a weak and tipsy-sounding whisper.

"I locked the door." He drew my skirt up and over my hips. "They'll have to knock."

"Michael . . ."

He scooted down on the bed and kissed my right thigh in the small slip of space between the bottom of my girdle and the top of my stockings, amid the jungle of cream-colored garter straps.

"Michael, please . . ." I sat partway up, but he ran his right hand up the length of my stomach and eased me back down to the mattress, where I closed my eyes and begged myself to draw a calming breath. I clenched my fists by my sides and told myself that no one was watching.

Michael's lips tasted my inner thigh, teasing with a touch so gentle, it soothed me, yet so enticing, I allowed my knees to fall open. He inched his mouth farther and farther up the length of my leg, and when my breathing heightened, he kissed me through the thin satin layer of my panties. Without fussing with all of the other trappings of my underclothing, he pulled the panties down far enough to expose my mound of curly brown hair. Cool air brushed between my legs, but in a moment warm breath and a soft tongue replaced the sensation, and I found myself soon holding onto the back of his head and lifting my hips to better place myself in his mouth. He squeezed my outer thighs and moved his tongue faster.

Without any warning, a knock came at the door.

Michael's head shot up. "Who is it?"

"It's Mrs. Harkey."

I froze, my knees still hanging open, Michael still clutching my thighs.

"Did you have any clothing for me to iron?" she asked.

Michael scrambled to his feet, and I adjusted my underwear, pushed down my skirt, and sat up. Spots of gold buzzed in front of my eyes, but through the disorienting fog of my dizziness, I spied that gaping keyhole, just sitting there beneath the brass knob, observing *everything*. I envisioned Mrs. Harkey on her knees, pushing her eyeball against the hole, catching Michael's head between my legs.

Michael dabbed at his lips with a handkerchief and clicked open his suitcase. "I might have a coat that needs ironing."

"There's no need to dress too formally," called our hostess. "Just make sure you choose something warm."

He tugged his charcoal-gray dress coat out of his suitcase and strode to the door on his sock-covered feet. He fumbled with the lock, and, after what felt like an hour, he managed to open the door to the awaiting Mrs. Harkey.

She smiled with dimpled cheeks and folded Michael's coat over her arm. "I'll have this done in a jiffy. Anything for you, Mrs. Lind?"

I couldn't even look her in the eye. "No, thank you. I travel so often, I pack clothing designed to withstand suitcase journeys."

"I'll give this back to you when you come downstairs, Mr. Lind."

"Thank you."

She turned and left, and Michael closed the door.

I shot off the bed and opened the largest of my two trunks to locate a dress proper enough for a Christmas Eve dinner—one that truly didn't need any ironing.

Michael sauntered toward me, smoothing down his hair. "Do you want to—?"

"No!"

"You don't even know what I was going to ask."

"I told you I heard someone out there. I knew we weren't alone."

"I don't think she was standing there the whole time."

I tugged out a long-sleeved gown made of emerald crepe.

"Do you, um . . ." He stuffed his hands inside his pockets. "Do you want me to leave while you change?"

"Yes, please. Mrs. Harkey is apt to knock again."

"I'll put on my dress shoes and then give you some privacy."

"Thank you."

Out of the corner of my eye, I saw him again dab his mouth

with a handkerchief, which made me both blush in embarrassment and crave a finish to our moment of intimacy.

I stood up with the dress spilling over my left arm and wondered if the next time we entered that bedroom alone—after dinner, after the Christmas Eve ghost tales that Mr. Harkey spoke of at the depot—my connection to the hotel would be blatantly apparent, which might further alter our relationship. Michael might view me differently. *I* might view myself differently.

He sat down on the other side of the bed and tied the laces of his black dress shoes.

"Michael?"

He peeked over his shoulder, his eyebrows raised.

"I'm going to show you something." I laid the dress on the bed and walked over to him with footsteps that made mere murmurs against the unvarnished floorboards. "I want you to witness a detail about me that might have something to do with my other life . . . if, in fact, another life is at work."

He continued tying the laces, his right leg propped over the left.

I closed the maroon drapes of the window beside me. Between the darkening sky and the snow blowing in the wind, I doubted that any brave souls would be wandering about enough to catch a glimpse of me up there on the second floor, but one couldn't be sure.

I pulled my sweater up and over my head, exposing the cream-colored slip that covered my breasts.

Michael's eyes hovered at the same level as my chest. He swallowed. "What am I looking at?"

"This." I stepped forward and put my fingers to a brown birthmark that marred the skin above my heart. "What does it look like?"

"I don't know." He swallowed again, this time with a discernible ripple of his Adam's apple. "A freckle?"

"Does it look like a bullet hole?"

He blinked as though startled. "Were you shot?"

"No, but I've often dreamt that I was."

He reached up and brushed a thumb across the marking, his movements cautious.

"Sometimes," I said, "I dream of a man kicking open a door and shooting me with a rifle. I've experienced the nightmare ever since I was a child." I sat beside him and took hold of his right hand between my palms. "I want you to know this information in case anything like it comes up when we learn the stories of this house. Just as I did with my investigation into Janie's claims, I want to lay all evidence out in the open before comparing notes with the residents."

"Are you going to speak to the Harkeys about your suspicions?"

I pursed my lips and debated his question. "I don't know," I said with a sigh. "I can't yet tell how responsive they'd be to the concept of reincarnation. I'm also worried they'll patronize me and go along with whatever I say just to give me a good show."

"Do they really strike you as that sort?"

"I don't know what sort they are, but the house seems so bland and unsettling. I can't imagine guests typically coming here for any reason other than hunting down gruesome details about murders and ghosts."

The door rattled behind us. We both jumped.

"What was that?" I asked.

Michael detached my fingernails from his arm. "Just the wind."

"I'm not so sure . . ."

"Listen to it howling outside. It's bound to slip through all the cracks in this drafty old place."

I stared down that thin wooden door and couldn't stop imagining an eye blinking on the other side of the keyhole, watching us, wondering when we'd strip down naked and finish the deed.

"I'll leave so you can dress." Michael got to his feet. "I think we both ought to have some food and a drink."

"Stand in front of the door while I change, will you?"

"How's that?"

"Block the view from outside."

Michael looked to the door and then back at me.

"Please, Michael. I really do feel as though someone is out there. I know it makes me sound like a paranoid ninny, but I can't shake the fear that someone wants to watch us."

His face paled at those words. He rubbed the side of his neck, and despite previously blaming the wind for the noises, he did as I asked with his own eyes locked upon the keyhole.

CHAPTER 29

Another door in the house perturbed me even more than the one in the bedroom.

The front door.

Michael had gone downstairs to fetch his coat while I remained upstairs to arrange my hair, and on my way down the wooden steps, the air in front of me blurred like rippling waves of heat. I saw the door's black wood and oval glass pane through the ethereal haze of a dream. The music of a nearby piano muted into a distant hum, and I imagined a man kicking the door down and blasting me in the chest with a bullet that burned through my flesh.

"Oh, good," said Michael, ducking out of the front parlor in his freshly pressed coat. "I thought I heard you coming downstairs."

"Yes," I said—a sound that escaped my lips as a flutter of air.

He joined me at the bottom of the stairs and took my hand. "Mr. Harkey has been serenading me with a depressing private concert in there. All I've wanted to do is run back upstairs and be with you."

I pulled my attention away from the door. "Are you all right? Are you feeling depressed?"

His eyes moistened, but he mustered a smile. "I don't want to talk about any of that right now."

"Are you certain?"

"Come along. I've heard drinks are on the way."

Inside the parlor, upon an upright piano, Mr. Harkey was playing "The Coventry Carol"—a song that inevitably set my skin awash in chills, no matter where I heard the somber melody or whatever frame of mind in which I happened to be listening to it. Thick green drapes sealed off our view of the outside world, and candles and kerosene wall lamps provided scant light. Shadows darted to and fro across the plaster ceiling—monstrous movements. Playful demons.

"Hot toddies are coming soon," called Mr. Harkey from over his music.

"Yes, so I heard; thank you," I called back, and I joined Michael in front of the fire, where we warmed our hands, our fingers rigid, our breathing shallow.

Footsteps rounded the corner. I glanced behind us and found Mrs. Harkey traipsing our way with two glass mugs of a golden beverage that, indeed, smelled like hot apple toddies, minus the kick of whiskey.

"Your drinks," she said, handing us the mugs, for which we thanked her.

"I hope you're not going to too much trouble over us," I said, and I forced myself to meet her eyes, still petrified she had viewed me with my legs spread wide open.

"No, it's no trouble at all." She wiped her palms on the apron tied around her waist. "Is Al's music too much for you? It's a little grim for Christmas Eve, isn't it?"

"A little," admitted Michael.

"Al!" she called over the piano.

Her husband ceased playing and raised his face. "What is it?"

"Mr. and Mrs. Lind aren't here for the ghosts, remember? Stop filling the parlor with atmosphere."

"Oh, come now," he said, and the lowest keys rumbled beneath his fingers. "They seem like good sports." He winked and embarked upon Beethoven's melancholy "Moonlight Sonata."

Mrs. Harkey tightened her apron strings. "I'm sorry. He gets a little carried away for my tastes sometimes. I hope it doesn't spoil your stay."

"No," I said. "Don't worry about us."

"I'll be back straightaway with the appetizers."

Before we could thank her, she dashed out of the room.

Michael and I blew on our steaming toddies, and a potpourri of nutmeg and sweet apples flooded my nose. Once again, homesickness for Mother's holiday cooking assailed me. The entire family must have been wondering where I'd gone by that point. It wasn't like me to disappear.

"Shall we sit down?" asked Michael.

I opened my mouth to agree but became distracted by the sight of a peculiar object to my right: a lone photograph, mounted on the yellow-brown wall directly across from the fireplace. It was a studio portrait of an imposing woman with blond hair pulled back from a stern face that glowered. She wore a high-collar dress with a cascade of white ruffles gushing from her throat, and she sat in a dining room-style chair, her thick hands clasped in her lap, her feet planted against the floor in high-buttoned boots. She looked as though she wanted to spring off that chair and batter a person with a rolling pin. Her eyes conveyed the message, *I do not want to be here.*

I knew that picture.

Oh, Christ.

"Who is that?" I asked Mr. Harkey, nodding in the direction of the image.

"That is the grande dame," he called over his sonata. "Mrs. Cornelia Gunderson, former owner of this hotel."

I approached the photograph, parked myself in front of it, and, *yes*, recognized it—just as Janie had reacted to the picture of Nelson Jessen standing with an arm around his bride. Without a doubt, that pose, that scowl, that lusterless fair hair yanked back from a severe forehead—*everything* about the woman struck me as familiar, even though I couldn't put my finger on the precise date and time that I'd viewed the portrait in the past. My gaze dropped down to a small metal sign, mounted below the wooden picture frame. COR-NELIA OGREN GUNDERSON, AGE 24, it said, and my eyes latched onto another name that stood within those block letters.

"She doesn't look like she's having much fun," said Michael, now beside me, sipping his toddy.

"Do you see it?" I asked him.

"What?"

The name seemed so obvious to me, the letters almost fatter and taller than the ones surrounding it. Annoyance entered my voice. "Don't you see it, Michael?" I pointed to the center of the name Cornelia. "It's sitting right there. *Nel.*"

He squinted and leaned forward.

"It says, 'Nel,'" I said again. "I recognize this photograph. I've seen it before."

"Are you sure?"

"I'm absolutely positive. I'm linked to this woman—I can feel it. It would make all the sense in the world, wouldn't it? A girl, calling herself 'Nell,' swearing she came from the Great Plains, from a place called Yesternight . . ."

Michael's face remained still, but his eyes shifted toward me.

"She's why I'm here," I said. "I'm certain of it."

He swallowed with so much force I could hear the ripple in his throat.

"What is it?" I asked, stepping back. "Does that idea frighten you? Or . . . or are you debating whether I've gone off my rocker?"

His eyes softened. "Alice, you're a prim and proper school psychologist. A kind woman. This battle-ax, however"—he pointed to Mrs. Gunderson—"sounds to have been a killer."

"I am not prim and—"

I stopped myself, for Mrs. Harkey had reentered the room not more than four feet to our left. She carried two pewter trays, one smelling of oysters and catsup; the other, of eggs.

"I have oyster cocktails and ham and egg balls for everyone," she announced, and she set the delicacies on a lace-covered table butted up against one of the chair rails.

Her husband abandoned his musical accompaniment, and for a moment, ghosts and somber carols, unnerving photographs and savage killings were all but forgotten as we assailed the food and piled small plates with towering stacks of appetizers. My stomach growled, whether from hunger or anxiety, I did not know.

Michael and I took our plates and forks to a salmon-pink settee at the center of the room, where we sat down together, side-by-side.

"I'm not simply a prim and proper school psychologist," I whispered out of the corner of my mouth. "Or have you already forgotten what we just did upstairs?"

"I'm not saying that you couldn't have been Mrs. Gunderson. It's just that you don't strike me as the reincarnation of a madwoman from the prairie. But if you feel as though you might have been her . . ."

"I do."

Not more than a minute after I'd uttered that proclamation, Mr. Harkey took a swig of his toddy and said, "Well, then, dear guests. Would you care to learn more about the bloody past of the Hotel Yesternight?"

Michael and I shared a hesitant glance.

"Yes." I nodded and sat up straight. "Please tell us as much about the history as you can. And there's no need to embellish with theatrics. Just the plain facts will do."

Our host broke into a smile. "You're so entertaining, Mrs. Lind."

"Why do you say that?"

"Because the plain facts are far more theatrical than anything I could ever make up."

Once again, I peeked at Mrs. Gunderson's photograph, wondering if she agreed.

Mrs. Harkey took a seat in a whitewashed rocking chair and didn't take a single bite of her oyster cocktail, which she held in her lap in its frosted glass.

Her husband strolled into the middle of the parlor with his toddy in hand, and the echoes of his black shoes volleyed across the ceiling. Something banged against the house outside—presumably from the wind—which elicited from the fellow a cunning smirk that emphasized the youthful playfulness of his dark eyes. He looked like a Boy Scout, poised to regale us with ghost stories over a blazing campfire.

"Let's begin this blustery Christmas Eve night," he said, "by discussing precisely what happened inside these walls thirty years ago. Please steel your nerves for a tale of madness, of murders grisly and abhorrent."

"Oh, Al," said Mrs. Harkey under her breath with a frown of disapproval.

I lowered my fork back to the plate, for my appetite had soured, and my nose now rejected the smells of oysters, horseradish, and Worcestershire sauce, all intermingling with the sharp vinegar of the catsup. Michael crossed his legs and scooted an inch closer to me.

"Our story begins in Kansas City, Missouri," said Mr. Harkey, his voice deeper, more serious and a little less stagy than before. He stepped in front of the fire, where the flames outlined his figure in an otherworldly orange glow. "In 1888, a Swedish-born shop-keeper named Frans Gunderson set off for Nebraska with a dream of building a hotel that would attract the merchants and business-men traveling westward. Accompanying Frans was his young bride, Cornelia, also born in Sweden, a woman of solid build and strong character. She detested the idea of leaving behind her family, as well as the civilization of the city. But she was Frans's wife, so leave she did." He gulped down another swig of the golden drink, as if to punctuate that last statement.

Beside me, Michael ate ham and cheese balls with tidy jabs of his fork. I myself couldn't eat one bite. I couldn't move.

Mr. Harkey swallowed and licked his lips. "Frans threw his entire life's savings into paying to have lumber hauled out to the middle of the prairie. He built a lavish inn that he named the Hotel

Yesternight, and he purchased livestock and seeds for sustenance. But very few customers arrived. Money diminished. Frans sought work elsewhere, picking crops, building railroads . . . whatever he could do to supplement what little income they gained from the hotel. Cornelia stayed here and fought to keep the dirt and the rattlesnakes out of the house, as well as the snow and the rain and the wind. She cleaned and cooked and tended the vegetable garden, and she hosted the occasional guest, completely on her own, without a man or a weapon to protect her. She lost several unborn infants because of her fatigue and malnourishment."

I squirmed, as did Michael.

"She lost hope," continued Mr. Harkey. "Folks say the barbarity of the conditions, the long absences of her husband, the months spent entirely on her own in the middle of these vast grasslands, turned her stark, raving mad."

"'Prairie madness,'" I murmured under my breath.

"Yes!" Mr. Harkey touched his nose. "Precisely. From the years 1890 to 1895, individuals who had last been seen traveling in this direction suddenly disappeared off the face of the earth. Even Frans Gunderson disappeared, around 1892 or '93. He had made trips into town for supplies every few months, but those trips abruptly stopped. People grew suspicious about the goings-on in this establishment. Sheriffs poked around the place. Cornelia kept the inn spotless, so no one ever spied even the smallest droplet of blood. She collected no records of her lodgers, so no one could link the names of the missing to the guests who had entered her hotel. No one smelled the decay of bodies or noticed odd holes dug into the ground. And yet people continued to go missing."

Mr. Harkey peered at Michael and me through the dimming

light. Beyond him in the rocking chair, his wife's eyes shone in the firelight, while the rest of her face slipped into blackness. Wind blew down the chimney and snapped the fire about, and drafts pestered the flames in the lamps.

Mr. Harkey wrestled a handkerchief out of his breast pocket and dabbed at his brow. "Cornelia Gunderson's downfall came in 1895 when she attempted to murder a young man by the name of Nathaniel Stone, the grown son of a former Civil War major living in Bern, Kansas. Nathaniel was the only person to ever survive one of Mrs. Gunderson's attacks. He became the sole witness to recount what happened within these walls, and I shall tell you what he said."

I leaned forward on the settee.

"According to Nathaniel," continued Mr. Harkey, "he checked into this hotel when traveling as a land surveyor. He found himself the only guest here, but such was the case in several other inns in which he'd lodged during his travels. He slept in a bed in one of the upstairs rooms and noted nothing out of the ordinary . . . until Mrs. Gunderson burst into his quarters with a hammer raised above her head, yelling, 'Stop spying on me! Stop spying!'"

My eyes widened, and a cold and agonizing attack of paralysis solidified my every muscle.

"The hammer came down upon Nathaniel's head, once, twice, three times. He hollered and fought to stop her, and she whacked him yet again. Somehow, by some sort of miracle, young Nat pushed the massive woman aside, hard enough to knock her head into a wall. He ran out of this house and into the night, his skull bruised and badly bleeding."

Mr. Harkey swallowed and fixed his gaze upon me alone,

which made the muscles stiffen all the more. My chest flared with a suffocating pain that stole the breath from my lungs. *He knows,* I thought. *He knows, he knows, he knows.*

"Major Stone did not take kindly to the near-murder of his son," said Mr. Harkey, still seeming to stare me down, although the light had grown so fragile, I couldn't be sure who was looking at whom. "Nathaniel spent days in bed with a concussion, and when his father heard what happened, he loaded up his shotgun, mounted his horse, and came galloping over from Kansas. He stormed inside this house and shot Cornelia dead."

I didn't gasp. Or flinch. Or whimper. I took great pride in my composed reaction, as a matter of fact.

"Where did he shoot her?" I asked with the same tone of professionalism I employed whenever quizzing children in schoolhouses.

"Where in the house?" asked Mr. Harkey with a smile. "Or where on her body?"

"Both," I said.

Our host took another drink before answering. "That's hard to say." He smacked his lips. "Some people claim a sheriff found her on the staircase. Others say she was killed in her bed, or out on the front porch, or even out by her line of laundry. Most people say that Major Stone shot her in the heart, but others insist that he blasted her straight through her head and her belly."

"Oh, Al, really," said his wife, sucking in her breath. "We still need to maintain appetites for dinner."

"Sorry, Mabel." He pulled at his collar. "Whatever the specifics, Major Stone ensured that the she-devil no longer breathed. He rode away and left her lying in a sea of her own blood. No one knows if she ever used more than just a hammer to kill her guests.

To this day, no one even knows what she did with all of the bodies, but thirty-eight deaths have been attributed to the woman, including her husband's."

"No one ever found the bodies?" asked Michael.

Mr. Harkey shook his head. "After the woman's death, authorities dredged the nearby lake, to no avail. They dug up the basement and excavated various other sites around the house, but, still, no one was ever found." He squeaked his finger around the rim of his glass. "Mabel probably doesn't want me mentioning this either, but cannibalism was suspected. Mrs. Gunderson lacked for food, after all. The darker legends suggest that she burned the bones and dined on her guests when she had trouble maintaining the livestock."

I felt the pressure of Mrs. Gunderson's eyes, watching us speak of her savagery from her photograph across the room.

"Did . . . did she have a nickname?" I asked, clasping a hand to my stomach.

"A nickname?" asked Mr. Harkey with a lift of his chin.

"Yes. You told me in the car that your grandmother went to school with her in Kansas City. Did she ever go by any pet versions of Cornelia?"

Mr. Harkey shrugged. "I'm not sure. Corn, maybe? Corny?" He chuckled. "I don't know what a nickname for Cornelia would be."

"Nell?" I asked.

"Maybe." He smiled. "Yes, Nell sounds about right."

Michael's leg tensed next to mine.

Mrs. Harkey scooted forward in her chair with a swish of her satin skirt. "Why do you ask, Mrs. Lind? Do you possess information concerning Mrs. Gunderson?"

"No." I laid my plate of food aside on the settee. "It's just that—" I drew a breath that tasted rotten, like boiled vegetables. Like decay.

"Alice?" asked Michael, folding his right hand over the back of my left one. "Do you think . . . ? Is that what you meant by showing me the bullet hole mark? Did . . . did you know she'd been shot?"

"No, I didn't know a thing about her before coming here today. I didn't even know her name. Or . . . at least . . . I don't believe that I did." I strained my eyes to see Mrs. Gunderson's photograph through the barriers of darkness and smoke. Candlelight reflected off the glass of the frame, but the face within hid in shadow.

Michael squeezed my hand "Do you truly think . . . ?"

"Do *you* think?" I asked, turning his way again.

"You said you experienced those nightmares . . . that you spoke often of this hotel . . ."

"Do you feel a connection to Cornelia Gunderson?" asked Mr. Harkey, stepping closer. "Are you Spiritualists, after all?"

"Should we tell them?" asked Michael.

"I don't know." I cradled my forehead in my free hand. "They might not understand . . . n-n-not without knowing what we've learned through Janie."

"We're reincarnationists, not Spiritualists," said Michael without any further ado, to my shock. "We've come here to trace Alice's connection to the hotel."

"You have a connection?" asked Mr. Harkey, eyes shimmering. "Is that what you meant by taking an interest in this place since childhood?"

I shook my head. "I don't want to discuss such a thing if past lives seem ridiculous to you."

"They don't," said his wife from the rocking chair. "We entertain guests who believe in just about everything. And when a person spends every single night of her life in the cold and miserable darkness of this house, surrounded by walls that have witnessed unfathomable horrors and violence . . ."

"Do you believe you were one of her victims?" asked Mr. Harkey, pressing his mug against his stomach.

"No." I averted my eyes. "I'm embarrassed to admit this, but in my heart I feel . . ." I clenched my fingers around Michael's sweating palm.

"You're *her*," said Mr. Harkey. "Aren't you? Is that what you're feeling?"

The fire sputtered with a suddenness that made my heart skip a beat.

"It . . . it would explain so much about me," I said, and tears soon stung my eyes.

Mr. Harkey trod closer still, his visage a barely visible slip of white. "Do you know where she hid the bodies?"

At that, I gave a short laugh. Somehow, we'd jumped straight from testing the waters for the acceptance of reincarnation to rummaging around in my head for Mrs. Gunderson's secrets. My eyes watered all the more. My temples ached. How desperately I wanted to answer his question, though—how I longed to solve my lifelong riddles and spring back into the car with a sense of completion, just as Janie did at the Rooks' house.

I'm ready, she had said.

I'm ready.

I swallowed down a bitter taste. "Has anyone ever dug up the vegetable garden?"

Mr. Harkey straightened his neck. "No, not that I know of. Should we?"

"Perhaps. I've loathed the taste and smell of vegetables all of my life. I . . ."

Just eat them, Alice, Margery had said through her teeth at the Thanksgiving table, and, my, how those green and finger-like pods had reeked of rotted flesh.

My children are watching. They'll wonder why they need to eat their vegetables and not you.

What's wrong with you?

What's wrong with you?

Should she die?

Should she live?

How many beatings did she give?

"Yes, perhaps you should check the garden." I drew my fingers away from Michael's, and a tear leaked out of my inner right eye. "They're in there; they simply must be. As sure as I'm sitting in this room, that's where the bodies are buried. That . . . that . . ." I struggled to catch my breath; Michael pressed a supportive hand against my back. "Yes—that would explain absolutely everything."

CHAPTER 30

Just as the Rooks had led Janie to Violet and Nelson's log cabin, the Harkeys guided me to a back sitting room, where they excavated a collection of fine china from the velveteen depths of an old steamer trunk with dirt caked in the seams of leather straps.

"People say that Mrs. Gunderson feared getting robbed by her guests," said Mrs. Harkey in a small voice. Upon a table, next to a stack of saucers, she rested a teacup painted in a pattern of rich blue ribbons. "Investigators found this trunk of her belongings buried behind the hotel in one of their searches for . . ." She gulped. "For skeletons."

Both of the Harkeys added several more heirlooms to the table, and with utmost care, my fingertips caressed each looped handle of the fragile cups, each gilded edge of the white plates. Everyone watched as my hands explored those cold and beautiful portals to the past.

What a relief, I thought, *to understand that it wasn't I who wreaked havoc upon my own life. These flares of violence that awaken now and then are no more than residual traces of a personality long gone—ashes sprinkled across my memories. Only occasionally do they smolder with the heat of that old, lethal fire, but it has nothing to do with me as Alice Lind.*

What an astronomical relief.

"Thank you," I said to the Harkeys, with Michael at my side. "This collection helps immensely."

"Do you feel certain?" asked Michael.

"Yes." I picked up a pale-pink sugar bowl so fragile, I feared it might crack to pieces in my hands. "I believe I do."

No one touched the vegetables at dinner. Boiled cauliflowers, pickled beetroots, and mashed turnips—all harvested from the local soil—lay on the far edges of pearl-colored dishes. We all concentrated instead on the breaded mutton chops and roasted venison and brushed aside anything that had risen out of the earth.

"Never in my life," said Mr. Harkey, with brisk slices of his knife through his mutton, "have I wanted to dig in a vegetable garden so desperately."

"There's a blizzard, Al," said his wife. "Don't even think of it until the ground thaws."

"Snow acts as an insulator to the ground." Mr. Harkey tilted his left ear toward his plate, as though the china had just whispered that information to him. "As soon as the storm passes, I'd love to shovel the snow aside and test out the softness of the earth. If you're still here, will you help me, Lind?"

From across the table, I eyed Michael for his reaction, to gauge his current state of mind. He focused all of his attention on his food at the moment, but he poked at the meat with his fork more than he consumed it, as though Janie again weighed on his thoughts.

"Mr. Lind?" asked Mr. Harkey.

Michael's head shot up. "How's that?"

"I said, if the blizzard dies down by tomorrow morning, shall we see if your wife's prediction about the vegetable garden leads us to those long-concealed bodies?"

"Al, please," hissed Mrs. Harkey, and she lowered her fork and knife. "Don't use the word *bodies*—not while we're eating. It's Christmas Eve."

Michael cleared his throat. "Sure. I'll help you dig."

His words elicited a pleased smile from our host, whose face now flushed with the ruddiness of excitement. "Can you imagine, Mabel"—he leaned toward his wife across the table—"actually announcing to the public that we'd found the victims? The newspapers, the local radio shows, they'd all be scrambling out here for an interview. The publicity would be astounding. And of course"—he looked at me—"we'd have to bring you out here throughout the year, Mrs. Lind. I'd give you free lodging in exchange for your time. You could sit in the parlor and spin stories of your memories as Mrs. Gunderson."

"But I don't have all that many memories . . ."

"If those"—he glanced briefly at his wife—"*items* in the vegetable garden prove that you were, indeed, our Yesternight Killer, then it wouldn't matter if the memories you shared were real or false."

"That sounds a little shady," said Michael under his breath.

"It's advertising," said Mr. Harkey. "It's what the public wants."

I opened my mouth to object.

"Mrs. Lind," he continued before I could make a peep, "people travel for miles and miles in search of even the smallest glimpse of the mysterious, infamous Cornelia Gunderson, and I've given a great deal of thought about why this is."

"And what have you concluded?" I asked, choosing to hide my psychology credentials until he explained.

He shifted his weight in his chair. "I've realized that people in this country are both terrified and obsessed with death, and yet we're still too repressed a society to admit how we truly feel about it, even in this era of libertines and bright young things. We dress death up in church hymns and ghost stories to make it palatable, but we rarely actually talk about it."

"You certainly do, Al," murmured his wife from behind her napkin.

"People like Mrs. Gunderson," he continued, "they sicken us and fascinate us because they're death incarnate. We could discuss them for hours and hours because they're symbols of the unspeakable emotions buried inside our minds. Death is like sex, in fact: it's part of life; everyone partakes in it at one time or another. But we're all afraid to admit we possess strong feelings about it, so we sit back and make jokes about it while also gawking at it in awe—or else we make ourselves feel guilty for thinking too much about it. We isolate ourselves so terribly because of our guilt and fears, you see, and we do our damnedest to scrounge around for connections to other people through popular culture and legends . . . through these *symbols* of our forbidden obsessions."

"Hmm." I resumed cutting my food, impressed by his insights into human nature. "That's an interesting way of looking at the American people."

"Am I wrong?"

"No." I slipped a slice of mutton into my mouth.

Mr. Harkey bent forward in his chair with a creak of the wood beneath him. "Will you help us, then? Will you do all you can to use your beliefs about this past life of yours to assist in making this hotel extraordinary?"

I finished chewing my food and sighed. "Cornelia Gunderson is simply a part of my past that I've been struggling to understand for years, just like any difficult memory. And to be most honest, I'm a practicing psychologist who works with children—one of whom recently demonstrated to me resounding proof of spirit transmigration. I'm interested in reincarnation as a science, not a spectacle, and so is Mr. O—" I stopped myself before saying *O'Daire*. "So is . . . my husband."

The mood in the room deflated. My bluntness had shrunk Mrs. Harkey's neck into her shoulders, and I'd disappointed her husband, I could tell from his vexed eyebrows. He wanted a show. He wanted tall tales and bursts of feral wildness, perhaps even a dash of blood—something he could photograph and slap onto a promotional poster.

I would not give him that.

AFTER DINNER, MRS. HARKEY and I bundled ourselves in jackets, scarves, and mittens and braved the blizzard to make the twenty-yard journey to the outhouse. She carried a copper lantern, inside which a weak flame gasped for life, and we clung to each other to keep the wind from smacking us down to the snow.

My hostess graciously allowed me to use the facility first. She hung the lantern on a hook inside the wooden structure and helped me to close the door against the storm. I then embarked upon one of the most terrifying outhouse moments in the whole history of mankind. The weather-chewed boards groaned and swayed and threatened to crack against my skull, and an ice-cold wind blew through the slats, inflicting pain on every square inch of exposed skin. My backside hovered over the opening in the seat. My knees wobbled as I bunched up my skirts with freezing fingers. I pictured a humiliating death that would involve the gentlemen of our group finding me curled inside the outhouse wreckage with my underwear hanging around my ankles.

Mrs. Harkey went next, which left me huddled against the outer walls in the dark. She was quick about it, however, and we were soon plodding back through the knee-deep snow and yanking the kitchen door open.

The men journeyed out after us, while I washed up at the kitchen sink.

"You seem quite ordinary for a person who lived such a terrifying past life," said Mrs. Harkey, and she handed me a dishtowel printed in bright-red cherries. "You seem so . . . *normal.*"

"Do I?" I took the towel and dried my hands and face. "I believe that's the first time anyone's ever said that of me."

She tittered. "I'm relieved you don't seem wicked."

"Oh, please, don't be frightened of me. In the short time I've spent exploring reincarnation, I've learned that the personalities of the past often fade over time. The person standing before you today was shaped far more by her present life than by any experiences as Cornelia Gunderson." I blotted my cheeks. "I'm just not sure my family will be too keen to hear about my discovery. I'm certainly not going to dash off any letters over the holidays, informing them of what I've found."

"Oh, that reminds me." Mrs. Harkey went over to a kitchen table that housed cookbooks and envelopes. "Someone sent you a telegram before we even knew you were coming."

"Oh . . . yes . . ." I lowered the towel to my chin. "Your husband told me as much when I telephoned. Are you sure it's for me? No one knew that Michael and I would be coming here."

"Oh, it definitely says 'Alice Lind.'" She rifled through the envelopes. "It was so strange. I almost returned it to the telegraph office, thinking it was a mistake, but then Al told me you'd telephoned and made a reservation. Here it is." She brought an envelope my way, studying the words upon it as she went. "It says 'Miss Alice Lind,' but perhaps the 'Miss' is a mistake."

"Yes." I took it from her. "As I said, we're newlyweds. Didn't I say that? The sender probably forgot . . . it's an easy mistake to make when one is newly married." I sweated, despite just having climbed out of a blizzard.

Mrs. Harkey offered a small nod, her round cheeks pinking up. "Well . . . I'll let you read it in private. I need to clear the dishes."

"Thank you for remembering that you had this. I forgot Mr. Harkey's mention of it."

She smiled and left the kitchen.

The moment her footsteps reached the dining room, I ripped the envelope open, now worried that some unspeakable tragedy had befallen Mother or Father, or one of Margery's children, and that Bea had thought to find me here. I'd spent so much time fretting over the O'Daires . . . fussing over myself . . .

I tugged the telegram out of the envelope, and yes indeed, the name BEATRICE LIND jumped out at me as the sender. My gaze dropped to her message.

I FEAR YOU'VE GONE TO YESTERNIGHT TO FIND OUT WHO YOU ARE, BUT I WAS THE ONE WHO

TOLD YOU ABOUT YESTERNIGHT WHEN WE WERE CHILDREN, ALICE. I BROUGHT HOME A BOOK ABOUT CORNELIA GUNDERSON. I READ IT TO YOU WHEN WE WERE BOTH TOO YOUNG FOR SUCH THINGS. WE PLAYED THAT WE WERE MURDEROUS MRS. GUNDERSON FOR FUN BUT ONE DAY YOU TOOK IT TOO FAR. I FELT GUILTY AND NEVER TOLD MOTHER. I'M SORRY. PLEASE STOP LOOKING TO FIND OUT WHO YOU ARE. YOU'RE ALICE LIND, A BRIGHT YOUNG WOMAN WHO SIMPLY HAD A HARD TIME OF THINGS TWO AND A HALF YEARS AGO. IT'S NOT YOUR FAULT YOU LOST THE BABY. NOTHING IS WRONG WITH YOU ASIDE FROM SOME ROTTEN LUCK WITH MEN AND A SISTER WHO SHOULD HAVE TAKEN CARE NOT TO DARKEN YOUR YOUNG MIND.

ALL MY LOVE
BEA

My mouth stretched open. It gelled into a horrified, rounded, silent scream of an expression that made my lower jaw pop and ache. I thought of Mr. Harkey offering free boarding and a regular stay in exchange for my knowledge of the hotel; the kindness of his wife; Michael's reassuring hand on my back; his support of my claims; my fingers rifling through Mrs. Gunderson's belongings. I had convinced myself so thoroughly. No . . . I *had* to have been "Nell" Gunderson. Alice Lind did not beat former lovers over the head until they collapsed to their knees on the ground. Alice Lind was not paranoid for no good reason. Alice Lind had always prevented the personal struggles in her adult life from unraveling her completely.

YOU'RE ALICE LIND A BRIGHT YOUNG WOMAN WHO HAD A HARD TIME OF THINGS TWO AND A HALF YEARS AGO.

I crumpled the paper into a ball, not caring at all for the implication that an overactive imagination and the loss of my baby had led to all of this. It was just a late and painful menstrual period; that was all. A bit of blood. Some cramping. A minor inconvenience. I felt nothing afterward. *Nothing.*

Voices neared the back door—the return of the men.

I darted out of the kitchen and bolted upstairs.

CHAPTER 31

Up in the bedroom, the flames of candles and kerosene lamps fluttered upon blackened wicks. I remembered Mr. Harkey mentioning something about lighting the lamps as his wife and I ran out to the outhouse, but, still, it shocked me to see signs of life in the empty room.

Inside that smoky haze of light, I dropped to my knees and buried Bea's telegram deep inside one of the suitcases, beneath dresses and nightclothes and toiletries.

I was the one who told you about Yesternight when we were children, she had said, and a vague memory of a book came to mind. A slim red volume that may have, perhaps, included Cornelia Gunderson's photograph.

Pretend we're eating fingers from the garden, I remembered an eight-year-old Bea once whispering beside me with a giggle when she chomped on a fresh green bean at the supper table. *You're eating fingers, Nell. How do they taste?*

Child's play.

Simple child's play, used as a means to work out feelings about the mysteries of death. "Funeral play," as one professor called it.

But one day you took it too far.

"I think I just escaped a horrifying death by outhouse," said a voice by the door.

I shot up to a standing position and hid my hands behind my back, even though they carried nothing.

Michael closed the door and worked the knot out of his blue necktie. "I'm sorry. Did I startle you?"

"It's just the house." I tried to shrug, but my shoulders merely twitched. "I'm so terribly jumpy."

"I think this house might be more afraid of you than you are of it, Alice."

I lowered my face. "We're still not positive that I'm her."

"You sounded so certain. And that bullet mark . . ."

"It's not like with Janie. There's no sister to verify my statements."

"Maybe there is." He strolled toward the bed and slid the tie off his neck. "Maybe Mr. Harkey's grandmother talked of Mrs. Gunderson having a sister—"

"Don't be an idiot, Michael. Mr. Harkey probably lied about his grandmother knowing Mrs. Gunderson. He's a huckster who admits to selling bunk to saps."

"Why are you snapping at me?"

"Please"—I sat on the bed and tore my right shoe off my foot— "forget what I said about Cornelia. It all sounds so stupid now that I'm upstairs."

"But—"

"This was a mistake. I knew I shouldn't ever be with a man again. I knew it!" I tugged my left shoe off my heel and felt him staring at me.

"What's wrong?" he asked.

"Oh, there's something definitely wrong all right—just ask my sisters, because apparently they know everything about me. They can tell you all about how I'm an emotional wreck and an embarrassment to the family, not because of any past life, but because of a far more pressing issue that even Mr. Harkey seems to think we should all be discussing."

I tossed the shoe to the floor and cupped my hands over my face.

"What pressing issue?" he asked. "What are you talking about?"

I sighed into my fingers. "I love sex, Michael. I'm an unmarried woman, and I absolutely adore climbing into bed with men. It's been killing me for years."

"What do you mean, it's killing you?"

"It's so terribly dangerous—so terribly wrong for me to love it."

"Dangerous?" He breathed a short laugh. "I don't understand—"

"A girl could get pregnant. She could lose her career. She could have people calling her 'loose' or 'slut' and render everything else in her life—all of her work and hard-earned respect—*meaningless*. I feel absolutely worthless when people think of me that way, especially my own sister Margery. And I feel so awful for raising your hopes for a better life, when here you are, stuck Christmas Eve with a broken woman who's desperate to blame her problems on someone else."

"Alice?" Michael laid his tie over a corner of the bed. His voice softened. "Why are you saying these things? Have people been cruel to you? Has another guy . . . ?"

Tears strangled my throat. I clasped my hands around the back of my neck.

"Alice . . . come on now . . ." He wandered over to my side of the bed and sat down. "I don't think poorly of you. I love sex, too, as a matter of fact. Desperately."

"You're a man. You're allowed to."

"I swore to you before, I won't get you pregnant."

"How can you be so sure?"

"I'll pull out in time."

I huffed. "That doesn't always work."

"I've had practice. It does."

I shut my eyes and ground my teeth together. "I'm such a wreck, Michael."

"So am I." He placed a warm hand on my lower back and stroked my spine. "You don't know how badly I'm falling apart inside. But your wanting to be with me is helping me survive. It's the only thing getting me through."

I sniffed and unlocked my fingers from the back of my neck. "Is it?"

"Yes." He scooted closer. "Please, let's forget about past lives. Past pain. Past lovers. We both want each other right now, in this life, tonight, so why should anything else matter?"

"If I become pregnant—"

"You won't." He swallowed up my hands in his, his flesh as bitter cold as the wind howling at the window. "I promise."

ALL IT TOOK was that one promise.

One more kiss.

One hand placed just so.

Before long, we had buried ourselves beneath the blankets on the bed, our clothing forgotten on the floor.

"I want to kiss every single part of you," he whispered against my neck, "but it's just so damn cold."

"Stay here, then, with your lips against mine."

All around us, the blizzard blustered. It breathed through the cracks in the walls and froze our skin, and yet our kisses led to caresses, to tasting, to tingling, goose-pimpled flesh and pounding hearts.

"Don't forget your promise," I whispered.

"I won't," he said as he climbed on top of me, just before that marvelous sensation of pressure pushed between my legs.

I wrapped my arms around his back, and the mattress purred beneath me, while the wind rattled through the boards and shuddered across the windowpane. I closed my eyes and gave myself up to the recklessness of it all, no longer thinking, only feeling—hungering and reacting and rising above my anxieties for as long as we could dare let the moment linger. Sighs and whimpers escaped my lips. My toes curled against the bed sheet.

Michael quickened his pace, and our arms and stomachs clenched against each other. His breathing loudened next to my ear, and he whispered with dreamy reverence, "Oh, God. Oh, God."

"Is it almost time?" I asked. "Should we—"

A rush of warmth.

A groan of pleasure.

He shook against me, and my eyes flew wide open. I grabbed him by his hair and cried out, "No! Stop!" And yet he shook and shook and shook.

"Michael!" I pushed at his shoulders to get him off me. "You promised! You swore to me you wouldn't do that."

"I'm sorry . . ."

"Get off of me." I wriggled my legs.

"Alice—"

"Get off me!"

He lifted his chest away from mine, and I maneuvered around his locked arms and slid off the side of the mattress.

"Damn it!" I bundled up my clothing in my arms. "Damn! Damn! Damn!"

"Don't panic so much."

"Don't tell me not to panic!"

He eased himself up to a seated position and wobbled as though drunk.

I slung my slip over my head. "Oh, Christ, you men have it so easy."

"Don't turn this into a sexist thing. We both agreed to do that."

"What does it feel like to be able to screw and know you can walk away without consequences? What does it feel like to not have to worry about your parents ripping you out of their lives and your hard work collapsing around you?"

He staggered around in the darkness of the other side of the bed and hit his knee on the bedside table. "Damn!"

"Did you 'pull out' so expertly when you shacked up with your nurse at your training camp?"

"I told you not to bring up past lovers."

"Did you knock her up?"

"No!" He tugged his pants up to his waist and buttoned them up. "If you must know, we used French letters. Condoms."

"Why didn't you bother to get any for me?"

"Because we're in the middle of goddamned nowhere, Alice. You know that. I did the best I could right now. Don't invite me into your bedroom if you can't handle a fuck."

I grabbed up one of my shoes.

Don't invite me into your bedroom if you can't handle a fuck, I heard him say again, and my fingers gripped the smooth leather.

Aw, you're so loose, Stu had told me, *some other chap was bound to knock you up anyway.*

Michael plopped down on his side of the bed and turned his undershirt right-side out before pulling it down over his chest.

I didn't even remember walking over to him.

All I saw was the side of a head of golden-blond hair that resembled Stu's, and then blood, spattering my cream colored slip from a strike of the sharp edge of the heel against his skull.

Michael's mouth opened wide. He dropped to his knees on the floor and held his head, and I hit him with the shoe again, this time behind his ear.

"Alice!" he shouted. "What are you doing?"

He tried to reach out with his left hand, but I hammered his head a third time.

"Stop it!"

More blows. More blood. Tears drenched my face, and I wanted to stop, but I found myself being rushed on a gurney down the too-bright halls of a hospital, my womb contracting, people staring, staring, staring, and blood everywhere. *Four months pregnant,* they'd told me, and I pretended that was nothing. I pretended I hadn't wished for the loss to happen. I pretended I didn't care . . .

Michael grabbed the vase of geraniums from the table behind

him and whacked it against my skull with a blinding pain that knocked me sideways, onto the edge of the bed.

"What have you done?" one of us yelled—I wasn't sure who.

I fell backward to the floor, and the room blurred; my ears blared with a horrendous ringing commotion that drew vomit to my throat. An orange light blinked and throbbed in front of my left eye, *on and off, on and off* . . .

"Is everything all right in there?" asked a garbled voice in the distance.

"Oh, Christ. Get up, get up, Alice." Michael shook my shoulder. "This doesn't look good—you in just your slip, bleeding from the head. They're going to think I attacked and murdered you if you die. They're going to think *you* fought back, instead of the other way around."

I rolled back and forth against my shoulder blades, my arms and head too heavy to lift off of the floor.

"Get up—please!" Michael stared down at me with his fingers wrapped around the vase, his teeth chattering, his eyes damp, his forehead bleeding. "Oh, God," he said. "Why did you hit me? Why'd you go nuts just like Bec did? You're all ripping me to pieces right now. Get up!"

His face turned dim and distorted and then faded from view as my eyes no longer stayed open.

Someone slammed his weight against the door from the other side. More voices. Stern voices.

"Oh, Christ, Alice," cried Michael. "I'm done with all of this. I'm done!"

The vase shattered against the floorboards.

A window opened.

Cold wind blasted through my hair.

CHAPTER 32

I woke up with surges of pain pulsating through my left temple—surges that brought on a dire need to vomit. Bandages squeezed the top of my head, and the smell of fresh gauze only added to the nausea. I crawled across the bed on my elbows and my belly and threw up on the bare floor below.

More sleep ensued, and then I awoke with a start, remembering.

Down on the floorboards at the foot of the bed, blood betrayed our violence. Piles of discarded clothing lay about like naughty children unwilling to hide their misbehavior. I still wore nothing but my slip, and I couldn't imagine what the Harkeys had thought when they found me lying in the middle of the room, half-naked, a wound gaping from the left side of my head. I remembered the sound of the window opening and wondered if they'd found Michael gone, or if he had stood there cradling his skull that I'd pummeled over and over again.

Not a soul seemed to stir downstairs.

I dressed and tiptoed down the staircase. A sickening wave of dizziness rolled through my brain, but I gripped the banister and called out, "Is anyone down here?"

Mrs. Harkey tromped into view upon shoes with sturdy heels that summoned more bile to my mouth. She wrung her hands and burst into tears. "We've called the police . . . and the doctor. No one can come until the roads get plowed."

I stiffened. "You—you called the police?"

"He attacked you and left you for dead. It was horrifying, finding you that way."

"Where is he?"

"He left."

My heart stopped.

"We don't know how far he got," she added, biting her lip.

"But . . . there was a blizzard."

"He escaped out the window before Al could pry open the door."

"There was a blizzard!"

"I bet it was this awful old house that did it." She wiped at her eyes with her hands. "Did he think he was attacking Mrs. Gunderson? Was it Al's obsession with death—or his stories about cannibalism? It's too much, isn't it? I always tell him, it's too damn much!"

I left the bottommost step and froze in place, for I spied Michael's black overcoat, still hanging beside my jacket. His gloves and his scarf drooped out of the pockets.

"Do . . . do you know why he attacked you?" asked Mrs. Harkey, still sniffling.

I shook my head, not knowing how to answer—too confused to properly decide whether I needed to lie about the entire situation. I couldn't stop staring at Michael's coat and gloves.

Mrs. Harkey coughed and choked before sputtering out, "Al's out digging through the snow in that vegetable garden. The storm passed, and he couldn't wait. The house is driving him out of his mind, too. All he talks about is those disgusting bodies."

"I've got to find Michael." I sprang for the coatrack and grabbed my jacket.

"The snow's deep. Please—wait for the police."

"If he's still alive he'll need help."

"Mrs. Lind . . ."

"He's not wearing much clothing." I slung my arms through the sleeves.

"Mrs. Lind, I'm so sorry, but unless he made it back inside the house without us hearing . . . There's nothing but open fields out there . . . Even if he had worn his overcoat . . ."

I muffled a sob and buttoned up my jacket, my chin tucked against my chest, my throat swelling shut.

"The police will probably want to know why he hurt you. If it was marital abuse . . ."

I wrapped the scarf around my neck, not caring that it choked.

"They won't understand what this house does to people." She rubbed her hands along the sides of her skirt. "I know you said you don't behave like Mrs. Gunderson anymore, but . . ."

My hands went still on the scarf's yarn. I met her eyes.

"Do be careful how you answer their questions."

"What do you mean by that?" I asked.

"Don't bring up that you were once Cornelia. The police might worry about you, too. Things that sound normal inside this house don't sound quite right to outsiders' ears."

"But I wasn't Mrs. Gunderson—that's the thing. There's been a mistake. I got caught up in the excitement of reincarnation and put too much stock in coincidences."

"But—"

"Michael lost his temper and attacked me. That's what happened. He attacked, and I fought back, but it had nothing whatsoever to do with Mrs. Gunderson. *Nothing.* He attacked me first. It had nothing to do with my past."

The woman just stood there with her arms by her sides.

"Do you understand?" I asked. "Do you believe me? I was never Cornelia Gunderson."

She gave two blinks of her bloodshot eyes, her pupils noticeably constricted, as though she partook in laudanum to endure the Hotel Yesternight.

"F-f-fine," she said—the same old response I myself was trained to give to the schoolchildren.

MY EARS ACHED from the lack of sound in that open field of endless, virgin snow. A troubling stillness had seized the land, and it seemed to thicken the air I breathed.

Twenty to thirty yards to the south of the house, a figure in a brown coat and Homburg hat shoveled snow away from a patch of earth. I saw Mr. Harkey's breath curling into the air and heard the faint swoosh of his blade digging into the powder, but he didn't even notice me out there.

My legs sank into snow clear up to my thighs; my muscles strained to clamber through the piles. I scanned the prairie as I went, in search of a stripe of color, an uneven hump, a patch of blond hair . . .

I saw him.

Oh, dear Lord.

To the east, a snowdrift the size of a man broke the flatness of the land. I covered my face with mitten-clad fingers and breathed with strangled gasps.

You must go to him, I told myself. *He once reached out to you in a storm. Go.*

I slogged through a sea of snow over three feet deep with my eyes tearing up from the cold and the pain, and again Bea's warning from Thanksgiving haunted my head.

Don't insert yourself into other people's stories.

Don't. Don't. Don't.

But I did.

He was Janie's father. *Janie's father.* How I envied that little girl for her newfound sense of peace—for the love and acceptance heaped upon her, even when she behaved in the strangest of ways. Everyone swore how much they protected her, and look what I did.

LOOK WHAT I DID.

This was not the life I was meant to lead.

This was not who I was.

Michael O'Daire lay flat on his stomach with his face angled toward me, his right cheek pressed against the frozen ground, his eyes faded to the coldest shade of blue. He wore only his undershirt and trousers and a pair of untied boots, and snow dusted them all. His skin had turned purple; his lips and the tip of his nose, a shocking black. Traces of blood stained his blond hair behind his left ear, above his forehead, on the top of his skull . . .

I wheeled around in the other direction and clasped my hands beneath my chin, shaking, crumbling into a thousand pieces. Tears hot and bitter burned my mouth and my tongue.

Mr. Harkey's shovel whooshed through the snow, and the Hotel Yesternight rose up in the near-distance, its slanted roof stretching toward a colorless, unwelcoming sky. Sunlight reflected off one of the upstairs windows—the one through which Michael had made his exit. My vision blurred, and the reflection seemed to be a wink, as if the house were telling me, *You may not have ever lived here, Alice, but, my goodness, you sure do behave as though you did.*

I sank down onto the snow in front of Janie's father and contemplated whether I should stay by his side and freeze into the prairie along with him, or if another chance still awaited me.

If this was the end, or a beginning.

If I would always have to be this Alice, or if I could heal myself into something entirely new.

Part IV
JOHN

CHAPTER 33

November 12, 1930

Faye Russell, a seven-year-old girl with bobbed red hair, sat down in the chair across from my desk at the Portland elementary school in which I now worked on a full-time basis. Naturally, the child reminded me of Janie O'Daire, as redheaded little girls were apt to do.

I took a moment to compose myself. Another incident earlier that day had already thrown me out of sorts, and the timing of Faye's arrival half-convinced me that the universe aimed to put me on edge. To taunt me. To test me. I aligned my pencil next to my notebook and engaged in the soothing breathing techniques Dr. Benoit had taught me in our sessions.

In through the nose, out through the mouth,
In through the nose, out through the mouth . . .

"Welcome, Faye," I said, and I folded my hands on my desk. "As you may already know, Mrs. Schmidt sent you into my office because she's concerned about you being so sad in her classroom. Is everything all right at home?"

Faye pulled on the skirt of her blue and yellow dress, which hung over a frame that lacked any meat. I anticipated her answer before she even said it. In fact, our attendance at the school was dropping at an alarming rate because of the response I knew her to be on the brink of giving.

"Daddy lost his job," she said, her tone hushed, her big brown eyes cast toward my desk instead of at me.

"This has been the case for many fathers over the past year, I'm afraid." I unclasped my hands. "How has your life at home changed because of him being out of work?"

"Who's that?" Faye pointed at my photograph of John, taken in a studio two months earlier, to commemorate his fourth birthday.

I'd forgotten that I had turned his photograph away from my view when I'd first sat down that morning. Feeling guilty for doing so, I slid the frame back toward me and saw the fair hair and striking eyes that so resembled his father's.

In through the nose, out through the mouth,
In through the nose, out through the mouth . . .

"That's my son," I said.

"Did *his* daddy lose his job?"

The question chilled the backs of my arms. Again, I straightened my pencil and debated how best to answer without sharing much of my private life—without causing more fears about fathers and loss.

"His daddy hasn't worked for a long while," I said, my mouth dry. "Now, tell me about your father. How is he behaving now that he's without work?"

Faye proceeded to share with me the same accounts of family hardships I'd been hearing from far too many children ever since the crash of the stock market the autumn before. Fathers hunted for jobs with stooped shoulders and dark-ringed eyes. Tables wanted for food. Mothers cried and spoke in nervous voices. Tummies ached. Children dropped out of school to help out at home.

My troubles of the morning seemed so odd, so petty, in comparison to what the pupils endured.

Twenty minutes later, Faye walked out of my office, her tears dried, her emotions purged, and, after her, at least a dozen other children entered my unfussy little quarters that day. I assisted the students, consoled them, tested them, dabbed at their tears with handkerchiefs, and, hopefully, sent them away standing a little bit taller than when they had first slouched their way through my door. One boy described a dream he kept having about eating lamb chops with mint jelly, but most students didn't share their dreams with me. None of the students ever spoke of past lives—to my great relief. Until the day when I would open a newspaper and read about Janie O'Daire breaking codes, developing theorems, or whatever she might do with her fantastical mind, I didn't care to think about the topic of reincarnation anymore.

I was done with that chapter.

At the end of the school day, I buttoned up my coat and fitted my wool hat over my head.

"Have a good evening," said our principal, Mr. Carver, with a pat of my shoulder. "Keep doing what you're doing to cheer up these kids. We lost two more today."

"Yes, Mr. Carver." I nodded. "I'll do my best."

"You're a treasure."

"Thank you."

He peeked over the shoulder of his smart gray suit and straightened a lock of auburn hair that had fallen across his forehead. We'd slept together once, in the squeaky backseat of his Oldsmobile, my legs and black shoes raised in the air, his pomade greasing my cheek, a condom providing an essential barrier between us. Dr. Benoit had called the tryst a detrimental step backward and warned me I could get fired from a job that represented a vast improvement in my career.

I considered it progress.

I hadn't shed one drop of Mr. Carver's blood in the aftermath.

JOHN AND I lived with Bea and Pearl in the same Northeast Portland neighborhood in which the elementary school was located, one neighborhood to the north of my parents' house. A November chill had arrived in just the past week, and my walk to fetch John from my mother proved more painful to the cheeks and hands than in recent days past. Normally, I would stride with a brisk step through such weather, but today my legs lacked the enthusiasm to rush. My chest hurt too much to exert myself. In fact, I had to stop and grip the edge of a picket fence with my feet braced two feet apart, while my shoes disappeared into a blanket of red and gold leaves.

You must have imagined what happened this morning, I told myself. *It was just your nerves, frazzled by the drinks you shared with the blond fellow you met in Dr. Benoit's waiting room last week. That's all it was. A touch of guilt.*

I pushed onward to Mother's; to my son.

And yet I couldn't stop dwelling on breakfast.

John had dawdled as usual over his food, taking a hundred years just to finish a slice of buttered toast.

"Hurry up, John," I had said, carrying my own dishes to the sink. "Grandma's waiting."

He didn't respond at first, and I assumed him to be doing as I'd instructed, eating his breakfast posthaste. I lowered my glass to the sink and filled it with water, and I thought nothing of the silence, or of the fact that John might be watching me. The water spilled over the edge of the glass, so I reached for the faucet and turned it off.

"Do you remember when you hit me in the head, Alice?" asked a voice from the table behind me.

I whirled around, my plate still in hand, and the room tilted sideways. John smiled and broke off the crust of his toast.

"Wh-wh-what did you just say?" I asked him, my knees bent.

"You took your shoe and went"—John lifted his right hand and brought it down like a hammer—"*whack, whack, whack, whack*. Do you remember that"—he grinned again, a dimple marking his left cheek—"Alice?"

My plate slipped from my fingers and broke against the tiles with a crash that brought Bea running into the kitchen.

"Is everyone all right?" Bea skidded to a halt when she saw me clutching the edge of the sink. "Alice?"

I couldn't breathe; I couldn't move. John had resumed chewing his toast and refocused his attention on the crumbs scattered across his plate. He snaked his left pinkie through the mess.

"Alice?" asked Bea. "What happened? Why are you so ghastly white?"

I couldn't answer. I couldn't do anything. Bea rubbed my aching-cold back and assured me that everything was all right, but even she didn't know the full story. No one did. No one but Michael had known about the shoe. My family believed we had gotten caught in a blizzard and that Michael heroically left the car to seek help. My parents and Margery even believed that he and I had married in Kansas. I'd told his mother, when I'd telephoned her to break the awful news, that Michael had gone on from Kansas to Nebraska to escape his problems on his own, and I'd followed after to check on him, after the storm blustered northward, but I'd found he'd perished in the blizzard. I penned the same story in a letter to Tillie Simpkin, and she'd written back to thank me for watching out for him. Mr. Harkey had dug up only one single, questionable bone in his garden. He couldn't add to his show any photographs of a mass grave; no discoveries made by "Mrs. Gunderson Herself!" And yet he and his poor, frazzled wife remained so generous and helped me with all arrangements and police interrogations. *A violent dispute between a married couple,* was the official report. *The deceased abandoned the scene of the fight from a second-story window, banged up his head on the drop down, and subsequently froze to death.*

"Please don't ever call me Alice," I told John when at last my throat relaxed. "That's not what you call your mother."

"I didn't."

"I heard you, John."

"My name's not John."

Bea mussed his blond hair. "Finish your breakfast, little monkey. Mama's waiting."

"My name's Michael."

Bea's jaw plummeted. Her head whipped my way, and she sent me a look that mimicked my own state of shock.

I fled the room and spent the next ten minutes with my head wedged between my knees, forcing blood to return to my brain.

And now, as I approached my parents' house that November afternoon, five years to the day after I'd arrived at the Gordon Bay Depot, I thought of all the books my little boy enjoyed—the mysteries, the seaside adventures, the tales of wandering dreamers. His little drawings of ships and seagulls and houses perched on ocean cliffs decorated the walls of our home, as well as Mother and Father's. I'd never once taken the child to the coast. I used to believe the drawings represented his longing to see where his father had been born.

But . . . now . . .

No, don't go down that road again, Alice. Don't assume.

I inhaled a breath that puffed up my chest and opened my parents' front door.

"Hello!" I called, my voice ringing through the front hall. "I'm here!"

John galloped out from the kitchen in the back and cried out, "Mommy!"

"There's my darling." I bundled him up in a hug and smelled chocolate in his hair. "Grandma must have baked you cookies."

"He insisted upon helping," said my mother, moseying our way, untying her apron from her waist. "He's quite the little chef."

I stood up and took hold of John's sticky hand. "Has he been a good boy today?"

"Of course," said Mother, straightening the back of his collar. "He bumped his knee on the kitchen table and had a cry about it, but Grandpa lured a penny out of the knee and made him feel much better. Didn't he, Mikey?"

I stiffened and inadvertently squeezed down on John's hand.

"Ow!" he cried. "Mommy! You're squishing my fingers."

"I'm sorry." I slid my hand out of his. "Why did you just call him Mikey, Mother?"

"He insisted that's his name today."

"Well, I'm not so sure that I like it. Don't you remember . . . ?" I gritted my teeth. "His father's name . . . ?"

"He was only playing, Alice." She bent down and kissed the child on the top of his golden head. "I'm sure it's a natural thing to pretend, especially for a boy who's never met his father."

My own father jogged downstairs and also said his good-byes. He helped John into all of his outer garments, gave him a pat, and then John and I set off for home, our gloved fingers intertwined, his little feet scrambling to keep up with mine.

"Slow down, Mommy."

I kept my lips pursed and peered straight ahead at the path of leaves and shedding trees before us. For each one of my footsteps John traveled three.

"You're going too fast!"

"Do you remember the snow, John?" I asked.

He fell silent.

"Do you remember a hotel in Nebraska?"

John snickered and pointed at the yard that we passed. "There's a cat sitting in that tire swing over there."

"John!" I squatted down in front of him and grabbed him by both arms, which frightened him enough to flinch. "Tell me what you remember. Why did you say that thing this morning about a shoe?"

He merely blinked.

"Why are you insisting that your name is Mikey? It's John Lind O'Daire, not Michael. Your name is John."

"It is now, Alice." He cast me a sidelong glance. "But it didn't used to be."

His words knocked the breath straight out of me. His eyes—that beguiling O'Daire palette of blues and greens—glinted with a knowing expression.

A moment later, his attention switched back to the tire swing. "Oh, look! The cat's rocking the swing."

I stood up but lost my balance. My arms and right foot shot out to save me from collapsing.

John tiptoed into the yard with the cat. "Can you write down a story for me when we get home?"

"Wh-wh-what story?"

"A story about the swinging cat. If I tell it to you, will you write it down?"

I closed my eyes and swallowed. *In through the nose, out through the mouth* . . .

"Yes, darling, of course." I rolled back my shoulders, drew more air through my nose, steadied my nerves. "I'm . . . I'm always happy to write down your stories for you."

John skipped back over to me and retook my hand. "I think I'll name the cat Jolly."

"That's a fine name for a cat."

"I think so, too."

"Sh—shall we go home and tell Aunt Bea and Aunt Pearl about Jolly and your day with Grandma and Grandpa? Was it a good one?"

"Yes." He jumped over a crack in the sidewalk.

"Are you a happy boy?"

Another jump. "Yes."

"Good. Let's be quick so we can warm up. I don't like walking in the wind when it's so unbearably cold."

"Me neither."

"I know, sweet—" I cleared the thickness from my throat. "I know you don't like the cold, sweetheart."

I squeezed his hand and urged him onward, through the leaves and the breeze that shivered against our ears.

About the author

About the book

Insights,
Interviews
& More . . .

Read on

Meet Cat Winters

Tara Kelly

CAT WINTERS writes books for teens and adults. Her debut novel, *In the Shadow of Blackbirds*, was named a Morris Award finalist and a Bram Stoker Award nominee. Her second novel, *The Cure for Dreaming*, was named to the Amelia Bloomer Project and the Tiptree Award Long List. Her other books include *The Uninvited* and *The Steep and Thorny Way*, and she's a contributor to the YA horror anthology *Slasher Girls & Monster Boys.*

The Peculiar Realities behind *Yesternight*

TYPICALLY, my novels take months or even years before they evolve from a handful of basic story ideas that I've stored in the back of my mind to an actual, workable book plot. However, I can say for certain that *Yesternight* came into existence on one specific day: March 25, 2015.

During that morning, I went online and spotted a link to an MSN article titled "10-Year-Old Boy Says He Remembers Past Life as Hollywood Actor." Intrigued, I clicked the link and learned about an Oklahoma boy named Ryan who, from a young age, told his mother that he once lived as someone else. He experienced nightmares and homesickness for Hollywood.

I clicked another link—one that led to a segment about Ryan on the *NBC Nightly News* website. A filmed interview with Ryan and his mother gave me chills. Major chills.

With the help of a photograph in a book about old Hollywood, as well as the assistance of Dr. Jim Tucker, associate professor of psychiatry and neurobehavioral sciences at the University of Virginia, Ryan and his parents were able to trace his purported past-life memories to a real person named Marty Martyn, a movie extra who become a successful film agent during Hollywood's Golden Era. Ryan gave dozens of details about his past life that matched up to Marty Martyn's ▶

3

The Peculiar Realities behind *Yesternight*
(*continued*)

real life, including information about family members, car colors, and even Marty's age when he died.

On the same day that I learned about Ryan and Dr. Tucker, my agent, Barbara Poelle, called me about another book proposal that I was working on. I told her, "I think I might be onto something new," and sent her the link to the video about Ryan. She, too, was astounded.

That afternoon, we emailed my HarperCollins editor, Lucia Macro, and pitched her the idea of a novel about a seven-year-old girl in the 1920s who states that she lived a past life that ended in a tragic death. In the message, I told Lucia that I planned to write the book from the point of view of a young psychologist trying to make a name for herself in her field. At the time, I didn't know much about the role of women in psychology in the 1920s—or that the psychologist herself would be carrying around her own baggage from the past. However, in less than twenty-four hours, *Yesternight* grew from a basic idea sparked by a real-life modern child to a rapidly forming plot for a full-fledged historical novel. I'm so grateful that my agent and editor encouraged me to take this concept and run with it.

As with all of my books, *Yesternight*'s characters, as well as many of its settings, are fictional, but actual people and places served as inspiration. The following is a list of characters and locations from the novel with ties to strange, fascinating, and sometimes horrifying realities.

Alice Lind. In 1967, real-life psychiatrist Dr. Ian Stevenson founded the University of Virginia's Division of Perceptual Studies to conduct parapsychological research that included the study of children who claim to remember past lives. Dr. Jim Tucker, the psychiatrist who worked with Ryan, is one of the researchers who carried on Dr. Stevenson's work after he passed away in 2007.

Instead of creating a modern-day character based on these two pioneering gentlemen, I decided it would be interesting if my fictional past-life researcher was a woman living in an era when entering the fields of psychology and psychiatry proved challenging in itself for females. I wanted the odds to be stacked against my protagonist so I could explore how much a person would be willing to give up for the sake of pursuing a compelling case that defies explanation.

Once I learned that school psychology was a path open to women in the 1920s and that some school psychologists traveled to rural towns to administer intelligence tests, the character of Alice came to life, and her journey toward discovering Janie O'Daire commenced.

Janie O'Daire. Janie's behaviors when describing her life as Violet Sunday, as ▶

The Peculiar Realities behind *Yesternight*
(continued)

well as her reactions during her visit to Violet's Kansas home, were inspired by Dr. Stevenson's and Dr. Tucker's accounts of real-life children who claim to remember past lives, including Ryan from Oklahoma (see the Further Reading section for a list of books by both Dr. Stevenson and Dr. Tucker). Janie is not meant to be one specific child, but a representation of dozens of the children discussed in reincarnation texts. Any mistakes made in my portrayal of such a child are entirely my own.

Michael O'Daire. Michael is an entirely fictional creation, and his role as the owner of a speakeasy can be traced to countless tales of regular people who illegally sold alcohol during the heyday of Prohibition. Full Prohibition came to Oregon in 1916. By the time the Volstead Act went into effect across the entire United States on January 17, 1920, Oregonians already had plenty of practice in finding creative means to procure their liquor, including fetching booze from Canadian ships that parked in international waters off the Oregon coast.

Gordon Bay, Oregon. Gordon Bay is a fictional town, loosely based on the coastal city of Rockaway Beach, Oregon, as well as other towns that turned into tourist stops once the railroads connected the Oregon coast to the inland cities over the mountains.

Hurricane force winds do, indeed, occasionally hit the region during intense storms, and a lady is likely to lose her hat.

Winchester Mystery House. The house that Alice mentions as being a prime example of the "séance frenzy" and America's "bizarre fascination with sideshows and amusement parks" actually existed in the 1920s . . . and it still operates as a tourist attraction to this day (I've visited it twice). Sarah Winchester, widow of the heir to the Winchester Repeating Arms Company fortune, built the elaborate 160-room mansion over a period of almost three decades in the late 1800s and early 1900s. During her lifetime, rumors circulated about her supposed madness, although modern-day books and articles refute that claim. Publications of the era stated that she hired workers to continuously expand the house in order to appease the spirits of all of those killed in the Old West by Winchester rifles.

Sarah Winchester died in September 1922, and in the spring of 1923, the house's new owners, John and Mayme Brown—a couple with ties to an amusement park in Canada—opened the property for guided tours.

The attraction is located at 525 South Winchester Blvd., San Jose, California. Its website is www.winchestermystery house.com. ▶

The Peculiar Realities behind *Yesternight*
(continued)

Violet Sunday. I decided to make the fictional Violet Sunday of Janie's past a mathematical genius when I read that children who remember past lives sometimes bring the skills of their former life into their new one. "Mathematical pioneers" is a category of women's history that doesn't often receive much attention, but nineteenth-century ladies did, in fact, make their marks on the worlds of mathematics and computing (especially when their families actually allowed them to receive a higher education). Two prime examples are Ada Lovelace and Philippa Fawcett. From 1842 to 1843, Lady Lovelace, daughter of famed poet Lord Byron, created the first algorithm ever to be used on a machine. She is credited with being the world's first computer programmer. In 1890, Philippa Fawcett became the first woman to take top place in the prestigious Cambridge Mathematical Tripos, shattering long-held beliefs about the inferiority of the female brain.

Cornelia Gunderson. From the beginning, I imagined Alice Lind's investigation into Janie's past life leading to grisly discoveries about a serial killer in the Great Plains, simply because several of the most notorious mass murders in United States history occurred in farmhouses in the nation's heartland.
　　Some examples:

From 1871 to 1873, a group of innkeepers known as the Benders of Labette County, Kansas, brutally murdered an estimated one to two dozen guests in their hotel. The "Bloody Benders" have gone down in history as America's first documented case of serial killers.

In 1912, an unknown attacker killed eight people with an ax in a farmhouse in Villisca, Iowa. The "Villisca Ax Murder House," incidentally, now operates as a tourist attraction that includes overnight tours and ghost hunting (www.villiscaiowa.com).

In 1959, two ex-convicts out on parole tied up and murdered a family by the name of Clutter in their home in Holcomb, Kansas—an incident that Truman Capote turned into the bestselling true-crime book *In Cold Blood*.

For Cornelia Gunderson's character, I combined the crimes of the aforementioned Benders, who reportedly attacked their Bender Inn guests with a hammer before cutting their throats, with traits of Belle Sorenson Gunness, a Norwegian-born Indiana woman who murdered somewhere between twenty-five and forty people in the late 1800s and early 1900s, including her two husbands, her children, and numerous suitors, the latter of whom she lured to her "murder farm" through newspaper ads in lovelorn columns. According ▶

The Peculiar Realities behind *Yesternight*
(continued)

to numerous reports and rumor, both the Benders and Belle Gunness fled the scenes of their killing sprees when they came close to getting caught and went into hiding for the rest of their lives. Investigators found multiple bodies buried on the grounds of both properties.

Friendly, Kansas, and the Hotel Yesternight, Nebraska. Both locations are fictional; however, all of the homes and the inn discussed in this Author's Note—as well as my own visits to reputedly haunted houses and hotels—influenced the creation of the Hotel Yesternight. ༄

Reading Group Guide

1. *Yesternight* is a novel where the known and unknown collide and paranormal events are definitely a possibility. Have you ever experienced something in your life that can't be explained away rationally?

2. At one point in the novel Alice maintains that "psychology explains everything." Is it possible that psychology can explain Alice's increasing conviction that Janie is indeed Violet reincarnated?

3. Alice's life at first seems like an open book. However, as the novel progresses we discover that her family represses not only their acknowledgment of her sister Bea's sexuality, but also any acknowledgment of Alice's sexuality. And Alice herself has repressed her memories of her unwanted pregnancy. Did the Linds' tendency to avoid such subjects strike you as normal behavior for the time period? Or did you find the family's repression to be extreme?

4. Is it possible Janie is a child prodigy with high mathematical ability? Is it possible Alice was just a child with behavioral difficulties? Or do you feel that the only way they could know what they do is to truly be the products of reincarnation?

5. Bea insists to Alice, "Don't insert yourself into other people's lives." ▶

How do you think that Alice's tendency to do this has affected her life so far?

6. Hotels play a large role in *Yesternight*. Alice stays in Michael's hotel at the opening of the book, as well as in the Hotel Yesternight and others. What do you think hotels symbolize with regard to the story?

7. Is Rebecca right to be suspicious of Michael's motives with regard to their daughter? Is he a man who only wants to discover the truth, or does he want to exploit his child for profit?

8. What do you think the police think happened to Michael that would make him run off into the blizzard?

9. What do you think of the ending? What do you believe is really going on with John?

10. What do you think will happen to Alice in the future? ❧

Further Reading

"Barriers against Women in Early Psychology," from *Research Methods: A Process of Inquiry*, Eighth Edition, by Anthony M. Graziano and Michael L. Raulin (Pearson, 2013).

Captive of the Labyrinth: Sarah L. Winchester, Heiress to the Rifle Fortune, by Mary Jo Ignoffo (University of Missouri Press, 2010).

Children Who Remember Previous Lives: A Question of Reincarnation, by Ian Stevenson, M.D. (McFarland, 2000).

Flapper: A Madcap Story of Sex, Style, Celebrity, and the Women Who Made America Modern, by Joshua Zeitz (Broadway Books, 2006).

"Grandmothers I Wish I Knew: Contributions of Women to the History of School Psychology," by Joseph L. French, *Professional School Psychology*, vol. 3, no. 1 (1988), 51–68.

Heartland Serial Killers: Belle Gunness, Johann Hoch, and Murder for Profit in Gaslight Era Chicago, by Richard C. Lindberg (Northern Illinois University Press, 2011).

Life before Life: Children's Memories of Previous Lives, by Jim B. Tucker, M.D. (St. Martin's Griffin, 2008).

Mad in America: Bad Science, Bad Medicine, and the Enduring Mistreatment of the Mentally Ill, by Robert Whitaker (Perseus Publishing, 2002). ▶

Further Reading *(continued)*

Return to Life: Extraordinary Cases of Children Who Remember Past Lives, by Jim B. Tucker, M.D. (St. Martin's Griffin, 2013).

A Saga of the Bloody Benders (A Treasury of Victorian Murder), by Rick Geary (NBM Comics Lit, 2007).

Twenty Cases Suggestive of Reincarnation, Second Edition, Revised and Enlarged, by Ian Stevenson, M.D. (University of Virginia Press, 1980).

Villains, Scoundrels, and Rogues: Incredible True Tales of Mischief and Mayhem, by Paul Martin (Prometheus Books, 2014).

Where Reincarnation and Biology Intersect, by Ian Stevenson, M.D. (Praeger, 1997).

"The Woman Who Bested the Men at Math," by Mike Dash (Smithsonian.com, October 28, 2011).

For more information about current studies on children who remember past lives, visit the website of the University of Virginia, Division of Perceptual Studies: https://med.virginia.edu/perceptual -studies.